A. F. Brady is a New York State Licensed Mental Health Counselor and Psychotherapist. She holds ⸻ ⸻ ⸻egre⸻ in Psych⸻logy from Brown Uni⸻ ⸻ gr⸻es in Psy⸻ ⸻ Counse⸻ ⸻rom Columbia University. She is a life-long New Yorker, and resides in Manhattan with her husband and their family. *The Blind* is her first novel.

The Blind

A. F. Brady

ONE PLACE. MANY STORIES

HQ
An imprint of HarperCollins*Publishers* Ltd
1 London Bridge Street
London SE1 9GF

This edition 2018

1

First published in Great Britain by
HQ, an imprint of HarperCollins*Publishers* Ltd 2017

ISBN: 978-1-84845-719-5

MIX
Paper from
responsible sources
FSC
www.fsc.org
FSC™ C007454

This book is produced from independently certified FSC™ paper
to ensure responsible forest management.

For more information visit: www.harpercollins.co.uk/green

Printed and bound by CPI Group (UK) Ltd, Croydon CR0 4YY

For the misunderstood

"Oh, you can't help that," said the Cat: "We're all mad here. I'm mad. You're mad."

"How do you know I'm mad?" said Alice.

"You must be," said the Cat, "or you wouldn't have come here."

—LEWIS CARROLL,
ALICE'S ADVENTURES IN WONDERLAND

PART ONE

OCTOBER 18TH, 9:40 A.M.

I'm kneeling on the floor in my office, tying the top of the garbage bag into a knot and squeezing out the excess air as I do it. The maintenance guys always leave extra bags at the bottom of the garbage can, so I can replace this one with a fresh one and just dump the tied-off bag into the bin. I find this is the most discreet way of hiding the rank stench of alcohol when I throw up into my garbage can. I want to believe that my tolerance is high enough that I never throw up, but the truth is, more often than not, I find myself on my knees in my office the morning after.

My name is Sam. I'm a psychologist, and I work in a mental institution. It's not like the ones you see in *Rain Man* or *Girl, Interrupted*. It's in Manhattan. It doesn't have sprawling grassy lawns and manicured hedges. It doesn't have wide hallways and eleven-foot doors like in *One Flew Over the Cuckoo's Nest*. It smells like a combination of antiseptic and bubble gum because they added bubblegum scent to the antiseptic. The lights are fluorescent and the toilets are always broken. The elevator is the size of an airplane hangar and it's always full. I've been working here for six years and I've never been in the elevator alone. Someone pushes the alarm button every day.

The ceiling tiles in the unit have leak stains in the corners. All the doors are painted gray and have oval windows with chicken wire in the glass. Except the office doors. There are no windows on the office doors, and they're painted pale yellow. They all have paper signs on them saying things like Lunch and In Session and Do Not Disturb. We have to make new ones pretty regularly because patients write stuff on the signs.

It always feels like once you walk through the front doors, the world gets smaller. It's impossible to hear outside sounds and, even though I'm in the loudest city on Earth, I can't hear it in here. There's only one group room that faces the sun and that's where the plants are, but it's always dusty and no one likes to go in there.

We have a lot of different kinds of patients here, 106 of them. The youngest is sixteen and the oldest is ninety-three. The oldest used to be ninety-five, but he died a few months ago. There's one wing where the men live and another wing where the women live, and pretty much everybody has a roommate. If a patient is violent or something, they can get a single room. Once patients find this out, they almost always become violent. What they don't realize is that a single room is just a double room with an accordion divider running through the middle, and when the room splits, someone loses a window. The institution is called the Typhlos Psychiatric Center and I've never asked why.

It feels fraudulent and silly and sometimes even comical, but I'm not any different from anyone else here. The clinicians are supposed to instill hope. We're supposed to take our talents and patience and hard-earned degrees and apply our education to the betterment of others. We pride ourselves on having it all together. We fancy ourselves the shepherds. We are told that this is noble and upstanding work, and a benefit to society. But it's all a pile of shit. We're no different from them. There's no line in the sand. In the end, we don't have canyons that divide us. We barely have a fissure. I have a key and an office and they don't. I came here to save them; they can't save me. But sometimes, the lines get blurred. People say "If you can't do, teach." Well, if you can't save yourself, save someone else.

OCTOBER 19TH, 11:12 A.M.

There is a new patient starting this week. No one wants to work with him. His file is nearly empty, and the rumors churning among the staff have been filling in the blanks with horror stories and nonsense. *(He murdered his last counselor; he refuses to do paperwork; he'll be a nightmare patient.)* Even *I* don't want to work with him, and I'm the one who takes all the patients no one wants. No one really knows what he's all about; what's true, what's a rumor. He has one of those charts where nothing is clear. He obviously hadn't answered the questions during the psychosocial evaluations. Most of what was written was garnered from his physical appearance and intake materials. He was definitely in prison; those records are clear. For twenty-some years, although somehow the charges aren't written in his file. Then halfway houses for years after prison. And now he's mandated to treatment as a condition of his probation.

We take so much of our power for granted; it only really exists because our patients aren't aware of their ability to fight against it. And then this guy comes in and starts unsettling everything. I guess I respect him, in a way. I had been napping in my office hoping that something would change, and I guess this guy may be the one to change it.

"Okay, guys, what does *hereditary* mean?" I'm running a group counseling session. This is a psychoeducational group, so I'm supposed to be helping my patients understand their diagnoses. So often psychiatrists will tell a patient that he or she has something and then never explain in plain English what it means.

"It means it runs in your family, right?" This is Tashawndra. She had eleven children. Every single one of them has been removed from her custody by social services. She isn't sure of the whereabouts of most of them, and she believes that two of them are dead, but isn't positive. This is her reality.

"That's exactly right—it means there is a genetic component. So which mental illnesses have a genetic component?" I'm up on top of the desk, where I usually sit.

"Cancer. My mom had breast cancer and I had to go get checked for it because she had it, but I didn't have it." Lucy.

"That's right. Cancer has a big genetic component to it, so it's important to get checked out if someone in your family has it. But what about *mental* illnesses? What about the kinds of things we treat here?"

"All of 'em, right? I know that if your parents or your

brother is addicted to drugs that you will probably get addicted to drugs, too. And people here are getting treated for that. You treat drug addicts here. And sometimes, if your family is depressed, you could get depressed, too." Tashawndra.

"Yeah, that's a big one," I say, wagging my finger in her direction. "Depression has a genetic component. So does schizophrenia, bipolar disorder and many of the other problems we treat here."

"So you're fucked, huh? If your mom is schizophrenic, then you can't stop it from happening to you, huh? It's like you're born fucked over. You're born to be crazy, right? Ha, like 'Born to Be Bad,' that song? Born to be crazy." Tyler. Tyler has schizophrenia. At twenty-two years old, he's very advanced for his age. He seems to have a greater understanding of the world that the rest of us missed somehow. He's at peace with things that the rest of us struggle with. Tyler has forgiven.

"Well, no, not always. And watch your language. When you have a genetic predisposition, which means when someone in your family has a disorder, then sometimes you will get it and sometimes you won't. It depends on what else happens in your life. It depends on whether or not you are exposed to things that will help you stay well, or things that will make you get sick." I'm bouncing my heels off the front of the desk.

"What kind of stuff makes you sick? Like drugs and stuff?" Tyler. "Because I know my brother did drugs in school with his friend, and then he was crazy after that. He got locked up but he was crazy, man. He never acted like that before he did those drugs."

"Drugs, sure. That's a significant one, actually." I'm nodding and explaining, bright-eyed. "Also, poverty, abuse, growing up without both parents, not being able to get enough food or go to school. They are kind of like strikes against you. So, if you have the gene in you to get depression or schizophrenia, and then you have these strikes in your life, too, you could end up with the diagnosis."

"Like three strikes, you're out, right?" Tyler. He and I talk baseball in the hallways. I'm afraid of running into him one day at Yankee Stadium.

OCTOBER 20TH, 7:44 P.M.

When it's almost time to go home, I start to look at all the things I've been avoiding all day. I don't have a drink or a cigarette with me to help me look at these things, but I start to peer into the abyss anyway.

I know when I get home and I am alone, and my phone isn't ringing, I'll be looking at this, so I may as well get it started now. Maybe it will ease the burden. Maybe I won't cry so hard when I'm at home. Inevitably, the only thing that happens is I am going to be forced to wear sunglasses on the train home because my face will be swollen with misery and my eyes will be brimming with tears that somehow, every single day, manage to cling to my eyelids until the very second my apartment door swings open.

It didn't always feel like this. Sometimes things made sense. Back when I felt like I understood what was going on, and I wasn't just going through the motions.

The subway is down. There is a fire on the tracks on the A/C Line, and I have to get off the train a hundred blocks from my apartment. For whatever reason, I am walking now. I tend to think when I walk, which is probably not a good thing, because I don't have any cash and I can't stop somewhere for a drink to help me stop thinking.

It's cold out. The kind of cold that makes your knees hurt and your lips get solid, so it's hard to talk. My eyes are watering, but I'm not crying. I'm smoking back-to-back cigarettes, and I don't have gloves, so I have to keep switching hands.

Even though it's freezing, there are families out in the street. I've seen them since I got off the train. There is a mother pushing a stroller on the other side of the street, and we have been pacing each other for blocks. She looks like me. Well, she looks like my mom, and I guess I look like my mom, too. We're blonde, and I'm guessing the woman has blue eyes like we do, even though I can't see that far. She's small, like my mother is. I'm much taller than they both are; I always thought my dad must have been a pretty big guy. Now I'm stuck thinking about my own family as I walk south in this bitter city.

It was just me and my mom growing up. My dad is somewhere, but I don't know where. I've never met him, but it doesn't really make a difference because Mom was almost too much to manage on her own. Sometimes she sang his praises—*Your father is a wonderful man*. And sometimes she shit all over him—*He's just some mick fuck who doesn't deserve me*. I wonder if that baby in the stroller knows her dad.

My name is Samantha because my mom's name was Samantha. I think that's why I go by Sam. Our last name is James. So I have two first names. I always told people never to trust someone with two first names.

I can see my apartment now. It's the only one on the floor with no lights on. It's in an old limestone walk-up building in the middle of the block. I've been living in New York City for a few years. I bounced around different studios and tiny one-bedrooms in Brooklyn and Manhattan after I came here for graduate school. My current apartment has three closets, which is practically unheard-of, and a bathtub. I have a desk and a coffee table and it could pass for a grown-up apartment if I could just buy food to put in the fridge. My couch is brown and I have different pillow covers for different seasons. Now it's the dark blue ones. I have a carpet that's mostly sun bleached because my windows face south, so the summer sun is in here for the whole day, and I used to like the colors but now I think it looks like a little girl's carpet. My kitchen is very clean and has a window above the sink, so I can look out while I'm washing wineglasses and see what everyone else is doing. The radiator makes noise, which is comforting because if it didn't, there would be no sound in here. I never turn on the TV because it makes me feel small.

The front door to my building has a tricky lock, and it always seems to get stuck right when the wind picks up and starts to make my ears hurt. The dark green tile floors in the lobby always look dusty and I'm afraid I'll slip on them and crack my skull. The stairs are wide and rounded, from a New York era long forgotten, and as I wind up them to my apartment, I peel off my outside layers.

I'm opening a bottle of wine that I bought at the liquor store across the street last night. I always make sure to be delicate and grown-up about my drinking. I drink every night, but that's okay because it's expensive wine that I drink out of expensive wineglasses that I always remember to wash before I go to bed. I also always clean my ashtrays, because even *I* think it's gross to have stale butts around the house. I quit smoking a few times, but then I gave up quitting because something else is going to get me first anyway. Desperation makes you hold on to funny things.

OCTOBER 21ST, 8:55 A.M.

I'm sipping the acrid, burned coffee from the lounge, waiting for my boss, Rachel, to start the clinical-staff meeting. My nails are grimy and dirty, and the nail polish is mostly peeled off. I look up to catch my colleague Gary staring at me. He immediately looks away when our eyes meet, but then he quickly turns his head back to me.

"Yes?" I ask him, eyes wide.

He brushes the side of his temple with the back of his left hand and juts his chin in my direction.

"What?"

He does it again.

I put down my red pen and coffee cup and wipe the sides of my face. I pull back my left hand to see a streak of un-blended cakey makeup across my pinkie. Crispy little bits of scab are dotting the makeup.

Rachel begins the meeting.

"Good morning, team. Nice to see everyone bright-eyed and bushy-tailed this morning."

Muffled laugher and sarcastic snorts.

"I know it's been getting a little overwhelming with all the new patients starting, but as you know, there are seasons and cycles that are at play with mental health, and with winter almost here, even though it's only October—" she shakes her fists at the windows "—with the shorter and colder days come more depression, seasonal affective disorder, hopelessness and the like. I'm not telling you anything you don't already know. That being said, as you're already aware, we have another new patient, and he is starting today."

The staff begins to look around nervously; people start adjusting their shirts, looking down at notepads, trying to disappear into the noise.

"I've heard a lot of chatter in the hallways. I understand that it's natural to speculate, but it's very difficult to maintain unconditional positive regard, an unbiased attitude and an open mind when rumors are being spread in this manner. You all know what I'm talking about." She glares at us like we should know better.

"Well, can you give us a little more insight into the story with this guy?" Gary.

"I'm not really privy to any more information than you are, so we're in the same boat. But I am urging you to put your preconceived notions away, set down these ideas you have about him and focus on the little information that we *do* have. He is coming here for treatment, for help, and your job is to provide that treatment without making the man into a monster."

"Look, I'm all for positive regard and unbiased treatment, but isn't it important to ensure the safety of the staff?" Gary again. "I mean, I heard his file is incomplete because he attacked his last counselor. I heard he refuses to answer intake questions, and won't discuss his history, and if you pry, he goes ballistic. I mean, he's forensic, and I'm not sure I'm comfortable treating a patient who is known for attacking his counselor."

"Well, we are not in the business of turning away problematic patients." Rachel lowers her head and shuffles out the file. "And there's nothing in here that indicates he has been violent with staff in the past."

"That's because there's nothing *in* there at all! The file is nearly empty. It says he is a big dude and wears a hat and doesn't talk. It says he's been in jail half his life. But, somehow, it doesn't say on what charge? Hmm? That's insane! You can't have a forensic patient with no history, and no psychosocial, and no diagnosis, and nothing in his file, just waltz in here, and we're supposed to figure this all out from nothing!" Gary is exasperated. Gary used to be a social worker in the finance world. He worked for a firm that did corporate layoffs, and Gary's services were offered to those individuals who lost their jobs. He always ended up feeling like the messenger and he couldn't hack it anymore, so he ventured into something he thought would be cushier, less dramatic, more sustainable on a daily basis. He went from the frying pan into the fire, and he is still looking around, bewildered, wondering how he got here.

"Then what exactly do you think we should do, Gary?" This is David, who usually stays above the fray in these meetings.

"Send him somewhere else!"

"That's ridiculous. We are the 'somewhere else.' This is the last stop. Would you rather he was out on the street? With no treatment? No chance?" Me, wiping coffee stains from the conference table.

"Look, I mean, I just don't want him on my caseload. I don't have a lot of extra time on my hands, and being tasked with completing an entire file of pre-intake data *in addition* to everything else needed for him, for a guy who will probably stab me and doesn't even talk? No. I'm sorry, but no, thank you." Gary folds his arms across his chest and leans back in a huff.

"Then why are you working here?" Shirley immediately regrets these words, and she cowers back into her seat, hoping this comment didn't open her up to the possibility of being the new guy's counselor.

Rachel jumps in, taking control of the discussion. "It's important for all of us to have a forum in which we can discuss the concerns we have with the patients, and to bring everything out in the open. These meetings are exactly that forum. We are not here to attack each other. I want you all to talk to me and each other about what you've heard and what makes you so nervous about our new patient Richard. But I will continue to caution you—rumors are usually unfounded, and we need to be careful how we color this man."

Gary slumps farther down in his chair and disengages from the discussion. Julie, the bubbly princess, pipes up that she is fearful for her safety, and she worries that she's too physically weak and defenseless to effectively treat someone who intimidates her. Other female staff members coo in agreement. Julie has wormed her way out of taking anyone else onto her caseload for weeks.

"Why was he in jail?" Shirley.

"I honestly don't know." Rachel. "As I said, I have access to the same records as you, and I don't have that information."

"But isn't that weird? Shouldn't we know?" Julie.

"What difference does it make?" Me. "If he were in jail for racketeering or armed robbery or whatever. It doesn't make a difference. It could be drugs. It could be the third offense for something small, and with the 'three strikes, you're out' law, he could have been in jail forever. It's not a sex offense, because he isn't registered—I looked it up. It really shouldn't matter what he was in jail for. But it's important to know that he *was* in jail. His perspective is obviously altered, and he has probably been subjected to some pretty horrific stuff in there." As I say all of this, it occurs to me that I am completely uncomfortable with not knowing why he was in prison for so long.

"I heard he doesn't talk, *at all*, and that he is very aggressive. He refuses to follow protocol, he doesn't get along with other patients, he doesn't do paperwork." Shirley.

"Well, I think it's clear that he's not cooperative with doing paperwork, but beyond that, I am going to ask everyone to chalk this all up to speculation and the tendency to fill in blanks with drama when we don't have sufficient information. The fact of the matter is he is here, and he is going to be working with us." Rachel is no longer looking at anyone and getting ready to drop the bomb. She's stalling. Everyone starts to shift uncomfortably.

"Sam—" she looks up and tightly smiles in my direction "—and Gary." He slumps back into his chair, defeated. "I'm going to put Richard with you, Gary, and Sam will be your backup. You can learn a lot from this patient, and I think you're up for the challenge. And, Sam, you have the best success rate with difficult patients, and you're a ranking member of the clinical staff. I prefer to start Richard with a male counselor and see how that goes. We will all be here for extra support should you need it, but I'm sure you'll be able to handle this."

Shirley and Julie give each other exaggerated looks of relief, and everyone breathes a sigh. David gives me a conciliatory squeeze on my shoulder. Gary huffs up to Rachel and lolls his head to the side as she hands him a copy of Richard's intake materials. He says nothing, and instead looks to me with wide eyes and an impatient bend in his leg.

"No problem, Rachel. I'm on it." I gather my papers and

coffee, and as we all bleed into the hallway, Rachel hands me my own copy of Richard's file.

Gary assures me that he has no problem taking Richard's case, and I will not need to participate in his supervision. Gary is an idiot.

"Well, that's all well and good, Gary, but I'd like you to come to my office so we can discuss a plan of action. Not because I don't believe you can manage this, just because I want to stay in the loop if I'm going to be your backup."

"I really don't have time right now, and I'd like to get an initial meeting with this guy done today." He stands at the door to the conference room with his whole body and one outstretched finger pointed toward his office.

"Come on. It'll only take ten minutes." He expels a giant, frustrated moan and follows me down the hallway to my door. "Sit down," I say, waving my hand at my patient chair. He flops down dramatically and lets his Gatorade slosh onto the carpet in front of him.

"I'm going to find him on the unit and bring him to my office for a meeting this morning. I'm going to talk to him like a man, and I'm going to treat him like he's not scary and no big deal. I'm sure all this crap about him being scary is just because he was incarcerated and prisoners scare people. Well, not me; I'm not scared." He rubs his Gatorade spill further into my carpet with his shoe.

"This is the extent of your plan? You're going to talk to him like a man?" I'm not even bothering to write this down.

"Yeah. It's not rocket science, Sam. He's a patient and I'm a counselor. So, he has to answer me. I don't see why everyone had so much trouble before."

I shake my fragile, hungover head to try to clear the stupidity of Gary's response. "Can you please give me something a little bit more specific? *How* do you plan on getting through to him when clearly no one has been able to until now?"

"Like I said, by talking to him like a man." He slowly enunciates the last three words.

"What does 'like a man' mean?" I hover my pen over my notebook and avert my eyes. I can't look at him for fear of his response.

"You wouldn't understand because you're not a man." He stands up to leave my office and pats me condescendingly on the shoulder as he leans down to add, "I'll make another meeting with you after I've gotten some answers out of him, okay?" And he's out the door.

OCTOBER 23RD, 11:37 P.M.

I have been avoiding garbage day for about a week now, and the recycling bin is overflowing. There isn't much space under the sink in my kitchen, and since I drink more than I cook, I have the big recycling bin between the front door and the fridge. It looks more like a hamper.

The blue see-through bag has been pulled under with the weight of the bottles, and I need to yank it up by the red strings to get it out of the can. The clattering sound it makes is absolutely insufferable. There is a leak at the bottom, and the putrid stench of week-old wine and booze, mixed with the acidic smell of the Tropicana bottle from this morning's screwdrivers, is making me gag. There's a reason I always put this chore off until the last possible minute.

The noise the bottles make as I pull it along the carpeted hallway is not as bad as it would be if I were to pick it up and haul it over my shoulder, Santa Claus–style. I will have to carry it that way when I walk down the old marble steps to the basement.

I push open the refuse-room door, and I see skittering bugs as I turn on the lights. They've come inside to hunker down for the winter, and this room is a veritable buffet of gnarly shit for them to feast on. I flip over my huge sack of booze bottles into an awaiting plastic can, and it sounds like several of them smash. I feel the ooze that has spilled down the back of my pajama pants, and I try to dry it off with a rag that was hanging on a hook by the door.

I get back up to my apartment and clean up the smears on the floor. I put the two forgotten bottles of beer into a fresh blue recycling bag and line the can with it. I have two bottles of scotch on my bookcase shelf that I never finish. There's always at least four fingers left in each bottle so if I have company, it looks classy and sophisticated. I usually have a bottle or two of wine in the fridge, too. Not because I'm saving it, but because I buy in bulk.

OCTOBER 26TH, 3:35 P.M.

Gary is loitering in front of my office door as I return from running a women's group.

"Hey, Gary. Did you need something?" I can see the desperation in his eyes, and I know what he came here to discuss with me.

"Yeah, I need to talk to you. Do you have a minute?"

"I sure do, come on in."

Gary slumps low in my patient chair and rakes his sweaty fingers through his hair. "This is making me crazy. I can't get a word out of this guy, and I've had meetings with him every day since Friday."

"You mean Richard McHugh?" I know exactly who he means.

"Yeah. I brought him in on Friday, like I said, and I tried to start the evaluations and assessments for his patient file, right?" He's leaning on my desk and waving a meaty paw in my face. "And he doesn't say a word. Not a *word*. He just sits there, and I thought he must be deaf or something, because he just didn't say anything. He didn't get mad or anything; he just sat there. I kept asking him the same questions, and he just looked at me or looked out my window. So, then I figured maybe he wasn't ready. I told him about me, tried to relate to the guy, said I would treat him like a man if he treated me like a man, and still *nothing*." Gary is genuinely surprised that his presumptuous macho plan didn't work. Half of me wants to laugh in his face, and the other half wants to be professional and help him develop as a counselor.

"Okay. So, the original plan didn't work. You said you met with him every day since then. Did you change your approach?"

"Yeah. I mean, I did everything I know how to do. First, I was just trying the 'talk to him like a man' thing, and that didn't work. Monday, I asked him to come back to my office, and he didn't put up a fight or anything. So, I figured this time I would just be all business and make him answer the evaluation and assessment questions. But he didn't answer a single question! He started reading the newspaper. He brought this huge stack of newspapers with him to read and wouldn't even look at me when I asked him questions."

"Okay, and I imagine the sessions yesterday and today were more of the same?" I'm already tired of hearing this.

"Yeah, total silence. He doesn't even say hello." Gary leans back, satisfied that this is my problem now.

"Gary, you've made four attempts to talk to a man who apparently doesn't like to talk much. So, you shouldn't be surprised or disappointed that conventional methods aren't working."

"I don't think it's my methods, I think it's me. I think he just doesn't like me." Gary is saying this to appeal to my ego, so that I offer to take over for him and he doesn't have to ask me.

"How would you like to proceed?" I'm not letting him off that easy.

"I think *you* should take him. I don't have this kind of time to waste on someone who doesn't talk, doesn't want to be helped." He is crossing his arms and shaking his head in fast, erratic twitches that make him look like a frightened woodland creature.

"I can't make that call. You're going to have to speak with Rachel."

"Oh, come on, Sam, can't you just take this one for me?"

"I've already taken Shawn for you." I sigh. "But if Rachel signs off on it, I will take him. Until then, he's yours." I close my notebook for effect and open my door, allowing Gary to go find Rachel and deal with this.

OCTOBER 28TH, 9:12 A.M.

We have a 9:00 a.m. staff meeting most mornings to discuss our patients and any administrative nonsense that needs to be addressed. Everyone usually drags ass in the meeting except for me and my boss, Rachel.

Rachel is a linebacker. She is a formidable presence, and her booming voice and sharp intellect scare the shit out of everyone. She was born to run an institution, and her lack of a private life really helps her excel at her job. Her stringy, mousy brown hair is pulled back with a velvet scrunchie and she is always wearing a sweater set and chinos that are too tight in the hips and it makes the slash pockets stick out like little ears.

Rachel likes me because she needs to believe that I really am always energetic and positive and a barrel of sunshine. Whenever I am out on the unit, I am a superhero. I am a troubleshooter, and a problem solver, and the go-to gal to get stuff done. My coworkers hate this about me. Until I cover their groups, or take their patients to the ER, or finish their case reviews/progress reports/treatment plans; then they love this about me. I make self-deprecating jokes as a defense mechanism. I always ask people about their weekend and how they're doing because people are narcissistic and won't ask me how I'm doing in response. This way I don't have to lie to anyone.

"Frankie's back in the hospital." Shirley begins her report. "Apparently he was standing in the middle of the street trying to direct traffic. This was an intersection on Broadway, and it's amazing that he isn't dead. Supposedly, when the police tried to stop him and arrest him or whatever, he started running away from them, bouncing off of cars, running in between them... It was a mess. Eventually they tackled him, I'm not sure, and they brought him to the psych unit at Columbia University Medical Center. He is on suicide watch right now, and I keep getting calls from the docs telling me that he's not cooperating. I'm not sure what I'm supposed to do about this." Shirley is both disengaged and disenchanted and ran out of empathy years ago.

"You go to CUMC, Shirley," Rachel responds, irritable, frustrated, possibly menopausal. "You talk to the doctors. You make sure they know you're the point person in his continuing care. Eventually, Frankie is going to be coming back here for inpatient services once he is cleared to go, and he needs to be aware that he wasn't abandoned in the psych unit at CUMC.

"Remember, all of you." She is looking at us like bad kids who ate all the cookies. "We are the only resource for many of our patients here. We are their mothers and fathers, their caretakers and confidants..."

I didn't sign up to work on this unit to be anyone's mother or father and I resent her for saying this as she drones on with the lecture she has delivered so many times. I sip my coffee and stare out the only window in the conference room. There is construction going on across the street; I can hear it a little bit, but mostly I just watch the men in jeans and reflective vests glide up and down this building as they work the planks and rods of the scaffold, and I wonder what would happen if someone jumped off.

"In other news," Rachel continues, "I'm announcing a caseload change this morning, as well. Gary has been working hard to reach our newest patient, Richard McHugh, but unfortunately, he hasn't gotten anywhere. I met with Richard yesterday to discuss a change in his counselor, and he asked for you, Sam, by name. So, tag—you're it. Good luck." Rachel told me about this before the end of my shift yesterday, so this is nothing more than a performance for the rest of the staff.

Rachel pulls me aside and thanks me for playing along. I rejoice in being her golden girl, and whenever she has faith in me, it helps me to have faith in myself. She reminds me again that Richard specifically said he wanted to work with me, Samantha James.

Julie is waiting for me outside the conference-room doors. "No wonder Gary couldn't handle that guy, I'm sure you're going to do a much better job. I can't believe Rachel even wasted our time assigning him to someone so incompetent." Julie, always looking for someone to tell her *she* isn't incompetent. She is huddling next to me like we're girlfriends of twenty years, holding my arm and whispering her hot-coffee whisper into my hair.

"I just think it's stupid to have these meetings at the ass crack of dawn when everyone is still hungover and can't even read yet," I say, trying to lose her.

"You're hungover?"

"It's a figure of speech, Julie. I am not literally hungover." Lies. Lies. Lies. I would be much better off wrapped around a toilet right now, but Julie will offer me no solace.

"Oh—I know—I guess I just thought maybe you went out last night again. When are we going to go out together? Are you doing anything tonight?"

Julie likes me and wants to be my friend, but I find it impossible to like her. As much as I appreciate her for being an idiot who can't get over high school, I still can't tolerate listening to her inane musings and cotton-candy problems with her debutante friends and country-club life. David walks past us and gives me a knowing smile and chuckle.

"I never make plans this early in the day. I will let you know, though; we should definitely grab a drink sometime." I smile broadly and disengage from her grasp as we are getting close to my office. I juggle my coffee and my case files to try to get the keys out of my pocket when I see that my door was left open anyway.

Nothing is amiss. I must have just left it unlocked. Maybe I'm still drunk. My iPod is still sitting tangled in the headphones on top of a stack of books on my desk. That wouldn't be there if anyone had come into my office. My sneakers are in the corner where I leave them every morning. A couple of months ago, Shirley left her door open during one of her group sessions and the batteries got stolen out of all her electronics.

OCTOBER 28TH, 11:00 A.M.

My initial meeting with Richard is already happening today, and I have been fixing my desk and my hair and my face and my office for the past hour to prepare for it. I am afraid of him, and I haven't had this feeling since I started on my first psych unit nearly fifteen years ago. I was barely twenty-two. I never feel like this anymore. I've sat across from lunatics and psychopaths, diplomats and dignitaries; it's all the same to me now. I haven't been scared like this in ages.

My office is configured the way it's supposed to be, with the desk chair closer to the front door than the patient's chair. This is done just in case the patient gets violent and the therapist needs to escape, but we say it's done so the clinician can obtain emergency services more quickly should the patient need it. I've never had a patient get violent in my office; it usually happens out in common areas. I realize I have the scissors closer to the patient's chair and I move them to the drawer. Sometimes I sit on my desk so I can gaze out the window and pretend I have a different life.

The door knock is so loud and jarring that my already frazzled nerves just explode and lodge themselves in my throat, making it hard to speak. I have to appear calm no matter how scared I am.

"Hi, Richard. Come on in, have a seat." I remain standing, holding the door open for him. I'm waiting for him to sit, then I close the door and begin to get dizzy. He sits in my patient chair and places a large stack of newspapers at the corner of my desk. "I am going to be your counselor. I wanted to set up this initial meeting so we could get to know each other a little bit, and maybe get started on some of the clinical documentation we need to do." I sit down as I say this.

Richard doesn't say anything in response. Instead, he lifts the top paper from the pile and makes a show of opening it up and finding his intended section. He slips off his hat. It's a brown herringbone newsboy cap. He places it gently on top of the newspapers. As he turns his neck, I notice two small, round scars under his collar.

I rustle the papers of his blank file and begin again. "Why don't we start with the family history section? This way you can tell me about your family, and we don't have to dive right into talking about you personally."

He turns away from me, folds his paper in his lap and focuses his attention on the men climbing the scaffold across the street.

"Okay, no family history. What about goals for treatment? Would you be willing to talk about what you'd like to achieve while you're here at Typhlos?"

He raises his eyebrows, releases a breath and adjusts his seat to get a better view of the construction workers.

"Okay, that's a pretty obvious no. How about telling me a little bit about yourself, informally, and I will gather whatever information I need. How's that?"

Richard glares disapprovingly. "You want me to sit here and tell you all about me? Like a job interview?"

"If that's how you want to look at it, yes. A job interview would be great."

"No." Blunt. Decisive.

I'm barely making more progress than Gary did. It looks like I'm going to have to work on this guy a bit more than I'd anticipated. I feel exhausted just thinking about it.

I sigh an enormous, frustrated sigh, and I intentionally blow it in Richard's direction. I hope it stinks of booze and vomit and coffee so he knows how much his resistance is pissing me off.

OCTOBER 28TH, 10:01 P.M.

I'm on the train, watching the people in front of me arguing. It's packed, and it's cold outside, but the body heat from the rest of the riders is making me sweat into my scarf. The sways and jolts of the train are lulling me into a trance, and all I can hear is the woman in front of me telling her boyfriend that she has had enough.

I am currently seeing someone. I don't know why that is the terminology we use—"seeing" someone; usually, I say "seeing someone" in reference to a therapist, but this is how I describe my relationship because I don't want to say "relationship." We have been involved for a while.

His name is Lucas. On paper, he is the type of guy you're supposed to marry. He does something in finance, and he calls it "finance," which makes me want to punch him. He knows the difference between Cabernet and merlot and wants me to taste the tannins. He has a King Charles spaniel named Maverick, which of course just makes him wildly out of my league. He went to Cornell, and he actively parts his hair. In the morning, he uses a fine-tooth comb and creates a straight line down the left side of his head, and he tucks stray hairs behind the line. I am anal, but he is crazy. He wears shoes that he keeps shoe trees in. He finds it very important that when he gets home from work and he takes off his shoes he immediately puts the shoe trees into the shoes because they are warm from wear and more susceptible to morphing into an undesirable shape. I care less about shoes than he does. He has dirty-blond hair, is tall and wears suits with pocket squares that he has to have folded just so. He's prettier than I am.

He talks to me about getting married. I find this completely ridiculous. I am not the girl you marry. The only reason I have stayed with him for such a long time is because I am trying to rescue him. This is a well-known pattern in my life, and I have only recently become aware of it and okay with the fact that this is what I do.

He has all the things that girls are looking for: the stability, the money, the good looks, the education. But underneath it all lies a very damaged, very insecure little man, and *that* is who I am dating.

I do not want this picture of perfection; I do not want this combed, shoe-treed, elitist, country-club gentleman. I want the broken-down little puppy inside of him who is desperately trying to play pretend. I want to find that puppy, I want to rub his belly and give him a good home, and then, when he's better, I will leave. This is a project. This is a way of making sure that I don't get hurt, and making sure that someone values me.

I have no way of getting value from within, so I get value from without. As soon as I see the reserves beginning to dry up, I will walk out of his life and move on to the next well of validity. The truth is, this plan isn't working, and hasn't been working, but I'm not ready to give up just yet.

OCTOBER 31ST, 10:25 A.M.

Richard is in my group this morning, and I suddenly feel like I am performing more than facilitating a therapy session. He's sitting next to a relatively new kid named Devon. Devon is my age and surprisingly stylish. Today he's wearing designer jeans, distressed black leather shoes that extend too far out and look like cartoon cowboy boots, a gray athletic T-shirt and a pretty badass leather motorcycle jacket. Not the kind you pick up at a department store for nine hundred dollars; the kind guys who actually ride motorcycles wear. His long dreads are twisted into a thick ponytail. If I had seen him under different circumstances, I might have said he was hot. Except for the shoes.

Devon is diagnosed with schizophrenia, disorganized type. This isn't particularly common here; most of the patients with schizophrenia are diagnosed with paranoid type. People outside these walls call it paranoid schizophrenia, but when I'm here I have to say it the right way.

He sits with his legs twisted around each other, at the edge of his seat, constantly wringing his hands together and twisting his arms around one another. At several points during today's group, he looked like he was about to tip over.

After a few groups, Devon began standing up in this position. He would perch on one bent leg with the other leg twisted around it, holding his arms out in front of him and eventually doing something that looked like martial arts. He would shadow box standing like that; he would move his arms in slow, concentrated motions like tai chi. This was both fascinating and distracting.

I'm seeing Devon twitch and perch now, and I'm inwardly terrified of how this is going to affect the other patients—particularly Richard. I'm watching him with one eye while keeping the other eye on the group. Richard is keeping to himself; he's arranged it so there's more than one chair between him and any other patient, but he is looking up from his papers over his glasses, and he is noticing Devon. The other patients start to become wary of Devon's behavior, and some become obnoxious and say they don't want to be around this weirdo and I should kick him out of the group.

"No one is getting kicked out, Barry. Take it easy." I lean back on the desk.

"Nah, man, this dude is weird, I don't want none of his weird getting on me, man. He distractin' the group! He shouldn't be in here!" Barry likes to be the peacekeeper while not keeping the peace at all. He frequently causes uproars in the name of justice and the betterment of the group process. I think Barry makes big scenes to distract himself from the voices in his head.

"Barry, since you've elected yourself to be the spokesman for this group, why don't we follow your lead and talk about stigma." Everyone hates when I do this.

"Aww, Miss Sam, can we *not*? I'm *tired* of talkin' 'bout stigmata."

"Stigma."

"Whatever you call it. I'm tired of it."

"Okay. First of all, what is stigma? What does it mean?"

"Stigma is like prejudice, right? Like when you an ass-hole to someone because of how they look, or being black or something, right?" This is Lucy. Lucy is seventeen. She wears sexy outfits and too much makeup. She has bipolar disorder. Some days she is so with it, I want to send her to Harvard, and some days she can't tell you her name.

"That's right, Lucy. Good job. Stigma is a lot like prejudice. It's a negative belief that exists about a member of a group that is based solely on group membership. Anyone ever have experience with that?" Sometimes, I'm more of a teacher than anything else. When I get into a good discussion, I start kicking my heels against the front of the desk. We are not supposed to be sitting on the desks; it's another one of the rules about making sure we keep a proper level of separation between "us" and "them." The longer I'm here, the less I care about this separation.

Everyone raises their hands to indicate they have been stigmatized in the past. Even Richard has his hand up. Devon is the only one who doesn't respond. I call him out.

"Devon, you see everyone else has their hands up? This has never happened to you?" I'm trying to involve him, not alienate him, but I fear I've made the wrong impression. He looks at me and seems to say something.

"I'm sorry, Devon, I can't hear you from all the way up here. Can you say that one more time?" He responds again, this time unlocking his chin from his neck and seemingly trying to project.

"I'm sorry, still can't hear you."

"He says he stays away from people." Stephan.

"Thank you, Stephan. Sometimes it's hard to hear. So, Devon, you stay away from people? Is that to avoid being stigmatized?"

He nods.

"It hurts to be the victim of stigma, doesn't it?"

He nods.

Everyone else nods.

"What kinds of things do you think other people believe about people with mental illnesses? What kind of stigma have you experienced?"

"People say we're crazy." As Stephan says this, I start writing the words on the blackboard behind me.

"Lazy. Uneducated. Stupid." Barry.

"People say we a burden. Like we don't do nothin' to help America." This is Lucy again.

"Dangerous." I'm surprised at who this is coming from. Adelle is about a hundred years old. She is as frail as they come, and I wouldn't imagine she experiences the stigma of being dangerously mentally ill. Then I remember that while off her meds, Adelle once stabbed a man in the chest with a pair of scissors.

"Dirty. Disgusting. People don't want to stand near us. Even we don't want to stand near each other." Darryl says this. Darryl is suffering from a traumatic brain injury that resulted from a self-inflicted gunshot wound to the head. He still struggles with major depression, but he swears he will never attempt suicide again. His wife left him after the incident because she couldn't bear to look at him with the resulting disfigurement.

"Alright, I'll say it: they say we're *weirdos*." This is Barry making amends. He looks at Devon. "Sorry, man, you don't need me calling you a weirdo when everyone else already does."

Devon nods.

"Thank you for that, Barry; that was very nice of you. What else, guys? What are some other stigmas you've experienced due to mental illness?" I see Richard looking at Barry, seemingly approving of his apology.

"People think they could catch it from you. Like if they have sex with you, they could get bipolar." Lucy.

"Does anyone know if that's true or not?" Me, I'm trying to teach without making the patients feel like they're in school. I'm looking at Richard, but his head isn't in the room.

"Nah, you could get AIDS and shit, but you don't catch crazy." Barry.

As I'm writing all the words on the board, I'm beginning to feel guilty because I've held every single one of these beliefs. I feel simultaneously sad and defensive.

As the group finishes, I wait for everyone to file into the hallway. I am walking around the room putting the chairs back into a semicircle, picking up the garbage left by the patients. As I walk past the chair that Devon squeezed into the corner, I notice little flakes, like paint chips or confetti, scattered at the base of his seat. I brush them onto the floor and keep walking.

I erase the board, making a mental note of all the words written, wondering how often I've felt stigmatized. Wondering how many of these things people think about me. Wondering, not for the first time, if *I* fit a profile.

NOVEMBER 1ST, 11:11 A.M.

I've given Richard a schedule with weekly one-on-one sessions with me, as well as several group therapy sessions most days of the week. Patients often respond well to structure, and I want to keep him busy while I figure him out. We have our regularly scheduled Tuesday 11:00 a.m. session this morning, and he is shuffling and wiggling and trying to get comfortable in my patient chair. He is too large for my office. He looks like a doll two sizes too big for the dollhouse. He is holding that stack of newspapers under one arm while shifting his weight back and forth in the seat. When he finally finds a comfortable position, he drops his papers onto the corner of my desk and awkwardly bends his elbow on top of them. His left arm bows at a strange angle, and he holds his wrist rigid, so it looks like he has a prosthetic arm.

"So, now that we're settled, I'm going to try to get going with your file again. Can you give me a few minutes of attention to get this ball rolling?" Hopeful, positive, maybe even energetic.

"What's this? Another test?" he asks. He doesn't take off his hat, which pisses me off because I think it would be polite if he did. I realize that the best way to suppress my fear might be to replace it with anger, so I momentarily dwell on being pissed that he is impolite. It's still the tweed newsboy cap, like the ones R & B groups made popular in the '90s.

"I'm not doin' no more paperwork." His voice is calm, masculine. He isn't arguing with me, simply stating a fact.

"*Any* more…" I absentmindedly correct him while sifting through my files and avoiding eye contact.

"Look, I'm here because I chose to be here, and I know that I don't have to fill out the forms, and I have confidentiality and privacy, and I don't have to answer any of your questions, and if you want to kick me out then that's fine. I know my rights. I heard you were the best counselor here and I didn't think you'd give me trouble like that last dud they put me with." He shifts farther away from me as he says this. He wrings each hand individually, as if he were wiping something off his thumbs. He is fidgety. He is nervous.

"You don't have to do anything you don't want to do. But you're going to make it harder on yourself if you avoid me. I am the person you're going to be working with for the duration of your time here. I am here to help you and to make your stay as painless as possible. If you need anything, I am the person you come to. If you have problems with anyone else on the unit, and you need an intervention, I am the person you come to. But I can't help you until you help me." Rehearsed.

I think the masking-scared-with-pissed ploy is working. He says nothing. I am looking at his eyes for the first time and I realize they are blue. For whatever reason I hadn't expected this. He keeps them squinted. I can't decide if this is because he is using his scary face or if he has sensitive eyes. They are light blue, much lighter than mine.

He is unfurling his hands now, and I see his fingernails are well maintained. This is notable only in the fact that it is completely opposite from every other patient. Even the women who spend their last dime on a fancy manicure will allow it to get gnarly and grow out so far that they have a quarter inch of real nail visible beneath the green, sparkly talons of a month ago.

But he remains silent. I can't tell if this is because I have stumped him or he is about to rip my face off for talking to him like that. I know no one else has said as much as this to him, and right now I can't imagine what gave me the balls to do it.

"Let's start with something light." I put on my glasses and I reach for a pen. "Name?"

I want to hear him pronounce his last name, because I am afraid he will be offended if I say it incorrectly. McHugh. I don't know if you're supposed to say the *h* or if it's silent or what. I've got him talking, and I don't want to compromise my progress.

"Richard McHugh." Sounds like *mah-Q.* Okay, now we have that settled. "Am I supposed to call you Doctor, or what?

"You can call me Dr. James, but I prefer Sam."

"Why do you prefer Sam?"

"Well, Richard, to be honest with you, I prefer Sam because it's easier to yell down the hallway. Why do you use your full name? Richard has so many appealing nicknames." Am I being obnoxious? Flippant? Nonchalant? I feel exhausted, like I can't conjure the energy I need to be a professional here, or to fake it anymore. I feel like there is a miscommunication happening in my brain and I am accidentally betraying my real feelings in a session and not putting on the appropriate mask.

"I like Richard. No one's calling me Dick."

"Okay, sir."

"No, I didn't ask you to call me *sir*; I said *Richard*."

"Okay, Richard." I've never seen a reaction like that. Who doesn't like to be called *sir*? "Moving on— Date of birth?"

"July fourteenth, 1960. It was a Thursday."

"Really?" Now I'm interested. "How do you know that?"

"My mother told me. She said it was the worst day of her life and that's why she always hated Thursdays." I can't believe we're getting somewhere. I am afraid of reacting incorrectly and shoving the turtle back into its shell.

"Well, I love Thursdays." *Benign response, please don't shut down. Please open up to me.* "Whole weekend in front of me. And where were you born, Richard?"

"Queens."

"Ah, right here in New York, huh? Siblings?"

"No." Back to one-word answers.

"Family history…"

"No."

"It's not a question; we are moving to a section regarding your family history, your backgr—"

"No. I'm not answering any questions about family." He cuts me off again.

"Okay, well, I understand completely if you're not comfortable, but it's vital for your treatment, and—"

"No. I said no. I'm not saying anything else." It's over; the turtle is back in his shell.

"Okay, you don't have to do this now; we can come back to it another ti—" He stops me before I can appease him.

"Are we done? I want to leave." Before he even finishes his request to leave, he is out the door and halfway down the hall. I am facing the bookcase instead of the desk because he brushed my chair and spun it off balance. What just happened? What did I say? How did I lose him?

NOVEMBER 2ND, 10:53 P.M.

I'm going to meet Lucas for drinks. We don't live together, but we spend enough time at each other's places that sometimes I wear his clothes instead of doing my laundry. Dating Lucas is like dating two people, and I can't take one of them out in public. The scabs on my scalp are itchy and raised, but I still go to him, and I still tolerate this treatment.

Ninety percent of the time we go to the same bar and meet up with the same people. Some are friends; some are just other bar regulars who have become friends; sometimes David from work comes to the bar. But tonight Lucas and I are going somewhere different because he said he doesn't have the energy to party tonight.

Somewhere different turns out to be Flatiron Lounge on Nineteenth Street. The drinks are really interesting and expensive, and it's dark and none of the seats are actually comfortable, and the waitresses are hot enough to make me feel insecure, but Lucas looks really nice in candlelight, so I try not to worry that he might have brought me here to break up with me.

"You look great tonight, honey." Lucas. His voice sounds

a little bit like what I would imagine a diesel engine covered in melted butter would sound like.

"Well, thank you, my dear. I have been sober for a shocking number of hours, and I'm sure that's a good look." I have trouble being serious when I'm nervous. Even though Lucas is a project, it's not part of my plan for him to break up with me, and it's not part of the plan for the relationship to end *now*, so I hope this is about something else. Inevitably, this forces me to remind myself of why I'm with Lucas to begin with and why I continue to put up with this.

"I just didn't have the energy for all the guys tonight, you know? It can be so exhausting going to Nick's Bar every night." He really does look like he has it all together.

"Yeah, I hear you." I lie. On the inside I really want to be at Nick's because everyone there knows me only just enough to think that I am fabulous and attractive, and they have no idea that I am actually a mess. That's the kind of crowd I need to be around. When someone else believes this show, when a whole group thinks this act is real, when scores of intelligent human beings look at Lucas and me together and they see us as stable, rational, healthy adults in a stable, rational, healthy adult relationship, then *I* can believe it. I need to believe it. This fancy show we put on, this ruse, this bullshit we sling, I need it. I need to make people believe that I am alright, because if they think I am, then maybe I can think I am, too. And that's why I tolerate it.

Right now, as I'm looking at all these leggy Europeans, I am starting to feel smaller and uglier and more and more in need of alcoholic sustenance, but I am drinking something made with frothy egg white and it isn't going to cut it.

"Also, I have to admit, that's not the only reason I wanted to go somewhere quiet tonight." He is looking at me with what I would describe on someone else as sexy eyes, but on him I just find it comical. He is very handsome, but I'm nervous and I think he looks like a cartoon.

"Oh, yeah? Whassat?" I can feel the sweat starting to bead between my boobs.

"I wanted to talk to you again about the idea of you and I moving in together." He leans even closer to me, and his elbow takes up the entire cocktail table between us, and I am suddenly aware of how small this bar is, and the lights start to look like they're pulsing, and I am getting that dizzy feeling where I want to put one foot on the floor, but both my feet are already on the floor, and the music is too loud, and someone is asking me if I want another drink and I think I'm going to pass out. Lucas reaches his hand over to stabilize me, knowing the look I have on my face.

"I'm not pressuring you," he lies. "I just want to open up these lines of communication again. I know you're not a fan of cohabitation, and I know you want your independence. But my place is too big for just me, and you would have plenty of space there." He has leaned back and let go of me.

I'm gesturing to the bartender, so he looks at our waitress and sends her my way. All seven feet of her approach the table and bend down to hear me croak out an order for four shots of Patrón Silver. Lucas gives me a condescending eye that he likes to use on me in places like this because he wants the other guests to believe that he doesn't binge on booze every single day, and at this club he can keep up that appearance. And Lucas thrives on appearances.

"I like the way things are going with us, Sam. I think we could really make something here."

"I like us just fine the way we are, Lucas. I don't think we need to change anything."

"Why do you have such a fear of commitment?" Crossing his arms, getting defensive. People don't usually say no to him. *I* usually say no to him.

"I don't have a fear of commitment; I'm as committed to everyone in my life as I possibly can be. I'm committed to you, aren't I? So why can't I keep my independence?" I may be talking louder than I should.

"You can have your independence *and* live at my apartment, you know. It doesn't have to be mutually exclusive." He can tell that he is getting nowhere. He usually gets nowhere.

The shots arrive, and I throw back two of them before we even have a chance to cheers. Lucas gently picks up the third shot glass, and as I'm reaching for the fourth, he says the same stupid toast he always says: "To being the best at everything, all the time."

I don't bother clinking glasses when he leans in, because I think his toast is ridiculous and pompous, and I throw back my third shot. The waitress promptly appears with more napkins and some pretentious artisanal beer, and I wonder if Lucas is living in an alternate universe.

NOVEMBER 3RD, 8:31 A.M.

Richard is in my office. He was standing outside my office door when I came in this morning. Something is bothering him. I am just putting my game face on, still stinking of my morning cigarettes, and I'm not sure I am ready to manage this particular crisis.

"Well, I'm not going to be in groups with her anymore," he says.

"Richard—" exasperated, tired, extremely hungover "—*why* can't you be in groups with Julie?"

"She doesn't know what she's talking about. She's telling me that if I eat beets my shit will turn red. What do I care about beets? I'm not eating beets. You don't give us beets here, so where am I gonna eat them? I don't need to learn about the color of shit from this woman. I'm not going to her groups. I'm not. Give me something else."

"It's a nutrition group. These are topics that come up."

Eyebrows.

"Okay, fine. What other groups do you want? Who *can* you tolerate?"

"What do you teach? I mean during that time, what group do you teach?"

"The group I run at that time is not appropriate for you. We have a lot of different kinds of patients here, and many of them require more specialized groups. I run a group like that."

"Can I have free time? Or computer-room time?"

"Well, I think we should look into what your goals for treatment are and how your time would best be spent."

"My goals? I certainly don't need to learn about beets and shit."

"Excrement, Richard. Feces. Don't say *shit*." Which defeats the purpose, but who's keeping score anyway? He's seated in my patient chair now, and he leans back and glares out the window with his arms crookedly crossed over his chest.

"You don't want me causing a scene and yelling at Julie in group."

"This is true, but it seems to me that you're a rational adult, capable of controlling yourself and being respectful. If that group is unhelpful, I will take it off your schedule." I sit down at my desk and reach into my drawer for his file. "What we need to do is work together to figure out what you need from treatment. That includes you completing the clinical evaluations—" I shake the unfinished sheets at him "—and then I will be better able to recommend a group schedule for you that could help you to reach your goals."

"Again with the goals."

"Yes, most people are here to strive toward therapeutic goals."

"Fine."

"Fine?" I ask. The hangover headache is gripping my eyeballs, and I want nothing more than to close my eyes and lie down. "Shall we take this time to discuss your goals?"

"I'll think about what I want to get out of my time here." He walks out as he says this. I realize that I have achieved nothing but giving Richard the upper hand. Now he doesn't have to go to one of his assigned groups, and I am not closer to completing his file, or having any clue what he's doing here. I swallow two Advil with a long pull of coffee and prepare to face the day.

My phone rings before the Advil has the chance to take effect. It's David.

"Good morning, sunshine," he says in his happy, sober voice.

"Good morning. Please don't need anything from me. I'm dying from a hangover."

"Well, that's a nice change from every other morning. Did you steal my Advil?"

"Yes. Is that why you're calling me?" I'm rubbing the bridge of my nose with one hand and turning the volume down on the receiver with the other.

"No, I'm calling because I didn't bring anything for lunch today, and I want you to come with me to that new place on Riverside."

"You want me to *walk* to Riverside Drive?"

"Stupid question, huh?"

"Yes. Very, very stupid. But you should feel free to bring me a sandwich when you come back." I smile to myself. I don't know what I'd do if I didn't have David here to bullshit with.

NOVEMBER 6TH, 6:14 P.M.

I'm sitting on the roof of Lucas's apartment building with his dog, Maverick. Maverick is wearing a cashmere sweater, and we are waiting for Lucas to come back up here with a bottle of wine he's been talking about. Lucas wanted to come up to see the sunset before daylight saving time turns the city dark at 4:30 p.m. It's Sunday, and other people seem to have had the same idea. Manicured boxwood hedges are separating the section we are sitting in from other seating areas on the roof, and every now and again, I see the plume of someone else's cigarette smoke.

There are lots of those big space heaters that look like giant silver dildos wearing beanies, and Maverick and I are sitting close to one. He's on my lap, on top of a huge orange horse blanket with a big *H* in the corner that Lucas insisted I bring upstairs. If I owned an Hermès blanket, I probably wouldn't actually use it, let alone bring it to the dirty outdoors.

Lucas rounds the bend from the elevator, carrying a crystal decanter filled with burgundy liquid and two spotless glasses. Maverick doesn't pay him any attention and instead burrows farther into my lap. Lucas makes a big show of waving away the smoke as he walks by another couple holding cigarettes, as if he were the only one allowed to poison his pristine lungs. He gently lays the two glasses down on the teak coffee table and swirls the wine around in the decanter.

"This is the one I was telling you about when we were at dinner the other night. I've been thinking about it, and tonight seems like a good time to bring it out."

"Sounds good to me." I wipe some stray hairs out of my eyes and watch as he pours about three sips' worth of wine into each glass. He hands me one and leans back into his chair with his nose buried in the other as he puts his feet up on the table. He closes his eyes and inhales deeply. He tells me to do the same.

"What can you smell?" he asks, his eyes still closed.

I stick my nose into the glass of wine and swirl it around like he showed me. I smell wine. "Leather," I say, because I've heard him say that before about red wines. I pull out a cigarette and place it between my teeth. "And tobacco," I add.

"Good. What else?" He is in a different universe, his pretentious wine world, where there's no such thing as just having a glass of wine. There's no such thing as drinking. There is only a full-body, total-immersion experience. I light my cigarette. His eyes snap open at the scratch of the flint. He pulls his feet off the coffee table and swiftly grabs the cigarette out of my mouth. The filter sticks to my dry lips, and, as he snatches it from me, he pulls away a piece of skin. "You can't *smoke* while you're having an '86 Margaux! You're going to ruin the experience. For yourself *and* for me. Jesus, Sam. Pay attention!"

His scolding cuts me, like I'm some petulant child who can't follow directions. His look of disappointment and contemptuous attitude cram me further down into a feeling of emptiness. When I lose his approval, he seems to get so big, and I feel so small. He was being nice today, and I had to go and fuck it up.

"I'm sorry; you're right. I didn't mean to ruin it. What should I be smelling?" I suck my bleeding lip and try to listen to him. I lean forward and hold the glass to my nose, but now all I can taste is the metallic blood in my mouth, and when I sip the wine, it stings. Maverick notices the tension and begins to get restless. He sniffs around my mouth and awkwardly re-adjusts himself on my lap. As I try to hold him and stabilize his little paws, I tip the glass and spill the tiniest drop onto the orange blanket. The dribble of wine seems to escape my glass in slow motion as I hold Maverick, whose furry paws are slipping off the cashmere blanket, and try to catch the drop back into my wineglass. My ears are hot and full, and I watch helplessly as the drop of '86 Margaux splashes onto the big *H.* I look up to catch Lucas witnessing this, and already angry, he drops his head. Before I can apologize and blot the stain with the sleeve of my sweater, he picks up his decanter and walks away. Maverick laps at the wine. I wipe at it furiously with my fingers, but it's not helping. It's hardly even visible, but I know that to Lucas, I've wrecked the blanket.

I gather my cigarettes and wineglass into one hand and put on Maverick's leash with the other. My heart is beating in my throat as I fold the blanket the way Lucas likes it folded and tuck it under my arm. I push the chairs back into their original position, and steel myself to go downstairs and face him. He had a perfect plan designed in his head, where we would drink his perfect wine, and watch his perfect sunset, and his perfect dog would sit calmly on his perfect blanket, and I spoiled it all. I shouldn't have lit that cigarette. I shouldn't have spilled the wine.

I push the button for the elevator, and my stomach squeezes and flips. I step inside the mirrored elevator and see the fear on my face. Maverick sits on my foot and looks up at me as we descend. The adrenaline is pumping fast now as we walk toward Lucas's apartment. And then it subsides when I see his front door. My handbag, the contents of which are now strewn around the carpeted hallway, is upended in front of his door. This is my invitation to leave. I bend down and gather my things, shoving everything back into my bag. I hook Maverick's leash to the doorknob and gently place the wineglass on the carpet. I fear for a moment that Maverick will try to lap at the wine and knock the glass over, so I gulp down the Margaux. Doesn't taste like such a big deal.

I see a pad of yellow Post-it notes in my handbag, with bits of fuzz and tobacco stuck to the gluey line at the back. I fish a Typhlos pen out of a zipper pocket and write "I'm sorry I ruined your evening" on a bent note with frayed and blackened edges. I peel it off and stick it to the door. I snuggle Maverick's face as the first tear falls, and I think to myself that this humiliation is better than the alternative. If he had left the door open or invited me in, I would be recovering for days.

NOVEMBER 8TH, 11:03 A.M.

It's Tuesday at 11:00 a.m., and Richard is about to come sit in my office for an hour. To date he has said nearly nothing to me until I ask him to focus on paperwork, and then he squeezes out one-word answers or angry refusals to respond. I am still scared of him, but it's getting better. I'm trying to show Rachel that I am capable of managing this, that I will be the singular psychologist able to get through to him and eventually give him the help he needs. I need to maintain her approval, keep her A-plus rating. It keeps me functioning.

Despite wanting to save the day, my mind is elsewhere this morning; I'm harping on what could have been on Sunday night, so I am thinking of bailing on the attempt to work on the files with Richard. I haven't yet made more progress than any of my predecessors, but I can't handle another issue right now.

I hardly notice as Richard walks through my door and sits down with his stack of papers. He takes his hat off in my office and gently sets it atop his pile of newspapers. Sometimes he wears the tweed newsboy cap; sometimes it's a gray one. He seems to have gotten more comfortable around me, now that we've had a few sessions and groups together. He sometimes says good-morning, sometimes nothing, but today I wouldn't have heard him if he had greeted me.

After a short while, he speaks. "You're different today."

"Nope, I'm the same today. Same old Sam, right as rain." I'm not even looking up.

"How come you're reading that same page over and over, then? You haven't turned that page in twenty minutes."

"I'm concentrating."

"On what?" He is incredulous; he is noticing. He is supposed to be crazy and I am supposed to be able to get away with my mind wandering sometimes.

"If you're not going to work on your file or talk about treatment goals, then please, read your papers and let me do my work in peace." Calmly, softly, defeated.

"I've never seen you in peace."

What are you, my therapist? You'll never see me in peace, Richard; stop looking.

We resume ignoring each other, and I sit quietly wondering what I'm doing with my life. Richard is shifting and wiggling uncomfortably in his chair. He reaches his crooked left arm out in front of him, as if trying to straighten it out properly. He huffs, and he's distracting me.

"Something bothering you, Richard?"

"Yeah, what's going on with that kid from the group you were running the other day?"

"I'm not sure what's going on with Devon. Why do you ask?"

"He always does this contortionist act when he's in group. I find it very distracting. And he always wears a jacket even though it's practically boiling in here. He leaves confetti wherever he goes. He's making me uncomfortable. How am I supposed to get better in an environment like this?" It seems it's his size that's making him uncomfortable, but I'd rather hear him complain than continue to avoid speaking altogether.

"Okay, what exactly is it that you would like me to do here?"

"I don't know—you're the shrink, not me." Richard waves his hands at me dismissively.

"This seems like more of an administrative problem. Or even a janitorial issue. I can ask that he refrain from contorting in groups. But, you have to remember, this is an institution, and we need to live with the foibles and behaviors of others."

"Within reason."

"Yes, Richard, within reason, but a little shadow boxing never hurt anyone. Maybe what we need to talk about is your ability to tolerate frustration."

"I tolerate it fine. I'm just not interested in being in groups with a man in a leather jacket who leaves confetti and makes himself into a pretzel."

"Noted. I will follow up, and should I discover anything, I will let you know. Fair?"

He raises his eyebrows at me, unconvinced, and returns his gaze to his newspaper.

"And he stinks, too. Just sayin'." One last jab and now he's finished.

NOVEMBER 9TH, 10:00 A.M.

Jenni is nervously twisting the hem of her shirt in my patient chair. She has a long history of being abused, and associates anyone in a position of authority with fear and danger. She hasn't been at Typhlos for very long, and she is still healing physically from the abuse she experienced before she got here.

"How are you getting along with your roommate?" I usually try to start sessions with something light and administrative so patients can get comfortable before we address anything serious.

"Tashawndra? She's good. We make good roommates, I think. She's clean and she keeps her stuff on her side, and I try to keep my stuff on my side, too. She's been here for so long now, she knows all about everything, so she's helping me get used to stuff. She lets me use her lotion."

"I'm glad to hear that. Tashawndra is very nice. I'm glad you are comfortable in your living space. How have you been feeling since detox?" Jenni had to go to detox before being admitted to Typhlos because she was addicted to heroin and going through withdrawal.

"Better, but it still hurts. I'd never been so sick before. The smack just takes the life out of you, and when you can't get any, it takes the life out even more. I thought I would never get better. It's scary, when you get heroin sick. It's very scary." She holds her stomach and rocks back and forth as she says this.

"It is, and you're very brave for committing to treatment so you'll never have to have those withdrawal symptoms again. Now that your physical addiction is under control, we are going to be spending more time focusing on the psychological and the emotional components of the addiction. I've changed around your group schedule a little bit to include some recovery groups, and some dual-diagnosis groups, as well. You and I are going to spend time in our sessions talking about your addiction, too. You think you're ready for that?"

"What's duo diagnosis?" she asks, scraping at the edges of a scab on her head.

"Dual diagnosis. That's when you have both an addiction to drugs or alcohol and a diagnosed disorder or mental illness. When you're struggling with both those things at the same time, you've got a unique set of circumstances, and we want to make sure that you can get all the support you need."

"Okay, that sounds good. What are we going to talk about in our sessions with you and me?" Jenni rolls up the sleeves she'd been tugging on and I can see the track marks still dotting her arms, from the crook of her elbow all the way down to between her fingers.

"Well, I wanted to start today by asking you to tell me a little bit about your history of drug use. When did you start, how did you use, those kinds of things. You ready for that?"

"Yeah, I'm ready." She takes a deep breath and pulls what's left of her hair into a stringy knot on top of her head. "I started doing drugs when I was really young. I was still in school, and I dropped out in tenth grade, so I must have been twelve or eleven or something like that.

"My mom was always out of the house; she worked two

jobs and when she was finished working, she would go to the bars, so my sister and I were alone at home a lot. My sister, Jackie, is four years older than me. She had her friends and boyfriends over to the house all the time, and they would sit in her room and smoke weed and cigarettes and drink alcohol and listen to music. Her room was the garage.

"Sometimes I would come to the garage when she was with her friends, and I would just sit there and watch them, but I wouldn't smoke or anything. She didn't mind. Some of her friends were nice to me. There was one boy who came over who liked me, I think. His name was Ronnie.

"One time, he came over and sat next to me while they were all hanging out. I was in the corner next to the garbage cans, and he came over and asked how old I was, and if I had ever smoked weed before. I said yes, even though I hadn't because I didn't want to look like some lame kid."

I silently smile at this notion, remembering being a kid among the older crowd, claiming to have personally experienced adventures I had seen on after-school specials.

"So, he handed me the joint and he told me to prove it. I took a hit that was way too big because I thought it was like smoking cigarettes, and I had smoked a cigarette before. I started coughing really hard, and I knew I was going to get sick, so I ran out into the driveway and I barfed all over the place. Ronnie came out after me and was rubbing my back. He told me I did good, and I could come and sit with them." She looks at me and smiles a sad, nostalgic smile. "I don't know why but I remember that night really well. After that, it all sort of gets hazy and blends together. I started sitting with them whenever they came over, and I started smoking weed every day. I was scared at first because I know you're not supposed to do drugs, but they all told me that weed was a plant from the earth and that made it natural and only the chemical drugs were bad for me. They made it all sound like everything we were doing was okay. It was normal. Ronnie was always sitting next to me and rubbing my legs and my back.

"Sometimes he made me uncomfortable because he was so much older than me, but I liked the attention, too. I knew Jackie would never let anything bad happen to me. Then he started bringing in junk. They said that heroin came from a plant, too, the plant where the poppy seeds for the bagels came from, and they told me that if I was okay having a bagel with poppy seeds, then it's the same thing." She snorts and shakes her head. "I can't believe I thought that bagels and junk were going to be the same."

Jenni continues her story, telling me about Ronnie tying her arm off with a rubber band because the belts they were using on their own arms were too big for her skinny adolescent body. As with so many other patients here, she tells me of becoming dependent on both heroin and Ronnie, and the tables turning after a while—Ronnie starting to demand something in return. Jenni has been desensitized to all this and retells the story as if she were reciting a grocery list. The word *rape* has lost its meaning, and she reports that sometimes her sister, Jackie, would step in and offer herself in place of Ronnie raping her twelve-year-old sister.

"Jenni, we are getting to the end of our time today, so I wanted to stop and thank you for being so brave and honest about all of this. I think I'm going to add you to a women's group that we offer here, where survivors of sexual abuse can work together to manage what happened to them." Jenni cheerfully nods along as I talk.

As she walks out the door, I look at the scabs on her scalp, I see the missing chunks of hair. I see the track marks on her arms and thank God alcohol leaves less of a trace. I think of

Ronnie taking advantage of her, pushing her into a corner with heroin and then not letting her leave. I think of Lucas. I wonder if I can walk away with all of my hair.

NOVEMBER 9TH, 4:46 P.M.

Richard is still complaining about Devon and his jacket; he's become obsessed, and he isn't letting it go. He spent half the day today indicating that something must be done about this man and his jacket and his confetti. We didn't have a session together, but he showed up at my door over and over again, demanding action. I'm going to Shirley's office. Shirley is Devon's counselor, so she must know something.

"Shirley, what's the deal with Devon? The jacket? I have a patient who is completely disturbed by his jacket. Don't ask me why."

"What jacket?" Shirley is eating a fruit cup with a plastic spoon.

"Really? Shirley? The leather jacket he wears *all* day *every* day. The old, scrappy motorcycle jacket? You can't tell me you haven't noticed this. He wears it every day. And what's up with the confetti he puts everywhere? Every time I have him in a group, he leaves these little brown scraps of paper or paint or something behind. Do you not notice this?" I'm looking at her chair, and it's covered in the confetti. It's covered in everything.

"Oh, the shit jacket."

"What? The *what*?" I've never heard Shirley curse. It's like Grandma taking a whiskey shot or smoking a blunt—what the hell is this? "Shirley!"

"He wears that jacket as a repellent."

"A repellent from what? From who?"

"Whom. It's a people repellent. It's his shit jacket. He learned this while he was homeless. He was constantly getting harassed while sleeping on the streets. He needed to find a way of surviving out there, so he smeared shit all over the back of his jacket so he would stink and people would stay away from him." She says this like she is telling me the turkey is done. She is nonchalant and unfazed by this information. I'm fascinated and repulsed.

"Oh, my God, Shirley! They're shit flakes? You mean to tell me the confetti all over the unit is really a pile of dried shit flakes! Jesus *Christ*!"

I'm slamming her door; I'm barreling into the bathroom. I'm scrubbing my hands, I'm fuming. I'm shocked. How is it possible that we have all been *handling shit flakes*, and Shirley never bothered to tell us any of this? Jesus, no wonder Richard was disturbed by the jacket.

I sit down at my desk and compose three emails. One to Rachel to ask her to confiscate the shit jacket now that I know it's a fucking biohazard. One to the head of the maintenance staff asking for a deep clean of the group rooms. And finally, one to the staff to let everyone know that the confetti they have been surrounded with is actually dried shit flakes, and in case we had forgotten, we are surrounded by insanity. With the pressure to keep myself sane—the need to ensure that something exists to keep a line between me and my patients—days like these help me believe that there really *is* a reason that I have keys and they don't.

NOVEMBER 11TH, 8:36 A.M.

"Good morning, Rachel," I say with a sunshiny voice as I saunter through Rachel's door and sit in her patient chair.

"Morning, Sam. You're very chipper today." She clears away a corner of her desk for me to put my files down so we can begin our supervision session. Rachel does very minimal supervision of the staff because she doesn't have the time, and she is forced to believe that everyone is able to take care of themselves. There's been a recent influx of new patients, and Rachel is preoccupied with placement and intakes, so she's been putting off traditional supervision and replacing it with encouragement to call her if we have questions or problems.

"Chipper every morning," I lie, swallowing my hangover heartburn. I put on my reading glasses and pull out Richard's incomplete file. "So, I figured since we only have a short time together this morning, I should jump right into business." Rachel nods, sips her coffee and swivels her chair to face me. She crosses her giant calves and waves me along. "Richard McHugh and I have been meeting weekly on Tuesdays at 11:00 a.m. There was a lot of speculation that he was uncooperative, but he always shows up to our sessions, and he's always punctual. He seems to like the structure. Now, that being said, he is extremely uncooperative *during* the sessions. He is absolutely unwilling to complete the psychological assessments and gets very defensive and cagey when I try to pull any information out of him."

"Do you feel safe in sessions with him?" Rachel asks.

"Sure. He isn't threatening or violent, he's just very quiet and guarded. I don't imagine that he would hurt me. He seems to be protecting himself by staying quiet. He doesn't like to share his story."

"Have you been able to determine why he was in prison?"

"No. This is actually one of the other issues with his chart; there isn't a lot of stuff in his continuation-of-care section. I have the names of the halfway houses he attended, but no contact number or contact person there, no sponsor or mentor. I have the names of the prisons he was in, and the dates he was there, but no further information. It's all very unclear. There are some xeroxed pages with huge swaths of the page blacked out. There is no information about the charges, so there's no way to know what he did to end up in prison. And he certainly hasn't made any effort to tell me."

Rachel nods. "I was the one who did his intake, actually, and I found the same thing. There was very little information available to us, but he was strangely insistent on coming here. He didn't tell me much of anything at all, but he was polite, if standoffish. It's a complete question mark. I got in touch with the teams at Revelations and Horizon House, the halfway houses, but they didn't have anything on him. The staff turnover at those places is ridiculous, and they don't seem to keep proper records." She's reaching around her desk and pulling at scraps of paper poking out of various in-boxes and out-boxes. She's looking for something.

"Have you had patients like this before? I'm not entirely sure how best to proceed. He's a giant question mark, like you said, so I don't know how to properly place him in groups, and I'm not sure how to draw out the information we need to help him." Rachel loves it when I ask her for advice.

"I'm looking for his original intake stuff. I gave him a blank sheet to write on when he refused to fill out the intake materials. I asked him about his goals for treatment and that kind of thing. I know he scribbled something down, but I can't remember what it said." She pushes her chair around the office, opening file drawers and checking inside a massive disorganized cabinet.

"For now, I'm just going to keep up our weekly sessions," I reassure her, "keep him in some of the high-functioning, intellectual groups, and see if we can get him comfortable with me, and maybe then he'll come out of his shell." Rachel doesn't seem to be listening to me anymore as she's seeking this document.

"Here! Here it is," she says, pulling a page with rolled corners from the back of a notebook. "See if this can be useful to you."

I take the page from her hands and look over Richard's handwriting. He was using a dull pencil and the lines of his cursive are blurry and uneven. He made a heading that says "Goals at Typhlos" and he filled in the section with bullet points: "To get better. To forgive. To reenter life." He specifically writes *Typhlos* in various places on the sheet. He obviously wanted to come *here* in particular. There are several other sections, but the pencil lines have been smeared and I can't read much. Under another heading called "Therapy," he wrote something that looks like *open up* and something else that looks like *Samantha*.

NOVEMBER 14TH, 12:34 P.M.

It's snowing outside. I'm up on the corner of my desk, staring out the window. The guys on the scaffold are still working, despite the change in weather. It's been brutally cold, but for some reason, when the snow starts, it feels warmer. Like the snow is creating a blanket that covers the world and keeps it safe. The flakes are fat and wet and sticking to the cars parked on the street below. In the city, the snow only stays beautiful for a couple of hours. Once the plows come through, the perfect white shroud becomes a thick, gray sludge, sometimes piled to waist height. The only thing I miss about my house growing up is the way the snow stayed untouched.

My door is slightly ajar, and I hear the chatter of patients in the hallway. My office is across from the computer room, a popular spot for patients to try to break into porn sites or gather to chat with each other. There are two dilapidated couches and someone is always asleep in there.

I hear an unfamiliar voice outside my door, probably someone leaning against the wall outside the computer room. It's a man's voice, Brooklyn accent, and the hiss of missing teeth. His voice is loud and abrasive, but he hushes it down to a whisper scream to add a conspiratorial air to his story. I move to the crack in the door and listen to him without showing myself.

"It's women—women get you into these places, man. No matter what you do, you can't please 'em."

"A woman got you in this place?" Another male voice I can't quite recognize.

"Yeah, she did. My ex."

"What did she do?" Whoever is telling this story is certainly commanding the attention of his listener.

"Well, she broke up with me, first of all. Then she went and started fuckin' my best friend. Mmm-hmm. And you *know* that ain't right. So, I had no choice; I had to get her back. Ain't nobody gonna disrespect me like that."

"How'd you do it? How'd you get her back?"

He hushes his voice back down to the whisper scream: "I killed the bitch."

"You killed her?" The listener gasps.

"Man, shhhhhh! Shut the fuck up, yo. I ain't gonna tell you nothing you keep hollerin' like that."

"How'd you do it?" the listener whispers back. I'm still eavesdropping from my office. I'm not concerned yet—these kinds of grandiose stories are not uncommon here. Some patients treat the unit as if it were prison, and the scarier they make themselves appear, the safer they feel, so bullshit stories about murders are rampant.

"Ha. I'll tell you how I did it. She had a house in the Bronx, right? And she would let her dog out the back to run around and piss and whatever. So one night, I went to her house, and I waited for her to let that dog out. Once I seen the dog, I jumped the fence and I grabbed him."

I hear chairs from the computer room scooting across the floor, followed by a few short footsteps. The story is getting more listeners.

"He was some old shaggy piece of shit dog. I had a can of lighter fluid with me, and I dumped it all over that dog. He was so stupid, he started to lick it off. He liked it, too. Just kept lickin' at that lighter fluid. But he stopped when I lit him up."

"No shit? You lit the fuckin' dog on fire?"

"Damn right, I did! And he starts barkin' and yellin' and shit, so I pick him up, and I throw his ass through the back window of the bitch's house. It smashes the window, and the curtains got lit up, too. I could hear the dog, and it was screamin' and then I heard Alisha, and she start screamin', too. And she trying to put the dog out, and he dyin' and the fire just getting bigger and bigger." His voice is getting loud now, and I can feel my fists clenching.

"So, she says 'fuck the dog, I gotta get out,' and she runs out the back door, and where am I? Right there waitin' for her. And it's dark out, and she don't even see me, so she runs right into me. I grab her and turn her around so she has to watch the house burn. I put my hand over her mouth so she can't scream. You see that?" I can almost hear the craning necks looking to see what the storyteller is showing them. "Bitch started biting my hand. But she stopped biting when I popped her in the mouth.

"The house was going up fast, I mean *fast*, and it started to get hot and the smoke made it hard to see, so I pulled her back into the alleyway behind the house. She was kickin' and pullin' and she knew she couldn't save nothin', and so she stopped strugglin' and just watched it burn. The fire was mad loud, and then when the trucks came, you couldn't hear nothin', not even screamin'. So I took my hand off her mouth, and I told her: this is what she gets for fuckin' with me."

"And no one saw you? You didn't get caught?"

"Nah, man. Nobody even knew we was there. And she starts beggin' and sobbin' and slobberin' all over, and that's when I finished it. I just put my hand around her neck, and I squeezed. Didn't even take that long."

I feel my face contort into an angry grimace as I hear this macho bullshit. I find myself overwhelmed with disappointment at the pathetically appreciative response from the listeners. This sociopathic story, this admiration from peers—I'll never understand this shit. The more I keep hearing it over the years, the more I feel like it's seeping into me, disturbing my sanity. I keep listening and I hear some of the guys relaying bits of the story to latecomers. I even hear what sound like high fives. And then I hear raspy, almost panicked breaths. I hear a familiar voice now, shaking, furious. Tyler.

"You set a woman's dog on fire? You threw her dog into her house and her house caught fire?" Tyler has obviously been listening, and he is appalled.

"Yeah, bro, and what?"

"And what? You murdered her? For cheating on you?" His voice is getting higher.

"You got problems, bro?"

"Yeah. Yeah, I got fuckin' problems."

"Hi, guys!" I shout as I open my door and pretend I haven't been listening. "What's happening? How's everyone?" It's clear there's tension in the hallway, and various patients have fled to the safety of the couches in the computer room. Everyone's eyes are glued to Tyler and the storyteller.

"Hi, I'm Dr. James. I don't think we've met." I extend my hand to the storyteller, who has his eyes trained on Tyler. He ignores me. "What's your name?"

"Floyd." He still won't take his eyes off Tyler. Floyd is about a foot shorter than Tyler is, but has probably sixty pounds on him. Tyler is vibrating with anger.

"Miss Sam, I don't think you should be here right now."

"Really, Tyler?" Chipper, unaware. "How come?"

"This man got no respect for women." Tyler is shifting his weight from one foot to the other, clenching and unclenching his fists. Floyd doesn't move. He stares, unblinking, at Tyler, waiting for him to act.

"Pitchers and catchers report in a couple months, you know." Talking Yankee baseball with Tyler is my ace in the hole to defuse this without security or backup. "Floyd, are you a baseball fan?" I ask as I move to the space between them, and the air is thick with perspiration and rage. "Tyler and I are huge Yankee fans." I'm a little taller than Floyd, so when I'm up close to his face, he has to shift his gaze to make eye contact with me. I'm obscuring his view of Tyler, so he's forced to address me.

"Yeah. I could watch some baseball, miss."

"America's pastime. It's a beautiful thing. Now—" I clap my hands together "—where are you gentlemen supposed to be? I'm sure there's something productive we could all be doing instead of loitering here in the hallway, huh?"

No one responds to me, but several patients observing from the computer room peel themselves off the couches and move on. Tyler is backing up slightly, but I can still feel his breath at the back of my neck.

"No? Okay. But I've got things to do. Tyler? Want to walk me to my next group?" I know Tyler is a gentleman and he wouldn't let a lady walk by herself if she asked for an escort.

"Alright, Miss Sam." I hear his teeth grind as he steps in front of me and starts slowly moving down the hallway. I pull my glasses down my nose and glower at Floyd.

Tyler and I walk down the hall, and I again ask him about baseball. Completely distracted, trying to shake the story from a moment ago, he falters and mumbles. When we reach an empty group room, I step inside and ask him to follow me.

"Tyler, when you hear something like that and you react,

it just feeds the beast. He was telling that story to get a reaction out of people. Let's not give him the satisfaction, okay? When you're disturbed by somebody, you walk away. You don't engage. Come find me or another staff member if you feel you're not able to take it, okay?"

"He killed that dog. I just got so mad when he said he killed that innocent dog and that innocent lady."

"Yeah, me too, Tyler. Me too. But we can't let it get to us, okay? We have to rise above it."

"You think it's bullshit? He's making it up to scare the other patients?"

"Maybe. Maybe he's making it up. But even if he didn't kill an innocent dog or an innocent lady, you and I both know that there are innocent ladies and dogs getting killed every day. But we can't go to pieces and get in fights because of it. You're here to take care of *you*, not to worry about anybody else. Right?"

"Yeah. I know you're right, Miss Sam. I'm here to worry about me. And the Yankees, because, last season, our pitching wasn't looking so good."

"You're damn right about that."

NOVEMBER 14TH, 9:21 P.M.

I'm sitting on my couch waiting for Lucas to show up with takeout. He said he was going to be here an hour ago, but he's not here yet. I'm trying to read a book, and I have to close one eye to see the words. I'm distracted and hungry, and I keep checking my phone to see if Lucas is going to text me. Nothing. I texted him thirty minutes ago, asking when he's planning on arriving, but I didn't get a response. I reread the same page over and over again.

My glass is empty now, and so is the bottle next to it. When I'm anxious, I drink faster than I should. Even though it's cold outside, colder than the last few Novembers, I'm still drinking white wine. I carefully wipe up the condensation on the coffee table with the sleeve of my sweatshirt and tiptoe to the recycling bin. I plop the still-sweaty bottle into the bin and crack open the twist-off lid of another one. It's better if Lucas doesn't know that I already drank a whole bottle. As I'm tiptoeing back to the couch, my phone buzzes and my foot catches the leg of the coffee table.

It's Lucas. Buzz me in, forgot my key.

I write back, You have to push the button first; it won't work if you don't buzz.

The buzzer blares a long and angry scream into my apartment, and I depress the button to release the door. I can see Lucas's bad mood on the grainy security camera. He slaps the up button for the elevator. He usually takes the stairs, because I'm only on the third floor, but when he's pissed, or drunk, or carrying something, he takes the elevator. Tonight, it seems he's all three. I leave the front door ajar and return to the couch. I pour a small glass of wine and clutch it as I wait. I pull my knees up to my chest and hunker down into my pillows.

Lucas marches in the front door and promptly dumps the take-out bag on the floor. He shoves it into the kitchen with his foot and angrily peels off his coat.

"Well, you could offer to give me a hand." He huffs at me. I pop up off the couch and greet him with a kiss on the cheek. I pick up the take-out bag, which is filled with something that has gone cold, and I lift it onto the kitchen counter. Lucas is very obviously on drugs. His hair is matted down to the back of his neck and his collar is soaked with sweat. He is clenching and unclenching his jaw, and he has thick white spit gathered in the corners of his mouth. Cocaine. He doesn't say anything else to me and instead walks to the bathroom to tidy himself up. As I hang his coat on the back of a barstool, I reach into his pockets to see what I can find.

A half-smoked pack of cigarettes next to an unopened pack. A black Bic lighter with gouges at the bottom from using it to open bottles. A crumpled credit-card receipt from First Wok with today's date on it. The time stamp was from two hours ago. I stuff the contents back into his pockets and reach into the breast pocket. A rolled-up fifty-dollar bill with one end wet and the other end powdery, and a tiny empty bag that used to house a gram of cocaine. Adrenaline burns in my stomach as I drop the contraband back into his coat.

I sit down on the couch and take a big gulp of wine. I light a cigarette and wait to hear the toilet flush. He usually muffles the sounds of his snorts by flushing the toilet. He probably has another bag in there with him. My building is old, and so is the plumbing. He overflowed the toilet once from flushing too many times because he was snorting so many lines. Somehow, he still thinks I haven't figured out what he's doing in there. I hear the telltale flush, and then he appears outside the bathroom door.

"Whew, sorry about that," he says as he plops down on the couch next to me. "Been a long day, and I'm lugging this Chinese food here, and I can't find my keys, and I just got frustrated. Hi," he says, turning to me and kissing me on the mouth. "How was your day?"

I can taste the coke and it immediately makes my lower lip numb, so I pull away from him and wipe my mouth. "My day was fine. How was your coke?"

"Oh, Sam. I don't want to get into this." He rolls his eyes and flaps his hands at me. "I had a long day and I needed a pick-me-up. Brian from the office was holding and he gave me a bag as we were leaving. We were working on a very important merger, and it was sort of a celebration. I'm sorry I didn't tell you, but I knew you would make a big deal out of it." He reaches down and takes a sip of my wine. He is leaning forward on the couch, hovering over the coffee table, picking at the label on the wine bottle. He's not looking at me. I'm not responding. Instead, I stand up and walk to the kitchen to get him his own wineglass. The adrenaline kick sobered me, and I feel like I haven't had anything to drink at all.

He keeps picking at the label until I sit back down and pour him a glass of wine. I refill my own glass and lean back, silent. I know the coke isn't going to let him stay quiet for long, so I wait and give him the rope to hang himself.

"I'm not trying to lie to you," he implores me. "It's just that we've had this coke conversation so many times, and I told you that I was going to cut down, but honestly, it just comes with my business."

"This isn't the '80s, you know."

"Maybe not wherever you live, but in the finance world, the '80s are the revered decade. Everyone is hoping to get back to that, and sometimes, we behave as if we *are* back to that. It's not a big deal; it's not about *you*."

"Lying to me *is* about me." We are both smoking cigarettes now, and the smoke is hanging in the air like a gray aurora borealis.

"I shouldn't lie to you, you're right." He turns to look at me and squeezes my knee with his left hand, his cigarette tucked between his fingers. He holds his wineglass with the other hand and continually slurps tiny, noisy sips. He is looking at me with wild eyes between his little sips, and he begins rubbing my thigh.

"Why were you so late tonight?" I ask.

"Because Brian and I were doing drugs, Sam. How many times do I have to explain this to you? You don't need to punish me; I've already admitted it. Can't get anything by *Detective Sam*." He pulls his hand back, and his cigarette leaves ashes on my pants.

There were about thirty seconds when I had the upper hand as he was apologizing, and now I see it falling out of my grasp and rolling under the couch. Of all the things that Lucas does and then lies to me about, for some reason I have attached myself to the cocaine. The Serenity Prayer has taught me that there are some things I cannot change, but for some reason, I think his coke use is one of the things I can. Baby steps. I'm chipping away at the vices. One day I'll have the strength to stop him from all the other damage he does, to me and to himself.

Lucas is reeling now, angry that I caught him. I'm contemplating my exit strategy when he suddenly pops up to his feet and offers me a hand to help me off the couch.

"Why don't we eat something? There's all this Chinese food in the kitchen; let's just have a bite to eat and forget this shit ever happened, okay?" He is clenching my wrist and pulling me into the kitchen. He takes two plates out of the cabinet above the sink and slaps them both down on the counter. He reaches into the First Wok bag and pulls out two white cardboard containers. Lucas drops my wrist and it falls to my side with a thud, and he begins unloading lo mein and sesame chicken onto the plates. I can see him getting angrier and angrier with each shake of the to-go containers; I start slowly backing out of the kitchen.

"Where the fuck are you going? You asked me to come over and bring dinner, and here I am, preparing dinner for us. Don't *sneak* out of here and pretend you didn't ruin our evening together with your accusations and your detective work. Here—" he shoves a plate of cold Chinese at me "—eat this. It's what you wanted, isn't it?" He leaves his plate on the kitchen counter and stalks toward me with his head bowed and his eyebrows clamped in rage. I'm holding my plate between us with both hands, backing up.

"Thank you for bringing Chinese food, but I didn't ruin our evening. You're the one who came over hours late and coked up." I keep backing up.

"So, I ruined the evening?" he growls.

"Look, the evening doesn't have to be ruined at all—" I implore him, but as soon as he's close enough, Lucas slaps the plate out of my hand, and sesame chicken and lo mein and broken shards of plate scatter on the floor around us. He pushes the mess out of his way with his foot and keeps lumbering closer to me. I hold my hands up against his chest and try to push him off me, but he is too big, and too angry, and already nearly on top of me.

"Hit me," he says calmly, with a twisted grin. "Hit me, since I fucked everything up. I ruined dinner, didn't I? So hit me." He starts yelling and chest bumps me, sending me stumbling back into the wall. "Hit me!" He points to his jaw and chest bumps me again, and now I'm pinned between him and the wall, and I can't find the room to squirm out. I feel the handle to the closet door with my left hand, and I try to pull it open, but Lucas's big arm is over my head, holding the closet door closed. "Hit me," he says again as his other hand rises up and grips me by the throat. "Hit me!"

NOVEMBER 16TH, 9:14 P.M.

I'm at Nick's talking to a friend, and although I've been told that he's very sexy and charming, I haven't noticed it until right this minute. He's standing in front of me, and we're flirting. Everyone else we know here is behind me, jammed in near the DJ booth. He's looking at me with a pair of eyes that I have never seen in his head, and I feel like the universe is shifting and my stomach is flipping. He is devouring me and I don't want him to stop.

He's a player—we all know it; I have always known it. I watched him hook up with a prepubescent neophyte yesterday and he has been picking the low-hanging fruit for years. I see every woman fall for him; I laugh at them and silently hope they remember to wrap it up, and I giggle at the girls who are mad at him for the fuck-and-run. I've always considered him a decent soul, and at the same time I don't see any of this right now. All I see is man. Man who can take my whole world and turn it upside down, just by paying me the slightest bit of attention.

Someone has taken out their camera phone, and of course this is a problem because everyone here knows Lucas, and I'm dating Lucas, and I should be thinking about Lucas, but

I can't even remember his name right now. I'm absentmindedly pulling my scarf up around my neck to keep the bruises from the other night obscured. We are all crammed together, taking pictures that someone will inevitably post on Instagram, and then all infidelity will be exposed and I'll be the bad guy and Lucas will run from me and I will be alone and I can't have that.

So I pose and I smile and I pretend that all the feelings I have rushing through me—the fire, the heat that's pulsing in my veins, in my stomach, in my pants—all of this is not happening. And of course, *he* comes to stand next to me for the pictures, and he is almost in front of me, and he is kissing my cheek for the photo.

The group is closely huddled together, and without anyone else seeing, while we're no more than a quarter inch from all our friends, he reaches his hand behind him, between us, and holds my breast. He's killing me and he knows it and I love it and all I want to do is stay and take more pictures and have him keep his hands on me and all over me and take me away from here and make me something better and never, ever, ever leave me.

Somehow it's all over and in a whirlwind, I'm on the street walking home. When we said goodbye he kissed me on the lips, but we all kiss each other on the lips, so this didn't mean anything to anyone witnessing it. But we had never kissed on the lips before and mine are burning with man all over them, and I am walking home toward Lucas and I want to turn back and run into the arms of man, but Lucas will leave me and I can't have that. But I need to see this guy again. When will we be able to do this? This is a mission and I must accomplish it, and I will have him no matter what it takes. His name is AJ. I don't even know what it stands for.

NOVEMBER 18TH, 12:03 P.M.

David and I are sitting in his office, avoiding the world, eating our lunches. He usually brings something in, and I end up stealing half of it, or we go to one of the sandwich shops down the street. There's a halal truck on the corner, and today we both got chicken over rice. We usually eat when the patients get their lunch, whether we're hungry or not—that way we're less likely to have visitors or intruders.

"Did you see Julie in the meeting this morning?" I ask, plastic fork between my teeth.

"Yeah, I saw her. Why? What'd she do?"

"She was doing her makeup in a Chanel compact at the fucking conference table."

"Is that a big deal?"

"She works in a *mental institution*. Why does she care so much about how she looks? It's pathetic."

David laughs at me. "You really hate her, huh?"

"I don't *hate* anybody. I just think she's incredibly silly and she doesn't belong here. She should be working at Bloomingdale's."

"You ever sat in on any of her groups?"

"No, have you?" David rarely engages in Julie shit-talking

and gossip with me, because he's mature and above it all, so I love when he descends to my level.

"Yeah, I was at the one that your patient stormed out of. The new guy, big dude."

"Richard? The thing with the beets?"

"Ha!" David opens his mouth to laugh and a single grain of rice flies past me and sticks to the window. "Yeah," he says, wiping his lips, "she was trying to delicately explain that some foods can change the color or consistency of pee and poop, and he just bolted. I think she wanted to get the message across that people panic when their shit turns red, thinking it's blood, so she was trying to preemptively quell the anxiety."

"Sure, which would make sense if anyone ever had beets here. What an idiot! Such a princess. I told you she shouldn't be here."

"Yeah, Rachel asked me to keep an eye on her because she's been racking up complaints."

"Really? How wonderful! Maybe Typhlos will give me an early Christmas present and fire her!" I joyfully scoop another forkful of chicken into my mouth.

"Yeah, don't hold your breath. How is the new guy, by the way? Last we talked you were getting nowhere."

"I'm still getting fucking nowhere. It's confusing. He's so high functioning, seems to be completely normal, so what is he doing here? Why is he in treatment?"

"What's his diagnosis?"

"Oh, right. Like there's a *diagnosis* in his chart. That would be too easy."

"Do you think he's diagnosable?"

"If I were to slap something on him, like for insurance pur-poses, I'd say adjustment disorder. And that's a *stretch*. There's got to be something that I'm completely missing. It's too weird for this guy to be admitted to a mental institution. Aside from being uncooperative and stubborn, he seems normal."

"You want me to meet with him? See if I can figure something out?" David is always incredibly helpful, always willing to go the extra mile for me.

"No, thanks. But keep an eye out if you notice anything." David smiles his sweet, protective smile at me and clumsily pats my knee with his free hand. I try to examine his thoughts as he turns toward the window; I'm looking for a place inside him where I could fit.

NOVEMBER 22ND, 11:06 A.M.

Although we haven't made progress with his file, it seems that Richard is getting more comfortable with me. He may even be developing a foundation of trust. He's speaking now, not about anything relevant to his mental health, but he's saying words out loud. He tells me about books he's read, or ones he's heard of that he hasn't had a chance to pick up yet. I tell him about what's happened in the music industry, and he's never happy to hear it. Today is another session with us just warming up to each other.

"You have a cell phone?" he asks me. He hasn't shaved this morning, and I can see the prickles of a pale beard poking out of his fat pores.

"Yes, I have a personal phone. Why do you ask?" I've got my legs crossed and I've twisted my chair to face him. We usually sit this way, even if the sessions are uncommunicative. It's a therapeutic technique. People are uncomfortable with silences, so often if a therapist faces a patient like they're talking, the patient will feel obligated to fill the silence.

"That was a shock to me. I was away when those things came out. Now even the homeless people have them."

"You were in prison when cell phones became popular?"

This is the first time he has acknowledged his incarceration to me, and I want to draw more information out of him.

"We didn't even have personal computers. Now everyone has a supercomputer in their pocket."

"Did you have computers available to you in prison?"

"Well, the phones are even more advanced than the computers now." He's not going to engage on this with me.

"It's true. They really do make communication much easier." Hint.

"Not just communication—everything. It's got a camera now, the internet, the emails. You can read books on those things! It used to be you had to have a whole suitcase worth of stuff to have everything that these phones have now. And they're this big." He holds out his wide palm to indicate the size of today's cell phones.

"A miracle of technology."

Richard shakes his head in wonder and returns his attention to his newspapers. Maybe I can draw him further out of his shell if I tell him that I addressed the issue with Devon and his shit jacket.

"Before you disengage completely, I wanted to let you know that I looked into the issues you were having with Devon."

"Oh?" He raises his eyebrows in anticipation.

"I put in a request with his counselor to take up the issues that you conveyed to me, including the hygiene problem and the disruptive behavior in groups. It has since been addressed with Devon personally, and I hope you will show some patience and tolerance as he adjusts."

"Well. Thank you."

"Is that a commitment to give the guy a break?"

"Not exactly."

"What is it, then?"

"It's a thank-you. I haven't said thank-you to anyone in a long time. I appreciate that you followed through." Richard bows his head to me.

"Maybe since I've shown you the respect of following through, you'll show me the same, and we can work on completing your file." Once last try for today.

His eyes return to his papers and he brushes his cheek with the back of his hand, as if he's brushing away my request.

My chest tightens as I draw in another disappointed breath. It's been almost a month now and all I have are his basics. I'm running out of ways to get through to him.

NOVEMBER 23RD, 2:14 P.M.

Julie is buzzing the intercom looking for me. Her shrill, piercing voice is making my eardrums explode, so I pick up the phone as quickly as I can and hold the receiver about a foot from my face.

"Yes, Julie?" I grumble from a safe distance. "What do you need?"

"Hi, Sam!" I can hear the syrupy ooze of her voice falling down the telephone line, threatening to come trickling onto my neck through the receiver. She pauses, waiting for me to return the cheerful greeting. I say nothing. "Um, I wonder if you have a moment to come to my office? I'm meeting with one of your patients right now; we had a little incident in group." She says *little incident* like she's talking about a kindergartner who wet her pants during nap time.

"Which patient?"

"I'm with Tashawndra." She enunciates each syllable slowly, fearful that her inability to properly articulate Tashawndra's name will indicate she's racist, or out of touch, or not relatable.

"Give me a minute." I hang up the phone before she inundates me with more pleasantries, and begin the slow walk to Julie's office.

I knock loudly on her door and realize that though we've worked together for several years, I've never seen the inside of her office before. She pulls it open, and I see Tashawndra with a shamed expression on her face, sitting on a blue plastic group-room chair. Looks like there weren't enough office chairs for Julie. She invites me in, and I take in my surroundings.

She doesn't have books or files or anything visible that would indicate this is a clinician's office; instead she has a large stuffed bear wearing a green Ralph Lauren sweater sitting on her bookshelf. She has pictures of her family with quotes about sisters etched into the white wooden frames. As she closes her door, I hear the plink of bells, and I turn to see she has two coat hooks, one with her pale camel-colored coat with a pink plaid scarf over it, and the other with a stuffed fabric wreath with lacy edges and bells hanging off it. The final straw is a framed plaque of faux reclaimed wood with intentionally worn writing and painted flowers that reads Live, Laugh, Love. I can feel the bile and undigested lunch rising in my throat, and I hesitate to stop myself from projectile vomiting directly into her perfectly combed hair. The look of disgust on my face must be apparent because Julie reaches out to touch my arm and ask me if I'm okay.

"Sam? You alright?" I yank my arm away from her and nudge her out of the way as I take a seat in Julie's desk chair. There's a scent diffuser somewhere in here, and it smells like baby powder.

"Tashawndra?" She hangs her head, and I lower mine to catch her eyes. "You wanna tell me what happened?"

"Can't Miss Julie tell you?" She hides her face in her hands. Her hair is twisted in ropes and dreads of various lengths and rigidity, some poking straight up out of her scalp and others falling forward into her eyes. She twists them when she gets nervous, and when she's feeling happy, she ties ribbons and strings to the ends. She's pulling at one of the strings now, a yellow piece of yarn tied to a dread on the left side of her face.

"I'd like to hear it from you, if you're willing to tell me. I want to know what you think happened." The yarn pops off between her fingers.

Tashawndra releases a snort like a bull about to charge. "I was in Miss Julie's group, minding my own business, and out of nowhere, I look over and I see that Barry is staring at Miss Julie, and his mind ain't right, and I know what he's thinking."

"What was he thinking?" I ask. Julie is hovering over us, blushing as her name is mentioned.

"He was thinking he like to sink his teeth into those legs!" She gestures toward Julie's panty-hosed legs, exposed beneath her admittedly work-appropriate skirt. Julie involuntarily bends and covers her knees with her hands.

I can't help smiling as I listen to this. "And then what did you do?"

"I threw my coffee cup at him." Tashawndra leans back and crosses her arms over her chest. She is braless as usual and her pendulous breasts fall into her armpits.

"Was there coffee in your coffee cup?" I'm nearly laughing as I ask.

"No! It was empty. I should have slapped his face."

"What's going on between you and Barry?"

"Well, nothing now! But before he decided to get all inappropriate with the counselor, we was seeing each other. Been a couple of weeks. He brung me flowers from the table in the lunchroom last week. And before that, he gave me the rest of his pack of cigarettes. He told me I was the most beautiful girl he ever saw, and we had lunch together and we smoked on the smoking balcony together, too. But all that over now!"

"Anything else going on between the two of you?" Sexual

contact between patients is strictly forbidden at Typhlos, although it's nearly impossible to enforce. With the growing number of patients, it's hard enough to keep track of where everyone is all the time, let alone try to figure out what everyone is doing. Patients have sex with their roommates at night, whether they're gay or not, in the bathroom stalls, out on the smoking balcony in broad daylight. Sometimes right in the open in the hallways and group rooms. Tashawndra has lost privileges and been isolated because of sexual misconduct many times before, but Barry has never been her partner.

"Nah. I know I'm not allowed to bang nobody while we doing treatment here." She fiddles with the yellow string, and I believe her that they weren't having sex. She seems to care about him, and she rarely has sex with people she cares about.

"Good. I'm glad we're making progress on that front. And you know you can't throw anything at anyone, whether they're looking at another girl or not, correct?"

"Yeah, I know." She shoots her arm out in an aw-shucks gesture and throws the yellow string onto the floor. "He gave me these yarns for my hair, too."

I pick up the string and hold it in my fist. "Tashawndra, I know it hurts when someone you like looks at someone else, but it's important to react appropriately. Do you want to say anything to Julie?" Julie's been leaning over us like an eager water boy during the halftime huddle. Her mouth hung open as she observed our interaction, and now that she's being addressed, she pops up straight and composes herself.

"I'm sorry I got jealous in your group, Miss Julie. I know people gonna look at you because you beautiful, and I know it don't mean that I can throw things at anybody." She tugs at her dreads.

"Thank you, Tashawndra. And I think you're beautiful,

too." Tashawndra blushes as a shy smile spreads across her face, and she pulls her shoulder up to her chin.

"You gonna talk to Barry about this?" I ask her.

"Yeah, I guess I could forgive him."

"I'm glad to hear that." I hand her back the yellow string, and she ties it into one of the dreads flopping down over her eyes. We walk out of Julie's office together, and I take a deep breath of institutional air to clear my nose of the insufferable scent from her diffuser. It's days like this that make me feel like a zookeeper, and I'm in awe of the level of shit I can continue to tolerate.

NOVEMBER 26TH, 12:45 A.M.

I find myself at Nick's again, waiting for David to show up. Lucas and I came together, but he is too drunk to function, so he parked himself at one end of the bar, staring at his phone, while I schmooze with our buddies. Everyone at Nick's thinks that Lucas and I are the perfect couple, and it's a very delicate dance, because we know this perception, and without speaking, we do everything we can to uphold it. Even if I'm afraid he might end up killing me when we are alone, in front of others, we put on the show that we need to put on to pretend to ourselves that each of us is fine, and that together we are the ideal couple: the beacon of domestic bliss that shines amid the crumbling failures of their past. It gives hope, and I am in the business of giving hope.

If I told them that he beats me, or that he had sex with a faceless hooker in the back room of a porn store earlier today, or that he is currently wolfing oxycodone in the bathroom, it would ruin their night, and I certainly don't want that. This perception that Lucas and I are perfect…it helps me believe it. And it's one of the last strings I have holding my life together.

David just walked into the bar, and he's scanning the room trying to find me. I'm waving with one hand while drinking a Jack and Coke with the other. He's probably the only person who knows the truth about me, the truth about Lucas and some truth about me and Lucas. Our offices share a wall, which means he can hear everything that goes on in mine. When I'm throwing up in the garbage can, or crying into my coffee, he tends to ask questions. Over the years, instead of lying to him, I've let him in, and he hasn't used it against me yet.

David is my best friend. Not just my work best friend, but the closest thing I have to a real-life best friend. I've never slept with him, although maybe I should. He has a crush on me, I can tell, and I flirt with him and humor him just enough to make the crush continue, but I'm careful to never allow it to turn into something that would require reciprocity. Just the way I like it. He walks over, we look at each other, and without saying anything, he drinks from the straw in my drink. I signal to Sid, the bartender, for another round.

David and I stand too close together and gossip. We find safety in our bubble and use that safety to dismantle the other people around us. David pretends not to notice Lucas. I can't tell if he's being polite or defensive.

Lucas is in a state now. His tie is partially loosened and partially tight, one of the middle buttons of his shirt is undone, his jacket is strewn in a booth somewhere, his glasses are all greased and cockeyed on top of his head, and he needs to lean on the bar for support. Despite this, he's become even more disarming and lovable to everyone in the room. The cocktail waitresses are huddled in the corner talking about him, and he has his hand on the panty-hosed leg of someone else's girlfriend. No one seems to mind.

When I approach, his hand slides back into his own lap.

"Act like you love me, you stupid asshole," I say with a smile.

"I do love you, you dirty whore," he replies, and he might not be joking. "But I'm tired, and I have a long week coming up, so I'm going home." He pulls his coat into his hands and makes a show of looking around the bar for his suit jacket. "If you see my jacket, will you bring it home with you? I don't have time to go searching for it now."

"No problem," I say, hiding the cigarette and lighter I have clutched in my fist, as if I wasn't about to step outside. If I give him a seamless exit, I can save myself from another one of his drunken attacks.

"You don't have to come with me. I'll get home fine," he slurs, and I give the panty-hosed girl a side-eye. We perform our saying-goodbye act, with big hugs and kisses, and after he doesn't bother to pay his tab, he stumbles out the door. I pretend not to notice the panty hose follow him out.

"You gonna be okay if I go, too?" David asks, joining me in pretending he didn't see anything.

"Yeah, I'm probably only going to have one or two more."

After tugging his coat over his shoulders, he leaves a fifty on the bar and wraps me in a bear hug. "I'll see you on Monday, but call me if anything stupid happens, okay?"

"Thanks, David. I'll see you Monday. Home safe."

Now that David and Lucas are both gone, I can turn my attention to AJ. He's been sitting at a booth with some people I don't know, but from the looks he's been giving me, I know that we're both waiting for the moment—the moment in time when it's going to be okay and we can run into the other room, the other world, the other universe where we can wrap up in one another and not worry what anyone else thinks, what anyone else knows, what anyone else can see, but at the same time, we know that that's never going to happen. So we have to live in between the lines. We have to be somewhere only he knows, and only I know, and no one says anything, because there's nothing to say. Where we can walk in daylight and hear no voices.

Even though it's the same bar we're always at, somehow the walls seem new to me. All the things around us seem to be brighter. The cheeky quotes written in chalk on the blackboard behind the bar are funnier. The music sounds like something I haven't been listening to for the last two months. There's something about the way he looks at me that takes down every single wall I have ever erected in order to keep people out.

He's standing at the DJ booth now, putting on a song and pointing at me across the bar. I'm doing everything I can to stay as far away from him as possible. He sees this and he sees me, and he puts on my favorite song and mouths to me, *This is for you.* I nod like I don't care but my life explodes and all I can think of is jumping into the rabbit hole with a guy whose full name I don't know.

No one is watching, and he walks to me and pulls me toward him, and I bury myself in the crook of his neck, which feels like the safest and most dangerous place in the world, and he tells me, "I like you...more than just sex." And I laugh at this because I can't do anything except laugh at this, and he pulls me into his neck and he smells like man, and he tells me he wants to take me away from here, and he asks me again why I'm going out with someone, and I say, "Am I going out with someone?" He tells me that he knows I have a boyfriend, and I say, "It's because I didn't know you first," and he laughs, and he pulls me in closer.

When he puts my face into his shoulder, a new life flashes in front of me, and then he breaks away. He walks to the bathroom. I check to see if anyone's looking at us, if anyone's noticing what's happening, but no one seems to notice that lightning is striking in this bar, and I follow him to the bathroom. He's in a stall, and I stand in front of the sink washing my hands and wait for him to come out but I pretend I'm not waiting.

He comes out and he didn't expect to see me, and he notices me so he starts washing his hands, and he looks at me from under his eyebrows and I act innocent like I'm not here for him, and he walks out the door before me, and I think my chance is lost. He dodges into a closet and as I'm walking past the door he reaches out and grabs my hand and pulls me in. The light is on, but he turns it off, and he kisses me and my life catches fire.

He's holding me with one arm and using the other to keep the door shut. I'm running my hands through his hair, then down to his ass, and his dick is getting hard against my belt. All I want to do is turn off the world and stay here until it doesn't hurt anymore.

He stops kissing me, and he holds my chin and says, "Look at me." I peer up at him, into the gray abyss of his eyes. The intensity is so brutal that I feel like I will melt into a puddle of sex on the floor. He says, "You're so beautiful," and he starts kissing me again, and I finally do melt into a puddle of sex on the floor.

I have never cared less about Lucas in my life, and I wouldn't be able to pick him out of a lineup right now. We're furiously making out, and all I want to do is stay, stay, stay here…

And then it's over.

He peeks out for onlookers, then sends me out first when the coast is clear. No one's the wiser, and I'm holding on to this secret like it's the nuclear codes. After he says goodbye to the people we know, he kisses me in front of everyone, but still no one notices, and he walks into the night.

NOVEMBER 29TH, 9:11 A.M.

Before I can settle into my chair and dig some Advil from my handbag, I hear a steady, slow knocking on my door. I know this knock. It could only be from Eddie, who raps on my door like this incessantly. Eddie does this to David also. I can hear him shuffling between our offices and knocking his pathetic knock. He usually waits outside the conference room for the morning meetings to be over, then walks behind me or David to ask us questions. If he misses this opportunity, he'll take turns at our doors, knocking until one or both of us has to leave, let someone else in, or we just break down and open up for him.

"Ssaammm, Daaaviiid." Eddie strings together his sentences as if each one is a very long word. He upturns the ends of each sentence so everything becomes a question, and he very nearly slurs while still managing to sound lucid. Eddie is not one of my patients, and he isn't one of David's, either. He works with Gary, but he has become attached to me and David. Why the two of us, I don't know—it could be as simple as the accessibility of our offices. The shuffling continues.

"Ssssaammm… I-know-you're-in-there… Please-open-up-for-me, Eddie…"

He sounds like a tire deflating. I pick up my office phone, put it to my ear and loudly start saying "Mmm-hmm." With my glasses on, I crack the door and peer out at Eddie like I haven't heard him this whole time. Eddie takes this as an invitation, and he sticks one laceless, dirty sneaker through the door to try to eke his way in. I mouth the words *I'm on the phone, we can talk later*, thinking this should be sufficient, but thinking wrong.

"Nnnnooooo, Sssssaaaammm… I'm-heeerrreeee-to-talk-to-you…" He has both his hands on the door and is pushing but not hard enough.

I make a display of covering the receiver with my free hand and say, "I know, Eddie, and I want to talk to you, too, but this is a very important call. We'll have to do it later."

"Oookkkayyyy… In-an-hour…?" I nod my head as I'm closing the door. I will not answer it in an hour when Eddie returns. I wish I could summon the strength and the energy it would take to give Eddie what he needs, but today I just can't do it. I couldn't be bothered to wash my hair this morning, and I woke up with a bloody butterfly stitch stuck in it, so I just put it in an elaborate bun that covers up the bandage. I take off my glasses and put down the phone, and I wonder how much more I can take of this.

Eddie has been living at Typhlos for God knows how long. In the six years that I've been working here, I think there have been three separate instances where he has been pulled from the unit and sent to emergency psychiatric. All of them were due to suicidal behaviors or threats. It's one of the hardest things about being in this business; we're supposed to be able to tell whether every suicidal gesture or remark should be taken seriously and then act accordingly every time. But when you have patients rubbing paper clips on their wrists until the red welts squeeze out the tiniest droplet of blood, and everyone else is saying "If I don't get my orange juice, I'm going to kill myself," it can get hard to differentiate.

After the third time that Eddie was removed, about four months ago, we had a morning meeting dedicated specifically to his case. I remember Gary was sweating profusely through-out the entire thing. He would regularly take giant gulps of cherry Gatorade, which left a wet red ring around his upper lip. Gary was scared that he'd be sued if Eddie ended up kill-ing himself. In order to protect himself, Gary would go over every service plan, treatment outcome, case note and evalu-ation with a fine-tooth comb to check for errors, typos, cof-fee spills, printing and reprinting these documents until he had a file he believed would render him blameless. Of course, Eddie has no family, so the idea that anyone would sue anyone should Eddie end up dead was somewhat ridiculous.

I remember Rachel took the meeting over from Gary, who proved himself totally unable to calm down and report on what was happening. She'd made several highlighted photo-copies of the important bits of Eddie's file that she passed out and asked us to share with our "neighbor." My neighbor was David, as usual. I had been extremely hungover, again, and David was quietly pointing out that I had a cigarette butt in my hair. He removed it without drawing attention, then we silently turned our focus to the handouts. Even though it was only a portion of Eddie's file, it was thick and riddled with cross outs and updates and changes to his diagnosis. There were Post-its stuck to other Post-its and stapled to several cop-ies of the same documents with black lines bisecting the pages. This was a file that had been tossed around from clinician to clinician after each one had reached the end of his or her rope, and Eddie was slipping through the cracks. One of the greatest sorrows of this business is seeing someone drowning and not being able to save his life.

I remember David and I flipped rapidly through the pages, scanning for buzzwords, and we simultaneously noticed a statement signed by W.D.R., initials neither of us recognized, dated 2003, that said "Unsalvageable. Beyond help."

"What the hell is this?" I unwittingly interrupted Rachel midspeech to express my outrage at this message. "What the hell *is* this, seriously?"

"What's what?" Rachel asked.

"'Beyond help'? Aren't we in the business of helping people? Isn't that what we're doing here? There's no such thing as 'unsalvageable.' This is a *human being*. Not a house after a hurricane. Jesus."

"Sam, I agree with you, but remember, Eddie hasn't been responding to treatment for years." Rachel.

"Fine, but when you give up on someone, what the hell are they supposed to do? It's our job to *not* give up, right? Am I crazy?" David put his arm around the back of my chair and used his thumb to rub my shoulder. This calmed me down, and when he whispered "easy, tiger" into my ear, it soothed me even more.

"No, Sam. You're not crazy at all. I feel the same way." Still Rachel. I felt overprotective of Eddie because he was so attached to me and David. I still have a soft spot for him.

As I sit remembering this meeting from months ago, I am suddenly overwhelmed with the idea that I should have opened the door to him. I should have taken the time to talk to him; if no one else was saving him, *I* should have. I could've dived in and rescued him from drowning. But my head is too full of thoughts of Lucas, thoughts of AJ, paranoid ideas of what Lucas would do if he knew about the closet at Nick's. I can't muster the energy to focus on Eddie today.

DECEMBER 1ST, 5:30 P.M.

Every year, each staff member who works on the unit has to have a psychological evaluation. Given that so many of the employees here are licensed professionals, capable of performing a competent psych eval, we've been doing each other's evaluations for years and then presenting the results to a representative from the New York State Office of Mental Health, which we just call OMH. Should any of the employees be deemed in any way unfit to be working in such a stressful and sensitive environment, some kind of action is taken. Of course, it seems ludicrous to insist on these precautions, considering you must be crazy to actually want to work here.

This year, due to a major change in the country's national awareness and vigilance about mental health, we're not allowed to give each other the evaluations. Instead, there are several highly trained, ruthless and not at all cozy psychiatrists independently contracted by OMH to come in and provide in-depth weeklong evaluations of each one of us. Each member of the staff, especially those who have access to all the patients, all the files—not to mention all the *drugs*—are to be interviewed by two separate psychiatrists. These interviews will include a battery of psychological exams and interrogations, as well as thorough background checks. Needless to say, I am shitting myself in anticipation. The batteries begin on Monday. I am promising that I will not drink myself into a stupor this weekend, because I know I have to be lucid on Monday. *Lucid on Monday. Lucid on Monday. Lucid on Monday.*

I've spent the day willing the hours to pass so I could get to this moment where David and I can escape our real lives and wander down a drunken rabbit hole. The days at Typhlos are always long and tiring, but with the new patients coming in and the responsibilities escalating, the possibility for a truly relaxing exodus is diminishing. I have been looking forward to dodging out of here with David and evading anything that could be considered a grown-up obligation.

"Hold on one sec, Julie just texted me," David is saying. I theatrically roll my eyes, indicating I do *not* want Julie to join us, and just as David is formulating his text rejection, a bubbly Julie appears before us in all her cashmere and Burberry splendor.

"Hey! David, I just texted you. What's up, you guys?" How anyone could be this energetic at the end of days like these at Typhlos, I have no idea.

"I was just writing back," David says as he tucks his cell phone into his back pocket.

"Were you guys gonna go out? I would *love* to come with you if you are?" Her wide eyes are wet and pleading, and I almost don't have the heart to lie to her. Almost.

"Yeah," David responds before I can sidestep her advances. "We're headed down to Jimmy's. You in?"

"Ugh, Jimmy's? Is that where we said we were going?" I am forcing nonchalance. "I slept with the bartender and he didn't stop calling me for like, a month. I can't go there. You guys go; I'll catch you next time." I'm already walking down the hallway, taking my cigarettes out of my bag and fishing for my lighter.

"Wait, Sam, I—I..." Before he has even finished his sentence, my mind explodes in rage, screaming inside my head that he cannot invite this pathetic little worm to one of *our* bars; she can't come and ruin the sanctity of *our* friendship! *Why* would he let someone else in? Why would he choose her over me? I have to save face. He can't abandon me for her! I'm leaving. I will leave. He can't leave me if I leave him.

"Don't worry about it. See you tomorrow." I'm out into the dark afternoon, I'm fumbling with my lighter. The fucking wind is blowing it out, and I can't light this *fucking* cigarette. I want to scream into this wind, I want to blame this wind for the tears in my eyes. I want to run to the subway and hide in the last car and pretend I don't want to murder David and damn him for leaving me! *Me!* After the friend I've been to him! For all these years, and he just chooses Julie. Julie, that incoherent, ridiculous parody of a human being! Jesus *Christ*!

I am curled into the fetal position in the handicapped seats on the C train. The C rattles and sways more than any other train, and it's helping to soothe me. I need to find solace somewhere. I need to do something to make up for this rejection. I need someone to love me. Where the hell is AJ?

DECEMBER 1ST, 7:06 P.M.

My phone has been beeping at me since I got off the train. It's David, and I'm still not answering. I read every text he sends me, but none of them will be able to make up for him choosing her over me. He doesn't even understand why this would be such a terrible thing to do to me, to abandon me for some shiny, plastic replacement.

I'm at Nick's, saying hello to everyone with cheerful kisses and hugs and questions about their well-being, and amid the faux sincerity, I'm scanning the bar for a friendly face, or the person I came here to find.

Walking into this bar is like standing behind a bus. The cold, windy silence of outside is replaced by an arresting wall of heat, noise and movement. It's always dark in here, as if it's lit to make you look your best even when you're at your worst. There are too many TVs showing too many programs at the same time, and the lines to the ladies' bathroom are always too long. The DJ gives me a wink and I collapse into my favorite stool in the middle of the bar. I haven't even said hello to Sid yet, and I can see him pouring me my Jack and Coke.

"Sammy!" he says with his Irish accent. "How are ya, doll?"

"Sid Vicious! What's up, baby?" Whatever is happening in

my life or in my head, I will always be this happy caricature. Precious few will think to look behind it, and even fewer will actually see.

The Jets game hasn't started yet, so I'm watching the pre-game show. I'm trying to keep an eye on the door while ensuring I don't look like I'm keeping an eye on the door. I don't know how to will AJ to walk in without calling someone to find out his number and asking him to come. I'm leaving it to blind faith. When Sid returns with a refill, I realize I'm putting these drinks away much faster than I should. I notice Claire, the hottest of the young, blonde cocktail waitresses, approaching me.

"Hi, honey!" She leans in to kiss me on the cheek with her tray of empties balanced in her left hand. "Where's Lucas tonight?"

"Where's what?" I heard her, but I need another minute to formulate a response. What shall I say? He's sleeping with someone. He's doing drugs. He's buying flasks of Jameson at the store to drink on his way to the bar. He's icing his knuckles from the last time he...

"Lucas! Where's Lucas?" she says with a smile.

"He's at work still. Some major finance thing keeping him at the office. I don't even know what he does all day."

Smiles, only a hint of recognition that she's in love with him. "Well, it's great to see *you*!" She walks to the service station and drops her tray. I give her the no-teeth smile.

I start looking through the messages David has been sending me. The first ones are all bewildered, wondering why I left. Those are followed by salvage messages telling me he isn't having fun with Julie and he wishes I were there. The most recent ones are clearly alcohol induced, and he's beginning to cross the invisible line that exists between friends and something more. I'm comforted by the idea that he may be in love with me, so I relax even though I may not get validation from AJ, but at the same time I am reminded that Lucas, my boyfriend, hasn't sent me a single message.

I'm getting the familiar feeling that my reaction time is slowing and my surroundings have begun shrinking. I am no longer looking around, and instead I'm creating the world I need within a two-foot radius. I have my drinks, I have my validation from David's texts, I can't make out whether or not Claire is looking at me waiting for Lucas to show up, and I finally have my armor back. I hear the sounds of Thursday Night Football in the air around me, and I feel in place; I find comfort in the status quo. I feel my phone vibrate in my hands and I look down to see another message from David.

She's superdrunk, and I don't know what to do. Where are you? I feel the twang of jealousy in my stomach and the metallic taste of desperation rising in my throat. He's taking care of her. I am not letting this get the better of me. I'm entrenched in my response.

I write and delete several replies before I settle on U know where I am.

There in ten. David is leaving her to come to me? This is unexpected. Do I want David to come here now? I haven't quite given up hope on AJ. I am watching the coin toss and trying to decide if I should dissuade David from joining me, and before I can make up my mind, he has materialized next to me.

"Why the hell didn't you come? I was stuck with her for hours! She can't hold her liquor. It was a mess." David is out of breath and exasperated, and I know he ran from the train station.

"*Me?* I'm not the idiot who invited her to come with us!" Am I glad that he is here or still enraged that he left me?

"Sam, you bailed. You could've come, too." He is signaling to Sid for a water.

"Whatever. You know I don't want to go out with *Julie.*" I can't bear to look at him while I'm saying this because I am afraid of seeing defense in his eyes, and if I see it, I know he will have moved away from me and over to her. Instead I lean to the left to avoid getting elbowed as he plops down in the seat next to me and catches his breath.

"She's such a lightweight! We didn't even make it to Jimmy's. She said she would rather go somewhere uptown, so we went to that place on Eighty-Fourth with the red-checked tablecloths? You know? And she had two glasses of sauvignon and was done." He's trying to appease me, and I don't want it.

David and I sit shoulder to shoulder watching the kickoff and I feel the intensity of his touch, but I'm too hurt to address him. He asks me if I want a shot without looking at me.

"Patrón Silver," I say without looking at him. David makes a mustache with his forefinger in Sid's direction, and Sid obligingly pours three shots—two Patrón, and one Jameson for himself. He brings the shots over to us and raises his glass.

"To keeping it classy." Sid jerks his head in the direction of some assholes in the corner and throws back his shot.

David holds his glass in front of me, imploring me to clink it. I see his ruddy cheeks and the sincerity in his eyes, so I put down my guns and toast with him. We upend our glasses with smiles on our faces, and I pull him in for a hug that could be considered intimate. Desperation will make you do funny things.

David and I are standing too close to each other by the bar, and when AJ walks in, my stomach leaps into my mouth. I immediately find myself straightening my shirt, fluffing my hair and sucking my teeth. David hasn't noticed my shift, so he keeps talking to me, and when I feel his hand creep onto my lower back, I jump like I've been burned. AJ hasn't spotted me yet, and I'm terrified of letting him know I'm looking at him. The entire bar turns into slow motion and I'm standing in the middle waiting for AJ to notice me, and I feel like the kid from *Scrubs* in that movie about New Jersey.

DECEMBER 1ST, 8:23 P.M.

I can't have AJ and David here at the same time. Oh, God, this is never going to work. If AJ sees me with David, he won't kiss me again, and I won't be able to lose myself again, and—oh, God—he sees me. He's winking at me from the doorway and now he's walking over.

He says hi to David; they give each other a handshake and man hug, and then he turns his attention to me. He pulls me into his neck and wraps one arm around my back. He kisses my neck with his scruffy face and leans back while still holding me, and winks again. I'm afraid my face will betray me, so I look down. He keeps his hands on me and swivels to order a drink. Sid gives him a two-fingered wave and makes a gin and tonic. It can't happen tonight; it can't happen with David right here with us. We are a tricycle when we should have been a bike. The music starts to fill my ears, my face gets hot, and I want everything to change.

I see AJ scanning the bar for familiar faces, and all the girls are looking at him. I feel the jealousy rising in my chest, so I reach for my drink, only to find David holding it. I pull it from his hands, and the straw stays between his teeth. He smiles his goofball smile, with the straw sticking out of his mouth, and I know that I love him, but I want him to dissolve into the barstool.

AJ is calling hellos to various people, and all I feel is special and scared that he's still holding on to me. David starts to notice this, and he takes it as a cue to return his attention to the Jets game. AJ sits on my barstool and pulls me to stand between his legs. He is asking me about my day, and although everyone is looking at him, he's only looking at me. I'm trying to be cool, but failing. My lips are trembling, and with the razor cuts to my self-esteem earlier, I'm too drunk to be able to manage this properly.

I feel the vibration of a text message in my back pocket, and if it's not David and it's not AJ, then I don't care who it is. But I need something to distract me, so I pull out the phone and unhinge my fingers from AJ's. I read the text message: Where r u? Lucas. I don't need this right now.

AJ starts playing with my hair. He's looking over his shoulder and talking to David, but both of his hands are smoothing the blond strands that have fallen into my face. I feel like I'm being crushed by waves while I debate what to say to Lucas. The electricity from AJ's touch is making it hard to concentrate on anything.

I put my phone back into my pocket and pretend Lucas's text never happened. I'm in the business of pretending and this shouldn't be anything new. AJ pushes my hair back and says, "So what are we doing?"

I can't imagine what a reasonable response should be, so I say, "Shots?" He smiles a Cheshire smile and pulls my face to his and kisses me on the mouth. For a split second the entire universe opens up and I am swallowed into a safe place where everything is warm and soft and the music feels like it is making my heart beat for me. He lets me go and turns to Sid.

The safety is gone and now I'm exposed again. AJ orders

shots and a wounded David looks to me for answers. My guilt is overwhelming and I can't have David upset with me, so I resume my flirtation with him. He's still facing the TVs, sitting in the stool next to AJ, and I put my arms around his shoulders and kiss his cheek. He asks me if I'm drunk, and I lie and say I'm fine. He pulls out his cell phone and looks over the messages he had been sending me that afternoon. He's clearly upset with me, and I can't handle it.

"What are we drinking to?" AJ spins his chair to face me, and David hands me a shot over his shoulder. "You okay, man?" AJ asks David.

"Yeah, man. Just had a long day at work." David turns to AJ to respond, but doesn't look directly at him.

"Oh, yeah? Well, sounds like you need this shot, then." AJ is smiling at me as he says this. I'm smiling back and struggling to care that this is hurting David. I pour the tequila down my throat, and the sweet burn helps me care even less. I put my glass down and close my eyes. I start swaying between AJ's knees and forget everything I know.

I feel David's lips on my cheeks as he leaves, and I reach for him, but he is already out the door. We are alone. I have been waiting for this moment, and now AJ and I are alone at Nick's, and Lucas is missing, and David is hurt, and all I can see is the pale of AJ's eyes and the dark of his eyebrows, and all I want is to fall into the abyss.

He puts another shot in my hands and bites his lips between his teeth while looking up at me. I throw back the shot and lean down to kiss his mouth. He tastes like hot alcohol and cigarettes and cinnamon gum. His tongue is soft and warm and it's sliding around my mouth, and I'm suddenly panicked with the idea that we are in public, so I pull back and lick my lips.

I'm still dancing, and the music is so loud, and the crowd

is packed in. There's a breeze coming in from the open door and it's so cold that I get goose bumps on my neck and all I can feel is the intensity of AJ's hands as they creep between my legs.

"Stop." I smile and pull his hands away. "We can't do this. I have a boyfriend. We can't do this."

"Can't do what? I'm not doing anything." His sly smile is so convincing, but I know we can't get caught making out at the bar.

"We can't do *this*, AJ. We can't." I'm biting my lower lip, giving him the opportunity to convince me otherwise. "I can't kiss you here."

"Where can you kiss me?"

He's fucking with me. He's fucking with everything.

"What are you doing with Lucas anyway?"

"Lying."

"Let's go." AJ is signing the bill, and he's leading me out the door.

"Where are we going?"

"We're going to my place."

"No, no, no." I'm pulling against his hands like a dog against a leash and trying to refuse to go home with him. "AJ, I can't—I can't go home with you."

"Yes, you can." He pulls me into his chest and backs me into the shuttered window of a bodega. He pushes me up against the cold metal and starts kissing me. His mouth is so warm, and the air is so cold. We are lapping at each other like hungry teenagers.

People are walking by and I don't care. I feel myself lifting my right leg to wrap around his waist, and he holds it up with his muscled arms and pushes me harder into the shutters.

I know he lives nearby, but I've never been to his place before. As we take the last drunken steps to his building, I feel like a movie star being shielded from the paparazzi by a hulking bodyguard.

We get in the same slot of the revolving door and walk into the warmth of his lobby, and all the while he hasn't let go of me. He greets his night doorman, who reports the Jets lost, and I shyly smile, knowing I shouldn't be here.

At the twenty-seventh floor, AJ leads me down the hall-way to his apartment. He has his keys in one hand and me in the other, and he opens the door to reveal a dark apartment that smells like aspen.

I'm taking mental inventory of his things, looking for red flags, looking for evidence of other women, looking for some-thing that would make me run the other way and save myself from making this terrible decision. I see nothing. Everything appears tidy and organized, except for a bath towel strewn over the handlebars of a bike.

He has several wineglasses in his sink, and I'm straining to see if there is lipstick residue on any of the glasses. He leads me to his living room couch and instructs me to sit down and take off my coat. He lets go of my hand and walks to his refrigerator.

"You want a drink?"

"Yeah, for sure." I probably shouldn't have another drink, but I need something to steady my nerves.

He brings two Heinekens over to the couch and sits almost on top of me. He leans forward and picks up a remote that I don't recognize, clicks on some unseen machine, and sounds of The National fill my ears. He leans back, and his shoul-der is crushing my shoulder into the couch cushion, and he places his hand on my knee and sips his beer.

I'm feeling exposed and nervous, and I'm struggling to ap-pear confident and sexy. When we were in Nick's, the crowd made me feel sure of myself, but now there's no noise to shield me, nothing to keep me safe.

He's looking forward, listening to the music, but attentively rubbing my thigh.

"I have to pee," I say, needing a temporary escape.

He points to the bathroom, and I grab my handbag and walk in. Everything is in order; he has extra rolls of toilet paper stacked on a shelf above the toilet, magazines neatly arranged on a small table and several open bottles of the same cologne in various locations.

I check my face in the mirror and have to blink away the drunk to see how I actually look. After wiping the errant flecks of mascara away, I fish in my handbag for my emergency sleepover kit.

I kick off my sneakers and pull my pants down so I can take off my underwear and replace them with the fresh ones stashed in my bag. I dab some concealer under my eyes, wishing I had a tan. Afraid I taste like cigarettes, I put a dab of AJ's toothpaste on my finger and run it over my gums. I pee and put my pants and sneakers back on.

When I walk back into the living room, I see AJ's face illuminated by the blue light of the television. He's smiling at me as I make my way back to the couch, and before I can sit down, he pulls me onto his lap. I'm straddling him with my face to the wall behind the couch, and he's pulling off my sweater. As I lift his arms up to remove his shirt, all my cares fall out of my head into a pile on the floor.

Our clothes are strewn about his living room, and he's lying on top of me on the couch. He pulls the cushions onto the floor, and a condom appears in his hand. My head is swimming and I can't see him put it on, but when the empty wrapper flies by my head, and I feel him going in, I close my eyes and succumb to the rhythm.

Flashes of Lucas pass through my mind as I realize that I haven't been naked with anyone else in over a year. The panting is making my mouth dry and I reach for my bottle of beer as AJ kisses my chest and tenses his arms around me.

I spill most of the beer onto myself and the couch, but I get just enough into my mouth. AJ is holding my lower back with one giant arm and bracing himself against the couch with the other. He's looking into my eyes as he glides back and forth on top of me, and I start losing myself in his eyes, and it's the most intense feeling I have ever had.

He doesn't look away from me, and the beads of sweat that are forming at his temples are the sexiest things I've ever seen. His mouth is hanging open, and he's breathing heavily, but slowly. He takes his eyes off mine and buries his face in my neck, and I can feel his sweat sliding down my collarbone.

DECEMBER 5TH, 9:21 A.M.

I'm sitting in one of the smaller group rooms waiting for the first in this series of meetings for my psychological evaluation. I'm steeped in coffee and it's making my jaw clench and unclench, and my hands are sweaty.

I have a very clear image of what this shrink who is coming to judge me looks like, and I'm counting the seconds until she arrives. She will be tall, makeup-free, with frizzy, unhighlighted hair swept into an unkempt bun with a few bobby pins poking out. She'll have horn-rimmed glasses that are slightly big, so they slip down her dinosaur nose when she talks, and she'll wear a turtleneck with sleeves that are a bit too short over a pleated skirt that looks like curtains. Under all of this, she'll have on oversize white Reebok sneakers that she bought in 1992.

She won't like me personally, but she'll think I am excellent at my job. She will not tolerate my witty banter. She won't find me amusing. As I'm thinking about this, and shaping how to behave in the face of this woman I've created in my mind, the door opens and a man walks in.

I'm immediately relieved because I am much more comfortable with men than I am with women, and he's young, just a bit younger than I am, looks to be about thirty-five. His rumpled hair is adorably unkempt. He seems to have had some trouble finding the group room, so he's a little late. He sits with a thud and unloads the contents of his canvas messenger bag.

"Hi. It's Samantha, right? I'm Dr. Travis Young."

"Hi, Travis. I'm Sam." I'm probably supposed to call him Dr. Young, but I don't.

"Sam, okay." He fumbles with his things for a minute, and I realize if I met him under different circumstances I would be flirting right now. "So, I guess you know what we're doing here, huh?"

"Yes, sir. Time for the unbridled fun of a psych battery!"

"Ha, well, yeah, something like that. The New York State Office of Mental Health requires that all employees in clinics and institutions such as this one have regular evaluations by external providers to ensure they are able to work with a psychiatric population." He has spewed this rundown so many times, he's boring himself.

"Here's a question, Travis: Considering that, by law, you can't fire someone for having a psychological disorder, what's the point of finding out if any of us have something? It's not like if you find out I'm psychotic you can fire me for it." I'm not flirting, but I'm not *not* flirting.

"Well, technically that's true, but if it's deemed that an employee is a danger to herself or others, their supervisor will review the evaluation and usually recommend that said employee be moved to a position that doesn't involve patient contact or access to confidential information."

"Oh, so just a demotion, then." I say this with a smile, trying to charm Travis into liking me.

Travis begins with the Beck Depression Inventory, a short assessment tool used to determine if I'm miserable. I imagine if I were filling this out for the first time, it would be quite different than it is now that I've taken and scored this test, formally and informally, probably a hundred times.

I'm afraid there's no possibility that any of our answers on any of these assessments could be considered wholly honest or truthful. We simply know too much to be able to accurately represent how we feel. I look at each of the inventory items, knowing exactly how the test was designed, how to score it, why the questions are worded the way they are, why there are so many similar questions, and I know what outcomes should be induced. Even though the test is structured to prevent manipulation, I can't *help* but naturally formulate my responses according to what I know—what to say to appear depressed, and what to say to appear perfectly happy.

I scratch my answers on the paper with a freshly sharpened No. 2 pencil. Travis is periodically glancing at me, like a proctor at the SATs, but generally minding the paperwork in front of him.

I slide my completed BDI over to his desk and look hopefully for the next assessment.

"Ah, done already. Okay. In the interest of time, I'd like to get a couple of the shorter inventories out of the way first; that way I will have a moment to score the ones you've finished while you're completing the next test. Is that okay?" He's shuffling through papers and handing me a copy of the slightly longer PDQ-4.

"No problem. You tell me what to do, and I'll do it. I'll be a very good patient." My adorable smile and accommodating attitude are lost on Dr. Travis Young.

I hate this inventory. We don't use it much here, and I hate it because everything sounds too familiar. It feels like some asshole wrote this thing for me, and the statements feel intrusive and belligerent. Asshole statements like "Sometimes I feel upset." What the fuck am I supposed to say—false? No, I've never felt upset before. Especially not *now*, while I'm taking this *asshole* test? I push my pencil hard to circle either the little *T* or the little *F* on the answer sheet.

I hand Travis my responses and the list of statements, avoiding the niceties I employed earlier. Wordlessly, he hands me the following test. I sit down at the table, and the back legs of my chair wobble. I shift back and forth to measure the degree of unsteadiness, and decide it's better to abandon this chair and find another one.

I'm standing next to a row of seats, pushing down hard on the backs and shaking them to see if they quiver. All of these chairs suck. The last one in the row seems to be the sturdiest, so I pull it across the floor to the edge of the table. I sit back down and resume the testing. I'm watching Travis watching me.

I'm filling out the California Psychological Inventory, which practically offends me, because this couldn't possibly be used to ascertain anything from seasoned professionals.

I trudge through more true-false questions developed to see my innermost psychological workings, and I'm thinking the same thing I thought before: *assholes*. This one is longer than the others, should take me the rest of our allotted session time to get it done.

I look up to catch Travis scoring the assessments I've just completed. His face isn't betraying any thoughts he may have. I try to concentrate on finishing this up quickly, so he doesn't have time to get a bad impression of me.

I stand before him with my completed CPI, and I see he has all the scoring sheets in front of him to expedite the process.

"You finished?"

"Yeah." I smile again, giving him another chance to notice me.

"We have another meeting scheduled for later this afternoon," Travis informs me. "I'm going to use this time to review the inventories you've given me so far, and later we can discuss them, okay?"

"Yeah, okay." I didn't realize the two hours were up already. "I'll see you this afternoon, then."

As soon as we finish, I walk into my office to compose myself. I've been giving these tests to patients for years, and still whenever I walk away from them I feel like I have been probed and exposed and left naked in the rain. The questions are all designed to ensure that you can't lie. There are all these little mechanisms in place to work out the inconsistencies. And now we're turning these powerful lenses onto each other, and it just feels fucked up.

"David." I don't have to yell through the wall for him to hear me, but today I really need him to come in.

"Yeeeessss?" He isn't screaming back.

"Can you come in here, please?" I can't have him upset with me for the way I behaved on Thursday night at Nick's, so I'm making an effort to pull him back in.

He doesn't respond and instead walks through my door, still drinking his morning coffee. "What's up?"

"Ugh, I just had part one of the probe. The shrink is hot, but it still feels like a soul gouging."

"That's delightful, Sam. I'm so excited to have my soul gouged tomorrow." David doesn't bother coddling me, because he knows I will reject it.

"It's a fucking nightmare. I suggest we go drink this whole icky feeling away as soon as possible."

"Don't you have another one this afternoon?"

"Yeah. I can't wait for all this to be over." I'm fidgeting in my drawers, looking for something to eat.

"I have to go to group. What are we doing for lunch today?" David is walking out.

"I don't know. What did you bring me?" He closes the door with a tight smile as I say this. I wonder if he finds me irresistible or wants to throw me out the window.

DECEMBER 5TH, 2:49 P.M.

I walk to the staff bathroom to find the Out of Order sign on the door again. I key it open and go inside anyway. I can't be asked to fix my face in the other bathroom and run the risk of letting patients see me grooming myself like a real human being.

I'm locking the door behind me. I check my teeth in the mirror, looking for poppy seeds from the bagel I had before meeting Travis. I'm delighted to see that I look reasonably good today. I have no war wounds to hide with that horribly cakey makeup that makes me look a million years old. There are no swollen red eyes resulting from hysterics or alcohol-induced dehydration. I guess my plan to take it easy this weekend in preparation for the evaluation *did* have a positive effect.

I peer into the stall to see if the toilet is noticeably blocked or broken. It looks perfectly fine to me, so I unzip my pants to pee. I squat and hover, and when I'm finished, I don't flush, just in case it would cause an overflow.

In the staff lounge, I pour a steaming cup of fresh coffee into someone else's mug, and dump in two tiny buckets of cream. I wonder how this cream doesn't spoil and every other dairy product needs to be refrigerated.

I walk back into the evaluation room and see Travis has finished scoring the three assessments I took this morning, and he's ready to continue on to the next phase. A Nalgene water bottle has appeared from his bag and is sitting on the corner of the desk. It's filled with something opaque.

"Hi, Samantha. You ready to get back into it?"

"Yes, I'm ready. Thank you."

"Good. Let's get started with some of the interview questions."

I sit back down in my stable seat and clutch my coffee. I keep the mug up to my face and blow at it. Travis begins by asking me about my upbringing. He sits with one leg crossed tightly over the other, his thick socks showing under his cuffed khaki corduroys.

"Well, I grew up outside the city. Small town a little over an hour north of here. Went to private school from kindergarten through twelfth. Grew up with my mom, no siblings."

"And your father?"

"I never met him." I blow at my coffee. "Don't know much about him."

"Were your parents ever married?" He doesn't look at me as he asks this.

"Nope. As I said, I really don't know much about him at all. My mom told me stories when I was younger, but they were very conflicting, and I don't know what's true."

Travis jots down some notes on a yellow legal pad, and I wonder how much he already knows.

"Go on."

"Um, well, I went to Vassar, and—"

"Right, I have your résumé here. I mean go on about your upbringing. Tell me more about your mom."

"Well, she *died* while I was at Vassar."

"Oh, I'm sorry to hear that." Standard shrink response. *You're not sorry, Travis. This is exactly what you wanted to hear.*

"Yeah. So, I guess I'm an orphan now. Never knew my father, my mother died when I was twenty, and here I am."

"How did she die?"

"Aneurysm." I hate talking about this. My mother died of a massive brain hemorrhage after a ruptured aneurysm, and even the words make me feel sick to my stomach. She was living alone in the house in Newburgh that her parents left her when they died. From what I could make out, she seemed happy. She was pals with the neighbors, and they did suburban shit together like share gardening tips, and bring each other baskets of dill and asparagus.

I would see her whenever I came home from school, but I couldn't bear to stay in her house. After one or two nights there, my anxiety levels skyrocketed, so I'd have to go back to campus, or take the train into the city and stay with friends.

She told me when I left for school that by going away from her—moving out of her house and leaving her alone—I was slowly killing her. She'd been feeding me the Kool-Aid my entire life, and I never had a different reality to help me figure out that her way of relating to people was dangerous and unstable. I thought it was every kid's upbringing to spend nights wondering if you would wake up with an angel or a monster. Turned out that wasn't quite the case.

"That must have been hard for you."

"Of course that was hard for me, Travis. My mother died. I wasn't there when it happened. Although the doctors told me there was nothing anyone could have done, and the speed with which the hemorrhage consumed her was unstoppable, you don't just tuck these things into your pocket and move on with life. It was a fucking nightmare, and the aftermath was no picnic, either."

"What do you mean, 'no picnic'?" Oh, my *God*, I liked this guy when he walked in the door. Now he is every psychiatric caricature I've ever seen. He might as well put on a tweed sports jacket with suede elbow patches and start smoking a pipe.

"I mean it was a mess. My mom hadn't worked for a long time, and although she kept up the impression—to me and everybody else—that she was perfectly comfortable financially, she was actually drowning in debt. I had to sell the house—immediately and *well* below market value—just to pay everything off and give her a decent funeral. I had to have her cremated because there wasn't enough money for a burial plot.

"She had made *zero* end-of-life plans and had *no will*, so New York State gave me all of her things, and everything was useless. It all went for pennies at a tag sale right before the house sold. It was like a final fuck-you to a twenty-year-old kid who still couldn't figure out which way was up. So, yeah, no fucking picnic."

"Did you always have a rough relationship with her?"

"Travis, this is a psychological evaluation that you are administering to the entire staff of a mental institution. The results of which are going to OMH to see if staff restructuring is needed. Is it really *relevant* to you to find out the juicy details of my relationship with my mother when I was a kid?" *Asshole. Voyeur.*

"Well, you're one of two staff psychologists here and you're obviously familiar with the assessment tools you completed earlier in this session. I'm just trying to ascertain why you may have shown high scores on most of the Axis Two, Cluster B criteria."

"What?" I sit up straight. "Personality disorders?"

"Yes. On all the inventories."

DECEMBER 6TH, 11:13 A.M.

Richard places his hat on his papers at the corner of my desk, as he does every other fruitless Tuesday morning, and turns his attention to whichever newspaper he has decided to begin with today. My frustration levels are already high, and my tolerance is lower than it should be. I've just been told that I scored high on personality disorders, which is absolutely impossible. I feel like the tables are unfairly turned with these OMH assholes here digging into my personal life, and I can't even get a patient to respond to me.

Although he's been talking, it's doing nothing to help me figure out why he's institutionalized. I just want to do my job and get to the bottom of this enormous, unknowable man. I have his nearly nonexistent file open on my desk, and blank documents open on my computer screen, on the off chance he decides to cooperate with me. I'm feeling more and more useless with each passing week.

"Richard." I use my coach-talking-to-the-star-player voice. "How about we get going on your patient file?" I tap the sheets on my desk with the eraser end of a pencil.

"I've been in this institution for quite some time now.

Haven't you gotten all the information you need from me?" He scowls.

"Actually, no. You haven't answered any of the questions I've asked you, and I'm still unclear about your goals for treatment."

"My goals for treatment are the same as everyone else's." He looks back down at his paper and sighs in frustration as he uses his finger to trace back to where he left off.

"And what goals are those? What does everyone else want out of treatment?" I poise my pencil to write down anything he gives me.

"To get out of here." More useless responses.

"Okay, so if you want to get out of here, the fastest way to do that is by helping me to understand what brought you *in here* to begin with." I poke the papers hopefully with my pencil.

"Shouldn't you be able to figure that out? Aren't you supposed to be one of the best doctors here? I keep hearing all this chatter from other patients about how you're the best, and 'Sam this and Sam that,' so shouldn't you have the powers of perception to figure out what I'm doing here? You're the professional, not me." *Asshole.*

"I'm not a psychic or a mind reader. I'm a psychologist. I can't use an X-ray and see through your skull into your inner workings. You're gonna need to help me out with that."

"Well, I *thought* you were supposed to be the best. I figured at least *you'd* be able to help me."

In the wake of Travis's accusations yesterday, Richard's words feel caustic and cutting and I want to stab him in the eye with my pencil.

DECEMBER 7TH, 7:22 A.M.

I'm staring at my face in Lucas's bathroom mirror. He has dimmers on his lights, and it makes it easier to look at myself, especially at this hour of the morning. But I can still see lines on my forehead that I never noticed before, and my perfectly straight teeth seem crooked on the bottom row. The marks that Lucas leaves on me are usually obscured by my thick hair, or along my ribs and hips, hidden by my clothes. This morning I see the creeping blue edges of a bruise sneaking onto my right temple. There's a matching bruise on the other side, but it's higher up on my head, and if I pull my hair back right, it can remain unseen.

I have a compact of makeup that's used to cover tattoos. There was a patient at Typhlos once who had worked on movie sets. She fell head over heels in love with the star of the movie, and he completely dismissed her. This was the trigger that sent her over the edge, and over the bridge, as well. She came to Typhlos after four months in rehab learning to walk and talk again. She told me about the makeup, and I watched her use it to cover her own scars. I have it in three different colors—a light one for the long winter months, and two darker ones for when I'm tan. Usually I have to mix them together in the heat of my palm to get the color just right.

I push the dimmer switch all the way up so I can see the details as I cover them. There are tiny blond hairs at my temples, and I have to be careful to avoid the cakey makeup getting caught in those, because nothing looks more obvious than matted-down baby hairs. I can't believe I'm here again, going through this routine again. But if I can just stay strong, it will stop. He cares so much about me; he's just not good at controlling his emotions. This isn't his fault. As I repeat these lies in my head, I put Visine in my eyes to erase the traces of tears, and scrub the grime out from under my nails.

Lucas is still asleep, and I'm dressed for work, prepared to walk out the door. I notice Lucas's espresso machine on the counter. I know he sets it to brew his coffee while he gets ready for work, so on my way out, I pop the plug out of the wall.

DECEMBER 7TH, 12:27 P.M.

I am back in the same evaluation room I was in with Travis, waiting for the new shrink to arrive. I don't have the same defenses geared up for the second wave of testing; instead I am exhausted and I desperately want to leave so I can smoke a half a pack of cigarettes in the warmth of my living room. As my eyelids begin to get heavy, the illustrious psychiatrist Dr. Brooks walks in.

She is female, but beyond that, she bears no resemblance to the woman I imagined on Monday. Dr. Jean Brooks comes into the room, as tiny as a fourth grader. She is substantially more put together than Travis, and she skips the formalities altogether. I'm so much bigger than she is that I find it almost comical that I'm supposed to answer her intimate questions.

Dr. Brooks is clearly reading over the information that Travis got from me on Monday. I wonder if she has already decided that I'm diagnosable, character disordered, a lost cause. She repeatedly clears her throat with a high-pitched, tinny squeal. She opens her mouth as if to start a sentence, then slams it shut and brings the papers closer to her face for a more thorough investigation. She seems both confused and interested, as if trying to decipher Travis's notes is an exhaustive but intriguing task. I'm sure Dr. Brooks will be able to see that I don't have a personality disorder like Travis seems to think I do.

"So," she finally begins, "you've already had some testing this week. How did that go?"

"It was fine."

"Good, good. Okay. Well, usually Dr. Young administers and scores various assessments and inventories, and then I take the second shift and focus more on interviews and discussions."

"Yes. And Travis took over some of the interviewing on Monday."

"Yeah—" She doesn't know how to take the fact that I'm calling him Travis. "Yeah—so, now we will simply continue with the interviews. I have been reviewing his notes, so there is no need to cover the same material if you don't feel it's relevant."

"Do you feel the death of my mother is relevant?" I should have smoked a *pack* of cigarettes before this.

"Not if you'd rather not discuss it. In fact, I am more inclined to take a structured approach to interviewing. Would you mind if I took the lead? We can take a ten-minute break at the halfway point of the session if you like."

"No problem, Dr. Brooks." I'm sitting in a chair with a desk attached. I have my coffee and a bottle of water on the desk, a couple of pens that I pulled out of my hair, and my daily schedule. My legs are sticking straight out in front of me, crossed at the ankles. I have my elbows cocked out with my fingers interlaced behind my head. This position is hurting my back, but I want to ensure that I appear laid-back and nonchalant. I can't be defined by these interviews. I can't be categorized.

"Dr. Young noted that you grew up in a single-parent

home and that your mother passed away when you were at college. Is that correct?"

"Yes."

"Did you ever receive counseling or therapy of any kind?" She's hovering a fat pen above a yellow legal pad, poised to jot down all the golden nuggets that spew out of my mouth.

"I was required to go to two years of counseling when I was in grad school. Every PhD candidate has to. But I'm sure you know that."

"I'm a psychiatrist, Dr. James. In medical school there is no therapy requirement. But, yes, I am aware of the practices in PhD programs. Did you ever have any other therapy or counseling?" She's already frustrated and competitive with me, and I wish I could care.

"When I was in ninth grade, the school psychologist recommended I see an external therapist because I was one of the only kids in school from a single-parent home. My mother agreed, and I was sent to a local psychiatrist. I'm not sure how long I went—not long. Maybe a couple of months."

"Do you remember the kinds of things you discussed?"

"Yes, I do. I remember that no matter what I came in with, what topics I had in mind to talk about, he would always steer the conversation back to my father. He had decided that the source of everything that was wrong with my life was the lack of a father figure. So, he would constantly tell me that I needed a father. But, of course, I didn't have one. He presented a solution that was unattainable, and the day I realized I was smarter than he was, I stormed out."

"You stormed out?"

"I tried to storm out. I stormed into the bathroom because the door was right next to the exit sign. So, then I had to storm back in and storm out properly. I forgot my jacket, too. It wasn't a very well-executed plan."

"You remember the details pretty well for twenty years ago."

"Twenty-three." *Don't antagonize me, medical doctor.* "He's one of the reasons I became a psychologist."

"This psychiatrist? How so?"

"I felt the field needed someone competent and empathic."

"And you could provide those things?"

"Precisely, Dr. Brooks."

"What happened next?" She is not amused.

"After I left his office? He reached out to my mother to try to get me to come back to counseling."

"And did you?"

"I didn't, but she did."

"Your mother?"

"Yes. In my place, my mother went. She took over my counseling sessions with my therapist and presented the problems that she believed I was having. She neatly and tidily extracted herself and her own behaviors from my issues and placed the blame securely upon my mystery father, who was not there to defend himself, because he existed primarily in her warped memory." I'm leaning on the flimsy desk, practically snarling at Dr. Brooks. "Is that what you want to hear?"

"Is that what you want to tell me?" I *hate* psychiatrists.

At the close of the session, I hold the door open for her, towering over her, and I momentarily wish I could slap the papers out of her hands so my answers are mixed up in the shuffle.

Desperation makes you do funny things.

DECEMBER 8TH, 4:17 P.M.

My phone vibrates and when I see it's a text message from AJ, my palms get sweaty like a teenager. He writes Miss you followed by a suggestive series of emojis. Everything he does is sexually charged, and it gets me every time. I feel no remorse that we superficially communicate almost exclusively in emojis and the exchange of bodily fluids. Just as my mind starts to wander, there's a knock on my door.

"Sssssammmm, it's an important day today, and I need to talk-to-youuuuu." Eddie pulls open my door and wiggles his way inside my office.

"Okay, Eddie." I tuck my phone into my desk drawer and shake the fantasies from my mind. "I have a few minutes between other important things I have to do. Why don't you come inside, and I can give you about fifteen minutes? How does that sound?" I've turned him down too frequently, and I owe it to him to listen.

"Yyyessss, Sssssammmm… Thhhank youuuuuuu."

Eddie shuffles into my office and composes himself on the patient chair. He takes his grimy trucker hat off his greasy hair and places it on his bent knee. He smooths his hair down on either side of his head, seemingly trying to make himself presentable. Once he gets what he wants, in this case some time and attention, the desperation in his voice begins to dissipate, and his strung-together words begin to disconnect.

"How come today is an important day, Eddie?"

"Anniversssssary."

"Oh, yeah? Anniversary of what?" I sip my coffee.

"It would have been my ten-year anniversary with my girlfriend."

"I didn't know you had a serious girlfriend. Tell me about her."

"It's hard, hard, hard to talk about her now." He shakes his head.

"Do you ever talk to her?"

"No, I can't talk to her because she isn't alive anymore."

"Oh, no, I'm so sorry. I didn't realize she passed away."

Eddie shifts in his seat and moves his cap up to the windowsill behind him. He leans in closer to me before he begins his story.

"She, she, she was depressssssssed for a long time, and sometimes there were days and weeks when she wouldn't get out of bed at all, and she would just lie there, and she wouldn't even read books, and I couldn't help her. She would look at old pictures, from when she was little. She had a ssssmall ssstack of old pictures, and she would lie in our bed, and she would look at the picturessss, and she would only have one little lamp next to her bed, and she put a sssssscarf on top of the lamp and it made the light in the room really orange, and she would look at those picturesssss."

He shifts again and wiggles his butt back in the seat as far as he can. He leans forward and puts his elbows on his knees, bends his head down and smooths his hair again.

"I was working then, and I was working long hours, and she was home alone all the time. We didn't have a big house, just a little apartment in east New York, and she didn't even get out of bed unless she had to go to the bathroom. She wasn't eating, and she got to be so skinny. I had to work. I was working for the MTA, and my cell phone didn't work underground. She didn't work, and she was at home all the time."

"How long ago was this?" I've known Eddie a long time, and I've never heard this story.

"Before I came here. I've been here eight years. So eight years ago, I guess. Or maybe more than that. I don't know. But you weren't here yet when I came here. And you came here six years ago."

"That's right. You were here first, and you have always made me feel very welcome." Eddie prides himself on his long tenure at Typhlos.

"Good, me too, Sssam. Me too, welcome here. But with the MTA, you have to do your work underground, and I didn't have my phone working underground, and my bosses just talked to me with the walkie-talkie, but my girlfriend couldn't get me on the walkie-talkie, sssssooo she was alone."

"What was your girlfriend's name?"

"Allison, Allissssssson. Allissssson and Eddie." He singsongs her name.

"That's a nice name."

"Yeah. And she was a nice girl, too, but too depressed. She would sleep all the time. And I would try to talk to her when I got home, but she didn't want to talk because she was too tired. I think she was tired and weak because she didn't eat enough and she didn't get any fresh air. I would make her some dinner, but she was asleep already when I took the dinner to her."

"What did you used to make for dinner?" Sometimes when I ask detailed questions, the patients can better pull up their memories.

"Soup. Ssssoup in a can on a hot plate. We didn't really have a kitchen, just a hallway with a mini-refrigerator and a hot plate, and some cabinets for spoons and bowls. We had a little sink there, too. But she didn't eat the soup. So I ate it.

"But then there was a time when it started to get better. She had this doctor who she would talk to on the phone sometimes, and he sent her medication to the pharmacy. And I would go and pick it up on my way home. I asked them at the desk for the medicine for Allison Swift, and they gave it to me, and it was ten dollars because of Medicaid.

"When she started to take the medicine, she didn't look at the pictures so much anymore. And then some days, she would be awake when I brought her the soup. And sometimes we would just talk, but sometimes we would talk *and* she would eat the soup, too."

"What kinds of things would you two talk about?" I'm actually very interested in Eddie's story. I get frustrated with him sometimes, and tired of trying to find time in my day for someone else's patient, but I have a soft spot for Eddie. I see him, and I want to be here for him.

"When she started to take the medicine and eat the sssssoup, then we could talk about getting married one day because she thought that if we could get married one day then she would be better. So, when I would leave work, and she was getting better, I wouldn't always come straight home. Sometimes, I would go to a store and look at rings for her. Engagement rings. And there were big ones with diamonds and gold, and there were silver ones with lots of little diamonds, but everything was so much money, so I was only looking."

I absentmindedly fiddle with my bare left ring finger.

"Whenever we would talk about getting married, she sss-seemed to get better, so I knew I had to go and get her that rrrring. And I was saving up and trying to work harder at the MTA, but it's hard work. Allisssson was all the time at home, and she couldn't work, so I had to pay all the bills and it was hard to keep up. She was getting some disability, but it wasn't much, and we had to eat, and we can't just live off of soup, so it was hard to save up for the ring. I told her I was gonna get her one."

Eddie turns around and pulls his hat off the windowsill. He smooths his hair down and puts his hat back on his head. He stands to hike up his pants, then returns to his seat.

"So, one day, I bought one. It cost $275 and it was probably too big, but the guy at the shop said that he could fix it if it wassss too big. It was gold and it had one diamond in the middle with a big ice-cream cone holding it up. It was sssshiny, and he put it in a dark blue box with silver writing that said 'Tony's,' and the box was soft and fuzzy. I brought it home with me, and I hid it in one of the cabinets high up in the kitchen so she wouldn't find it there. I knew that when I gave it to her it would be all better, but because our two-year anniversary was coming up, I wanted to wait and give it to her on a special day.

"We stopped talking about getting married because I was ssscared that I would get too excited and spoil the secret that I had bought a ring. But then she started to get depressed again. She put the scarf back on the lamp, and she took the pictures out again. She stopped eating the soup I brought her. But I knew she would get better when I gave her the ring, and there were only a few days until our anniversary, the sss-special day I was going to give it to her.

"On our anniversary, I had to go to work like I had to do every other day, but I didn't want to because I knew she would be so happy. I remember during lunch, my boss told me that my cell phone was ringing in the office, and I wasn't allowed personal calls at work. I said it must be an emergency, and he said if it was an emergency, then they would have called the office phone, and I thought he must be right. When the day was over, I wanted to rush home and surprise her. I was excited. She was going to be better now."

He squirms in his seat. I put a hand on his knee to steady him and gently nod my head.

"I got to the house and I took the ring out of the cabinet and I dusted it off and made sure it looked shiny in the box. I walked to the bedroom, and the door was closed. She never closed the door. But today the door was closed, so I opened it, and I walked into the room. She was lying in bed, as usual, so I went to wake her up. But when I tried to wake her up, she didn't move. She wasn't moving. Then I saw the medicine bottles on the table with the lamp. And they were empty, and there was a flask, and that was empty, too. I put the ring down next to the bottles, and I checked her neck to see if her heart was beating, but I didn't feel anything."

Eddie lowers his head and tears silently fall from his eyes onto his dirty sneakers. He tugs at the edges of his sleeves and pulls them down over his wrists.

It occurs to me that it's strange he doesn't mention the unsettling sensation of his girlfriend being cold. Every other time I've heard a story about interaction with a dead body, people will always remark about how their loved one was cold. And that this was terrifying. But Eddie doesn't say anything about Allison's body being cold.

As he concludes his story, he reaches into his pocket to show me a picture of her. He is looking up at me with wet, persuasive eyes as he hands me a worn and wrinkled printout of Reese Witherspoon when her hair was brown for *Walk the Line*.

DECEMBER 8TH, 11:28 P.M.

I'm wearing heels that are too tall and hard to walk in, so I'm taking tiny little steps and bending my legs like a velociraptor. Lucas is walking too fast for me and he refuses to slow down. He was the one who bought me these shoes and insisted I wear them tonight. I'm grasping his elbow, trying to keep up as he takes huge strides down the uneven pavement toward his building.

Dinner was awkward. It's not often Lucas brings me out with his work associates, and I didn't realize how much of a dog and pony show he puts on for these people. He had one hand under the table either on my thigh or my hand, and when he needed me to laugh on cue, or go along with a lie he was telling, he would squeeze far too tightly. I ended up squealing more than laughing, and I can see the finger marks on my right thigh rising up under my sheer panty hose.

"I thought it went well tonight. Don't you?" I say, stumbling behind him, trying to keep the cold air from freezing my teeth as I speak.

"It did *not* go well." He pulls his elbow out of my grasp and speeds up as we approach his entrance. The slots of the revolving door are wide enough for two, but he shoves his way into one without me, leaving me to push the heavy door alone. I'm embarrassed and nervous as I rush my tiny steps past his doorman, who greets me with a tip of his cap and a warm smile. Out of breath, I catch Lucas at the elevator bank, slipping into an open car and not planning on waiting for me. I wave my handbag in front of me; it catches the sensors of the elevator and the door opens wide to let me in. Lucas doesn't acknowledge me, and instead slaps the button for his floor over and over until the door closes behind me. I brace myself against the railing and pull off my shoes. I'm hopping back and forth to get the feeling back in my freezing legs and work the kinks out of my sore feet.

"Put your fucking shoes back on, Sam. We are still in public. Have some respect for yourself." He won't look me in the face; instead he looks at the shoes in my hand with wide, glaring eyes, until I pick up one aching foot to slide the shoe back on. When we arrive at his floor, he brushes past me and takes enormous strides down the hallway to his front door. If it weren't for the time it took for him to slide the key into the lock and open the door, my hobbling wouldn't have gotten me there in time to slip in after him.

He's pulling off his tie and pacing the apartment. I know exactly what's coming, and I remove my shoes and my tights to gain a better grip on the floor beneath me. I can hear him mumbling to himself as he flies between his closet and the kitchen, pulling off pieces of clothing and throwing ice cubes into a glass. Maverick runs to a corner farthest from the half bathroom and cowers near a large potted tree. He knows exactly what's coming, too.

My head is filled with the right things to say to Lucas to calm him down, and as I try to bring the sentences from my brain to my mouth, he walks past me and grabs me by the waist. I know he doesn't mean to hurt me, and I know that if I could just better sense the nuances of what he needs, I wouldn't piss him off so much. His arm is hooked around my middle and he throws me to the floor of the bathroom. My leather skirt catches on the tile floor, and I can hear the fabric ripping at the zipper. I hold up my hands to Lucas and push myself between the toilet and the wall, where he can barely reach me. He moves his drink from his right hand to his left and crashes a flat palm into the side of my head. My ear screams and vibrates and I pull up my shoulders to defend myself. I squeeze farther back into the corner and knock the toilet paper off the holder. Three more slaps come down on my ears and I'm pushing so hard against the holder that the shiny chrome is breaking the skin over my collarbone. My fists are clenched and my eyes squeezed shut when I hear the sound of his lighter and smell the first plume of cigarette smoke. It's over.

Maverick runs from his hiding place and jumps on top of my knees. I let the backs of my legs fall to the ground to give him room, and he anxiously licks around my face and neck. When Lucas passes by the door to the bathroom, I hug Maverick close to me, knowing he would never hurt his dog. Lucas throws an ice pack at my feet and stands in the doorframe, watching as I lift the pack to my temple and wiggle out of my corner. I close the toilet seat and sit down on top of it, with Maverick still on my lap. Lucas sits on the floor in front of me with his back against the wall. His drink is sweating on the tiles next to him. He rubs my calves with his left hand and smokes his cigarette with his right. Part of me wonders if I deserve to take a beating now and then. The other part of me wonders if I deserve to have a boyfriend who buys me Manolo Blahniks and takes me to dinner at the Four Seasons.

DECEMBER 9TH, 12:14 P.M.

The sessions with Travis and Dr. Brooks have my mind wandering back to growing up. I wonder how much of what I remember is modified by my education and experience, and how much of it actually happened.

I sit here and think to myself that I knew what she was doing the whole time; I knew that my mom was sick and that she was incapable. I was resilient and strong and resisted her attempts to control and decimate me. I look back through the windows of the house I grew up in, onto scenes of my childhood, and I color everything in with my current understanding of her disorder. I paint a happier picture for myself because I can't carry this baggage anymore.

I bring these thick and tangible memories with me as I walk through the group-room door and see a crowd of expectant eyes looking up at me.

"Hello, everyone. Good to have you here today." As I scan the faces around me, I notice that some of them aren't familiar. "I see some of you are new to this group—welcome. Why don't we go around the room and introduce ourselves? I'll begin. My name is Dr. Sam James, you can call me Sam, and I am a staff psychologist. Lucy, you want to go next?" Lucy is sitting at the edge of her chair, her short skirt riding up so her exposed butt is flush against the slick blue plastic seat. Her chair has a desk attached, and she's leaning on it with all her weight so that the back legs are upended. She lolls her head side to side and introduces herself.

"I'm Lucy. I'm a patient here. Been here awhile. I love Miss Sam's groups because no one gets in trouble for telling the truth." She smiles a huge, goofy smile at me, and I can see the wad of green gum clamped between her back teeth.

We continue around the room with short introductions, rarely as colorful and animated as Lucy's; usually just a name quickly blurted out. I'm told that we have additional patients joining the group because they're new and have nowhere to go, and roommates and fast friends have brought them to sit in on my group.

"Today's discussion is going to be about family. I've been thinking a lot about family recently, and it's an important part of who we are. Our families have a huge influence on us, both before we are born and all through our lives. Does anyone want to talk a little bit about what their family is like?"

I worry sometimes when I start these kinds of discussion groups because I know I'm opening a Pandora's box and the stories that could emerge may be too traumatic to bear. I convince myself this is for the greater good, and a trauma released is always better than a trauma retained, so I press on. "Anyone?" The patients shuffle in their seats and look around at one another.

"I know I must be one of the only ones with a story like this, but I grew up in a really happy home. We even had a dog growing up, and I had a turtle, too. We had a nice little house, and both my parents had jobs. Everybody got along with everybody." This is a new patient whose name I can't remember. He has the skinniest head I've ever seen, and his wide ears stick out like a car with the doors open.

"My mom was a great cook," he continues, "and she always made corn bread on the weekend, and my little sister and me would fight over who got the last piece. But then my grandma would always sneak in and pop it in her mouth while we were arguing. She lived with us, too. And while my mom and pops were at work during the day, my grandma would look after us kids. It was a nice time, growing up."

"Thank you for sharing that. Sounds like a positive environment to grow up in. I'd like to hear from others who may have had a similar experience as— I'm sorry, remind me of your name?"

"Paul."

"Thank you. If people have had a similar experience to Paul's?" I scan the room hopefully, with little expectation that many hands will rise.

"I had a nice childhood, too." June. "We didn't have too much money, and my daddy was away for work a lot, but everybody was nice and calm, and we never had any drama in the house." June is suffering from schizophrenia. When she was first prescribed antipsychotic medications in the mid-1990s, she developed tardive dyskinesia, a terrifying side-effect that permanently turns her hands into claws, slacks her jaw and tongue, and compromises her mobility. Her limbs sway and jerk involuntarily, and her neck bends to the left, so her shoulder is always to her ear.

She has taken to wearing oversize men's button-down shirts that she can leave open to compensate for her twisted body. I can't imagine making the decision to take the meds or leave them, to choose to maintain soundness of mind or body. June has been here for almost as long as I have, and I've never heard her utter a word of complaint.

"I know we always talk about how hard people have it, and growing up on the street with no one, and no money, and having to turn to prostitution and drug dealing to get by, but I didn't have any of that in my life, either." This is Susan. She is sitting next to Tashawndra and knows that her comments describe Tashawndra's upbringing. Susan places a hand on her friend's knee, assuring her that she's not trying to be offensive. Some patients shrink back into their seats, distracted by their own memories.

"We come from everywhere, don't we?" Stephan. "You can never really tell who will be touched with mental illness and who will be passed over. I had it in my family. We were riddled with it. My father was an alcoholic. My mother was bipolar. There was always anger and frustration in my house. Disappointment. Someone was always letting someone else down. And you can't grow up in an environment like that and imagine that you'll walk away unscathed. You can't come out of a dirty house and think you'll emerge clean.

"My brother and I both ended up the same as them. And their parents before them, too. They say that addiction is a family disease. So is mental illness. Unless you find a way to stop it or deal with it, it's going to get you if it's in your family." Stephan tells his story with his hands raised in surrender. He shakes his head and shrugs his shoulders as he continues.

"I went to college, for crying out loud. I got a good education. That doesn't stop it. It doesn't stop the disease from coming to get you. And you can learn everything you want about it. Find out what bipolar means, where it comes from. You can find out whatever you want. But that doesn't mean you can stop it. I bet I know as much as all these doctors, and still, I can't fix it." He closes his commentary with an exaggerated shrug and gently folds his arms back over his chest. The other patients are staring at him, wide-eyed. I fear the overwhelming sense of recognition and reality that he has released into the room. When the OMH results are in and the death sentence is doled out, I won't be able to fade into the background anymore. I feel the truth clawing at my throat, and I have to sip my coffee to stop from choking.

DECEMBER 10TH, 10:24 P.M.

Sid is mopping up the counter in front of me where my Jack and Cokes have been sweating. He's not very talkative tonight, which is good because I don't feel like talking. There's Christmas music playing in the bar, and string lights up around wreaths and garlands and festive holiday decor. It's making me feel even smaller and lonelier than I did before I came in here. I needed the noise of the bar to soothe me, so after finishing a bottle of red at home, I put on my coat over my pajama pants and sneakers, and came to Nick's. None of my friends are here. Seems the only people who go to bars on weekends are college kids and amateurs and pathetic, miserable drunks such as myself.

"Sid, can I have some cocktail olives?" I'm hungry, but I don't have the energy to go across the street to get a sandwich or a slice of pizza, so cocktail olives will have to be a makeshift dinner again. Sid puts a rocks glass full of fat green orbs in front of me, along with another drink. I reach for a stack of bar napkins and pull a pen out of my handbag. My thoughts are going too fast and I need to get something down on paper so I can try to understand what the hell has been happening. I think about the addiction groups I facilitate every week and the aspects of life that are negatively affected by substance abuse: work life, home life, interpersonal relationships, self-care, mental health... I check all the boxes in my head before I write them down on the napkin.

I still can't get a certain patient to really talk to me. I've been lying to Rachel and telling her we've been making progress, but in reality Richard won't say a useful word. He watches me and scrutinizes me, and I feel like he judges me when he sits in my office, but he won't let me in. I've always been the best with these kinds of patients, and Rachel is counting on me to be able to figure out a back door to his psyche. I can't do it. It's been six weeks since I took Richard from Gary, just as smugly overconfident as he was, and now I realize even I can't get this man to talk. I don't want to be replaceable. I couldn't bear the rejection if Rachel reassigned him to someone else, someone she found more capable. I need to be the capable one. I need to figure out what brought this man to treatment at Typhlos.

Sid leans on the bar in front of me and flashes his grimy horse teeth. "You want another one or something different?"

I look down to see that I've already finished the Jack and Coke. "Well, you're not putting any Jack in these drinks, so maybe a shot and a beer." I smile my charming smile at him and hope he doesn't think I'm drunk.

"Hardly a splash of Coke in there, my dear. Jameson and Miller Lite?"

"You know me so well." I return my attention to my list.

My home life and interpersonal relationships—how can I even begin to address those? Home life consists of buying booze, drinking booze and recycling bottles. Throw in the occasional shower and a meal from a deli bag or a plastic take-out container. Add a weekly carton of cigarettes and copious quantities of Advil, and I've got the painting of my home life.

It's Christmastime, and I don't have a family to buy presents for. I don't have a reason to pull myself together so that I can impress the guests at a shiny, top-shelf holiday party.

To complicate matters, I've got Lucas to contend with. But because I can't manage to face him or the fact that I can't ever change him, instead I will distract myself with AJ for physical feelings of love, and I'll keep David by my side for emotional support and intellectual feelings of love. As the words bleed through the deteriorating bar napkin, I look up to catch my beleaguered reflection and I can't believe that this is what I actually do. There's too much truth on this napkin. I drink my shot, crumple the napkin and stuff it into the empty glass.

The whiskey ring at the bottom of the shot glass begins to disintegrate my life that I've scribbled down. I don't want to be disposable. I don't want to be expendable. I need to be needed, and I see the crushing failures in every aspect of my life. Only at work do I have anyone relying on me for anything. And it's only because they *pay* me to be reliable. But I see that slipping through my fingers as soon as the OMH report comes through and exposes the truth.

Lucas doesn't need me; he needs a punching bag, and she could be anyone. AJ probably doesn't even know my last name, and the only purpose I serve for him is as a receptacle. David would be better off without me; he knows it and I know it. It's only my patients who need me. Only my patients who are forced to believe that I am competent and composed and able to save them from themselves. Eddie needs me, and Tashawndra needs me, and even Richard needs me.

I see my slack jaw and teary eyes in the mirror behind the bar, and when I catch the look on Sid's face as he notices me from down the bar, I know it's time to leave. I pull a wad of cash from my coat pocket and tuck it under my empty beer. I pop an olive into my mouth to get the boozy taste out and stumble toward the exit. I blow Sid a kiss and force my face into a happy mask as I walk into the cold night. I clench the other napkins in my sweaty fists inside my pockets and hope I can soak through them and erase the pathetic, hopeless words describing my life.

DECEMBER 12TH, 3:23 P.M.

I'm sitting on top of the desk in a group room, waiting for the rest of the patients to shuffle in before I get started. My plan is to use this group session to surreptitiously garner some information from Richard. This is a mixed group, filled with old and new patients, suffering from all types of mental illness. I like these groups because they show patients making progress for those who need inspiration, as well as the madness into which we can descend if we veer off the path of recovery.

Richard's stack of newspapers is neatly tucked under his chair, and he leans back with his ankles crossed, his big fingers interlaced over his belly. I notice Adelle sitting next to him. Normally in groups, Richard makes sure to keep at least one empty chair between him and anyone around him, but now that I see this today, I am reminded that he has been sitting next to Adelle in several groups.

Adelle has thin beige socks on with orthopedic sandals; she sits with her legs crossed at the ankles. Her cane is resting against the chair next to her, and she clasps her hands together in her lap. She looks like a sitcom grandma, wearing a fuzzy mauve cardigan. I wonder what makes her acceptable to him.

After a few more patients lumber into the room and take their seats, I begin addressing them.

"Good afternoon, everyone. Welcome. We're going to start off today's session discussing our progress toward goal achievement. We've got some newer patients here who haven't really defined their goals yet—" I stare directly at Richard, but he isn't looking at me "—and I'd like to get a sense of where some of you veterans are in your recovery." For whatever reason I've seemed to engage nearly everyone today, and a few hands shoot up offering to start the discussion.

"Yeah, Jenni, please. Why don't you go ahead?" I say with a warm smile.

"My goals are to learn how to stay away from heroin no matter what and to make better decisions about men." She launches her response into the room as if through a megaphone, gratified that she has a well-defined set of goals.

"What kinds of decisions did you used to make about men?" I ask, encouraging her to continue.

"The wrong ones. Well, the wrong *one*. I made the same wrong decision about all the men. Thought I had to give 'em something. Thought I wasn't good enough to leave when they weren't good to me." I'm absolutely delighted to hear that; Jenni must be going to her women's groups and embracing the notion that she is worthwhile.

I glance at Richard and see him looking over his glasses at Jenni. He catches me looking at him and gives me a knowing stare.

"Who's next?" Several more patients raise their hands and share their stories. I watch Richard and Adelle each time, and they seem to have similar reactions to each story. They both either nod in approval or grimace, turn away or disengage when they feel the stories are trite or phony. I wonder if they're becoming friends.

"Adelle," I say, breaching the exclusivity of their bond, "what about you? Do you want to share your goals?" I watch Richard for his reaction. He tentatively glares at me, but doesn't make a move to do or say anything.

Adelle regards me and seems to consider my request before delicately shaking her head no. Richard watches her shake her head, then turns to me and throws a gratified and superior smirk in my direction, complete with a flick of the eyebrows. He may as well have stuck out his tongue and called "nanny-nanny-boo-boo." *Well, fuck you, too, Richard.* He's protecting her—from what, I have no idea. But as we conclude the group, and I watch them leave, he hands Adelle her cane and helps her up from her seat. He slowly walks behind her into the hallway, and he tips his cap and bends politely in her direction as she carries on down the hall, remaining ever the enigma.

I walk back to my office, wondering how Adelle broke down Richard's tough exterior, and I find a note has been slipped under my door. I feel the anxiety crawl up my spine as my mind wanders back to the evaluation sessions with the OMH psychiatrists, and I wonder if my secrets will all come tumbling out and they're here in this note. I pick it up with apprehension.

It's a sheet of Typhlos legal-sized printer paper folded in three, with a Post-it note tucked inside. The Post-it falls out as I open the note, and inside is a message from David in thick, black Sharpie: "Found this outside your office. Had your name on it, figured it's yours. Don't leave your private stuff outside your office. You know how the patients can get." He signed it with a large *D*. I bend down to pick up the Post-it, which didn't come from any of the pads in my office. The back has lost its stick and is marred with gray newsprint. The front of the note says my name, followed by my home address and two different subway routes from my apartment to Typhlos. It's not my handwriting. It's not my Post-it note.

DECEMBER 14TH, 7:11 P.M.

When I get home, Lucas is waiting for me at my apartment, and I can see when I walk in the door that he's already drunk. I see several bottles on the coffee table, all with their labels facing the couch. Lucas is sitting in his work shirt and underwear, with the rest of his clothes piled on the back of a barstool.

He has red-wine mouth, which surprises me, because the only bottles I see are beer bottles. There are two packs of cigarettes on the table, both open, and a sea of butts in an ashtray that isn't mine. He's watching *Pulp Fiction*. He doesn't hear the door open when I walk in, so I make an effort to let it slam as a greeting.

"*Hey, baby!* Where you been? I been waitin' for ya!" As he says this, he's throwing his arms in the air and swaying like the waves are hitting him.

"Did you not have work today? Why are you so drunk?" I'm tossing my keys onto the console.

"I'm not drunk, I'm just happy to see ya! C'mere!" He's holding his arms out for an embrace and I walk to the stool and push his clothing onto the floor before hanging my jacket on the back of it. Though he notices his clothes dropping, he doesn't say a word, and continues to smile his drunken smile at me, and I feel like projectile vomiting right into his face.

"I've had a fucked-up week at work, and I'm not in the mood to babysit you tonight. Can you please pull yourself together?" I sit on the other end of the couch and avoid the attempted hug.

"Baby, I'm fine. You don't have to babysit anyone. Can I get you a beer? Or some wine? I opened a bottle of wine. I hope thatsh okay with you. I know you love your wine. I'll getcha some." He pinballs off the furniture on his way to the kitchen to get an open bottle of wine that has maybe half a glass left in it. I start smoking the cigarette he left burning in the ashtray. "Do you wanna glass or is the bottle okay? *Ha-ha*, I'm jush kidding, I'll getcha a glass for this wine."

After another spectacularly exhausting day on the unit, I don't have the energy to even bother fighting with this asshole, so I just lean back and inhale the smoke. Visions of AJ are clouding my mind. Sometimes watching the cigarette smoke come pouring out of my mouth makes me feel like I'm pushing out all the negatives from my day. When it hangs in the room like a ghost, I like to blow at it so it dissipates. For such a dirty habit, it really does feel cleansing.

Lucas is beginning to sway, and I can see him starting to hear the voices inside his head. I'm watching him change. I'm looking on as I see him shift from average drunk to violent offender. And then the full-blown switch to psychotic disaster. I brace myself for the onslaught. He's swaying in the doorway, holding himself up with one arm and smoking another cigarette. Something has crept into his head and he doesn't want to think about it. He has a half-empty bottle of Tito's Vodka sweating on the table next to him and a glass filled to the brim. I'm sitting on the couch, watching him not watching me, and I'm drinking Chablis.

"How long have you been drinking?"

Lucas gets defensive and arrogant when he's drunk. "I don't think that's really any of your business."

I look away from him as he says this, trying to avoid a fight. But I know it's coming.

"And you're just as drunk as I am, and you're the one who's drunk every fucking night. You're the one who gets so drunk you can't find your keys and you *pash out* in the hallway. Don't tell me *I* fucking drink too much."

"I didn't tell you that. You're yelling at me for no reason right now."

"It's not *no reason*. You're turning into your mother and I'm sick of watching you collapse. You're out at Nick's with all these guys all the time, and you *drink*, and you're smoking all day, and you always look like shit, and you're supposed to be my *girlfriend* and you act like a whore." He's holding the bottle in his hands now, and he left the full glass by the door.

"*I'm* a whore? You're out there with *actual* hookers, and you're calling *me* a whore?"

"Well, maybe if you were a better girlfriend, I wouldn't have to."

"You know what? Get out. Get the *fuck* out of my apartment. You don't even live here! You're drinking all my fucking booze—just get the fuck out." Now I'm standing up and pointing at the door. I'm showing him the way out, and I'm showing myself that I have the self-respect to demand to be treated properly.

"What the fuck? I'm in my underwear! I'm not going anywhere."

"No, put your fucking pants on, and get the fuck out. I'm not going to sit here and listen to you call me a whore. I have done *everything* for you! I take care of you when you're sick, I pretend not to know about the hookers, I put up with your drugs and your bullshit, and you're being an asshole now? You have *no right* to be an asshole! You should be kissing the ground I walk on! You should be thanking your lucky fucking stars for me. You prick! You piece of shit. You *fucking liar!*"

He's swaying toward me, and his hands are outstretched. Now I'm bracing to defend myself. He reaches for me, to pull me into a hug, to try to convince me to let him stay.

"No, get off me. You can't stay here." I tuck and move, attempt to get out of his reach. He slaps the cigarette out of my hand. It rolls under the coffee table and starts burning a track in the floorboards. He's grabbing both my shoulders with his sweaty hands, and his sour breath is in my nose. There's white spit gathering in the corners of his mouth, which makes me think he's on drugs again, too. I don't have the self-respect to make him leave. I don't have the self-respect to pull his hands off me, which are now digging into my shoulders so badly that I know I will have bruises by morning. I don't care enough about myself to pick up the phone and call the cops and tell them that he's going to hit me again.

He's almost on top of me now, and I see *Pulp Fiction* on the screen, and I hear Samuel L. Jackson's character saying he's trying, real hard, to be the shepherd.

When he shoves me into the wall, my mind skips to the safety of David.

When his eyes brim with tears and he tells me he doesn't mean to hurt me, I think of AJ.

When he lifts the bottle and spills vodka on his shirt, I think of a different life.

When he picks up the cigarette he slapped onto the floor, I think of my office garbage can.

When I wipe the tears out of my own eyes, and he hits the side of my face and my ears won't stop ringing, I think of Richard.

DECEMBER 15TH, 4:33 A.M.

I'm lying in AJ's bed, and I'm looking around his bedroom while he brushes his teeth in the bathroom. His sheets are soft and he has two windows in here. Beyond that, it's the most anonymous bedroom I've ever been in, which works for me right now, because I shouldn't be in here.

When Lucas lit that final cigarette after the violence, I knew he would leave like he always does after an outburst. Out of breath and sweaty, he put his clothes back on with a soggy cigarette hanging out of his mouth, threw his jacket over his shoulder and left me bloodied in the bathroom as he walked out the door. AJ was quick to respond to my text message and invite me right over. I cleaned myself up with a hot shower and tattoo makeup. The swelling is obscured in the low morning light, and my hair is down and wild to cover it even further.

AJ walks back into the room holding two glasses and a pitcher.

"Do you like margaritas? Do I even have to ask?" He's naked, and he looks like a Neanderthal in a display case at the Museum of Natural History. He climbs onto his bed and sits cross-legged in front of me, pouring drinks. He seems to have no insecurity that his dick is lying on the bed before him, and I can't help but gaze at it. We clink glasses, and when I lower my head to take a sip, I look at it again.

I'm naked, too, but I have the blankets pulled up under my boobs because I don't have the same confidence he has. I don't want him to see the bruises on my ribs, either. We drink wordlessly, staring at each other, smiling.

He reaches over and tugs at the covers. He smiles at me and pulls the blanket down past my stomach. He puts a finger in his glass and draws a heart with the cold liquid on my thigh. He gets his finger wet again and colors in the heart. It feels cold as it drips between my legs, and he leans down to kiss the tequila off me.

His warm mouth on my thighs, coupled with the intensity of my guilt, is making me quiver and shake almost uncontrollably. He's so much bigger than I am, and when I begin to shake, he pulls me into him and envelops me in his enormous arms. He breathes hard and wraps his arms around my back, lifting me to straddle him while he stays seated. My legs are wrapped around his back, and he traces more tequila up and down my neck and collarbones.

Each time he traces another line, when the drips begin to fall, he leans down and laps them up. I have goose bumps all over me, and I'm breathing in sharply with every touch.

My head and torso fall back onto his pillows, and I look up at his ceiling and wonder what I'm doing here. My mind is still in my apartment, in my bathroom, covering my head in the corner, but I'm trying to be here in the moment. The sun must be coming up somewhere because the city outside his windows is starting to show its edges. A familiar sense of fear begins to rise from my belly and crawl up into my mouth. Whenever the sun comes up and I'm still awake, I begin to feel like time is running out, and I have to grasp everything around me to make it slow, slow, slow down.

I'm gazing out his windows with my head and neck tilted back, so it all appears upside down to me, and the horizon is reversed. The outlines of the upturned buildings look like they're spelling out Lucas's name in giant, skyscraper block letters, and I have to flip my head away from the windows and blink away the image. AJ catches me as I sit back up, and my hair falls over his shoulders. He wraps his arms around my back again and pulls the glass from my hand. He places it next to his on a bedside table and lifts me up off the mattress. Wordlessly, he walks me to the windows, effortlessly carrying me, like I'm as tiny as a ballerina. He closes his curtains and buries his face in my neck. As I watch him close out the last traces of the brightening city behind him, he throws me onto his bed and climbs on top of me.

DECEMBER 15TH, 6:16 A.M.

The sun is peeking out over the buildings as I fumble with my front-door keys. I knew I shouldn't have stayed out this late, but after what happened with Lucas, I couldn't be alone. I had to go to AJ's. But, God, why did I have to drink so much? I look at my phone with one eye closed as I stumble into the elevator: 6:16 a.m.

I have time.

I can sober up with some coffee and a shower, and get to work in clean clothes.

I have time.

I have time.

I take giant steps from the elevator to my front door, as drunk people pretending to be sober do. I lean my left shoulder against the doorjamb and make several attempts to get the key into the lock. The key seems to be made of clay. After a few deep, concentrated breaths, I open the door. I squint into the sun and put on the coffee machine. I don't have time to wash my hair, but I can get the booze sweat off me in a hot shower. Or am I supposed to take a cold shower?

I step out of my clothes and get into a lukewarm shower. I'm spitting the boozy taste out of the back of my throat and brushing my teeth and my tongue so hard that it makes me gag. I push the toothbrush deeper into my mouth and gag again. I know if I get the booze out it will make a world of difference, so I keep pushing until I vomit all over my feet. I rinse off the toothbrush and move the showerhead around the tub to wash away the vomit. I scrub my skin with flowery-scented body wash and convince myself I can pull this off.

Stinging toothpaste and vomit burps crawl up my throat as I sit on the subway making my way uptown. I look at the passengers sharing the car with me, and none of them seem to think I look suspicious. This galvanizes me for the day ahead. I'm drinking my coffee out of a thermos from home, and I will stop by the bodega before I get to Typhlos. Grease. I need a greasy bacon, egg and cheese sandwich to coat my stomach. I look at my phone again, this time with both eyes: 7:53 a.m. I'm going to make it.

I'm eating the bacon, egg and cheese and drinking my second coffee in my office when it occurs to me that my hair stinks. I pull it out of the ponytail and waft it in front of my face. Smells like cigarettes and a long night out. I pull the bottle of Febreze from under my desk and spritz my whole head. I'm finger combing my hair as I walk to the bathroom to dry my hair under the hand dryers. This is humiliating, and I'm cursing Lucas under my breath for practically forcing me into AJ's arms, into his bed for solace. I knew I couldn't miss work today, dammit, Lucas. Asshole.

I'm dizzy walking back to my office. I know I need to stay seated for as long as possible and wait for the coffee and water and greasy breakfast to take effect. I'm hoping Rachel calls me in for our meeting toward the end of the morning. I pound the rest of my water and gently lay my head back onto the desk chair to rest my eyes for a moment.

David's knock on my door is spectacularly loud and

wrenches me from the grips of a drunken nap. I nearly knock myself off my chair as I jolt upright and fling open the door. Out of breath and wide-eyed, I stare at David.

"Hey, good morning. You okay?"

"Hey, David. Yeah, I'm fine. Just tired." My eyes take a moment to focus on him.

"Rachel asked me to let you know that she's ready for you in the conference room. You sure you're okay? You look totally out of it."

"No, no, I'm fine. I must have fallen asleep and you startled me."

"Are you drunk?" David whispers as he leans forward and sniffs in my direction. He closes the door behind him.

"No. No. No, no, no. Not drunk at all. Just didn't get enough sleep last night, and running on fumes right now." *Definitely still feeling drunk.* I look at my clock; it's nearly 10:00 a.m.

"Well, you better pull it together before you go in there. You look like you slept in a gutter."

"Fabulous. Thank you, David. But whatever, I'm totally fine. How's Rachel? What kind of mood is she in?" *Definitely not totally fine.* I smooth my hair into a bun and pick the sleep out of my eyes. I swish some Listerine in my mouth and spit it into the garbage can.

"Rachel seems okay. We just finished our meeting and everything went fine. Good luck." He walks out of my office, clearly disappointed, clearly disapproving. I can't be bothered to worry about what David thinks. I check my face in a compact, grab a stack of patient files and walk confidently to the conference room.

Rachel is sitting at the head of the table with her back to the door. The conference table looks enormous when there's only two of us sitting around it. I arrange my files in front of me as Rachel says hello, and then I stand to get myself another cup of coffee.

"Grab one for me, too, would you? Mine is the Tweety Bird mug." Rachel calls after me as I slip into the lounge.

"Sure, how do you take it?" I yell through the cracked door.

"Light and sweet, please." I prepare our two coffees, then walk them back into the conference room with trembling hands. As I place Rachel's cup in front of her, coffee sloshes over the lip and wets the table. "Thanks, Sam." She wipes up the coffee with a thin tissue and takes her first sip. "So, let's get started. Remind me how many of your patients are on meds here?"

We're in our monthly medication-management meeting. Each clinician meets with Rachel once a month to review how our patients are doing with their medication: Are they taking it? Do we suspect they're tonguing it? Is it having the desired effect?

"Everyone except Richard," I say.

"Okay. How's it going with Richard? Not really a med-management question, but still. We haven't had a chance to catch up."

"Making progress, I think. He's a tough guy, and he's still certainly not interested in answering questions about his incomplete file, but I'm beginning to sense that the violence rumors are nothing but hearsay. He's more like a stone wall than anything else." My eyeballs are jiggling inside my head.

"Well, I'm glad to hear you're making progress. We'll discuss that further at our next patient meeting, okay?"

"Great." I feel the hiccups starting to form deep in my chest.

"Last time we were here, we were discussing Adelle. Something wasn't working. I think we discussed changing her dosage or talking to the psychiatrists about trying a different medication?"

I flip through my files until I see Adelle's, and I have no idea what Rachel is talking about. I have no notes in her file about changes in medication. "Um, yeah. We were going to add in olanzapine, see if we can get her bipolar symptoms stabilized." *Does Adelle even have bipolar?* When I don't know what the fuck I'm talking about, I usually just throw around industry jargon and hope no one else is paying attention.

"Okay. Watch the interactions there. She's got a history of alcoholism, right?"

"Yeah, but she's been in treatment and away from booze for many years. She's in her nineties now, probably won't be an issue." My breath is hot and thick.

"Just monitor for liver function, and keep an eye out for anything seizure or tremor-like. I'll make a note of this. Hopefully, we find more success with the olanzapine than we have with the risperidone. I wouldn't want to compromise the system of such a fragile woman." Rachel writes something in her book.

"Okay." I scribble a wobbly note in Adelle's file to have her psychiatrist sign off on olanzapine. I feel the hangover sweats soaking the armpits of my sweater.

"What about Shawn? We've gotten some reports that he's completely out of it in groups. Very forgetful, confused. Have you determined if this is med related?"

Rachel is going too fast for me, and I'm having trouble keeping everything straight in my head. Shawn... Which one is Shawn again? I shuffle the files. "Uh, Shawn is fine. Actually—" I can see my brain forming the lie, and I want to stop myself, but I don't "—he has been showing signs of memory improvement, less confusion. I think we should stick to his current medication plan as it is, let it do its job. Shawn

is only twenty-six. I assume the confusion is a lack of attention, honestly."

We continue moving through my caseload, discussing the
details that I can't seem to remember about all my patients.
A violent headache is taking hold of the tendons behind my
eyes, and I fake my way through the meeting, feeling both
drunk and hungover, until I can finally stand up to leave.

I hold the door open for Rachel as I walk out into the
hallway. She looks at me quizzically, still sitting in her chair.
"I'm staying here, Sam. I've got meetings with the rest of the
staff." She screws her face into a judgmental grimace. "Try
to get some sleep tonight."

DECEMBER 16TH, 2:12 P.M.

I'm covering a group for Julie, who couldn't be bothered to come to work today. She probably had a meeting with her wealth manager to discuss stock options and pork bellies. This group is a spectacular waste of my time, because the only counselor responsibility is to monitor what the patients are doing on the computers.

Porn and gambling websites are blocked all across the institution, as well as social media sites, gossip sites or anything containing dangerous keywords like *guns* and *drugs*. I can't figure out how to circumvent this blockage, but some of the young patients are tech wizards; they manage to find some way around it and end up jerking off in the computer room. So, this is essentially what I'm doing in the computer room right now: making sure no one is breaking into porn sites and decorating the underside of the desks. I'm wearing AJ's scarf, and I periodically pull it up over my nose to inhale his scent. It brings me directly to his apartment, and my legs start to tingle and my stomach gets warm.

Eddie and Adelle are next to each other, and both of their computers don't work. Eddie keeps pushing the button on the monitor and waiting for something to happen. Adelle is patiently watching him. Lucy is on the other side of the room, looking at academic websites. She's planning on taking her GED, and she wants to prepare herself. She has a stack of papers that she took out of the recycling bin and is copying down every word she sees on the screen.

Eddie leans over Adelle and pushes the button on her monitor. Nothing happens.

"Sssssssam, the compuuuter'sss broken."

"Why don't you try one of the other ones?" I say without looking up. I'm gazing into my coffee, searching for answers.

"This lady'ssss computer'ssss broken, too." Adelle turns ever so slightly in my direction, and I groan to my feet and walk over to them. I push the same button Eddie has been, with the same result. I get down on my knees and poke the button on the tower between the two computers. I listen for anything to happen.

"Hey! My computer died!" Tyler looks around trying to figure out what happened.

"Sorry, Tyler. Hang on a sec." I push the button again, turning Tyler's computer back on. I finally find the right one, and Eddie's computer creaks to life, but Adelle's stays blank. There isn't another tower down here. I peer back up onto the desk, and there isn't another tower up there, either. Adelle's monitor is attached only to the keyboard and the mouse, and it doesn't even have a power cord going to the wall.

The computers we have are ages out of date, the technology is about ten years behind, and here we are using dead monitors plugged into nothing to help our patients learn modern technology. Welcome to Typhlos. What a bunch of bullshit.

"Eddie, what are you doing on the computers today?" I ask, hoping he and Adelle can practice some patience and teamwork and do a computer project together.

"I don't know, Sssssam, what sssshould–we–dooo?"

I stand behind his chair and lean over the desk to reach for the mouse so I can find a game or an educational program that they can work on together. Eddie doesn't move his hand as I descend onto the mouse, and we end up holding it together, and I push and pull his hand and arm with mine. I open a program designed to help with recall memory and information retention.

"Would you two be willing to work on this project together? Maybe you can help each other to learn and remember?" I've already done more than I wanted to do in this joke of a group, and I'm getting fed up and frustrated. Adelle removes her Coke-bottle glasses and polishes them on her scrubs top. She perches herself at the edge of her seat and gently pushes Eddie's elbow, encouraging him to move the mouse and start the game. Eddie does, and the first box that pops up on screen asks for a name. Satisfied that they are willing to work together and I can go back to zoning out, I leave them and return to my seat by the door. After a few minutes of deliberating, I see Eddie and Adelle type "Eddelle" into the name box on the screen.

I look around the room and see various copies of the *Diagnostic and Statistical Manual of Mental Disorders* that mental health professionals use strewn about. Instead of drifting into a semiconscious state, I walk around and start tidying up. There's a copy of the third edition of the diagnostic manual, the *DSM-III*, opened to the section on personality disorders. This is more of a history lesson than anything else; so much has changed. There are notes in the margins, but they're in smudged pencil, so I can't tell what they say. Some of the pages have their edges bent down. I close the *DSM-III* and walk around the room to pick up the other books.

Two copies of the fourth edition are also out on desks. I read the familiar words and strain to see what the notes in the corners say. There are initials and check marks in the margins, as well. F.W. and S. something.

As I close the books and stack them in the crook of my arm to put back onto the bookshelf, I notice that one of the monitors was left on, and no one in this group is using it. I approach the monitor to turn it off and discover an open Wikipedia page about personality disorders, and to the right of the monitor is a Post-it pad. It's not a Typhlos one, but for some reason I think I've seen it before. I survey the room to figure out who could have been looking up diagnostic criteria, but no one in here knows how to work the computers well enough to find this. Suddenly I feel like I'm being watched, but as I scan the room again, all I see are patients slowly tapping on computers or dozing off in their chairs.

DECEMBER 19TH, 1:19 P.M.

I need to smoke. I can't go out now—it's freezing outside, and there are too many people between me and the door, and I don't want to look at anyone's face.

I pace my office, which is too small to pace, so essentially I walk in miniature, tight circles, and I realize this is making me feel insane.

My windows are on the left side of the building; they're not in the front where some staffer may see me if I were to lean out, but up on the third floor above the side street.

My Lunch sign is already affixed to the outside of my door, and I don't have any groups for another hour, so I would have time to air myself out and even brush my teeth.

Knowing that my coat already smells like cigarettes, I rationalize that it won't make much of a difference. I pull open the window and carefully tuck all my hair into my hood. I take off my shoes and stand up on the patient chair so the whole top half of my body is out the window. My gloves are on, which makes it hard to grip the cigarette and the lighter, but at least my fingers won't smell.

I finally get the cigarette lit, and all this concentration and effort is paying off. As the smoke fills my lungs, the unending sense of panic begins to fade. I focus on blowing the smoke away from the open window, and the thin white wisps disappear in tiny tornados of bitter cold. It's bright, and my sunglasses are in my handbag. Squinting, I watch the plumes flow out of my mouth. I look upward toward the warmth of the sun and suddenly choke on the cigarette smoke as I see Rachel hanging out of her office window.

"Sam!" I hear a flustered whisper scream call my name. It's Rachel. She's leaning out the window of her office, with her hood pulled over her hair, clutching a pink Bic lighter in her left hand. "Put out that cigarette and come to my office. Now."

Without saying a word, I throw my still-lit cigarette onto the street below me and pull back into the office. My heart explodes in my chest and the panic begins to rise like bile in my throat. What the hell is Rachel doing smoking out her window? I hurry to get my shoes back on and my coat up on its hook.

I grab my water bottle, take my toothbrush out of my emergency sleepover bag and brush my teeth, quickly spitting into the garbage can. I spritz on perfume and use the Febreze that lives under my desk to spray my sweater and hair.

Rushing up the back stairs to Rachel's office, I take the steps two at a time. My heart is racing from a combination of horror, fear and nicotine. I can feel my jugular straining against my neck.

I'm winded when I reach Rachel's office, and I knock despite the laminated In Session, Quiet Please sign on her front door. I try to camouflage my anxiety with the veneer of professionalism, but I feel the sweat trickling down my sides. I can sense the golden-girl image tarnishing.

Rachel inches the door open and pulls me inside, quickly

closing us both in before the smell of cigarettes can escape into the hallway.

"Sam, you're smoking?" Rachel has already hung up her coat and reassembled herself.

"Yes, I've always smoked. Granted, never out my window, but yes, I have been a smoker since I started here." I sit down in her patient chair, even though she didn't invite me to.

"But now? Still? You're still smoking?"

"I'm sorry, I totally understand that smoking out my window is completely impermissible and out of line. I promise you, it won't happen again." I hear the apology come out of my mouth and marvel at Rachel's hypocrisy.

"No, I'm not— I don't mean the rules, I just— I can't believe you would smoke while you're pregnant. Someone as educated as you are."

"*Pregnant?* I'm not pregnant! Oh, my God!" The spins are back.

"You're not pregnant?" Rachel seems genuinely shocked.

"No! Where did you hear that?"

"Oh, God. Samantha, oh. I thought—ahh. I came by your office the other day to discuss some things with you, and I heard what sounded like vomiting coming from your office. I guess I just assumed that you were having morning sickness, and you stayed in your office to avoid telling people. Oh, I can't believe I jumped to such a conclusion. I'm sorry."

"Oh—I…" I'm caught off guard. I thought I would have to excuse the smoking, but now I'm being called out on throwing up in my garbage can. *Fuck.* "Yeah—I've been really, uh, ill. I get these migraines, and sometimes they make me really nauseous. I don't often have time to make it to the ladies' room. It's an absolutely disgusting affliction, but, not quite pregnancy." I've had this lie sitting in my back pocket

for years, assuming I couldn't possibly go undetected forever.
I'm watching Rachel's eyes and hoping she buys it.

"Oh. Well, I'm sorry to hear that. I had no idea you suf-
fered from migraine headaches. My ex-husband had those.
They're quite debilitating."

"Yeah, it's fine. I've had them for a long time, so I'm used
to it at this point." *Are we going to discuss that we were both just
smoking out the window?*

"I've noticed you're slow to react sometimes in the staff
meetings—now I understand why. No wonder you looked
so exhausted and out of it when we had our meeting the
other day."

"Sorry if that happens. I try to hide it, but sometimes it
just gets the best of me." *Garner the sympathy, get the shine back
on me. I can masquerade a hangover as a migraine all day.* "What
brought you to my office the other day? You wanted to discuss something with me?" I need to quickly maneuver the
conversation away from anything that's making me look bad
or weak. Or pregnant.

"Uh, yeah. I did." Rachel shifts uncomfortably in her seat.
"But obviously we should address the elephant in the room."

I hold up my hands in a gesture of surrender. "Your secret
is safe with me, Rachel."

"Well, thank you, but it's absolutely inappropriate for me
to be smoking out my office window." She releases the breath
she's been holding since I walked in. "These are just very
trying times, and sometimes I get overwhelmed like anybody else."

I seamlessly switch to psychologist mode and furrow my
brow to listen. I cock my head slightly to the left and give an
almost imperceptible nod, encouraging her to keep going.

"Things have been stressful here," Rachel continues. "I'm
sure you, of all people, have been able to sense the chaos."

She makes a grandiose gesture with her hands, seemingly trying to indicate that the whole unit has gone up in flames.

I'm nodding along, interested and also somewhat guilty that I haven't noticed the severity of the chaos.

"We're in—" She leans toward me to tell me the details like little girls sharing secrets on the playground. "We're in, like, *extraordinary* financial straits right now." Rachel throws her back into her chair and spins it away from me, clearly uncomfortable releasing this information. She's rubbing her temples, and I notice for the first time that she has chewed her cuticles and they're red and raw.

"I haven't been disclosing any of this to the staff, and I know the other administrators have been playing it close to the chest, as well. But, frankly, I was just smoking, and since you were, too, looks like professionalism is out the window, so to speak." She looks over her shoulder at me and smirks. "And I trust you, Sam."

"Rachel, I'm so sorry. I had no idea that Typhlos was in such trouble." Things are starting to make sense; of course we're in trouble. The staff has been irritable, and the admins are nowhere to be seen. The sick days are adding up all over the place. The paint is peeling; the toilets remain unfixed. More and more patients are filing in and no more staff has been hired to manage them. Caseloads are case *overloads*. I begin to wonder how bad it really is.

"I didn't realize how much I needed to talk about this." Rachel sighs.

Looking around her office as she says this, I can see the results of the turmoil. It's in a state beyond disarray. There's a dark stain on the carpet in the middle of the floor, and it seems to be growing fuzz of some kind. Several umbrellas have dropped between the wall and the filing cabinet, none properly closed. The plants that line the windowsill are long dead, even succulents and cacti that are supposed to be un-killable. Under her desk, there are numerous pairs of shoes crammed into a plastic bag. From woolly winter boots all the way to sandals—obviously unattended for months.

"Well, I'm right here to listen to you. I have a group in forty minutes, but I could have David cover for me if you need to discuss what's been going on." Now's the time to so-lidify my status with Rachel.

She nods somberly, defeated, and I pick up her phone to buzz David on the intercom. He agrees to cover my group and doesn't bother to ask why.

"Covered," I say. "What's happening?" I feel like I should be uncomfortable; it's not normal for Rachel to allow profes-sional boundaries to fall, and it's certainly not normal for her to confide in me. But instead this feels like an opportunity.

"It's not just us—it's all the publicly funded facilities. The money just isn't there anymore. The city doesn't have it for us, the state, the federal government—no one. The money just isn't there. The mental-health-care world never recov-ered from 2008. Things were redistributed, and we got the short end of the stick, as we usually do.

"But now we have the same yearly decline in staffing be-cause people can't exist on these wages. We're losing adminis-trators who can't stand to live without a six-figure salary, and the workload and influx of patients is going in the opposite direction." Rachel isn't looking at me. She's facing away, with her head lolled back on her desk chair, her feet stuck straight out in front of her, and she's gently twisting left and right.

"How long has this been happening?"

"Months. Or, I suppose, I've known about this for months, but it's been building for longer than that." She abruptly spins back to face me and pulls a tin of something from her desk drawer. She plucks out a sour candy and offers the tin to me.

I politely decline, as I still have the taste of toothpaste in my mouth.

"The suits came for a meeting before it got really cold, maybe September or so; let me know that the wheels were coming off at Typhlos. Long discussions of staff loyalty and capabilities. Who would be able to handle a heavier caseload, who would maintain employment with us, despite increased work and no increase in pay. It's always such a *pleasure* to hear them commiserate with us as they take away the last crumbs of our survival. And preach the importance of patient care. I'm the captain of a sinking ship, and they're constantly calling me to remind me that they're fighting the good fight, and they're down in the trenches with me. They propose these preposterous solutions to keep team morale up. *Team morale?* They don't even know our names."

I'm looking at Rachel's desk. She has files and notes and binders stacked haphazardly all over the place. There are take-out containers underneath piles of documents and used tissues shoved into corners.

Her desperation is evident, not just in the fact that she's talking to me at all, but her voice, her office, her demeanor; everything about her suggests an air of madness.

"They don't even begin to comprehend that I'm alone here." She's nearly sobbing. "I'm alone in managing this crisis, I'm alone in knowing the crisis even *exists*, I'm alone in performing the bulk of the managerial duties. I even asked! I *asked* if I could promote one of the psychologists to a managerial position, so I could at least *talk* to someone about this! I had *you* in mind, by the way."

"And what did they say?" *Am I getting a promotion?*

"'We would prefer if the staff didn't get wind of the financial setbacks. We imagine it will be temporary, and we would prefer to have as few people aware as possible.'" She uses a nasal, cartoon voice to impersonate the higher-ups and pulses animated finger quotes at her temples. "Same nonsense as always. So, they're lying to everyone. Lying by omission."

"Well, I'm glad that you told me. Obviously, you need to get this off your chest and have the opportunity to share with another staff member. I don't expect any kind of promotion or change in title, but if you need my help, or some kind of backup while you're going through this, I am right here. Very happy to help. And I won't tell anyone what's happening." Doesn't seem worth it, but I might as well keep up appearances.

"I can't—I can't ask that of you. I've already put so much on your plate. I've given you all the impossible cases, you're running the most trying groups, and I can't risk pushing you to a breaking point. If I lost you, this whole place would go under, believe me. And Jesus Christ, I just accused you of being pregnant."

"Rachel, this is my job, and I love my job. And I'm good at my job. It would be impossible for me to know that this is going on, and to know that you need help, and not provide any. Give me something. Let me shoulder some of this burden for you."

I can see in her eyes that she desperately wants to accept my offer. She's been thinking about it. She's been waiting for an opportunity to come talk to me. The shine is back on me, and it's nearly brilliant now.

"I haven't been doing monthly med meetings with all the staff. I've been outsourcing supervision sessions, as you know. Sam, I haven't even reviewed the staff evaluations." She holds up the pile of folders. Still with the OMH seal tied over the stack like an unopened Christmas present.

So *that's* why I've been flying under the radar; the evaluations were never reviewed. "I should have had these finished and the report submitted to OMH as soon as Dr. Brooks and Dr. Young gave me their summaries. But the Office of Mental Health has the same problems we have—they're overworked, underfunded, understaffed. We're all in the same sinking ship."

I have never been so lucky as to have a golden opportunity to save my own skin fall into my lap like this. "Rachel, please, let me take something off your hands." *Give me the evals, give me the evals. Give. Me. The. Evals.*

"I'm just so overwhelmed, and I look at the patients every day, and I can't let them down." She's getting misty-eyed and a faraway look. *Give me the evals.*

"I can help with administrative tasks if you need. I can take over the intake responsibilities. I can cover your groups if something comes up—" *give me the evals* "—or I could even do the OMH evaluation summary for you." My heart is beating in my throat, and I can feel the blood and adrenaline pumping all the way down to my fingertips. The veins in my hands are starting to come to the surface, and the sweat is pooling at the back of my waistband.

She looks down at the handful of evaluations, but there is some disconnect between what she sees and what she's thinking. "I—I can't have our patients suffering because of financial issues. I can't have them losing out again; they've been through enough." Her voice gets smaller as her thoughts tangle and crash. Seemingly without consciously deciding to, her hand slowly extends in my direction, and she looks to me, slack-jawed and wide-eyed, opens her fingers and drops the evaluations into my outstretched hands. "I can't have the patients feel these changes. They need support..." Her voice trails off; my ears are full and ringing. My stomach is creeping into my mouth, and I'm elated and terrified that she may be giving me the ticket to my liberation. I run my hands over the smooth face of the top file folder with my sweaty palms and feel the weight of the package.

"What else?" I ask, my eyes glued to the stack of evaluations in my hands. I can't believe this is happening. Rachel is in a trance of anxiety and self-pity, and I'm not sure she can hear me.

"Here's what you can do for me." She's staring into the middle distance, as if she took acid and it just kicked in. "Don't tell anyone that I'm drowning. Don't tell the rest of the staff, not even David, that we're in trouble. Keep up the facade. Please, don't let anyone see the man behind the curtain, so to speak." She refocuses her eyes onto mine and clamps the outsides of my hands with hers as she says this. Her hands holding my hands; my hands holding my salvation.

I slowly stand up; I need to get out of this room with these evaluations before she sees right through me and takes them back. Rachel straightens up and meets my eyes again with a confused and tenuous look.

"I won't tell anyone if you won't." We shake on it; a pact. A pact between two drowning women to pretend that the other can swim.

DECEMBER 20TH, 3:46 P.M.

I have the package of evaluations tucked under my arm and I feel as if I know what it's like to be a heroin dealer concealing a shipment. The excitement is tremendous, but the fear is overpowering. Rachel has lost her damn mind and decided that the best person to review the evaluations and prepare a summary report for the Office of Mental Health is *me*. Mentally unstable, self-annihilating, awe-inspiring superhero Dr. Samantha James.

I have to work as quickly as I can because there is no way she will remain this brain damaged for long. Just because Typhlos is in trouble doesn't mean she needs to stoop to this level.

I tear the OMH ribbon from the package, and the files spill out like an open accordion. They're organized by department, and even though curiosity immediately sends me to read the files of my clinical colleagues, I restrain myself and create an organized and cogent system for summarizing the findings. I have to get something down on paper in case Rachel were to come check on me, so I start with the boring ones: the maintenance staff and the kitchen workers. I'll follow those with the security staff, then the orderlies and nurses, and fi-nally I will dig into the clinical staff.

My head is filled with the notion that Travis and Dr. Brooks gave us all a free pass and I'm not going to be found out. I don't know what I would do if I opened my file and discov-ered I was wrong. I place the folder with my name on the tab down at the bottom of the pile.

David is still covering the group I asked him to cover, so I could talk to Rachel. I imagine he will come in and tell me how it went when he finishes. I've got ten minutes, maybe fifteen, and after that, my schedule is clear for most of the afternoon. I should be having individual patient meetings; I should be working on case files and reaching out for continu-ing care. Instead I hang an In Session sign on my door, turn up the white-noise machine to full blast and clear my desk of all other work and debris. I pull out my phone to find a text filled with suggestive emojis from AJ. With a smile, I turn it off; can't have distractions now. I take out two pens: a red one for notes, a black one for the summary. I lay a white Typhlos legal pad next to the stack of evaluations, and it's off to the races.

Each folder contains the results of the assessments and in-ventories that were given to the staff member, as well as a brief summary of the findings. Then there's a separate synop-sis of the interviews. For the OMH doctor's reference, there is a copy of the Typhlos employment history and each indi-vidual's résumé.

After Travis and Dr. Brooks complete the probes and turn in their findings, it's Rachel's job to review their conclusions and make employment decisions for every employee. This is now *my* job. The actual OMH reviews go back into every-one's staff folder in the administration office, probably never to be seen again, and it's Rachel's final report that gets submitted to OMH. Now *my* final report.

I open the first folder—Salvatore Valbuena, maintenance worker. Employed with the Typhlos Psychiatric Center for eleven years. Education level? High school equivalency diploma. Assessment and interview conclusions? Unremarkable. Verdict? Fit to maintain current employment. I jot down some quick notes, carefully close his folder and place it upside down on my windowsill.

As I continue, I see that nearly all the maintenance staff has the exact same result, with the exception of Carlos, who showed erratic and unreliable responses on all his inventories, and the interviews were inconclusive. Clearly, this is because he doesn't speak English, and neither Travis nor Dr. Brooks spoke any Spanish. Instead of doing their fucking jobs, they decided to assume that his bizarre responses were due completely to the language barrier and despite the inconclusive results, they pronounced him fit to maintain current employment. To show that I am scrupulous and careful, I make a large red note on my pad requesting that the next time these evaluations occur, a Spanish-speaking doctor is available to those who are not proficient in English. *See? I'm perfectly capable of doing this.*

As I read through the evaluations and review the results of the assessments, I wonder if these things are being graded on a curve. If I had to guess, I would say that at least half of us are fucking crazy, and if we didn't come in here crazy, we went crazy while we were here. Look at Rachel—she was the poster child for being sane, and now she's beginning to come apart at the seams. Did the OMH clinicians give us some leeway? Did they take into account the stress levels that this environment produces? I wonder if they took it upon themselves to give some of us get-out-of-jail-free cards, just to keep us employed here while the seas of financial uncertainty swell around us.

I've gotten through the monotonous and uninspired evaluations of almost all the ancillary staff. My shift is technically over, and I could go home and open a bottle of wine now. A cold one. Maybe two cold ones. And I could smoke cigarettes in peace. Before I decide to fully pack it in, curiosity prickles my neck.

I flip to the bottom of the stack, shimmy my evaluation out and place it on top of the pile. I stare at it for a moment, wondering if I have faith enough to open it. I let it sit there, at the top of the pile, next on the list, waiting for me to gain the strength. Stashed somewhere is a giant Ziploc of nips. Where the fuck did I hide that thing?

I put my unopened folder back beneath the rest of the clinical staff and kick off my shoes. I can't bear the thought of finding out yet. I bring the remaining evaluations onto the floor and pull my coat off the hook. I make a little nest for myself, using my coat as a pillow. From what I've gathered so far from the other evaluations, this is going to be more entertainment than anything else. As I'm gearing up to get a good laugh, starting with Julie, there's a knock at my door.

"It's me. You still in there?" I reach up from my station on the carpet and open the door for David. "Hi. What are you doing down there?"

"Hi. Just some extra stuff that Rachel asked me to help out with." I can't even tell David that I've been given this opportunity to save myself. I can't admit what I'm planning on doing with my evaluation. "What are you doing?"

"I was heading home. Just wanted to let you know that your group was totally uneventful. You might want to check on Shawn's meds, though. He was super out of it."

"Will do. Thanks, David." I wave at him as he closes my door, and refocus on Julie's evaluation.

I pull out her résumé, and scan over any bolded information. Upper East Side address, high floor, 10021 zip code. Obviously. She included her GPA on her résumé. *Jesus Christ, what a kiss ass.* Graduated from college when I was defending my dissertation. She's only twenty-eight years old. Master's-level clinical staff, employed with Typhlos for two years. Her last three jobs before this were in residential programs. None of them lasted longer than six months. I see copies of two performance reviews. The first was completed just after Julie's six-month probationary period, and the next one a year later. Everything looks good; she gets three and four out of five-point ratings on most items. The comments section is what I'm interested in.

Lacking professionalism in patient interactions.
    Inappropriate use of hugging and physical contact.
    Energy levels distractingly high.
    Nonclinical language used in clinical paperwork.
    Can benefit from observing other clinical staff members during group sessions.
    Note: Please do not use smiley-face symbols on *any* clinical documentation.

Ha! I can't believe these things were addressed with her over a year ago, and she still behaves like a cheerleader, sorority slut on the unit. *What a joke.*

Her assessment summary states "unremarkable." *Just like the rest of her.* Nothing notable, nothing pathological, other than pathologically irritating. The interview summaries indicate her bubbly personality may not be suited to this particular field, although it concludes that she is fit to maintain her current employment. Maybe I should grab a fat black Sharpie and change that conclusion. At the bottom of her interview summary, I find another golden nugget.

Axis 1 Diagnosis: None (rule out anxiety)
Axis 2 Diagnosis: None (elevated histrionic response)

The psychiatrists think she's got anxiety and a tendency toward hysteria. Freud would *love* this shit. I toss Julie's evaluation aside and continue through the counseling and social-work staff. I keep running notes in case I encounter anything interesting, but Travis and Dr. Brooks seem to have kept everything perfunctory and professional. Now and again there is a small blurb about a foible or personality trait that could be problematic, but no one has been deemed unfit so far.

Before starting in on Gary's file, I pop into the staff lounge for another coffee and a pack of peanut M&M's. Gary is the last in my master's pile, then I'm moving on to the psychiatrists, then the two PhDs: David and me.

I skip over Gary's résumé and give a superficial glance to his employment history and performance reviews. He has mostly three-point ratings. Average. Nothing special. I get to his assessment and interview summaries, and now it gets interesting.

Intense discomfort and anxiety related to completing psychological assessments and inventories.
Profuse sweating and heavy breathing noted during each assessment and interview session.
Frequently asked for bathroom and water breaks.
All assessments inconclusive; erratic answer patterns; inconsistent control responses.
Fit to continue adjusted employment: recommend in-

creased supervision and continuing education, decreased patient contact.

Axis 1 Diagnosis: Generalized Anxiety Disorder
Axis 2 Diagnosis: None

I guess we didn't all fly by under the radar. I suppose Travis and Dr. Brooks had to be more scrupulous with the clinical staff. My heart begins to flutter as I get closer to looking at my own evaluation, no longer confident that I will have gotten away with anything. My palms are sweating as I quickly review the results from both our staff psychiatrists. Obviously, Travis and Dr. Brooks protected their own. MDs will always support other MDs, so there's nothing but egregious praise and penned blow jobs in the summary reports. Assholes. I throw these folders on top of all the other ones. Just two more to go now.

I slowly open David's folder, cautious not to get sweat stains or chocolate on his file, careful not to mar my best friend's clinical reputation. The goofy, reformed frat boy with a lopsided grin and permanently rumpled hair who I know and love is not the same David as the one he brings to work. He's not hiding his true self or pretending—he just has the capacity to turn his professional persona on and off.

Everything about David's file is perfect. Even the xeroxed signatures on his performance reviews are flawless. His five-point ratings rival my five-point ratings, and I never thought of him as quite as good as me. The recommendations at the bottom of his reports are thinly veiled compliments. Trying to make *perfectionist* sound negative, as if he is too good at his job. I thought *I* was the only one with this kind of reputation around here; I thought *I* was the golden child. He even charmed the OMH doctors. All compliments and no diagnoses on his assessment and interview summaries. This isn't fair.

I pull a shiny yellow M&M out of the package and let it sit between my fingers for a moment. Before I pack up for the night, leaving just one evaluation left unread, I smear the candy coating on the front of David's review. *Not so perfect anymore, are you?*

DECEMBER 21ST, 9:46 P.M.

I'm curled on the couch in Lucas's apartment. There's a bottle of Chablis chilling in a bucket that looks like it costs more than my rent, and I'm terrified of leaving water rings on the table. I'm wearing navy blue socks, and I don't want them to leave little fuzzies on his cream-colored couch. It's clear I don't belong here and that makes me extremely uncomfortable.

He lives in one of those buildings that's half hotel and half apartments, and he has access to all the hotel amenities—including the housekeeping staff. A cleaning lady is in here every single day, so everything is immaculate. His chrome furniture is perfectly shiny, and his fluffy white rugs are perfectly fluffed.

Lucas went shopping earlier, and he's now giving me a fashion show of all his purchases. He wants me to pick the best outfit for him to wear to some New Year's gala to which I am not invited. *Oh, I would bring you, Sam, but you know how boring these things are. I wanted to spare you the misery.* I'm sure it's because he's still mad about that dinner weeks ago with some of his coworkers when I didn't properly laugh on cue.

"And this one," he says as he saunters out from his walk-in closet, "is Armani. It's got a peaked lapel, which I usually don't go for, but this suit is cut so impeccably, and the stitching is just beautiful."

To me, it looks like another dark suit, the same as the thirty dark suits already hanging in his shiny, perfectly lit closet. "What's the difference between this one and the last one?"

"Well, first of all, this one is blue."

"But you're wearing black shoes. Aren't you not supposed to wear black and navy together?" I pull a cashmere blanket off the arm of the couch and drape it over my shitty socks and Old Navy jeans.

"Can't you see the difference in these suits? This one's got a completely different texture. Here—" he comes closer to let me feel "—touch it. The other was much lighter." When he approaches, I see the price tag hanging from the jacket sleeve. The jacket alone was $3,600. I wipe my hands on the front of my sweatshirt before touching his pristine suit.

"Oh. Yes, it's very nice." Maverick ambles into the room and jumps up to sit on my lap. I think he likes me better than Lucas.

He continues to show me various suits and shirts and ties and cuff links. He's putting together different combinations and different personas. When he goes back into the closet, he continues talking to me from inside, and I can't understand anything he's saying, but intermittently I call out an "uh-huh" or a "really?" so he thinks I'm paying attention. I'm picturing my evaluation in my head, hoping it looks as good as David's. Knowing it probably won't. Maverick starts licking the rim of my wineglass, and I let him share my Chablis with me.

"This one," he says as he exits the closet, "I think *this* is the one for the gala." Again, it looks exactly the same as all the other ones. His shoes look smaller than his feet should be, and his belt isn't closed.

"You think that's it? It looks good. It looks especially good with the coke you have on your face."

"With what?" He furiously wipes at his nose and mouth with both hands, then pulls his palms back to see if he got it. "I don't have anything on my face." He quickly turns into the bathroom and mops his face with a Frette washcloth.

"I thought you said you weren't going to do that shit anymore." I wrap my cheap viscose scarf around my neck and start throwing my things into my handbag.

"Sam, I'm *not* doing coke. I don't know what you think was on my face, but it certainly wasn't cocaine."

"Okay. And all this energy you have to talk a mile a minute while putting on and taking off enough suits to clothe all of Manhattan, I'm sure that's because of an afternoon espresso, right?"

"It's just excitement. Just regular old excitement about my new suits. Of course *you* have to make a big deal out of it. Of course you can't just be happy for me and help me pick something out. *You* have to force me to be one of your patients. Make me look sick so *you* can save me. As usual." He's always very quick to turn the tables and displace blame.

"There's a prescription bottle with someone else's name on it in your medicine cabinet, and I can see the 'spoon' you're using to take bumps. It's sitting right there, you fucking idiot." I'm walking past his closet to put on my coat, and reflected in the closet mirror is a small bag of cocaine with a gold collar stay sticking out of it. "So, unless you've recently changed your name to Michael Sumner, and you need oxycodone for some injury or surgery or whatever, then you're still a liar and you're still a drug addict. Merry Christmas, asshole." Maverick follows me to the door, his tail wagging dramatically. I bend down to kiss him goodbye. I wish I could take him with me.

"You're leaving? What are you—a saint? Too good to be

with me now? It's just coke, Sam!" He screams this and his voice just escapes the door as it slams behind me. I used to pause in the hallway after I stormed out. I would wait for him to come out and get me, to apologize and promise to change. To admit that he *is* a liar, but vow to make it better. Now I just head straight for the elevator. He's never come out after me.

DECEMBER 22ND, 11:34 A.M.

Richard is sitting in my patient chair, and we're still getting nowhere. He finds himself in my office on a Thursday because Christmas is this weekend and half the staff have taken time off, so the groups aren't running regularly. The heap of evaluation folders caught his eye when he walked in this morning, because they're in the spot where he usually leaves his load of newspapers. He gave the pile a once-over, sneered at it, then placed his stack precariously on the windowsill. I keep glancing at the evaluations. I've avoided completing the last file, *my* file, and it's been filling up my head ever since. After seeing that Gary's file, and even Julie's, were filled out with professional precision, and actual *recommendations* as opposed to just flying through and marking everyone competent, my convictions that I'm safe are faltering.

Richard is talking to me again today, but still not about anything useful. He's mentioning the weather, telling me about how this is good fishing weather, but the city is too noisy for fish. He's describing the way the city used to be when he was young, when it was still gritty and full of character. He says now it's gone soft, and only millionaires can play in its gilded playgrounds. The "soft hands," he calls them.

People who have never done an honest day's work. People who don't deserve their money, who don't deserve this city. He tells me how happiness doesn't come from money, so I ask him where it comes from, and he replies "How the hell should I know?"

"There used to be a time in this city when people walked the streets with their heads up," he says. "Before the stock market crashed, before the buildings went down. Everybody wasn't always so miserable. And they weren't always so coddled. These days, you hear about a kid who won't pay attention in school, and so they say he has some disease, and he *can't* pay attention. So they put him in a special class where he doesn't have to come in until later, and they give him special pills to help him concentrate, and it's all bullshit. Whatever happened to telling the kid to buck up and pay attention? Whatever happened to discipline? Now it's all lawsuits."

As Richard gets on his soapbox, I hear some kind of rumbling in the hallway. Not like a train below us, or construction noises, but some kind of disturbance. I keep one ear strained toward the door and half-heartedly listen to Richard continue on his tirade.

"The parents sit at home in their piles of money, and they hire all the nannies and the housekeepers to raise the kid—I bet you the dads don't even know their kids' names—and the moms are getting their fat pulled up and sucked out and their faces picked up and sliced out, and—"

In the middle of Richard's sentence, the intercom siren screams into my office, announcing a code blue on the second floor of the unit. The siren blares repeatedly, with a panicked, mechanical voice echoing "Code Blue, Code Blue" over and over. Before I can explain to Richard what's happening, I fly out my door and tear down the hallway. I run down the back stairwell to find a cluster of patients and staff standing in a tangle around some central commotion. Patients on the outskirts of the clump are jumping up to see over the crowd and assess what's going on.

I grab sweaty shoulders and bathrobes, pull people to one side or the other and shove myself into the middle of the fray. On the floor in front of me, an orderly is performing CPR on Adelle. A couple of female patients are crying hysterically, and another orderly is offering them oxygen. There's a backboard on the ground next to Adelle, and it keeps getting kicked around by frightened patients. Other clinical staff members are spangled among the crowd. I capture Gary's attention and do a helicopter with my left hand.

"Everyone out of here, Gary. Help me." Gary nods at me and starts with the people to his immediate left and right. The orderly who was offering oxygen to the women is enormous, and I think his name is Carl.

"Carl, help me get these people out of here. Adelle won't be able to breathe with all this around her."

"It's Kyle."

"Sorry, Kyle. Please help me." Kyle straightens and is even bigger than I remembered. His shaved head glistens with sweat under the fluorescent hallway lights. When he spreads his huge gorilla arms, his wingspan holds five bodies on either side. But his voice is not as booming as I would have imagined as he gently asks the patients to move back. I step in.

"Everyone *back*! Thank you for your concern, but we need you all to clear the area *now*. Please go to your *rooms*, or somewhere else, but we need this area clear *right now*." I'm holding my hands above my head, bellowing as loudly as I can. With Gary and Kyle helping to escort patients in the right direction, the crowd is thinning. I can hear the sirens of an ambulance arriving outside.

for your level heads and quick responses. Let's get back to our days, okay? Make sure you check in with all your patients, keep everyone's spirits lifted. Maybe I'll organize a game night tonight, or a movie or something..." She trails off and wanders toward Terry and Kyle, who have been standing by the elevator. Rachel shakes both their hands and bounces her head as they speak.

Shirley, Gary and I slowly walk to the rear staircase and silently make our way back to our offices. When we open the door to the third floor, a huddle of patients has been waiting for our return. We're greeted with a cacophony of "What happened?" and each of us ushers a few back to a group room or a lounge area.

I need to get back to my desk and go through my files to find out what I did to Adelle's medication. Did I take her off the risperidone before I added the olanzapine? Do I dare mention to Richard what just happened? After seeing their friendship in groups, I don't know how he would react.

Drained, I push open my door to find Richard's chair empty.

PART TWO

DECEMBER 27TH, 8:37 A.M.

Now that the unbearable loneliness of Christmas by myself is behind me and the vacationing staff is back in the madness, I have some time to face the task I've been avoiding. I'm staring at my evaluation, and I don't know that I want to bring myself to open it. I need to get the summary back to Rachel before she becomes suspicious; I figure I better shoot to have it done this week. There's no such thing as a good time to read this, but I can feel the headache that only comes with being hit in the ears, and I'm sure this can't be the best mental state in which to read about my fragile sanity.

I hide it in my desk drawer and finish my coffee to settle my nerves and counteract the remnant alcohol. I hang one of the more decorated In Session signs on my door. I can feel the evaluation staring up at me, like the monster under the bed. I'm frightened, and my breathing is panicked. I've never looked at a document like it was going to hurt me before. But I'm better off knowing than not knowing. That way I can focus on damage control.

I ease it out of the top drawer of my dented, rusty gray desk. Some of the papers are tucked neatly inside and some have their curled edges poking out, and this pisses me off because

I think it looks sloppy and unprofessional. I set the daunting sheets on my desk and watch them until I catch my breath.

My fingers and lips are trembling as I pull open the folder and begin to scan the results. The fear rising in my chest is tremendous, and my knees are involuntarily bouncing. *Please, slip through the cracks.* My eyes are periodically blurry as the tears form and fall, and it's hard to stay silent. The tiny squeals coming out of my mouth are beginning to border on hysterical, and the pain in the base of my skull is pounding. *Please, slip through the cracks.*

My hands are shuffling the papers before I can finish reading, and I'm moving too quickly between the pages to gain a full understanding, but I can't stop myself from trying to get to the bottom of this. I see words like *manipulative* and *unstable.* I see words like *promiscuous* and *impulsive.* I see sentences like "frantic efforts to avoid abandonment" and "possibly alcoholic." The summaries have comments like "extreme emotional disturbance," "consistent with assessment findings." *Please, no.*

I know this was all a mistake. I know this isn't really my evaluation and I know that no one thinks these things of *me.* My hands collapse at my sides and my head falls back against the desk chair as the intensity of this conclusion washes over me. I feel trapped under the weight of a diagnosis, and I know I can't escape.

I'm imagining the consequences. What will become of me? Am I a danger to myself? Am I a danger to others? Will I be fired, or demoted, or politely asked to find new, more suitable employment? If I'm the most valued clinician at Typhlos, can they afford to lose me?

I see vivid and colorful images of Rachel summoning security to watch me clean out my office and escort me out the door. I see trained professionals going through my handbag to ensure there are no stolen items I'm trying to take with me as I go. The scenes are playing out among the dirty ceiling tiles, and I have to furiously rub my eyes to make them stop.

If anyone finds out about this, I'm finished. Finished at Typhlos, reputation destroyed. Everything I've worked so hard to achieve—the name I've made for myself, the way people see me—it will all be gone.

As these menacing thoughts dance inside my head, I lean over my desk and try to grasp reality. I see myself from the ceiling of my office like I'm in a movie and the crew is using a wide-angle lens. This coffee doesn't taste like coffee anymore. I'm watching my arm lift the cup to my lips, but it doesn't feel like I'm the one drinking it. As I pitch forward to throw up in my garbage can, I see my hair fall over my face, but it doesn't feel like I'm the one vomiting.

I wander, dazed, into the hallway toward the staff bathroom so I can continue throwing up. The Out of Order sign is still on the stall, and I walk in again without a second thought. I wrap my shuddering arms around the bowl and violently heave into the gray water. The purge is bringing no relief, and the feeling of lunacy is creeping deeper into my bones. I see the lines that existed between my patients and myself mixing with the stagnant water and vomit in the toilet bowl, and as I try to flush it all away from me, the water surges back at my face.

I jump up onto my feet and scramble away from the upsurge of vile liquid. I nearly crash into Sal the custodian as I slip out of the bathroom, still wiping the tears from my eyes.

"Sal, hi. Um, we've got a little issue in the staff ladies' room here." I point at the door and hope he mistakes my tears for watering eyes.

"Hi, Doc. Just running to a call in a group room with an accident, if you know what I mean." He holds his nose with one hand and wafts his other hand dramatically in front of his face. "You know how to use a plunger?"

"Of course. Where can I find one?"

Sal tosses me a key from the giant ring clipped on his belt. "Grab one from the janitor's closet. Just make sure to lock it up again when you put the plunger back. Leave the key at the security desk." He's hurrying away from me, calling these instructions behind him. I watch him head down the hall and watch myself walk toward the janitor's closet. I feel like my eyes aren't the only ones on me.

DECEMBER 27TH, 11:22 A.M.

Richard has been sitting in my office for almost a half hour yet it feels like he just walked in. I see him reading his newspapers, but I suspect he's pretending. I'm terrified that he can somehow see through the walls of my skull and is looking inside my thoughts and he knows what happened. I can feel my psych eval in my desk blaring this diagnosis at me, and all I want to do is slam my drawer shut over and over again until it shuts the fuck up.

Everything I have known forever is no longer relevant. I'm looking out of new eyes, and I'm listening out of new ears, and I'm pounding new fists into the desktop, and I'm crying someone else's tears, and I'm wiping someone else's face, and I'm noticing Richard noticing me, and I'm hoping all of this is a dream.

"Did you get some bad news or something?" Richard sounds disgusted as he says this. "Are you sick?"

"Sick? No. No, Richard, I'm not sick."

"You look sick. You look like you need some help." He folds down the corner of his paper to look at me as he says this.

"Thank you. I'll look into that." I pull away from him and collapse into myself.

"You don't have to be scared of me," he says. "I'm not going to hurt you."

"I'm not scared of you. Do I seem to be scared of you? Do I seem to give a *shit* what you think of me? Do I?"

I'm holding my forehead. I'm not even trying anymore; I'm letting the truth hit me like a barrage of bullets and I don't know how to fake it. This is not about him, but he's in the path of a speeding train and is going to have to be the collateral damage.

"You give a shit about something," he says. He isn't fazed by my outburst. He has seen this somewhere before, clearly. He isn't worried that his therapist is unraveling in front of him. "It's okay, you know. You don't have to have it all together all the time."

"Of course I do," I somberly respond. "My job is to have it all together. My life is supposed to be together… I am supposed to have everything together."

I can't stop the tears from flowing. I can't stop the liquid snot from falling out of my left nostril and gliding down my chin. I can't stop my chest from heaving in erratic rhythms, or the veins in my forehead from coming to the surface like they're trying to break free. I can't stop my fists from clenching and unclenching like if I do it enough everything will go away.

I can't control myself, and I can't stop Richard from seeing this. The collar of my button-down shirt is wet and it's sticking to my neck and I can't stand this sensation. Richard is politely shutting the fuck up, and all I want is for him to leave so I can throw up in my garbage can.

I hear the doors to the group rooms closing outside my office, and as soon as all the voices are muffled, I open my door slightly and gesture for Richard to excuse himself. I'm hanging my head in case a stray passerby happens to peer inside and see my life collapsing.

Richard looks at me, looks at the open door. He reaches out a Timberland boot and gently kicks it shut.

"I still have time left." Mercifully, he looks back at his paper and doesn't acknowledge my state. "And I'm the only person you can lose it in front of."

I can't defend myself; I can't even remember how. I resign myself to managing this situation. I'm pretending that Richard isn't even in the office anymore, and he seems to be pretending that I'm not in the office disturbing his paper-reading peace.

As I ignore him completely, I try to wrap my brain around what's happening. I am not the superhero I thought I was. I am not the girl I've been pretending to be. With my head in my hands and my elbows on my desk, I sneak a sideways look at Richard's face. *You're the crazy one, not me.* The lines that divide us fizzle and fade, and I see sane all over his face and crazy all over mine.

I glance at my clock to see how much longer I have to sit with him, and I'm startled to attention by the phone ringing.

"Good morning, Sam James?"

Richard drops the corner of his paper to watch my call.

"Hey, it's me," Rachel sighs into the phone.

"Hi, Rachel. What's up?" I'm performing for both Rachel and Richard at this point, and I feel like there's a spotlight on my face.

"What's the progress with the OMH report? Have you gotten that summary together yet? I can't wait any longer. Brooks and Young gave me their report two weeks ago. If you haven't finished the review, I need to do it myself."

Holy shit. "Yeah, I'm nearly done with that. What's the next step? Just send it in to OMH? Or give it back to you or what?" I'm scrambling with the papers in my desk drawer, pulling together the notes from the evaluations. I haven't decided how I'm going to handle reviewing my own report yet. What am I supposed to do? Tell the truth? Or lie on an official government document like an asshole?

"Drop the whole pile and the summary up in my office when you finish. I got a call from the OMH representative this morning—all the summaries from the other New York City units and wards are filed. We can't delay this; it'll make us look incompetent and that could further affect our funding." She's exhausted, remorseful. Regretting letting me take this off her hands.

"Okay, no problem. I will get it to you right away."

She huffs a long exhale and hangs up the phone without saying goodbye. I hold the receiver to my face, pretending that Rachel is still talking so Richard gets the impression she didn't just hang up on me. I feign a cheerful goodbye and gently return the receiver to the cradle. No emotions show on his face, and he looks back at his paper for the last five minutes of our session.

DECEMBER 28TH, 3:20 P.M.

Rachel has called a last-minute meeting today, and she almost never calls for last-minute meetings. We're all supposed to convene in the conference room at 4:00 p.m.; we're supposed to end our groups and sessions early to have a staff discussion about something—about what, I have no idea. Is it the OMH evaluations? Am I about to be outed in front of the entire staff? Is this where I'm given my outright release and told that I'm not fit to treat patients? I haven't even given Rachel the summary results yet. Is it possible she was informed? Has she known my diagnosis all along?

The minutes are taking hours and I check my desktop clock every ten seconds, trying to will the time to pass so I can get the humiliation over with and drown my sorrows. My heart stops when there is a knock on my door. A panicked, rapid-fire knock. I open the door before I can think to make up an excuse to keep it closed. Julie is standing in front of me— she's shuffling into my office, she's collapsing into my patient chair, she's shaking.

"What? What happened?" I ask.

"We have a meeting. We're supposed to go to the conference room and Rachel is going to fire everyone." Completely disoriented, trying to sort out the gossip.

"What the hell are you talking about, Julie? Who's getting fired?" *Oh, my God, I was right, here it comes, everyone knows.*

"I heard from David, who was on the phone with his friend at OMH, and this has happened before. After they finish the evals, if people don't pass, we all get restructured and laid off." Julie is absolutely vibrating with fear, and she is behaving like she would have nowhere else to go should she lose this job, when in fact she has a trust fund bigger than most college endowments, and she will land safely on her Manolo Blahnik-ed feet. But I'm not supposed to know this information, so I play along.

"Your eval is fine. Nothing is going to happen to you. Calm down," I say as I turn away. She doesn't know I'm the one writing the summary.

"No, it's not fine. It's not fine at all. I know my performance at work could use improvement, and my service plans are postdated."

"Julie. You need to stop freaking out—nothing is going to happen. I promise you, you need to relax." I should leave well enough alone and let her wallow in her shitty patient files because if I can get it done, then a monkey can get it done.

"*You're* fine! You're going to be fine, no one can mess with you. Rachel *loves* you, so you have nothing to worry about." Julie flatters me. "But me..."

This is what I want everyone to believe. Somehow I have been able to keep up this appearance for my coworkers, but apparently not for OMH, and now I am found out, and everyone will know.

"I'm definitely not fine." I try to commiserate, but will never tell Julie the truth of the situation.

"Oh, whatever, you don't have to worry about getting

fired." She sighs and slides from the chair to the floor dramatically. The hem of her skirt is pulled up by the edge of the chair and I can see her underwear as she lays her head back against the radiator and rubs her temples. Her underwear is powder blue. For some reason, I'm surprised by this.

David hears the conversation through the wall and comes to knock on my door and join in the panic. He scoots Julie over and scrunches himself into the office chair, and as his pant legs lift, I can see he has mismatched socks. Julie is using the distress of the situation to be unusually flirtatious, a move with which I am familiar. She's leaning on David's leg, and he's gently touching her hair. Again with these two.

"You both have nothing to worry about," he says to appease us. "I'm sure this has nothing to do with anyone getting fired." Julie looks up at him with Disney-princess eyes, and I want to throw my stapler at her face. "My friend at OMH, he seems to believe that there's some issue with funding, so maybe Rachel is going to talk to us about that. *Maybe* layoffs are coming, but I imagine the ancillary staff will be the first to go. Don't put the cart before the horse here."

At some point while I'm on autopilot in this conversation, I begin to realize that I'm insanely jealous that David and Julie are using each other for comfort in this moment. I have no recourse, no one's leg to lay my head on and no one to touch my hair. Why are they using each other and not using me? David is *my* best friend, and Julie *wants* to be my best friend, so why the hell are they flirting with each other and not with *me*? Should I feel happy that they both chose to come to *my* office to feel better? Is it the fact that I'm in here that helps soothe them? Why isn't anyone touching *my hair*?

David checks his watch and taps the glass face. "Let's get going, ladies. The meeting is in two minutes." He helps Julie up off the floor, and I hold the door open for them. I momentarily wish I could stick out my foot and trip Julie so that her mouth smashes into the ground and her orthodontic work gets destroyed, but instead I calmly close my door and walk down the hall.

Now we're in the meeting, and it's clear that there have been several cliques who've been speculating in their offices about what's going to happen here. Rachel is huddled over a stack of papers at the head of the conference table, and each staff member is sitting unusually close to the person next to them.

I'm sandwiched between David and Shirley, and Julie is to David's left. I'm still reeling, ever so slightly, that I wasn't being touched and my hair wasn't being pet in my office. The stress of the impending conversation helps me to move away from the irritation of being left out, and I try to read Rachel. She isn't looking at any of us, which means that we either collectively did something terrible and she's debating the punishment, or she's about to clobber us with news that even *she* doesn't want to hear.

I'm bracing myself for the inevitable outing. The force of the panic is rising in my chest, and I have to keep swallowing to keep it down. I'm waiting for Rachel to open her mouth and look at me. I'm waiting for her to pull me aside after the meeting and explain that her hands are tied. I'm waiting for her to use the *DSM* diagnostic criteria to clear up any questions the other staff members may have as to why I was deemed unfit to care for a psychiatric population.

Finally, after what seems like hours of deafening silence, Rachel begins to address the group. I white-knuckle the arms of my chair.

"Thank you all for coming here today. I know it's last minute and I know how hard you've all been working, and I do appreciate it. I'm sorry to tell you this, but I brought you here to share some sad news." I can hear Julie draw in a sharp breath and I watch her clutch David's arm, and this immediately makes my head pound and my neck sweat.

"All of you have been here for long enough to know that sometimes we have a patient we can't help. All of you have witnessed the sad side of our business, and today is another example of this. I'm so sorry, folks. We've lost Eddie."

A collective gasp fills the room. The air gets warm suddenly, and we all look around at mouths agape, seeking answers from one another. A wet wave of shock hits me like a ton of bricks, and I fall back into my chair. I want to feel relief that this meeting isn't about me, but I can't.

No one knows what to say or how to proceed. Julie's hand holds David's, and he turns to me. His face is stoic, but his eyes are brimming. He takes his hand back from Julie and puts both his hands on my knee. He drops his gaze and over his shoulder, I can see Julie turn away and steeple her fingers over her face. David and I have a connection to Eddie that no one else has, or knows about, and although we took him for granted then, we can't take him for granted anymore. I think to when he pushed his laceless sneaker into my office to try to talk to me. When I promised I would see him in an hour.

He had been relying on us, and we let him down, but instead of ruining ourselves with thoughts that we should have saved his day, we find comfort in each other, and we whisper that there was nothing we could have done.

"He has passed from an apparent suicide." Rachel continues, "Sal the custodian discovered his body last night in a janitorial closet downstairs. There was no note on him or in his room, but we believe, based on his prior attempts, that this was likely a suicide."

Gary can no longer hold it in and bursts into projectile tears. His neighbors console him with back rubbing and cooing and promises that he couldn't have done anything to stop it. I put my clammy left hand on David's hands and he looks up at me like we're a hundred years old and we have all the answers.

Rachel keeps talking and tells us that we have therapists available to us should we need to explore our feelings about this. We all behave as if we hadn't even heard her. Rachel says she will leave us to discuss this without her. Julie immediately begins to panic. Her breathing becomes hysterical, and she's shaking, so Shirley ushers her to the ladies' room to calm down. Everything around us is fast and loud and anxious, but the bubble that David and I hide in is slow and calm and quiet.

DECEMBER 29TH, 12:47 P.M.

It's been almost twenty-four hours and the news of Eddie's death hasn't stopped ringing in my ears. I feel anesthetized and disoriented, and I'm having trouble concentrating on anything productive. The incident report has been filed, and I'm wondering if it'll help to go read it. If I put facts to this tragedy, will it be easier to take? Will I be absolved?

I drag myself out of my chair and slip down the hallway to the records room. There's a nurse leaning over the Xerox machine making copies of a flyer advertising a going-away party complete with cheese *and* cheesecake in the staff lounge on Friday. I'll be sure to miss that one. She gives me a sweet smile as the intermittent copy light illuminates her white teeth.

I walk to the patient files and punch my code into the keypad. Eddie's case file is fat and disorganized, and the incident report is conspicuous from the outside, as it's the only piece of paper sticking out without frayed or bent edges. I photocopy the report without looking at it, then tuck the original back into the folder.

The two-page report feels heavy in my hand, and I sit with a thud on the carpet in my office to read it. His name is written Edward "Eddie" William Bailey. The formality that comes with death is making this harder to read. His birthday and the date he died are written next to each other, and I didn't realize he was only forty-one. My own fortieth birthday is only a few years away, and I can't believe a life could get so ruined and so lost while still so young.

I feel the trembling begin at my shoulders, travel down my arms and over my jaw to my chin. The tears are already welling up in my eyes, and I hear distant echoes of Eddie's telltale deflating voice. I will never hear it again. I will never push his laceless sneakers out my door again. I will never tell him I don't have time for him again. Never is too long, and I can't handle it. My chest heaves; I blink away the tears and keep reading.

The incident report isn't an autopsy; a medical examiner doesn't sign off on it. It's just an additional document that gets filed when something big happens. Something big, like a fight, or a medical emergency, or a threat. Or suicide. My fingers fumble with the pages, and my tears are crimping the margins. The cause of death states suicide. And in the description, I read on to see what Rachel didn't announce to us in the meeting. Eddie hanged himself. He pried open the metal piece of a janitorial mop, pulled out those long gray dreadlocks and tied them together to make a rope. He tied one end to a hook inside the janitor's closet and the other around his neck.

The closet is the width of a mop bucket, and he was found with his feet in the bucket and his hands in his pockets. His knees were bent against the edge of the bucket, and there were purple ligature marks around his throat. He died of asphyxiation. There was no snapping of his neck; it wasn't an instant end. He slowly watched the inside of the closet go dark, and he didn't even struggle against the creeping shroud of death. All the items in the closet other than the dismantled mop were reported undisturbed. He hadn't touched a thing. He probably didn't want anyone to have to clean up after him. The lock on the door wasn't tampered with, it wasn't broken; someone must have just left it unlocked. Someone is going to pay for that.

My hands fall to my sides, and the incident report crumples under my sweaty palm. Eddie had come to me for help, and I turned him down. I said no. I said no to a man who just wanted me to listen to his stories. Whether they were true or not shouldn't have mattered. He just needed me to listen, and I turned him away. I said no… I said no.

I'm a fraud. I'm not the golden girl. I'm not the hero of the institution, saving the days of all the lost souls. I'm a fucking con artist who plays the part only too well, and I let one slip through the cracks, and he died alone in a murky mop bucket with his defeated hands in his pockets inside of a fucking janitor's closet because some asshole left the door open.

A prickle forms at the base of my scalp and I feel a wave of nausea building. Oh, my God, is it possible that I forgot to lock the door when I borrowed the plunger? *Fucking Christ, what have I done?* I slump down to the carpet, hearing myself moaning, begging for forgiveness. I'm at once embarrassed at my sniveling self and unable to get it together.

I pull off my left shoe and throw it at the door. It slams into the knob with a satisfying thunk, so I take off the other one and throw that, too. I pull my handbag off my chair and as it falls to the ground next to me, I pick through the contents for more things to throw. I hurl my Altoids and the tin explodes against the hinge of the door and tiny white orbs fly all over the office. *A fraud! I'm a fucking fraud!* Throwing the pack of Kleenex doesn't make me feel better at all, and the headphones are impossible to chuck. My book! I get up and grab the stupid fucking novel I still haven't finished and I tear the cover in my hurry to heave it at the wall. I stop myself from throwing it and tear at the pages. Just one at a time at first and then fistfuls, angry fistfuls of bullshit! *Eddie! I'm sorry! I should have been there for you. I should have been there for you.*

With thin, cheap paperback pages still clinging to my palms, I collapse back down onto the ground and I hold my head in my hands, paper sticking in my hair. My chest heaves out my last panicked breaths; I spit a clot of phlegm with a throaty cough into the garbage can and stabilize myself. I lay my head down to rest. The impossible apologies and the vastness of never seep into the cavernous places in my brain where I store things I can't handle. I concentrate on breathing, and a fuzzy calm begins to cloud my mind.

I see a coil of unfurled carpet fiber a few inches from my face, and all my thought and concentration is immediately transferred to it. The way it's catching the light is emphasizing the burgundy-and-eggplant polyester threads that make up this nothing- and everything-colored carpet. I push the coil down with my thumb and it springs back like a Slinky. I keep pushing it down and down and down again, and it keeps coming back up. It will not be defeated. This tiny corkscrew will not let me kill it. I flip over to my knees and lean as close to the helix as I can. I flick it with my fingernail, and it comes back like a weighted inflatable clown. I twirl it between my fingers, and my breathing steadies. I wipe the tears from my face and blow my nose. I can't take my eyes off the carpet fiber. I'm petting it, and protecting it, and before I can understand what's happening, I'm laughing. I'm laughing at the red-and-purple coil, and I've named it Eddie.

A soft knocking comes from my door, and I look up to see if I hallucinated. The knocking continues—a slow, constant, Eddie knock.

"Eddie?" My butt pops up off my ankles, and I reach for the door to let Eddie's ghost in and show him the perfect carpet ringlet I named for him. In a concentrated whoosh, David moves stealthily into my office and looks down at me, wide-eyed and concerned.

"Sam? Are you okay? I can hear you from my office. What's going on?" When I see it's only David, I crouch back down to the floor and refocus on carpet Eddie. I stroke the swirl.

David gets down on the floor with me and looks at what I'm doing. He observes the spectacle in my office. Torn novel pages and smashed contents of my handbag strewn all over the place. Shoes off, scarf in a tangle around the wheels of my desk chair. He must think I've gone crazy. I watch him scrutinizing the scene. I don't care. I don't *care* what he thinks.

Each time I touch carpet Eddie, David looks at me with apprehension and uneasiness. He glances at the incident report on the floor behind me and sees the used tissues in a pile by my feet. He takes my hands and pulls me upright.

"Sam, what's happening?"

"Be careful, don't step on Eddie."

"Sam, Eddie is dead."

"Not *this* one." I reach into my garbage can and find a small plastic cup from the water cooler, and I overturn it and place it over the coil so no one steps on him by accident.

David sits me down in my desk chair and puts his hand against my clammy forehead. "Sam, you're burning up. Did you take anything?"

"I haven't taken anything, David. I'm fine." I brush his hand away. I don't need him taking care of me.

"No booze today? I heard you crying earlier. Did you drink anything?"

"No. And I can't seem to find any of the alcohol I hid in here." I pull open my bottom file drawer and check under a shoe box full of crayons.

"Do you have any more groups today?"

"Yes, I have groups to run today. And I have individual sessions." *I'm a professional, David. Stop talking to me like a child.*

"Can I please see your schedule?"

"You know where it is. Stop bothering me; I'm fine." He's holding my face and not letting me look down at carpet Eddie.

"What happened in your office? Looks like a hurricane came through here."

"I want to stay here with Eddie, make sure he's okay."

"Who is Eddie, Sam?" I point to the overturned plastic cup, protecting carpet Eddie. David draws in a deep breath. "I'm going to get the rest of your schedule covered today, okay? I think you need a break."

"Fine. I don't care anymore. Do whatever you want."

David pulls a sheet of paper from my printer and a marker from the mug on my desk. He writes "Please Do Not Disturb" in big block letters and tapes it to the outside of my door. He gathers up the torn pages from my book and throws them away. He picks up the incident report, smooths it out and lays it flat on my desk, weighing it down with a psychopathology textbook. He arranges my shoes neatly to the left of the door and untangles my scarf from under my chair.

David steps outside the door, leaving it slightly ajar, and pops back in seconds later, holding a banana, a half-eaten bagel and a bottle of water.

"See if you can eat these, okay? You're very shaky right now. And drink this water. Take your time. I will get everything else covered for you today, and I'll tell Rachel something. I need you to just lie low and get yourself together, okay? You seem to be taking this news about Eddie really hard." The alarm in David's eyes is unfamiliar to me. I resign myself to the idea that I get to stay safe and protected in my office for the rest of my shift.

"Okay, I'll stay here. You can run my groups." It's starting to feel like I really *don't* care anymore.

"I have groups, too, so I'll get someone else to cover everything for you. But you don't need to worry or think about *anything*. I'll handle it. Just please, take care of yourself." David ensures the sign is securely stuck to the door, and he turns off my overhead light, leaving on my desk lamp. "Text me if you need anything, okay? I'll check on you later."

David leaves my office, and my eyes are heavy from crying. The last two strings holding my life together, my work life and my sanity, are finally unraveling. I have nothing left to hold me together. I take down my coat and lay it over my back. I flop the hood up over my face and check on carpet Eddie as I drift into an uneasy sleep.

DECEMBER 29TH, 5:11 P.M.

I wake up with a start and jolt myself into consciousness. What happened? Was it a dream? Is Eddie alive? I look around my office and see the remnants of the disarray earlier. It must be true.

What time is it? I wipe a sticky line of drool off my chin and check the clock on my phone: 5:11 p.m. I see several text messages from David. He sent them periodically throughout the day, but I didn't have my phone set to ring. He's been updating me. Checking in on me. Making sure I'm okay and letting me know that he spoke to Rachel, and she knows I need some time. Why didn't they just let me go home? He asks me if I ate the bagel. I look at the tinfoil package on my desk. Among the messages from David, I find another text from Lucas. I've avoided him since I caught him doing coke a week ago. He went home to spend Christmas with his family and didn't bother to invite me, citing our fight as his reason. Convenient. Now he's trying to make up for it by asking me to join him at a New Year's Eve party. As I finish reading these messages, I hear the click of high heels passing my office and a knock on David's door. Julie calls out her name, and I hear David invite her in. I immediately jump to my feet, nearly tripping over my shoes, and smash my ear against the wall, straining to hear the details of their conversation.

David starts. "I told Rachel that she was distraught over Eddie's suicide. She was very understanding."

"Is that really what's wrong?" I can almost hear Julie reaching her hands over to David's knees, eyes pleading with him, feigning concern for my situation. *Don't buy her bullshit, David. Don't fucking tell her anything.*

"Yeah, she's just having a hard time. Even though technically Eddie was Gary's patient, he was really attached to Sam. He went to her office all the time to talk to her. She had a soft spot for him."

I can't hear what Julie is saying now. I'm not sure if anyone is talking. What are they *doing* in there?

"I had to get some of her case files today, because I covered her individual sessions, too." *What?!* I'm outraged! *Julie* met with my patients today? She read my reports, she read my notes, my files? Fucking *Julie*?!

I rip myself away from the wall and tear at my scalp. I bury my face in the hood of my coat and scream a barely audible scream into the furry lining. I'm taking concentrated, gruff breaths, and I need to calm down so I can hear more.

"She's brilliant, you know. Her reports are absolutely flawless, and the clinical intuition is just…awe-inspiring." *Oh, why don't you just blow him, you whore!*

"She's extremely talented, I know; excellent clinician." *Et tu, Daveed?*

"There are a couple of questions I had, though—some of the medication stuff with a couple of patients. Seems a little off," Julie continues.

Wait a minute, what day is it? Oh, my God, what day is it? Did I have a session with Richard today? Please, Jesus Christ, tell me Julie didn't cover a session with Richard. I'm thrashing through my date book, trying to keep it quiet while riffling for the date, because I can't let Julie and David know I'm in here and I can hear them. Thursday. Thank *God*. She must have met with my patients, run a couple of groups.

My head is beginning to throb again. I'm going to have to make up for whatever idiotic bullshit she tried to feed the patients in my groups today. These groups were too advanced for her. She doesn't have the experience or the intuition to run these. I have no idea why David didn't get someone who isn't a moron.

Now what the fuck are they talking about? I cram my ear against the wall again. David is saying something, and I can hear movement and papers shuffling.

"Yeah, I'll just straighten out my office, and I'll meet you by the elevator. You want to go for a drink, or—" I feel my entire body go rigid.

"Yeah, a drink is great. I just want to talk about the paperwork. Reading Sam's notes—I mean, I just feel like maybe I'm not doing such a good job. She's got different methods, you know? And I don't understand her patient medication management."

"I'm sure you're doing a great job," David assures her.

"Thanks, I'd love your advice, I guess. Maybe, if you're hungry, maybe we could grab a bite, too?"

It starts in my ears—a consuming rage—and it travels slowly around the base of my skull, then forward toward my eyes. It feels hot and prickly, and I imagine that my whole head is turning crimson like a cartoon thermometer that eventually explodes. All my muscles tense up, and my left eye twitches. I've tried to stop these emotional attacks from coming before, and I just end up twisting an ankle or overextending a ligament. This time, I know to just let it come over me, let the fury and humiliation tackle me to the ground, where I can lie and stare at carpet Eddie for solace and comfort.

I never thought that David would betray me, but it goes to show that you can't trust anyone. Not even your best friend. Not even your best friend who acts like you're crazy and then locks you in your office all day long and gives all your precious patients and advanced groups to his unintelligent, pathetic slut girlfriend. What a fucking shame.

As my muscles and joints turn stiff, and the corners of my mouth curl into a furious scowl, I feel the vibration of my phone, which I didn't realize I'd been clutching. I hold the message up to my eyes and see it's from David.

Feel better, Sam. I'm heading home now. Call me if you need me. *If I need you? I needed you today, and you left me. You abandoned me for her, you duplicitous asshole.*

DECEMBER 31ST, 11:47 P.M.

It's New Year's Eve, the most overrated and disappointing night of the year. Especially in New York. People flock here from all over the globe to stand in the freezing cold, in the worst neighborhood on the planet, to listen to shitty pop stars and D-list celebrities through bad sound systems, and ring in the New Year by watching a Waterford crystal bomb fall. Hooray.

I'm in someone's penthouse on Seventh Avenue in the Fashion District, sufficiently south of Times Square that I can't smell the vomit and urine from their balcony, but close enough that I can hear the sounds and see the lights. I'm wearing a velvet dress, and I hate it, but Lucas bought it for me and told me how much it cost, so I feel like I have to wear it. I've gotten myself on the opposite smoking schedule from Lucas so that I can go outside without him and pretend we didn't come together. I've seen most of these faces before, I think, but I can't remember any of their names. These are the people Lucas tries to impress. He couldn't be happier that I'm avoiding him, because it makes it easier for him to fabricate whatever he needs to fabricate to ingratiate himself with these filthy socialites.

I'm champagne drunk already, which is different from other booze drunks because it feels more like drugs than alcohol. I'm woozy and disoriented. I feel like my head is a balloon and my neck is becoming the string attaching the balloon to my body. The cold air from the balcony and the smoke in my lungs helps me to bring my head back down to earth, but I don't want it to reattach enough to be able to think about what's happening to me.

I've been officially labeled by OMH now, and it's only a matter of time before the consequences descend upon me like a death shroud.

I look up at the bitter, artificial city; Eddie is gone. The lights of Times Square are lighting up the clouds and the mist, and it's reminding me of the dirty colors of Eddie's greasy trucker hats.

My left knee buckles, and I hold the railing for support. A caterer wanders onto the balcony and replaces my empty champagne glass with a full one, and informs me it's nearly midnight. He and I are the only ones on the balcony, and I hear the cries of the crowds below us, counting down. I turn to look inside, and the glow off the lamps and the Christmas tree lights are blending into one big, shiny blur, and I catch Lucas screaming the countdown with a blonde in one arm and a brunette in the other. I watch the women watching him, and just as the confetti begins to explode up from beneath me, Lucas draws the brunette in for a long, simmering kiss. He catches my eyes as he separates his lips from hers and sends me a smiling shrug. I raise my glass in Lucas's direction and pull the cater waiter's face to mine. I'm kissing a stranger, and my mind flashes to thoughts of David kissing Julie at this very moment somewhere. I pull away from him, and his startled expression makes my stomach sink.

I'm immediately returned to the grips of fear and paranoia.

I chug the champagne in my glass and pluck another full one off the waiter's tray. He retrieves a lighter from his pocket and lights my next cigarette for me before walking back inside, leaving me alone to watch the confetti snow fall around me and hear the distant sounds of singing. My thoughts wander to Lucas. I know he should be forgotten and never brought to mind. Never one to make New Year's resolutions, tonight, I decide that Lucas has to fade out of my life. I have to let him go for real this time. I lean over the balcony to throw up, and I see my balloon head float up above me, drifting into the shiny, synthetic-colored sky.

JANUARY 3RD, 11:40 A.M.

Richard and I haven't said a word to each other since the day he witnessed my collapse. We both have secrets thick in the air between us, and neither of us can face them. When I'm not at Typhlos, I'm able to pretend I didn't get shot in the chest by a speeding psych-evaluation bullet and I'm not slowly bleeding to death. But when I get off the subway in the morning and trudge to the institution, my heart sneaks up into my throat.

Is that why Eddie killed himself? Is that why Adelle nearly died? Because I'm an unfit therapist? Because my negligence made it possible? I haven't been fired; I haven't been demoted; I haven't even been approached. Is it possible I've managed to slip through the cracks?

Rachel already asked me once for the completed report and I haven't given it to her. It's complete now. Except for my own eval. Can I pretend that I left my report for someone else to do? Gave it to David? It's not even ethical for me to write my own summary but ethical guidelines seem to have gone the way of the dodo at Typhlos these days. Maybe I'll be able to get away with this.

Either way, I'm sure the evaluation results must have been a mistake; there's no way I could have been so careless as to drop my guard and let them see who I really am. As I'm formulating a scenario in my head as to how exactly this mistake happened, and what I'm going to do about it, Richard interrupts my musings.

"Okay, we have only fifteen minutes left. I'm ready to work on the file."

"The *what*?" I snap.

"The file. The papers that you're always trying to get me to finish? You know?" He seems genuine. He seems to be trying to stick to the plan regardless of the fact that he hasn't attempted to even begin his file since he got here.

"Oh, my God. You want to fill out *forms*? Right now?"

"This is what you said we have to do, so yeah."

"Oh, my God. Oh, my *God*, this isn't happening." I clench my jaw tightly. "Fine. You know what?" I say, smiling through my teeth. "Fine. We'll do the fucking documentation." I shuffle his file out of the filing cabinet and start tearing through the papers.

"Whatever happened to you probably isn't my fault. I don't think you need to take it out on me."

"You're absolutely right, Richard. Maybe right now isn't a good time for us to meet. Maybe you need to go to a group." I slap his unfinished file back into the drawer.

"That wasn't the deal. I can do the paperwork if you can ask me the questions. And then write the shit down."

"Watch your mouth."

"I think that ship has sailed, Sam."

"Has it?" I snatch his file back up. I'm so defiant, I'm so over it, I'm so ready to fall that I don't care how I hit the ground. "Okay, Richard. Why are you here? What's your diagnosis? What are your goals for treatment at Typhlos? Why were you in prison?"

"I killed my mother."

JANUARY 3RD, 2:00 P.M.

I hear a knock on my door and I'm not supposed to have any sessions right now. My head is detached from the rest of my body, only able to focus on the information Richard threw at me this morning. I open my door and lean back in my chair to see who's knocking. In walks a lanky young man with cornrows.

"Hey, Doc," he says and he plunks himself down in my chair.

"Hi. Can I help you?" Confused.

"I have my schedule." He reaches into his back pocket and pulls out a folded piece of paper with heavily frayed edges. "It says I have my meeting with my doctor now, so here I am."

"Does it say who your doctor is—" I crane my neck and check for a name on his schedule "—Shawn?" He looks at his sheet and scans for the answer.

"Uh, no. But today is Tuesday, right?"

"Yes, today is Tuesday. May I see your paper?" Shawn hands me his schedule with a worried look.

"I take this medicine, and it makes it hard to remember. So, I got this schedule with me. And I bring it with me wherever I go. That way, I don't forget the places I'm supposed to be. I go to my meetings, and my groups, and it says that my bed is in room 127. So that's where I go when I'm supposed to sleep."

I'm looking over this piece of paper, and nowhere does it say who Shawn works with. I know I've seen him before, but I'm not sure where or when.

"Shawn, have you and I ever had a meeting before?"

"Yeah, Tuesdays." He folds his paper back into his pocket.

"And on Tuesdays at 2:00 p.m., you come to my office?" Why am I not remembering this?

"Yeah, and we do the questions and answers here."

"Okay. Have you ever had a meeting with any of the other doctors here?"

"I don't know."

"Shawn, what's your last name?"

"Reynolds."

"Okay, I'm going to check something for a second, alright?"

"Yeah." Shawn leans back and wipes the sweat from his forehead. I pick up the receiver on my phone and dial #44, which connects to all the office intercoms.

"Staff, if you're in your office and not in session, please pick up. If you're in session, please mute the phone." I stay on for a moment, hear a few clicks and repeat the message. When I'm confident the staff in session have muted their phones, I talk to whoever is on the line. "Hi, everyone, it's Sam. Quick question, who belongs to Shawn Reynolds?"

"Umm, he *was* mine," Gary says. "Do you want me to come to your office?"

"Yes, thank you." I hear various clinicians click off the call, and Gary tells me he will be right over to talk to me.

"So," Shawn begins. "What questions should we talk about today?"

"Well, Shawn, unfortunately, I'm not your counselor. You work with Gary. Do you know who that is?" I feel bad for the kid; he's obviously confused, and I'm beginning to suspect that Gary fucked up his medication.

"Gary? Gary…" He looks at the ceiling as if to try to remember.

"What's the name of the medicine you take, Shawn?"

"It's the orange one."

"Do you take more than one?"

"Yeah." He pulls out his schedule again, and there's a handwritten note in the corner that reads "Orange in the morning, pink at night." He hands it to me again. "And the pink one."

"Okay. Why don't we wait for Gary?"

"Okay." His eyes glaze over and he slumps into the chair. Gary knocks on my door. I stand up to open it, and Gary walks in.

"Hi, Shawn," he says, and Shawn's eyes refocus.

"Hi, Doc," Shawn says. I offer my seat to Gary, who sits down and leans forward with his elbows on his knees.

"Will you do me a favor, Shawn? Can you wait in the computer room while I talk to Sam for a minute? It's right across the hall. I'll meet you there in just a minute."

"Yeah, that's okay. I'll wait in the computer room. Sorry for the mistake." Shawn lumbers out of my office, and I sit down in the warm of his chair.

"What's he taking?" I ask.

"It's the chlorpromazine."

"Oh, yeah. He said the orange ones. What's his diagnosis?"

"Sam…" Gary looks at me quizzically. "Paranoid schizophrenia and intermittent explosive. He's on diphenhydramine, too."

"If the chlorpromazine is affecting his memory this substantially, then you should take him off the diphenhydramine."

"Shouldn't *you* take him off the diphenhydramine?"

"You can't do it?"

"Sam, Shawn is *your* patient. The meds written on his schedule are written in *your* handwriting. He used to work with me, but then Rachel changed around my responsibilities. So she gave Shawn to you. Remember?"

"What? He's mine? That was my handwriting? I've never forgotten a patient; how could this happen?" I'm bewildered, a deer in the headlights.

"I don't know, Sam. Have you been feeling alright?"

Gary's the one who forgets patients; he's the one who can't do his job properly. Not me. This isn't like me. "Yes, I—I…" I'm stammering. I can't wrap my head around this. *I* fucked up Shawn's medication? I'm the one who had him under the fog of a heavy dose of diphenhydramine on top of chlorpromazine? Impossible! I would never let that happen.

As Gary stands up to leave, my phone rings.

"Hello? Sam James."

"Hi, Sam. It's Rachel. Did you get the Shawn issue worked out?"

"Uh, yeah. So sorry, I got momentarily confused and completely forgot that he was on my caseload now. All taken care of, though. No worries." I chuckle nervously.

"Is this another med-management thing?" Her voice is frustrated and exhausted.

Another one? "Nope!" I feign confidence and cheeriness and the self I used to be at Typhlos. "Just an honest mistake."

"Call me back if you can't handle this. I'm relying on you, Sam. I need to know that you're capable."

"Of course I am. You know me."

"Right," she says, sounding dubious. "I hope so."

JANUARY 4TH, 10:56 P.M.

AJ and I are sitting at some anonymous bar down in the East Village so we can get away with kissing in public without a second look. There's sawdust on the floor, and the barstools are uncomfortable. The TVs are too high above the bar—I have to strain my neck to see them to keep from looking at AJ. We shouldn't be meeting in public and pretending we have anything in common or anything to talk about. It's awkward, and the only way to manage is to get drunk, lose any inhibitions that may exist between us and let the sexual charge carry us through the evening. AJ doesn't smoke, so when the air gets uncomfortable, or there's an uneasy silence, I put on my coat and walk out the door for a cigarette.

My phone vibrates in my back pocket as I take the last drag off my Marlboro. It's Lucas. I'm sticking to my New Year's resolution and distancing myself. He's asking me about Maverick's medicine. Could be a ploy to look aloof but still require a response; he knows how much I love that dog. I resist the temptation, flick my cigarette and walk back into the bar.

"I ordered you another drink," AJ says. "Figured you would want one." He pulls me between his knees and kisses my mouth. He tugs at my scarf as I take off my coat and hang it back on my barstool. My scarf tangles in my hair, but AJ keeps pulling it. "What's that?" he asks as his clumsy scarf-tugging exposes bruises on my temple.

"Oh." I gather my scarf out of my hair and tuck it under my coat. "Just a little accident." Embarrassed, I curtain the bruises with my hair and immediately become aware of every movement my body is making.

"What kind of accident?" He brushes the hair away, and my self-consciousness explodes.

"Um, a taxi accident." He continues to gently stroke the bruises and it doesn't hurt, but I see the shimmer of the makeup on his fingers as he pulls them away, and my stomach twitches and wrenches, and I feel the panicked sweat beads forming on my lower back. "I was in a cab the other night, coming home from this thing I had to go to on the Upper East Side." I'm adding too many details because I'm lying and I haven't prepared. I grab the Jack and Coke from the bar and quench my parched throat before continuing. "I didn't put my seat belt on—I guess I *never* put my seat belt on—and we were flying down Park Avenue. I was looking at all the Christmas trees lit up on the median—so I was facing the driver's side window—and he slammed on the brakes to avoid some asshole who was turning west on Seventy-Fifth, and my face crashed into the plastic partition." I'm out of breath. I can't tell if he's buying my story because he's just looking up at me with puppy-dog eyes, and continuing to stroke my face and massage my neck.

"Did you go to the hospital? You could have whiplash or something." He seems both unfazed and unconcerned, but his words are kind, and my thunderous, discomforted heartbeat is pounding in both my ears.

"We were right next to Lenox Hill Hospital, so I told the driver I was going to go there and get checked out. I made a big deal of writing down his medallion number and license and name and everything so he didn't make me pay for the ride. But I just walked to the 6 train and went home. It probably looks worse than it feels." The lie forms so easily, it's almost as if I don't have to think about it, and the pieces of the story—the geography, the landmarks—they all seamlessly fit together. I can't have AJ knowing that Lucas was the accident who made those bruises on my face. AJ's not here to save me from Lucas, he's here to *distract* me, and I won't allow those lines to get blurred, too.

I order shots and try to erase my memory. Spending time with AJ is supposed to be my reprieve from real life—from my work failures and terrible romantic decisions. This is supposed to be the time I can pretend that I don't have a mental illness, that I don't forget who my patients are. When I'm with AJ, the only thing I'm doing wrong is cheating on my boyfriend, and I can live with that.

I take another shot and hope it brings me to a place where I can no longer remember the fact that I've been trying to draw the truth out of a patient who killed his mother. I want to slide into an ignorant bliss where I can't quite feel suspicious that everyone knows my secrets. I need to let the alcohol dull my senses enough that I no longer distrust everything I thought I knew.

JANUARY 5TH, 1:17 P.M.

I'm in the patient bathroom, scrutinizing my reflection and pulling at the skin of my cheeks. I look dead. I have swollen blue veins bulging under my eyes and crispy remnants of yesterday's mascara on my lashes. My skin is dry and greasy at the same time, and the color can only be described as sickly. Bruises on my temples that used to be blue are a yellowish green that I haven't bothered to cover with the tattoo makeup because it takes too much effort. My hair should have been washed days ago. I take the lip balm from my pocket and smear some of it on my cheeks, hoping the pink tint and shine will bring some impression of life back to me.

As I walk out of the ladies' room, head down, wiping my hands on the backs of my pants, I nearly crash into the mountainous Rachel. "Sam! I was just knocking on your office door. I'm glad I ran into you."

"Hi, Rachel, what's up?" I'm immediately self-conscious about the lip balm on my face, and I wipe at my cheeks to remove it before Rachel notices.

"I came by to pick up the summary for OMH. I need it today. I know you had a really hard time with Eddie's death, and I wanted to give you a bit of leeway, but at this point I can't delay any further." She seems disappointed and forgiving at the same time.

"I understand. I'm sorry for the delay. Eddie's suicide was a real shock to me, and I struggled to focus last week. I think I'm back to my old self again, so no need to worry." I wonder if she can hear my heart beating as loudly as I can.

"Good, glad to hear that. I figured I would take the evaluation files as well, since I've got a meeting down in admin later today, and I could file everything in the staff folders." Hopeful, optimistically anticipating that I won't let her down.

"Oh, no, no, no. I told you I would get that done for you. You don't need to concern yourself with filing the original evals; I'll take care of that!" I buoyantly lie to her face as the rush of panic takes hold of my sweat glands. "I'll get the summary to you this afternoon, and the files put away by the end of the day. Okay?"

"I need them *today*, Sam. No later. OMH is breathing down my neck." Rachel eyes me suspiciously, still encouraged but not convinced. She holds out her hand to shake with a tenuous smile on her face. My right palm is sticky with lip balm, but I'm afraid if I wipe it off on my pants I'll look like I'm hiding nervous sweats, so I grasp her hand and feel the gummy ooze of clammy balm transfer to her fingers. I flash an enormous toothy grin and trot quickly in the direction of my office, calling "See you this afternoon" behind me as I go.

I turn the corner and leave Rachel on the other side just in time to catch David and Julie standing too close together in front of his office. His door is open, and her hand is on his chest. Her back is to me, so I can't see her face, but David's is all smiles. He steps backward into his office without seeing me and waves his long fingers at her as she turns to walk away. I see her smile and sigh and clutch her files to her chest like the fucking head cheerleader after the quarterback asks her to prom.

She blinks herself back to reality as she sees me thundering down the hall, and I startle her to attention. She stumbles with words and slows her pace, as if somewhere inside her puny little brain she understands that she's fucking with the wrong person and owes me an apology. I'm picking up speed as she nears my office door, her mouth open, thinking of something to say, and I barrel right into her shoulder, never taking my eyes off hers. I continue to look her dead in the face as she staggers backward out of my way, and I shove my key into the keyhole. She stammers and lurches, attempts a statement, and I pat her hard on the shoulder as I open the door to my office. With a menacing grin, I slowly close the door and watch as she stumbles away from me with a smear of pink lip balm on her pristine white sweater.

JANUARY 5TH, 5:34 P.M.

I buzzed Rachel's office twice, and she didn't pick up either time. She must finally be down in the administrative meeting. Now's my opening to drop the evaluation summary in her office without having to face her.

I stack the evaluation folders in the crook of my left arm and lay the summary on top. The piece of paper looks as innocuous as an office memo, and I keep telling myself that's all it is. With my sweatshirt concealing the pile of folders, I head down the hallway toward the entrance to the stairwell and gently close the heavy door behind me so it doesn't slam and alert anyone to my presence. I can feel my heart beating in my ears, and it's echoing down the stairs. I creak open the door and step gently into the hallway. I pass the body of a sleeping patient curled in the fetal position on the floor. Normally, I would wake him, but today I tiptoe by and hope I don't rouse him. Rachel's door is only five more yards away.

I shimmy the summary out from under my sweatshirt, and my heart starts beating so hard I'm afraid it will wake the passed-out patient. I look it over one more time and bend quickly to shove it under her door. *It's over. No turning back now.*

Invigorated and empowered, I head toward the staircase

to run down to the first floor and get rid of the folders. I stomp clumsily down the steps, clutching the railing with my right hand until I come upon the giant push bar to the first-floor exit. I open the door and walk into the sticky heat of the administrative-records room. All the way in the back, where the light doesn't fully reach it, sits the old wooden filing cabinet with the Typhlos staff files. I shouldn't have access to this filing cabinet, and I probably shouldn't even be in this room, but no one bothered to change the access code since it switched from the staff lounge to the records room. I've worked here long enough to watch most of the secondary spaces get used up as the number of patients continues to grow.

Now I'm standing here, with the last pieces of contraband in hand, alphabetically depositing each summary into the appropriate staff member's file. I put away the file for Frank Ignacio, the security guard, and continue next to Mary Kinney, my favorite nurse. I have no *J* last names in this stack of folders. As I plop Julie Watson's file into her thin staff folder, I wipe the dusty remnants on the front of my shirt and throw my sweatshirt over my shoulders. I'm finished. All the files that I'm going to put away are safely in the folders where they belong. And now I need a tall, strong drink to help me forget what I've done.

JANUARY 10TH, 11:00 A.M.

I'm filled with whizzing thoughts and worries, crashing into one another in my head. I keep seeing a blaring red sign that says Murderer across Richard's face. I'm nervously glancing at him and then my mind skips over to wondering about Rachel. Is she going to look through the staff files for the original reports? Check to see if I completed the summary to her standards, or will she just trust me?

As I'm evaluating the possible outcomes, Richard puts something in front of me and it breaks my concentration. I focus my eyes on this small object he has placed on my desk. It's an airplane bottle of Jack Daniel's.

"What the hell is this?"

"Nip. You got the shakes," Richard says nonchalantly.

"Richard, you can't have alcohol on the unit. I could get fired for this. You need to get this out of here."

"No one knows it's in here. No one ever comes in here. Your door is locked, and you need it."

"I don't need… I don't. Take this away, Richard. I can't believe after all the concessions I've made for you—letting you sit in my office in peace while you don't even bother trying to do your psychological assessments—you take advantage of it like this. Get this off of my desk." I can't look at him, and I can't look at the bottle. He reaches in front of me and takes the nip away. *How the hell did he get alcohol on the unit?* My eyes are wide, and as furious as I am that he brought this to me, I realize how much I need that shot.

He cracks the top and hands it back to me. I hold it in my hands and watch him. He takes off his hat and pulls another nip of Jack out of his pocket. He opens it, clinks my bottle and throws it back. Almost without thinking, I raise the bottle to my lips and feel the sweet burn as I chug the contents.

He reaches over and takes the empty bottle that is still upended to my mouth. He carefully tucks both nips into his pocket and puts his newsboy cap back on. He looks back down at his papers as if nothing happened. I sit, stunned, for what feels like hours. When Richard peers over the top of his glasses at me, I right myself and reach into my top drawer for an Altoid. I offer the tin to Richard and he takes two without looking. We resume ignoring each other, although I'm more focused on him now than I've ever been.

JANUARY 12TH, 3:09 P.M.

I just woke up on my office floor after another unsettling dream. I haven't been sleeping well at night, so office naps are becoming more regular. This time the dream was that I was one of those models who holds up the big signs during boxing matches to show what round the fighters are in. I had a perfect body, and perfect hair, but I was miniature because the boxing ring was one of those Rock 'Em Sock 'Em Robots boxing toys from the '80s. Lucas was the red boxer and AJ was the blue one, and every time either one of them landed a punch, their robot heads would fly off into the crowd. Maverick would run into the stands and return the heads to their bodies and I walked around the ring with my big sign. When I looked out toward the spectators, every one of them was Richard.

I shake the dream out of my head and force myself not to look for meaning behind it. The OMH summary is done, and Rachel seems satisfied, so I'm trying to concentrate on every work-related task I have so I don't tear my eyeballs out with the fear of what will come of me if I'm found out. If I keep my mind occupied and distracted, I can pretend that everything is going to be okay.

Every week on Friday afternoons, we have family-visiting day at Typhlos. Patients who will benefit from interactions with family members give us the names of people they'd like to see, and after we properly vet and communicate with the individuals, they come in for visiting day. I have a list of names that my patients have given me but I haven't bothered to vet, and now I'm rushing through it so these people can come in for tomorrow's visiting day.

I have the files of all my patients stacked on my chair, and I'm reading through family histories and psychosocials, looking for evidence to show that a requested relative is either a definitive yes or no. I recognize the names of most of these people, and it's easy to stamp *approved* with my big red rubber stamp next to them on the request list. I continue working, happy to be doing something both mundane and useful, when I hear David's office door close with a thud, followed by a prepubescent giggle that could only belong to one person.

My spine tightens with disgust, and a prickle of sweat forms along my eyebrows. I loudly clear my throat in an attempt to disturb their peace, but I fear it won't be heard. Instead I cough dramatically, slapping the arms of my desk chair for added effect. I hear more giggling on the other side of the wall. Of course they can hear me. I could be *choking* in here. I could be *dying* on the other side of the wall and David would be too busy trifling with this empty sweater to come rescue me. Well, if I can't stop them, at least I can make it unpleasant for them. I look around the office for something to throw at the wall—anything that would be a nuisance, a distraction. Nothing is calling out to me as the perfect intrusion, and then I look down at my right hand and see the big red rubber stamp.

If I pull out my desk drawer and slam the stamp into the papers as hard as I can, it'll make a loud bang and rattle, and that would be sure to tamper with their flirtation. If someone comes in, I'm innocently working, stamping my vetted guests; there's nothing to say I'm trying to break up a fledgling couple, or save my former best friend from this terrible decision.

I slam the stamp down on the first sheet. A satisfying clang rings out, and the drawer shakes and jangles. I hit the next page. I keep slamming the red stamp into the pages over and over again as I grit my teeth and move quickly through the sheets. The sounds and shocks are annoying and I'm sure to disrupt their bullshit conversation now. I gleefully crash the stamp down again. I hear David's door creak open and the click of high heels on linoleum as Julie retreats, defeated. For good measure, I slap the stamp down on the last page of my list of family members. I look at a sea of ragged, red "approved" stamps and feel a warm blanket of success fall over my shoulders.

JANUARY 13TH, 9:50 A.M.

I've been plagued with thoughts of Rachel finding out I never filed my own evaluation summary, thoughts of David and Julie, and thoughts of Richard killing his mother. A crushing loneliness came with every text message David sent me. His words were almost good enough to fix this; they were almost convincing enough to make me feel like he still cared about me, and he didn't transfer all his energies to Julie. *Julie.*

Julie, with her genuine good heart and earnest attitude. Who would I be to hate someone whose sincerity is so apparent it's practically scrawled all over her perfect face? What kind of asshole would I be to tell my best friend that he should stay away from her and return his undying affections back to me, even though he knows it's a fruitless endeavor? *Me!* I would be that kind of asshole! But now it seems so useless. I'm not getting any benefits from hating her; nothing good is coming to me by being angry with David.

I pick up my phone and buzz David's office. He answers on the first ring.

"Hi, David." I realize I haven't planned out what to say. "Can you, uh, come in here, please?"

"Sure," he sighs into the phone, and I hear him scooting

his chair back. I know this self-righteous sigh, and I'm immediately pissed that I decided to forgive him. He walks in my
door and stands behind me, leaning against my filing cabinet
with his arms crossed over his chest. I have to spin my chair
around to face him, and when I do, my knees brush against his
shins because my office is too small for these kinds of games.

"David, can you sit down?" Frustrated, uncomfortable.

He stays exactly where he is, raising his eyebrows in anticipation of an apology. Like I broke the lamp and blamed
the dog. I'm shifting in my chair, trying to get to an angle
where he isn't directly above me, so I have to look up at him
and ask to be forgiven for clearly meddling in his affairs. He
planned it like this. *Asshole.*

"David." I'm slamming my chair into my desk, trying to
create more room, and it's making my skin prickle and my
collar starts to feel tight at my throat. "David, can you *please*
just sit down?" I'm raising my voice now, looking directly at
the floor. I hold my hand out to my patient chair, inviting him
to sit, but I don't raise my eyes to look at him. With a frustrated sigh, he takes one large step to the chair and sits down.

"What can I do for you, Sam?"

"Look." Flustered, annoyed. "I'm pretty fucking pissed that
you decided to pull this shit, but in the interest of avoiding a
nuclear holocaust, I'm going to forgive you."

"*You're* going to forgive *me*? For what?" He leans forward
and huffs his moral superiority right into my face.

"For *Julie*, David. She's literally the only person I can't stand
in this entire place, and you decide to start dating *her*? And
you don't even talk to me about it first? It's ridiculous! It's
completely unfair, and you should have bothered to consider
my feelings before you embarked on this stupid adventure. I
mean, Jesus Christ. Do you even *know* how it feels to share you

with her? How could you *like* someone like her and someone like me at the same time? You're making my stock plummet."

"Are you done?" If I had a father, I imagine this is the face he would have given me as a child when I royally fucked up.

"Yes." I lean back, satisfied that he should be able to understand his egregious misstep, and he will now apologize profusely and set things right between us.

"Sam, you're completely out of line." The lecture begins. "First of all, I am not dating Julie."

"Ha! Yeah, right! I can hear through the wall, you know!"

"Shut up and let me finish. Like I said, I am not dating Julie, and you have absolutely no say in whom I choose to date anyway. You're *not* my girlfriend; you're not even my *ex*-girlfriend. Your opinion is irrelevant, so of course I didn't consider it when I had several innocuous conversations with a coworker upon whom you have completely unfairly dumped your vitriol." David used one huge breath to launch all this at me, and as he reloads with another breath, I roll my chair back to the door and pull my feet up onto the seat to keep a protective layer between me and David.

"You're so malicious when it comes to anything that you *think* could compromise my feelings for you. But then you treat me like I don't even matter! I'm tired of it, and if Julie wants to pay me some attention, and I engage with her, it doesn't mean anything. But don't *begin* to imagine that I will tolerate your contempt. It's bullshit. You need to grow up and take some responsibility for yourself. You can't have your fucking cake and eat it, too; keep me dangling by a string, and then pitch a fit if I decide to look elsewhere. You're really losing it, Sam. You have got to get your shit together."

"I just—I just don't like it when someone comes between us." My ego deflates as I admit this. The scorn and the fury are settling down, and as I put my feet back down on the ground, I can feel the cruelty seep out into the carpet.

"She's not coming between us. But you can afford to open up a little and let her in."

"You know, I wanted you to come in here so I could tell you that I forgive *you*, and now it's all twisted."

"Well, I forgive you, too. And I'm glad you forgive me, even though there's nothing to forgive me for. Can we get back to normal now, please?" He stands up and offers me a hand. I take it and he pulls me to my feet. He wraps me in a warm hug and reminds me to stop being so hard all the time. I remind him to stop being such a pussy all the time. And with a grin of self-satisfaction, I slip back into David's number-one spot; exactly where I belong.

JANUARY 17TH, 11:08 A.M.

Today, Richard is running late, and what I'm coming to realize, as I wait for a man who murdered his mother, is that I have never felt safer with any other man in my life.

"Okay, no papers today." He hasn't even sat down as I say this, or put his stack of newspapers on the corner of my desk.

"No papers?" he says, looking hopefully at his handful.

"Yeah, no papers today. We need to discuss what happened here." It's my duty to remain professional, and I never should have allowed us to drink in our last session. I shouldn't have, but I did.

"I'm not telling anybody about the nips, Sam. We don't need to talk about it." He sits.

"I'm not worried about you talking to people about the nips. We sat in my office drinking together, and that can't happen. I am your therapist, I am a professional and I am in my place of work. I can't behave like this. *You* can't behave like this! You're here for treatment, for *help*, and I'm the one who is supposed to give it to you."

"How you gonna help me when you can't even help yourself?"

His words cut me; the truth in them is almost too much to take.

"I can help myself, I *do* help myself! You have no idea about my life. You don't know what I'm going through. You have no idea."

"Okay." He pauses, still looking at me but not saying anything. When I fail to continue, he reaches into his jacket and pulls out four mini-bottles. They're all Grey Goose, and like a gentleman, he opens my bottles before he opens his own. He puts two nips in front of me, and I look at my computer screen. The cursor is blinking at me accusingly, pushing me to finish all the paperwork I need to complete Richard's file. Pushing me to talk to him about what he told me, pushing me to put down my fears and not pick up the bottles.

"I can't drink these, Richard. I can't drink at work with a patient." I lower my gaze, not looking directly at him or at the bottles.

"Who do you think you're fooling, exactly? I've been watching you since I came in this place, and you've got *alcoholic* written all over you."

"Alcoholic? How do you figure I'm an alcoholic?" My head snaps back up.

"Well, first of all—" he pounds one of his airplane bottles "—I put a drink in front of you last week and you barely hesitated before guzzling it down. Second—" he drinks the second one "—how the hell do you think I got these?" He wags his empty bottles at me.

"Where *did* you get them?" My throat is suddenly parched, and I look down at the bottom drawer of my filing cabinet. I know exactly where he got them.

He sees me eyeing my drawer and throws up his hands. "See? Now, what kind of fucked-up shrink has a ziplock bag full of nips just sitting in her filing cabinet?"

I can't argue with this. I look down at my drawer and re-member the bag was hidden underneath some art supplies and a shoe box full of crayons. I had been collecting those bottles forever, and after a particularly bad week months ago I brought them to the office. At the liquor store near my apartment, the cashier would always throw a tiny bottle into my black plastic bag when I went in to buy booze. He got to know my favorites. I'm at that liquor store all the time. I would spend my whole paycheck in there; I probably single-handedly pay their electric bill. And now my patient has my bottles. All of them. There must be dozens.

"How did you find those?"

"I haven't just been sitting here reading the paper, you know. I'm watching you, and I see what's happening with you. I didn't know what I would find when I went looking, but I knew I would find something." He shifts forward, re-adjusts his seat.

"What the hell? You snooped through my office?" I stare at him, astounded. "You've asked me to make concessions for you, and I have." I'm holding out the fingers of my left hand, using the pointer of my right to list his infractions. "You've asked me to give you a break and let you sit in here with your papers, and I have. You've made it insanely difficult to be your counselor because you never say anything and I still have no clue why you're here, and I'm putting up with that! I'm forced to trust you and just keep trying with you, hoping to find out why you're institutionalized… Well, enough now! *Enough*. I'm not even gonna *ask* when you rifled through my office because I'm already angry. You want me to trust you and then you do *this*?" I slam my hand against my desk, and my water bottle falls over and clatters onto the floor.

"You left me in here while you attended to some emergency." He waves his hands as he says *emergency* as if it were an exaggeration.

"Because I trusted you! And you took advantage of that?" I'm staring at him in disgust. "You took advantage of me?"

"I needed some leverage. Because I want another compromise."

"Ha! Are you kidding? After *this* shit?" I return to my computer screen.

"You need it just as much as I do."

"Another compromise." I shake my head. My voice is softening now; I can't have passersby hearing this insanity.

"I've made the decision that I'm going to cooperate with you. I'm going to help you finish this file you keep bitching about."

I turn to him with eyebrows raised and a tight-lipped smile. I tuck the pages of his file into my drawer and straighten out the remaining documents on my desktop. "*You're* going to cooperate with me?"

"I know what it takes to stay here. I know I can't just stay silent. So I will complete the file."

"What's the catch? What's the leverage for?"

"I'm not going to be treated like a patient."

"You *are* a patient. How the hell do you want me to treat you?"

"Like a human being, an equal. I'm not going to sit here and spill my guts to you while you revel in the dirty details. I'm not a sideshow."

"You think that's what we *do*?"

"*Your* walls are coming down, too. You're not gonna stay silent and have all the power. I have collateral now, and I could get you fired in a second. I can expose you. You don't know where the bottles are. I've watched you losing it and I can show your boss the bag of booze, and when I tell her that's why you're not living up to your responsibilities, she'll know it's true. Look what happened to Adelle on your watch! And I could mention that *you're* the one who left the janitor's closet unlocked. I saw you take that plunger and walk away."

"Adelle is fine! She was released from the hospital with a clean bill of health! It was a false alarm!"

"A false alarm, huh? Well, a false alarm from a medication mistake by a drunk psychologist. And what about the closet? Eddie may not have done himself in if he didn't have a place to do it. That's what I could say."

"Why do you want to get me fired? How does that help you? And why are you following me?"

"I am not following you. And I don't want to get you fired, but I will. I can. If you refuse to agree to this deal. You need to tell me what's happening with you, just like I need to tell you about me. We're going to talk like equals. That's the deal. Take it or leave it."

"Let me get this straight." I rub my aching eyes and try to wrap my mind around what's happening in here. "You're willing to complete your file, and actually participate in therapy, as long as I share my personal stories with you? And if I don't, you'll show my boss the ziplock bag—which you *stole*—and I will be fired? You'll tell her that I'm responsible for what happened to Adelle and Eddie?"

"Yes." He responds as if this were a sane and reasonable request.

"How do you plan on getting away with this?" I need a cigarette.

"There's nothing to get away with. I've already gotten away with it. I already know about Adelle's medication and the unlocked closet. I took your booze, and now I'm holding it hostage until I get what I want. And it's what *you* want, too. Even if it's not the way you wanted it. It's the only way you can get me to finish my file. The only way you can prove to everyone how wonderful and talented you are as a therapist," he says with a whoop-de-doo face and twirls his fingers in the air.

How the hell does he know that I want to prove myself to everyone? I look him over with apprehension, wondering where he's keeping the rest of the stash. "And if I say yes?"

"Then you keep your job. And you give me the help I need. And you look like a hero."

"And where's my guarantee that you don't just turn me in anyway?"

He stands up and sticks out his hand.

"A handshake? After all this you think I'm going to trust a handshake?"

"I can't offer you anything else. I stand by my word, and if you shake on it, I give you my word. You hold up your end of the bargain, and I'll hold up mine."

Richard eyes me suspiciously, and I smile at him as I dump the two remaining Grey Goose bottles into my empty coffee cup and shove the empties toward him. I lift the cup in a gesture of cheers and pour the vodka down my throat.

JANUARY 18TH, 10:47 P.M.

AJ is abandoning me. It feels like everything is different now. He did what he came to do, and now he isn't interested in me anymore. I was just a mission, the proverbial notch on the bedpost.

I desperately need the distraction from my own terrible reality, but I'm afraid to see him now and cement this awful fate for myself. He won't love me, he won't want me anymore, and then I won't have anything. I'm forgetting that I started this thing not caring about him. I just wanted something to distract me from Lucas, and now I'm addicted and I need him to need me.

I'm willing my phone to ring. Now that I have entered into this clandestine thing with him, I'm vulnerable and exposed, so I'm constantly checking my phone. I will check it every couple of minutes until I fall asleep and I will check it again when I wake up.

I will pour another glass of wine and count the cigarettes I have left in the pack. There's a deli and a liquor store within twenty yards of my front door, but if there's any way I can avoid going outside, I will. I have six cigarettes left. Will that be enough to carry me through? Probably not; I'll call the deli and the liquor store and ask them to bring me some sustenance.

I'm giving up hope, and he's an asshole. I was using him! He wasn't using me. I just needed him for a minute as an escape from Lucas. And it doesn't matter. I don't need him. He isn't even that good-looking. He has that stupid smile that looks like a cracked-out Cheshire cat. He isn't even that sexy. He's stupid and childish. And then my phone beeps.

Hey, baby... My heart soars into my brain and I'm sweating, trying to decipher the ellipsis. Do I look desperate and needy if I respond immediately? I wait for what feels like hours but is actually only three and half minutes.

Hey, you. This response feels laid-back, but now I'm in that awful waiting period where I want him to write back something perfect and do it immediately to prove that he is thinking about me. I want the ball back in my fucking court. I wait. I wait for the three little oscillating dots to appear to show he's writing back. Come on, little dots!

And then, finally: You going to Nick's tonight? he responds. I wasn't planning on going to Nick's tonight, but now I'm thinking about it. But something is stopping me. I feel like there's an anvil on my lap, and I can't lift it.

Maybe all I needed was to hear that he is waiting for me at Nick's and I can choose to go or not go see him. Everything changed when he saw the man behind the curtain when my bruises were exposed two weeks ago. The shine came off, and we were no longer two wild kids sharing a frivolous and shallow frolic in bed. He saw something that he wasn't supposed to see; he saw me. Maybe, *maybe* he really likes me. What an idiot. This could be my opportunity to prove to myself that I don't have to do this anymore.

Think I'm gonna skip it tonight, I respond. Have fun without me.

Leave him before he can leave me. Hurt him before he can hurt me.

JANUARY 19TH, 10:19 A.M.

"Miss Sam! Miss Sam, come quick!" There's a slamming at my door, and I hear Tashawndra pleading for me to come help.

"What is it?" I say as I swing open the door. Tashawndra takes my hand and pulls me down the hallway.

"It's Jenni. She's freaking out. She's locked herself in a stall, and she won't come out. She's been crying all morning."

"What's going on? Did you call Rachel?"

"No, I came to get you, and Lucy went to get Julie."

"Okay." We hurriedly jog down the hallway and push the door into the women's room. Lucy and Julie just arrived, and Julie is asking questions through the locked stall door.

"Jenni, what's going on in there?" Jenni is sitting on the floor of the stall. We can see her lower back between the bottom of the stall door and the floor. She's slumped in the corner of the handicapped stall and is heaving from crying so hard. We can hear her cough and choke back her tears, and when she leans forward to throw up, Lucy widens her eyes and glares at me.

Julie sits down on the floor by the stall. "Jenni," she coos through the crack, "what's happening in there?" Jenni coughs and spits and flushes the toilet. She breathes in heavy breaths, and we can see her back moving up and down. Julie reaches her hand under the stall and lays it flat next to Jenni. I hand Julie some paper towels, and she passes them under. Jenni takes one from the stack and blows her nose.

Julie is now using her thumb to rub Jenni's back, and we can hear her breath beginning to slow. Tashawndra is crouching in the corner with her knees pulled up to her chest, resting her chin on her fists. Lucy is watching Julie, periodically turning to me and then looking at her own reflection. I'm watching Julie, trying to ascertain if she can handle this situation. Then Jenni speaks.

"I don't want to be in here anymore." Her voice is thick.

"Then come outta there, girl. We're right here for ya," Tashawndra calls from her corner.

"No, I mean *here*, in a mental institution. I don't want to be here anymore. I want to go home." She sighs a heavy sigh, and I see her hand drop to the tile, and I watch a needle roll out of her hand.

"Shit. Julie, go get medical. Now. And don't tell anyone what's happening! Go, but be discreet." I hike up my pants and use Lucy's shoulder for balance as I boost my foot onto the sink. I push myself onto the top of the stall door and shimmy through the space between the door and the ceiling. My feet crash down onto the toilet seat and skid onto the floor. She has a thick hair tie around her biceps and a green lighter on her lap. I look for a spoon, but don't see one. Then I notice the foil spinning in the toilet bowl.

Jenni's head is against the stall, with her jaw slack and her eyes in slits. There's no way for me to tell how much heroin she has taken.

"Jenni!" I holler directly into her face. "Jenni, it's Sam. Wake up. *Wake up!*" I'm shaking her shoulders, and her head bobbles and her chin falls to her chest. I reach over her and unlock the door. I push Jenni's body out the door and lay her flat on the cold bathroom tile.

Tashawndra is staring wide-eyed in the corner and starting to cry. Lucy sits next to her and puts her arm protectively around Tashawndra's shoulders. Julie comes running back into the bathroom.

"Oh, my God, Sam, is she dead? Oh, my God!" Julie hasn't let the door close behind her when she says this.

"No, she's not dead. She's breathing, but barely. Did you get medical?" I'm holding her wrist to monitor her pulse and putting my ear to her mouth to make sure she's still breathing.

"Yeah, they're coming, I called a code blue."

"Thank you, Julie. You did a good job. Please take Tashawndra and Lucy to my office, and wait for me there, okay?" I can't have her in here if she's going to get emotional and freak out.

"Okay," Julie says and stays motionless, staring at the scene on the floor.

"*Now*, Julie, right now." I throw her my keys.

"Oh, oh!" She jumps to attention and pulls the women up off the floor and ushers them out the door. As she opens the door, I can see two orderlies and two nurses approaching with a gurney and bags full of medical equipment. They shove through the bathroom door with a backboard and ask me what happened.

"Heroin, I don't know how much and I don't know when. Other patients told me she's been in here all morning, but they didn't mention any drugs."

"What's her name?" a large male nurse asks as he slides the backboard under her and picks her up.

"Jenni, her name is Jenni."

"We'll take it from here." He turns away from me and thumps Jenni onto the gurney. "Jenni! Jenni!" he calls into her ears. "How much heroin did you take, sweetheart?" He pushes her down the hallway toward the clinic as a crowd of patients and clinicians gather to witness the commotion.

I can't do any more for her, so I walk back to my office to find the three women on the floor, huddled together, crying.

"Hey, it's okay now. Sshhhh. Don't worry. She's at the clinic now. They're going to take her to the emergency room. You guys did a really good job, okay? You did the right thing to come get me and Julie. You probably saved her life." I'm wiping the sweat from my face and chugging water from the bottle on my desk.

"Where did she get the drugs?" Julie asks me, but I don't look directly at her.

"I don't know," I say and I see both Lucy and Tashawndra hide their heads when Julie asks me.

"Ladies, where did she get them? This is incredibly important; you're not going to get in trouble. Did she tell you? Do you know?"

Lucy looks up and shyly responds, "Jenni said her sister brought her the medicine she needs. We figured she meant drugs, but she didn't say for sure. And she never told us what kind."

The heroin-addicted sister. The one Jenni would use with. How the fuck did she get in here? As my breathing starts to normalize, I pull up a blank incident report on my computer and start filling it in. Julie brings Lucy and Tashawndra to a group room to talk, and I promise to meet them there as soon as I'm finished. I reach over to Jenni's file to copy down the pertinent information. The top sheet in her file is the visitation record and family-vetting sheet. I see a sloppy red "approved" stamp next to her sister Jackie's name.

JANUARY 20TH, 11:14 A.M.

The light coming in the office windows is especially intense today, and I have to pull the shades to see the screen of my computer without any glare. Even when the shades are down, the brightness in the office feels almost blinding. I fish for my sunglasses so I can concentrate on getting some work done. The stack of files on my patient chair seems larger and larger every time I look back at it. No matter how many documents I complete and move to the pile of finished files, the heap on the patient chair continues to grow. I'm drinking a flat Mountain Dew and it tastes like acid.

The buzzer on my intercom blares at me, and I see the flashing green indicator next to the security guard's line. Raul's voice fills the room. "Sam, there's a Lucas here to see you. I sent him back to your office; he had a guest pass."

A guest pass? Where the fuck did Lucas find a guest pass? He's never come to the office. Before I can snatch up the phone to tell Raul to get that asshole out of here and strip him of his fraudulent pass, there's a delicate rapping at my office door. I adjust my sunglasses because the light is still unbearable, then get up to pull open the door.

Lucas is standing in the hallway—there must be a dead bulb

because it's darker than usual out there—and he's holding a limp bouquet. It's a bunch of red roses, wrapped in green cellophane and tied with a thin white ribbon. The bouquet smells of piss and garbage, and before I can turn him away, he shoves me back into the office and crashing into my patient chair. The mound of files tumbles down on top of me, and I can't seem to find my footing to get back up.

My sunglasses are askew and I can only see bright light and the silhouette of Lucas's body as he lunges down toward me. I'm trying to protect my face and chest, and I find my hands are filled with the roses, and the thorns are stabbing my fingers.

I am kicking at him to get him off me, but every time I land a hit, my foot seems to absorb into his torso like I'm kicking a marshmallow. I can't get the roses out of my hands, and there's sticky blood spilling all around me, and Lucas knocks down my Mountain Dew as he reaches for the scissors from my drawer. The can lies upended on the edge of my desk, and so much liquid is coming out, it's beginning to fill the room.

My hands are lined with thorns and I can't clench my fists. My hair is trapped under the wheels of the chair, and the Mountain Dew level is rising to my ears. Lucas is looming over me, completely silent, holding the scissors above his head. The blades are glinting in the sun, and just as the Mountain Dew begins to choke and suffocate me, it's all over.

My office phone is blaring loudly, and I pick my face up off the floor and wipe away a stream of drool. This is the dream I keep having now. Sometimes I wake up sweating, sometimes crying, but always out of breath and exhausted. I crawl up onto my hands and knees and answer the phone.

Rachel asks me what happened in the bathroom with Jenni. We haven't had a chance to talk since then. I explain the details of the incident and let her know how it was managed. I even give Julie credit. As I'm telling Rachel that I will call her back as soon as I get an update from detox, she interrupts me.

"Before I let you go," she breathes heavily into the receiver, "thank you for the OMH summary. I really appreciate you doing that for me. Things are still such an *unbelievable* mess around here, but with your help, it's been a bit easier to manage."

"Of course, Rachel. We're all together in this," I say, holding the phone between my ear and shoulder. I scratch at the zipper marks on my face, leftover from using my coat as a pillow.

"Tell me, what happened to the original reports from the psychiatrists at OMH? I don't see them in my office?" My heart stops.

This was bound to come up at some point, and now I have to explain. If I can get away with this, I may be in the clear. "Right. When I dropped off the summary, your door was locked, so I couldn't drop off the folders, as well. I just slipped the summary under your door and filed the original reports in the records room downstairs. I hope that's okay." I hold my breath and clench my teeth, waiting for her response. I can hear her breathing heavily, shuffling papers around. My eyes are squeezed shut and tiny tears are starting to form in the corners. My shoulders tighten, and I hear a click on the line.

"Uh, yeah, that's fine. My other line is ringing, so I have to let you go. Thanks again, Sam." I hear her click over to the other call, and I release my breath. I unclench my muscles and hang up the phone. I pull open my desk drawer to see my OMH folder still sitting there, looking back at me. I gently slide it out and tuck it safely in my handbag.

JANUARY 20TH, 2:23 P.M.

David and I are having a late lunch together but I'm still licking my wounds from his comments a couple weeks ago, when
he called me malicious. So although we look like we're better,
I'm keeping him at arm's length. I haven't said a word to him
about the evaluations or stamping the visitor pass for Jenni's
sister or leaving the janitor's closet unlocked. As I take a bite
from my half of his sandwich, he pries into the Lucas situation.

"We gonna talk about what's going on with you and
Lucas?" he asks me with his mouth full, as if by being infor-
mal, he is minimizing the gravity of the question.

"What about me and Lucas?" I'm only going to give him
exactly what he asks for, and nothing more.

"I haven't heard anything about him in a while." David
holds his open palm in front of his mouth as he continues.

"Well, I haven't seen him in a while. We'd been fighting a
lot, and I didn't feel like handling his shit as well as the messes
that have been going on here, so I took myself a little break
from Lucas." I speak into my sandwich.

"How's he taking that?"

"Honestly? I'm not even sure he noticed. I bet he has plenty
of other women around to keep him warm. It's been like,

three weeks. He sent me a few text messages, asking if I am intentionally avoiding him. He knows I'm pissed. He kissed some chick at that pretentious New Year's Eve party, and before that, he was blowing lines again, and I couldn't take the lies anymore, so I took off. I think he's just giving me space." I sigh a long, ragged sigh and sip from a giant Coca-Cola.

"Didn't you kiss the waiter?" David raises one eyebrow at me, takes a bite of sandwich and wipes his mouth with a napkin. His office is a little bit bigger than mine, but whenever he gets haughty and superior, it feels like the walls are starting to close in.

"Yes, but I kissed the waiter in retaliation for Lucas kissing some random woman. I didn't go in there intending to kiss a waiter; he was the only person on the balcony when it was midnight. I would have kissed a fish if he were the only one on the balcony with me."

"Are you going to break up with him?" he asks.

"Ugh, I don't want to do this. I don't want to *talk* about this shit. I know you don't like him, and I know you sort of know what's been going on, but I don't have the energy for this, and I would love it if you could just leave me alone about Lucas." I'm whining and I don't want to be confronted about my decision making.

"I haven't seen any evidence of abuse for a while," he slowly points out.

"'Evidence of abuse'? Why do you *say* it like that? I'm not a patient. You don't have to treat me. You haven't seen blood in my hair or bruises on my face. I get it. Okay. Well, that's because I haven't been staying over at his place for a couple of weeks, and he hasn't been to mine. So… *God*. What do you want from me? I don't want to talk about this." I shove the rest of the sandwich into my mouth and hope that David takes it as a sign to stop prying and let me be.

"I think you'd be better off without him." He holds his hand up in surrender. "That's it, I'm done!" He pops the last of his sandwich into his mouth and claps his hands together.

I look out David's window at the scaffolding across the street. Now I'm forced to think about Lucas and wonder what I'm going to do. I've become so accustomed to hating him or loving him that I need him in my life so I can occupy my mind with *something*. Hate and love are the same fucking things, just positives and negatives of the same emotion, the same actions, the same feelings. And I long, desperately, for indifference.

When he's calling me, I have something to hold on to, something to be mad at, something to bitch about, but when those calls stop, where will I be? There's no one here to replace this bullshit, and I need my daily dose of bullshit to get by. I'm addicted, and that's why I can't get enough. I say I don't want it, I say I don't need it, I say I'm better off a thousand times without it; but pretty soon my head is going to start screaming for more.

JANUARY 20TH, 3:15 P.M.

I'm in a group session waiting for the rest of the patients to trickle in, lost in my thoughts. I realize now, finally, that my time has run out with Lucas. There is an expiration date, because that's how *I* want it. I've incited the part of myself that takes care of business by cutting off my affair with AJ. I know I need to officially break up with Lucas soon, or else I will lose my nerve and go back to him. I end up thinking for days that I'm going to be fine without him, and he won't be able to hurt me anymore, and I can't save him, and then my head explodes.

Everyone's now here and we're sitting in a circle, and as the side chatter dies down, the ladies look to me to present a theme.

"Hi, everyone. Today, I want us to discuss a topic that might be a little bit difficult for some of you. As you know, this is a safe space to discuss whatever is on your mind. Everyone who is in this institution is here to get better, to take some time for themselves and get back on their feet. Sometimes, it's important to face the scary things, and that's what we're going to do here today."

"We're going to talk about husbands?" Nancy asks.

"Maybe. What I wanted to talk about was domestic abuse. Violence."

"Huh—" Anna leans back and crosses her arms. "Husbands." I'm a bit surprised that Anna is using the term *husbands* being that she is gay and her wife was her abuser.

The ladies offer muffled giggles in response. I look around and see several patients absentmindedly touching scars, pulling their shoulders up to their necks, looking down. I notice myself squinting, blinking my left eye and matting down my hair.

"Do you mean to say that everyone in this room had a husband who was violent?" Tashawndra.

"Well, not always a husband, but yes, everyone in this room is a survivor of abuse." I hope they won't ask if I'm included.

"We supposed to share our stories?" Nancy.

"If you like. This is a safe space, and sometimes sharing stories can help. Would you like to begin?"

"Okay. I can start. Hi, my name is Nancy. I am a survivor of domestic abuse. I was married for a while and my husband, Glenn, used to beat me up when he was angry. That's my story."

"Hi, I'm Anna. I had a wife and she beat me up, too."

"That's great, ladies. Thank you for starting. Do you think that either of you would be willing to tell us a little bit more about your experience? I find it can be helpful to your recovery to talk about it."

"You could go." Anna, nodding toward Nancy.

"Okay. Umm, well, I was married for four years. I had a grown daughter from a different relationship, and she lived with me and Glenn on and off while she was between jobs. I liked it when she would stay with us because Glenn wouldn't beat me if anyone else was around. It's funny, even now when I think about him, I don't feel angry at him. I feel guilty. I feel sad and sometimes scared. I'm always looking for the things that I could have done differently so that he wouldn't get so angry."

"Yeah, me too! I always think of it like that." Lucy. "Like if I just remembered that he hated my pink skirt, then I wouldn't have worn it, and it wouldn't have gotten me in trouble."

"Yeah," Nancy continues. "There's always something that's gonna make them angry. Always something that'll make you get in trouble."

"One thing I want to talk about is leaving. How did you all get out of your own abusive situations?" Wondering if their stories could help me, wondering if any of us have any sense at all.

"Well, Glenn got arrested. So, when he went to prison, the situation didn't exist anymore. I had a social worker come talk to me, and she helped me get a lawyer and we filed for divorce while he was away. He's still in prison now."

"How did you get the courage to report him?" Tashawndra.

"I didn't. He got arrested for burglary. I never even told the cops or the lawyers that he beat me. I was too scared."

"Scared," I say, trying not to remember myself cowering between the toilet and the wall, covering my head with my arms. "Often victims of abuse are too scared to report it to the police. Why do you think that is? Shouldn't we ask for help? What is it that stops us?" Are these the pronouns I should be using?

"Because, what if you don't have enough evidence? The men always lying about it anyway, always saying they never touched you, and saying you fell down, or you got drunk and that's why you have marks on you. What happens if the cops believe him and not you?" Lucy.

"And they always say to you that if you tell anyone they'll kill you. Glenn said he would bury me and no one would ever know."

"When my wife was hitting me, or right when she was finished, she would tell me she loved me and she was so sorry. Sometimes she would cry and tell me she didn't mean to hurt me. I felt bad for her. I didn't want her to get in trouble." Anna, probing the long scars on her arms. I think of Lucas throwing me an ice pack.

"Right, and if this is what he does when he loves me, what will he do when he hates me?" I watch the words come out of my mouth as if they're encased in a cartoon speech bubble, and I want to suck them back in before anyone hears me.

"That's right, Miss Sam, and the best way to make them hate you is involving the cops." Nancy draws the attention away from me before I can be exposed.

"Scared that you've got nowhere to go." Diana. "The house was his. The car was his. If I get the cops involved and they take him away? I'm homeless again. The money was his, everything."

"So you feel you have to tolerate the abuse," I say, "in order to avoid homelessness?"

"Yeah. And the friends are his, too." Sue. "When I was trying to figure out if I could leave him, all my friends were *his* friends. I knew I would be all alone. We had been married for so long, and I was so isolated from everyone in my life before him, that everyone I knew was through him. So if I left him, or reported him, I would have no house, no car, no money and no friends. So, what's worse?"

Sue escaped her abuser using a network of survivors who shuffled her between various secret pickup locations under the cover of night in disguises. Before she left, when her name was still Rebecca, Sue was beaten nearly to death. Both her eye sockets were broken and a cracked rib had punctured her lung.

"That's interesting that you use the word *isolated*. Many abusers have a pattern of isolating their victims. Pulling them away from friends, from family members, sometimes even having them quit their jobs, leave their own homes. It's about control." I think about Lucas asking me to move in with him, to leave my apartment, to leave my independence, to force me to rely on him.

"I always had this notion that it was embarrassing." Chloe. "Like I should be able to handle it, I should be able to get him to stop. I thought that if I told anyone, they would pity me or judge me. I was afraid they would think I was weak."

Chloe is an Ivy League–educated woman who had a long career in finance. She worked at a large bank in Manhattan when women were scarce in the banking world. Her husband of nearly twenty years periodically drugged and raped her. She would wake up in clothes that didn't belong to her, in hotels she didn't remember checking in to or in neighborhoods she didn't recognize. Only when she hid a recording device in her handbag did she discover what was going on.

As the women continue sharing their tales of survival, I find myself drifting into my own story.

When weapons of choice were compared—belts, fists, bottles—I thought of Lucas always cornering me in the bathroom.

When Sue said her husband knew how to hit in such a way that he didn't leave marks, I wondered if Lucas had practiced on other women.

When Nancy said it was anger that triggered Glenn, when Lucy said that it was jealousy that triggered Julius, when Anna said she could never predict the triggers, I thought of Lucas and booze, and I wondered if it would stop if he were sober.

When we listed all the different ways the women escaped, I wondered why I haven't just left him yet.

JANUARY 24TH, 10:44 A.M.

"So, today's the first day of the new deal." Richard steps into my office. He looks encouraged and apprehensive at the same time.

"Is that what you're calling it? I'm calling it 'the blackmail.'"

"You going to give me shit the whole time? I told you this is for *both* our benefits."

"I'm not going to give you shit, Richard. Let's just get this over with—I need to finish your file. Start talking."

He awkwardly hovers over the patient chair while he contemplates his response. "I don't know what to say; don't you just ask questions?" I guess he only thought this through far enough to get me squirming in his hand.

"You don't have something in mind to start with?" I am terrified to ask Richard the details of what happened with the murder. Maybe now we'll both be squirming. "Well, why don't you finish the story you started a few weeks back, about your mother." I quickly look away after asking him.

"What story about my mother?" Richard is sitting down, getting organized. His papers are in a stack on my desk corner, he has pulled out two tiny bottles of tequila, and he is laying his hat on top of the newspapers. He takes the caps off both bottles and hands one to me. As our bottles clink, he says, "What story? What did I tell you?" We drink our nips.

"Richard. You said you were in prison because you killed your mother," I stammer. I'm holding out my empty bottle for Richard to stash in his coat pocket. He takes it and presses a fresh bottle between my fingers.

"You're gonna need more than one for this. I am, too." We go through the routine a second time before Richard begins speaking again.

"I had a real special mother. She was a single mom and didn't have a man to help around the house. I don't have brothers or sisters, so it was just she and I growing up. Woodside was pretty much an Irish neighborhood, so even though it wasn't so safe, being that we were Irish, she never seemed too scared of anything. My dad died when I was just a baby, and she had a rough go of it."

Richard is looking out the window while he's beginning his story. His legs are sticking straight out in front of him, hands clasped over his belly. The air is strange in here. I can't tell how I'm supposed to act. The tequila has dulled my sensibilities, but only slightly, and I'm on high alert because I'm frightened. I can't believe he's managed to get me to agree to this.

"I don't tell this story, Sam." He looks back to me.

"I don't drink in my office with patients, Richard. You're the one who asked for this. You said you wanted to be treated like an equal, not a patient."

"Fair enough. Alright. I don't... I don't know how to tell it."

"I want to hear everything you're willing to tell me." Standard response.

"Bah, '*everything*.' Women." He takes a deep breath and starts again. "It's complicated to try to explain what it was like.

I lived with my mother, Frances, in a three-family house on Sixty-Fourth Street, near Trimble. You know Woodside?" I nod, although the only thing I know about Woodside is that it's in Queens; beyond that, I have no idea.

"It wasn't nice, but it was enough for us. The elevated section of the 7 was nearby, so I could feel the trains coming all day and night. The walls would rattle and things used to fall off the shelves. I was sweeping all the time because things kept falling down and breaking." Richard is looking at the men on the scaffold across the street; he's rubbing his thumbs together. He shifts his weight and continues.

"My dad died when I was little and I don't remember him. I heard the stories from Frances, but I don't know what was true. She didn't have any more family except for me because her brother and sisters moved away when Queens got dangerous.

"She told me they went to Ohio, where it was safer to raise a family, but that she stayed because she wanted to be with my father and he had a good job in Queens. When he died she could've left, but she told me her family didn't want us in Ohio, because I was a 'bastard child' and that would reflect badly on them, so we couldn't leave Woodside."

"When did your father die?" I ask, sipping my coffee.

"I was a baby, so maybe '62, '63? I don't know exact dates."

"Did you ever find out what happened?" I instinctively pick up a pen and pull a pad to write his answers on. Before I jot anything down, I remember the deal; I'm not supposed to treat him like a patient, so I tuck the pen back into the mug on my desk.

"Well, I know that he was killed in an accident at work, but I don't know the details. Frances told me that because she and my dad were never married that the company wouldn't help her or me with any money or benefits. She was always mad about that. She never could let it go. Saying that she had a son because my father wanted a son, and now no one would be here to raise me. She hated that company."

"What kind of work did your father do?"

"Construction. He was a roofer, I think. There wasn't a lot of opportunity in the '50s for Irish guys with no education. You went to work in pubs or construction. So, he was a roofer. I guess he fell off a roof or something, but I never found out exactly what happened. After he died, it was just me and Frances."

"That must have been hard for both of you."

"Are you going to write all of this down? I don't want this story to be written down." The notebook is still out on my desk, but I haven't been taking any notes.

"I'm not listening to you as a therapist, remember? And you're not going to listen to me as my patient. This is one human being talking to another. Just like you said."

"So you're not going to ask me how I *feel* about all this?" He twinkles his finger at me.

"I'll try not to."

Richard gives me an incredulous sideways glare and puts his hands behind his head. His elbows are stretched out on either side, and in my too-small office, he seems to take up the whole space.

"She was a teacher, so I got to go to private school until the teachers' strike in '68. She went to all the protests and waved a sign around. She got angry with all the other women, but she never really wanted to fight *for* anything, she just wanted to fight. When the strike was over, she refused to go back to St. Teresa's because she said she had been too badly disrespected. She said she never wanted to see them again, and I couldn't go to school there anymore. I left after second grade and I had to go to public school.

"There was a problem to get me into another school because my birthday is in the summer, so they didn't know if I should be the youngest kid in fourth grade or the oldest kid in third grade. I could read pretty well, I wasn't a disciplinary case, and because the schools got so crowded and confusing after the strike, I got to skip third grade. I remember Frances told everyone in the neighborhood that I was the smartest kid.

"I was doing fine in the new school and it was pretty close by, but I would have to change again soon, because PS 78 only went up to sixth grade. I had to make good marks because Frances wanted to show everyone that I was smart.

"Things got bad for her around then. She wasn't working a real job, just cleaning houses some days during the week. She was so angry that she had to clean other people's houses to make a living. Whenever I got home from school, she would force me to clean *our* house.

"She would sit in this yellow plastic chair in the kitchen with a scarf tied around her hair and smoke cigarettes. She would ash them on the floor and then tell me to clean it up. Then the train would come by and something would break. She would always put these little trinkets and vases and delicate stuff up on this shelf where she knew it would fall off and break.

"I remember one time, she had a flask of vermouth on the stool next to her yellow chair, and when the train came the flask fell down. She had been drinking all day and all that was left in the house was the flask of vermouth. That was the first time she hit me. I was nine years old."

"Do you remember what happened?" I interrupt.

"Of course I remember what happened. No matter how much I try to forget it, you can't forget it. I remember what everything smelled like. I remember the color of the tiles and the specks in the grout. I remember wondering if linoleum can break. She had one shoelace untied, and I was afraid that if she saw that, I would get hit again, so I tried to tie it while I was cleaning up the ash by her feet.

"When the flask went down she screamed at me to pick it up. I was holding the broom and I was in the doorway to the other room. I walked to pick it up and she kicked me in the ribs when I bent down. She told me I was wasting it. She said that it was spilling and I needed to pick it up faster. I held it up to give to her and she slapped it out of my hand. She kept slapping the side of my head over and over again telling me I wasted her medicine. I don't remember if she hit me hard or not, but I remember the sound it made when she got my ear. I didn't say anything back because she was drunk, and I knew it would get worse. She pushed me away and told me to start cleaning again from the beginning."

The telltale ringing that only comes from getting slapped that way is rising in my ears, and I squint away the pain. I know this sound so well, and as I hear Richard telling the story, I can imagine myself in his position.

"We didn't have any cleaning gloves, so my hands were raw and sore from all the bleach and scrubbing. She would fall asleep then get back up and tell me to start again. I cleaned all night until I went to school the next morning. I had bleach all over me, and the knees of my pants had torn." His gaze returns to the men outside the window, and his voice begins to get small. He leans forward and looks at my desktop clock. "If I keep going, there won't be any time for you to talk."

"That's okay. This session can be all for you," I say, feeling that he's telling my story along with his own.

"That wasn't the deal." He readjusts his position. He's sitting ramrod straight with his feet tucked under the chair and his arms crossed over his chest. "What are you going to tell me?"

I shrug and throw my hands in the air, wide-eyed. "What do you want to know?"

"I want to know why you had all these bottles hidden in your drawer."

"Well," I begin, letting my guard down, "I needed them at the time. Everything was falling apart and the booze was all I could find to hold myself together. You already called it; I'm an alcoholic."

"That's it?"

"No, that's not it, but we're out of time, and if we're going to be breaking all the rules like this, then you're going to have to give me a minute to get used to it."

"Are you going to tell me what really happened to you?" he asks genuinely.

"Maybe I will tell you next time." I shuffle my papers and straighten my desk. "I don't tell my stories, either, you know," I say, wagging a notebook in his direction. "It's not an everyday occurrence that a patient blackmails me with my own bottles of alcohol, then feeds them to me and asks me the gory details of my life's story. So," I scoff loudly, "forgive me if I don't take to this like a duck to water."

"I don't have to feed it to you. I'm depleting my own warranty by bringing you these bottles. I just figured you could use a drink if you're going to spill your guts."

I throw the notebook into my desk drawer. Richard picks up his papers, puts his hat back on his head. As he walks out my door, I realize he didn't tell me anything about killing his mother.

JANUARY 31ST, 11:02 A.M.

Richard has settled into his seat in my office. His cap and newspapers sit on the corner of my desk. Four tiny bottles of Grey Goose have materialized.

"Frances started working at Shea Stadium in 1970. After the Mets won the World Series in '69 she figured she would make money at Shea because the team got so popular. The only job you could get there as a woman was waitressing or bathroom attending. She worked as a waitress. A beer maid, they called it. She would bring beers and hotdogs and what-not to the fans in their seats. Sometimes they would be drunk and she would get a big tip; sometimes they wouldn't give her anything."

"Did you ever get to go to games with her?" I ask.

"Nah, I've never been to Shea. I guess I never will. You a Mets fan, Sam?"

"Nope, Yankees fan." I reach for a Yankees flag behind my computer and wiggle it in Richard's direction.

"Yeah, Frances wasn't a Mets fan, either. She just went there for the money; she didn't care about baseball."

"How old were you when she started working there?"

"Well, it was 1970, so I must have been eight or nine. I was already at PS 78 then, I remember because all the kids there loved the Mets and everyone got so excited that my mom worked at Shea Stadium. They always asked me to bring them shit because they figured I got to go to games for free. I told them I did. I didn't want anyone to know that I had never seen a baseball game before."

"You *never* went to a ball game?"

"I couldn't go when I was growing up. Then I was in prison, so I don't get to go to baseball games."

"I guess that makes sense, but you've got to go. It's the best thing in the world. It's freedom, it's America, it's sanity. You have to go." I twirl the flag between my fingers.

"I'm stuck in a mental asylum and you're telling me about freedom and sanity?"

"Yes. Sometimes it's the only place I can go to feel alive." I'm imagining the field of Yankee Stadium; I'm trying to get the smell in my nose. I'm listening to Bob Sheppard and the crowd screaming. I'm watching the scoreboard light up, and suddenly, Richard brings me back.

"When I get out of here, I'll try to get to a game."

"You really should. Sorry, continue your story." I'm back in my office now, and the sounds of baseball have faded.

As Richard opens his mouth to continue, the back of my seat is bumped by my office door opening. I hear the creak of the hinge and the door swings open, and I turn around as fast as I can and scramble to my feet.

"Shawn!" *I can't believe I left my fucking door unlocked!*

"Hi, Doc. Is it time for our meeting?"

"Shawn, you startled me!" I push his shoulders and stumble over my chair, moving us into the hallway. There are four bottles of Grey Goose prominently displayed on my desk. I slam my door behind me. "I am in session with another patient now, Shawn. I can't have you just barging into my office like that, okay? I need you to knock on the door before you come in." I'm wild-eyed and disheveled, fearing I've been caught red-handed.

"Sorry, Doc. Thought it was time for our meeting." Did he see them? Did he see the bottles?

"Not now. Our sessions are at 2:00 p.m. Okay? It's not even noon yet. Go ahead and check your schedule. I have to get back to my other patient now, alright?" I'm sweating and out of breath. I turn into my office, lock the door and test the lock. I pull back the knob and it doesn't open. We're safe. I drop back down into my chair, and I see that Richard scurried the bottles away somewhere.

"Did you hide them?" I demand. "Jesus!"

He pulls open one side of his jacket like a man on the street selling stolen goods and shows me the necks of the bottles poking out of the inner pocket.

"Thank God." I let my head fall back onto my chair. I'm *already* hanging on by a thread here, and if Shawn saw this booze and says anything to anyone… My stomach is roiling with adrenaline, and my throat aches with worry.

"Where was I?" Richard says, pulling the bottles back out. He doesn't realize how close to caught we are, or seem to care.

"Shea Stadium, 1970." I'm still out of breath.

"Right, Shea. Frances started working there after the Mets won the World Series. Even though she didn't have to clean houses anymore and she had some money coming in, she still didn't get any happier.

"She would still sit in that yellow chair drinking all night, and she would still make me clean… I guess it must have been a really hard time for her, because when I was cleaning the kitchen, she would cry and tell me how no one appreciated her, and that she was always there doing things for everybody, but no one did anything for her.

"She never seemed to get a good night's sleep. She had headaches, and she would make me turn off all the lights and close the curtains when her head was hurting. She would tell me to shut up and get her some ice, and then she would lie on the couch with her feet up and moan. When the trains came by she would make a face like she was dying. I remember I wanted to help her so badly, but I was scared to go near her."

"Migraines, huh? I get those. Were you scared she was going to freak out if you approached her?"

"I never knew what she was going to be like. Even when she was in all that pain, she could still scream and hit me. Other times she would tell me I was the only person she cared about in the world. It was confusing, and I was too little to understand. So, it made me scared. Whenever she got nice, I was excited and I hoped it would last, but then she would pull the rug out from under me. It's like one day she loved me and needed me and the next day she hated me and said I ruined her life."

"You were so young then, Richard. There was no way you could understand." My heart is hurting for him. I have this image in my head of a tiny boy with ripped pants and a dirty muscle shirt holding a mop and staring at his ailing mother as the train passes overhead. All I want to do is jump inside this story and protect this little boy.

"Yeah. I remember feeling so confused. There was this one day, it was a bad day. It was a Saturday or Sunday, and the Mets game was in the afternoon. Frances was up for the whole night before, making me clean over and over. She had been drinking and crying again. Even when she was drunk or sad, she wouldn't ever go out in public looking a mess. And she wouldn't ever let anybody in the house unless she was ready for it. So she had gone to work at the game with her face all made up and a clean uniform on, and she was very pretty.

"It was a sunny day, and I went out with some of my friends in the neighborhood and we were horsing around. Frances always had me home before she got back from the games because she said she didn't want to worry about where I was, and she didn't want to burden the neighbors and ask them to look after me. I remember I was having fun with my friends that afternoon, and nobody had a watch on, so we kept guessing the time by looking at the sun. Nobody actually knew how to do that, but Jesse, a kid in the neighborhood, he always said it was noon so that none of us would have to go. Jesse was older, so we listened to him. After it had been noon for a few hours, we all said our goodbyes and went back to our houses."

I'm listening to Richard telling me the story, and scenes from *The Sandlot, A Bronx Tale* and *The Basketball Diaries* are playing in my head. Scenes with dirty boys playing outside. I'm imagining Richard again in a dirty muscle shirt, playing in a dusty lot, throwing big silver hubcaps like Frisbees.

"When I got in the front door, Frances was in her yellow chair. I said I was sorry that I was late. She was smoking cigarettes, and I remember the light kept catching the smoke coming out of her mouth, and I thought she looked like a dragon. She told me that something special happened at Shea Stadium that day. She told me that if I cleaned myself up, she would show me. I went to put on different clothes and wash my face, and I didn't hear her coming into my room. I was pulling up my shorts when I saw her in the doorway."

Richard is getting a faraway voice and isn't facing me anymore. He has his eyes fixed on the men up on the scaffold across the street. He's rubbing his thumbs together.

"She walked into my room with a big baseball bat in her hands. She held it out for me to see and told me it was Bat Day at Shea Stadium. When I reached out to touch the end of the bat, she started swinging it at me. She didn't swing it like a ball player; she choked up really high and hit me like she was hammering a nail. I tried to cover my head and duck and she yelled at me to stand up like a man. She said if I was going to disappoint her like a man, I should take a beating like a man. She just kept swinging and swinging. She finally stopped and fell on the floor crying. My room was all messed up now and everything was everywhere. She said, 'Look what you made me do.' Both of my arms were broken."

I can't help but gasp and cover my face when Richard says this. I blink away the tears that are forming in my eyes so he doesn't see them. His arms were broken; that's why he can't bend the left one properly and it juts out at that angle. He turns to me to finish the story.

"She saw that they were broken and I needed to get help. She went to her room to change her clothes and fix her makeup, and I tried to pull on my clothes even though it hurt so much to move my arms. I couldn't manage to get a shirt on, but I had on my pants and slip-on shoes. She came back to my room to get me; she wrapped her scarf around my shoulders and took me to the doctor down the street.

"In those days, the neighborhoods always had a doctor who took care of the kids when they got hurt. I don't know if anyone ever paid him or what. I never had an X-ray or a cast because we never went to the hospital. The doctor made me splints with pieces of wood wrapped in cotton and gauze. Then he bent my arms at the elbows and strapped them into slings. We walked home that night, and she told me that I couldn't tell anyone what happened because if people knew how bad I was they would take me away from her."

"Richard, you weren't *bad*. That wasn't your fault!" I wipe my eyes with the backs of my hands and reach for a tissue. "Your mom never should have done that to you." I'm not hiding the tears anymore, and as he sees them, he blushes. I know what it's like, I know what it feels like to get beaten and to believe the only thing I know how to believe: that's it's my own fault. That I brought this on myself. I know exactly how that feels. "She was sick, Richard. You couldn't have stopped her!"

"I know. She was sick. She was very sick." He's looking out the window again, and I know the story is over. He breathes a deep sigh and folds his hands in his lap.

"Is it your turn to talk yet?" he asks, finished with the emotional storytelling, trying to push it away from himself and lay the burden on me.

"I guess—I guess it is. But it's hard to focus on me after what you've just told me. I can't believe you grew up like that." Should I tell him about me? About Lucas? Should I tell him I know exactly how he feels?

"It wasn't always that way. There were days when everything was fine. She didn't hurt me all the time, but I figured the stories where things were good aren't the stories you want to hear. Right? In prison, every time they asked me about myself, they just wanted to hear the fucked-up stuff. No one wants to know that I had cereal and milk for breakfast, or that my mom always made sure I got good marks. They don't care that I never had to worry about food or clothes, even though we didn't have any money. They just get off on hearing the fucked-up stories."

"Did you tell anyone what you just told me?"

"Nah. I just kept to myself when I was in there. I did what they told me to do, but then I stayed alone and read my books. They said I could've gotten a degree in the joint with everything that I was reading."

"You really enjoyed the books, huh?" I'm not ready to tell

him about me just yet. I push the focus back to him and lean in to listen.

"Yeah. I always loved to read. Don't have to talk to the books."

I'm laughing inside at the image of Richard in a jail cell with pictures of Farrah Fawcett on the walls and cracked cement under his feet, reading dog-eared copies of *War and Peace* and the Koran.

"Did your arms heal properly?" I ask, even though I know they didn't.

"For the most part. This one bends funny, but it does everything a normal arm should do. I had to have those splints on for a long time, and it made it really hard to enjoy the summer, but I could still read my books. And when I stayed in the house, she didn't get mad as much, so maybe it was a good summer." He looks at me, at my clock and then at me again.

"You didn't tell me anything this time. So next time, you have to tell the stories." He stands up and gently pats me on the shoulder. He lumbers out of my office, and I'm left alone to rethink his story over and over. He grew up with no father, just like I did. He found himself abused and guilty and overwhelmed with rejection and confusion. Just like I did. Richard had to find a way out to save himself. Just like I do.

JANUARY 31ST, 12:01 P.M.

I'm licking the rest of the vodka off my lips as I walk toward my 12:00 p.m. addiction recovery group. I see all the group members sitting in their chairs in a haphazard semicircle, slouching, some in coats, some in pajamas. Nancy and Tashawndra are huddled close together, gossiping about something. Every now and again they look toward the other patients and laugh, mouths covered.

I'm walking in the door, pretending I didn't just drink two tiny bottles of vodka, and then I'm sitting on the edge of the desk. The blackboard behind me has scribbles from previous groups; words that look like *hypocrite, liar* and *fake*.

The best I could come up with today is to hand out printer paper, pass around a shoe box full of stubby crayons and ask the patients to draw their feelings.

As they pick their colors, I scroll through old pictures on my phone. Usually, when I break up w   ith someone, or stop sleeping with them, I go through all my photos of them and delete or edit them out of my life. For whatever reason, with AJ, I don't want to delete the photos. I'm scrolling through the ones we took at Nick's with the whole group— the ones where he's holding my boob and no one knows. I'm smirking to myself and trying not to laugh as I look through the pictures.

My mind is swirling back to images of AJ's naked, primate body, laughing on his bed, holding a cocktail in his hand. I'm entranced by a picture of him making the same face now. For a moment, I forget why I want to forget him. I forget why I decided to cut this cord, why I pulled away, why I let him fade. As I'm looking at his squinting eyes, I'm reminded why I jumped down the rabbit hole, and for a second my heart hurts as I remember the feeling of freedom I had when he first kissed me.

As I'm reminiscing, reconsidering all my decisions, wondering what prompted me to leave, feeling so lost and looking for a lifeboat to jump into, Lucy appears over my shoulder.

"Who's that? Your husband?"

"Lucy! You frightened me." I quickly lock my phone and put it facedown on the desk. "What's up?"

"He's cute, your husband. I knew you'd have a good-looking man."

"Ha, well, thank you, but that's not my husband. Just someone I used to know." The idea of climbing into AJ's lifeboat slips out of my mind and onto the floor, and rolls under the desk where I can no longer reach it.

Lucy hands me her drawing and asks if she's done. The page is covered edge to edge with pink crayon. I asked her to draw her feelings. Her feelings are pink. She pushed down so hard while she was coloring that large flakes of crayon stick up from the page. And just like that, AJ fades back into obscurity where he belongs.

I pick my phone back up to delete the pictures, and I see a text from Lucas: You're never going to make it out there without me. You need me. You'll kill yourself. You probably should.

This is the fourth text he's sent me since New Year's, and I turn my phone off without responding.

"Miss Sam, I was wondering." Nancy, clearly being egged on by Tashawndra. "Did none of you counselors ever have any drug problems?"

"I'm not sure, Nancy. Why do you ask?"

"Well, I think that if y'all had some drug problems, then y'all would be able to understand us better. But if y'all have been sober forever and don't even party, then how you suppose to help?"

"That's an interesting question, Nancy. Let's bring that discussion to the group, okay? What do you all think? Do you think it's necessary to know from experience what it's like to have an addiction in order to treat people who have addictions?" A warm vodka burp is climbing up my throat.

"I think that you'd be better at it if you knew how we felt." Stephan, trying to get the girls to notice him by defending their points.

"Do you think an oncologist would be better at treating cancer if she had cancer herself?" I ask, wondering why I'm playing devil's advocate.

"Well, nah. But maybe they could be better at making the patient feel good. Not necessarily at curing the disease, but their bedside manner, their compassion. Maybe those things would improve if they had their own experience." Stephan, now ignoring the girls, but intrigued by the topic.

"Okay, I agree." I engage with him. "I think if someone has a personal experience to draw from, they have a different level of insight into things, whether it's cancer, or addiction, or whatever."

"Yeah," Stephan replies, "but don't you think that sometimes they get caught up in their own experience, and they think the way they got better is the best way, or the only way, and sometimes it's better if you're *just* a teacher, or *just* a doctor, and you never went through it in your own life?"

"Stephan, I think that's a great point." I wave my arm around at the group. "Have you had experiences where other people in recovery have helped or hindered your progress? Tashawndra? Nancy? You ladies kicked off this discussion—what do you think?" I'm genuinely interested now, and I want to know if my diagnosis is actually helpful to my patients.

"Miss Sam, we just wanted to know if y'all ever partied. That's all."

The patients giggle and disengage, realizing that Tashawndra and Nancy were just trying to get gossip out of me, but now my head is filled with the notion that they may be onto something. Maybe it's a good thing that I'm a drunk. Maybe my history of choosing all the wrong men and all the wrong friends, and waking up with bloody scabs and black eyes, is somehow useful, somehow allows me to understand things differently than the other therapists.

I power on my phone and read Lucas's text message again. I delete it and the three others, along with his and AJ's photos.

FEBRUARY 2ND, 9:37 P.M.

I'm sitting at the dinner that we both knew was eventually going to happen. For whatever reason we decided that the fancier the restaurant, the better. I imagine it's because we both have some sense of decorum and would be less inclined to stab each other in the face if we were among better company.

Lucas is intelligent enough and aware enough to know exactly why we're here, but he's choosing not to acknowledge it. Instead of filling up any silence with some abusive rhetoric or regurgitated political views, he is slipping in compliments and showering me with unwarranted and unearned accolades. This may be a desperate attempt to stop the oncoming train, but I have somehow become immune to his charms. Despite his efforts to derail my intentions, I am now breaking up with him.

I feel like I'm in a movie, watching a character playing Sam James breaking up with Lucas instead of actually doing it myself. I see the camera panning around the restaurant at the two-tops occupied by wealthier, better-suited-for-each-other and happier people. I see the delicate plates of precariously balanced microgreens atop tiny portions of tuna tartare with some swath of green sauce. As the plates pass our table, perched on the upstretched arm of a strapping young server, the focus comes to Sam and Lucas.

Lucas is leaning back in his chair. His left leg is crossed over his right, and the stem of his wineglass is held tightly between his fingers. He's looking at me, but not looking at me. We are between courses, and we have at least a few minutes before someone approaches the table again. If ever there were a time in which I could blurt these terrible statements, that time is now.

"I can't do this anymore." The words are coming out of my mouth; I can even feel each one reverberating the vocal cords in my throat, but it doesn't feel like I'm the one saying them.

It's like watching a building burn. Slowly each room lights up and gets consumed. My head feels full, like I'm underwater. He's admitting to sleeping with Claire the cocktail waitress. He is begging for forgiveness but I'm just starting to feel hot. Now it feels like I'm *in* the burning building.

He starts crying at the dinner table. I'm embarrassed for him, and I don't want the stares that are coming our way. He is a mess. He goes back and forth between blubbering that he isn't being a good boyfriend to me (which is surreal because he has *never* been good to me, but he has also never admitted it to my face), and then he rages that it's not his fault and he has a problem, and isn't it my job to fix problems?

Lucas swivels and sways and his Jekyll and Hyde are melting into one sobbing disaster. Our waitress has the politesse to pretend this scene isn't unfolding and gently places our main courses before us.

I have never felt less interested in a steak. Lucas is probing his cavatelli with his fork and looking up at me with puppy-dog eyes. I am critically studying his face, wondering if there is a human in there somewhere. Wondering if he lost himself so badly that he will never be found again. Wondering why

I bothered to look for him in the first place. The emptiness I see in him is all-consuming and black. He isn't in there. No one is. And I have been waiting to see this for as long as I can remember.

"I can't lose you. I know that I need to get better, and I know that I can't keep doing what I've been doing, but I will change. I promise you, just please don't leave me." He sips his wine in tiny little sips between each statement.

Just as I'm about to respond, he clears his throat, and there's a notable change in him. His eyes seem to refocus and his brow furrows. His air of pathetic disaster seems to disappear and he re-forms into a cutthroat businessman with a billion-dollar merger on the table. He puts his wineglass down and signals to the waitress. The tears he was just crying don't seem to have reddened his eyes or left marks on his cheeks. Instead, it seems I imagined them; there are no traces of actual emotion anywhere on him. As the waitress approaches, he orders a double vodka martini.

"Sam, this isn't a reasonable negotiation. I am pouring my heart out here, and you're not even the slightest bit accommodating. How do you expect me to respond to this?"

"Wait—what?" I'm off balance.

"I ask you to move in with me," he begins, "and you refuse. I try to get you to understand the way you should behave, and you defy me. If you could ever be bothered to actually focus on me, and give me some of your precious attention, then maybe I wouldn't be sleeping with other women. Did you ever think about your role in all this?"

"You're telling me it's my fault that you're fucking other people?" I'm smiling and incredulous.

"No, Samantha, you should learn to listen. I said 'your role'; I didn't place all the blame squarely on your shoulders. I know I have some part in this."

"You know you have *some* part in this? *Some* part? I didn't stick your dick in someone else, you did. I didn't throw myself into walls, I didn't slam my face into toilet seats, I didn't punch the sides of my own head. *You did.*"

"And I've apologized for that. You know I have a temper. If you would just learn to keep your mouth shut, then I wouldn't have to get angry with you." He drains his drink and signals for another martini. The little stick with the olives is about to fall out of the glass.

I begin to realize that I'm negotiating with an emotional terrorist and I will never be able to get through to him. My eyes glaze over and my consciousness fades out of the conversation. I can feel my mouth moving, but I don't know what I'm saying. I sense the cool of the wine going down my throat, but I don't feel like I'm drinking. I see my hand reaching into my bag for my wallet, but I don't remember asking for the check. I hear the scrape of the chair as I push back and stand up, but I don't know the last words I said. I feel my thumbnail jimmy my key ring as I remove Lucas's keys and replace them with his copy of mine. I see the prideful smiles of the staff as they watch me go, but I don't feel my feet hitting the ground.

I am a house after a hurricane. I have to wait for the wind to stop blowing, but when it does, I will dig the debris out of the living room. I will sand down the floorboards and refinish them. I will pull out the broken windows and install new ones. I will walk around the neighborhood until I find my roof. I will drag the roof back to the front yard piece by piece; I will put it back together again. And the next time the cruel wind blows, and it pounds on my door saying "Little pig, little pig, let me in," I will say "Not by the hair of my chinny-chin-chin."

FEBRUARY 7TH, 11:22 A.M.

"The first time I was arrested was in 1977. Do you know about the '77 blackout?" Richard hands me two tiny bottles of Jack Daniel's and takes off his hat. Richard's plan to force me to treat him like an equal through blackmail has morphed into an easy routine of drinking and sharing stories. I need him to open up to me, and, so far, I've been keeping my own stories at bay to allow him to do that.

"Yeah, I wasn't born yet, but I know the story." After we almost got caught the other day, I brought in two small plastic cups from the water cooler today. "I'm pouring those in here; can't be too careful." He nods at me and hands me the other two bottles, as well. I open them and dump the whiskey into the little cups.

"Well, during the blackout, I was about to turn sixteen and I was acting a fool with my friends. We were bored, it was hot, and the lights were out, so we went with so many of the other kids and started looting the stores." He gathers the empties, tucks them into an unseen pocket.

"Are you serious? You were such a good kid, I thought." I wipe the whiskey from my lips.

"I was a teenager. Your mind's not right when you're a teenager."

"That's true." I lean back with my hands behind my head, listening to Richard's story. I used to steal bottles of liquor all the time. Didn't need a blackout. I remember wearing an oversize pair of pants, cinched at the waist with a ratty leather belt. I had on a regular pair of pants under them, and I would slide bottles into the pockets of the regular pants. The giant jeans would obscure the bulges, and the cashier would usually throw me out for being too young before he noticed I was stealing.

"We stole booze from liquor stores, and we went to get cigarettes and sodas. We thought we would never get caught because everyone was doing it. There were fires everywhere. The cops had no way of managing everything. But we got caught. All of us. Me and Jesse, and a bunch of other kids. We got thrown into the back of a paddy wagon and taken to booking. I remember we were so scared. We didn't say anything to each other in the back of the wagon.

"When we got to booking, it was so crowded. There was a long line of kids getting fingerprinted and photographed. I remember my hands were so sweaty by the time I had to get fingerprinted that they had to roll my fingers in the ink over and over again. I didn't have a driver's license, and back then none of us kids had any ID, and because it was so crowded, they just asked us for our names, and took us at our words. I didn't tell them my real name because I was afraid. I was reading *The American* at the time, so I told them my name was Henry James. And they printed me and booked me as Henry James. I wish I had a copy of that mug shot."

"They didn't even bother to check? You couldn't have gotten away with that." I finish sipping my drink.

"No, they didn't check anything. They were so crowded

because all the kids were looting, and there was so much chaos, it didn't seem to matter. Jesse and I were in the same holding cell, and there were so many other people in there, and it was so hot. Then they started bringing in all the blacks and the yellows, and it got to be a real mess."

"Blacks and yellows? We don't use those terms anymore. Come on."

"Back then we did. It was a really racist time. That's what's crazy about this story. All the mick cops were so racist that when the cells started to get too full, they just let the white kids go. They came into the cell with their billy clubs and pushed the blacks and the Asians out of the way, and they grabbed the white kids by the collars and they told us to leave. They were filling up the cells with just the blacks and the Asians. They let us go, me and Jesse."

"They just sent you home? They let you walk out the door? Did you get fined? A summons?"

"No. Nothing at all. It was like it never happened. It was so chaotic, and then suddenly Jesse and I are back out on the streets. We had to walk home because the trains weren't running, and it was so hot out. The air was thick and it made it hard to breathe. We kept running and then slowing down to look at everything that happened. There were cars turned over and buildings on fire. There were smashed windows and glass everywhere. People were just standing in the streets looking around, trying to figure out what to do. It smelled so bad, and all you could hear was the crackle of the fires."

"I remember seeing footage of it on TV, but I can't imagine what it would have been like. I was here for the 2003 black-out, but it wasn't anything like what you're describing." I put my feet up on my desk and lean back in my chair.

"It was a crazy time. I got home that night and Jesse left me at my door, and we promised we would never tell anyone that we got arrested. Jesse was over eighteen at the time, so it would've been worse for him if anyone ever found out. He told me the name he used was Jim Morrison."

"Did it ever come up for you again? That you had been arrested?"

"Yeah, of course. Because my fingerprints are my fingerprints. So when I went to prison, I was already in the system. But they didn't know my real name. I went to prison only two years after the blackout, but I still didn't have any ID. And I had no family, and no one to vouch for me, so I think there was some problem with my name. After the day I got booked in the blackout, I started liking to be called Henry, so sometimes I would tell people that was my real name."

"Sort of like a different identity, huh?" I wish I could have a different identity sometimes, hide behind something more resilient than just my professional reputation.

"Yeah, something like that. Maybe I wanted to be somebody else, because when I looked at my real life, it didn't feel so good to be me."

"When did you start going by Richard again?"

"I guess I started thinking of myself as Richard again when I was in prison. But no one calls you by your name in prison, so it was just in my head. When I got out, and I went to the halfway house, that's when everyone started calling me Richard again."

"What did Frances call you?"

"She called me Richie." He's reaching into his pocket for more nips that we haven't drunk yet. He's pulling out two bottles of Patrón. I feel myself stopping him as he puts the bottles on my desk.

"Let's not drink any more today. You've already told me your story for the day, and we don't need them."

"You sure? You haven't told me *anything* yet. You don't need one?" He dangles the bottle between his fingers.

"No. I need to do this with a clear head." I draw in a deep, cleansing breath and clutch the arms of my chair. "You asked me a few weeks ago why I stashed those bottles in my office."

"Yeah, I remember." He holds the bottles between his knees. Not quite accessible, but not quite put away, either.

"Well, I've been thinking a lot these days, and I'm getting a better understanding of why I drink so much. And I don't think it's just about fucked-up things in my life." I squeeze my eyes shut, not sure I want to see his reaction.

"I know."

"You do?" I open one eye to look at him. "Why do you think I drink?"

"People don't drink because fucked-up things happen, Sam. People drink because *they're* fucked up."

"You know I'm fucked up?" Now both eyes are open, and my hands slump down into my lap.

"I know you're not happy. I know you're not okay. I know you're holding on to the strings of your life and you feel like they're slipping through your fingers."

"How the hell do you know that?"

"All you have to do is look, Sam. You're not fooling anyone."

"Richard, I'm fooling *everyone*." Doesn't he see the professional superhero? Doesn't he know I've been hiding behind this mask of perfection at work, and no one is the wiser?

"That just means that no one's looking."

"And maybe that's the biggest problem of all."

"So why *do* you drink so much?"

I'm already terrified to share this story with him, and he's so astute and insightful, it's making it harder for me to admit the whole truth. "I have… I have this problem, this disease."

My heart is beating in my throat, and I'm preparing myself to say the words out loud for the first time. "This horrible thing. And I always sort of knew that I had it, and I always wanted to fix it, but I never got formally diagnosed. And I just did." My mouth turns into a dry field of razor blades and my stomach twists into adrenaline knots. I can't say it. I can't say the words out loud.

"You have borderline personality disorder?" Richard says it for me.

"What?" The saliva catches in my throat. "Do you know what that is? You know about borderline personality disorder?" The words fall out of my mouth like vomit.

"Yes. Frances was borderline."

"Oh, my God." I'm astounded, stupefied. He knows what this is? He knew that I had it? "Okay, enough. I can't talk about this with you." I immediately feel dizzy and slack-jawed. Where the fuck is the catharsis? I thought admission was supposed to make me feel better!

"You can't talk about it with anyone else."

My head is in my hands, the tears are flowing like rivers, and the slaps they make on the desk are audible. I need to escape.

"I know what it's like. I know you're suffering." Richard's voice is soft and soothing. I can't respond. The words are all stuck in my throat, and I can't make sense of anything.

"It's not your fault, you know. You're just sick. It doesn't mean you're bad."

"Please, stop." I choke back the tears and grab the bottle of Patrón from his lap. I crack the top and pour it down my throat. Richard obligingly opens the other bottle and hands it to me with one hand while taking the empty away with the other. I drink the rest of the tequila and throw my head back against my desk chair. My hair is down and it's stuck under my head and it hurts, but I don't move and I squeeze my eyes shut and let the tears dribble into my ears. I take deep breaths until the lump is out of my throat. I'm covering my face with my clammy hands, and I know it won't make him leave, but that's all I want him to do because now he knows too much. I should have kept my goddamned mouth shut.

"This wasn't a good idea. I can't talk to you like this. I can't tell you what's happening with me. I am here to help you; you're not supposed to have to worry about me. I don't care what fucking deal we made. This isn't right."

"I'm not leaving."

"You *are* leaving. We can't do this anymore. We can't have these meetings anymore. Richard, I seriously can't do this." I've held this secret in—safely, tightly—under my skin and my muscles and my rib cage, down in the pit of my stomach where it belongs, and now it's out, and it feels like I've released a toxic gas into the office and it's going to suffocate me.

He's leaning forward in the patient chair. He isn't leaving. Now he's leaning closer to me, looking at me, and I feel like his ice-blue eyes are piercing my soul and he knows something about me that no one else in this world knows, and he's a patient in my office.

I have to get out.

I have to get out.

I have to get out.

I'm breathing too quickly, my heart is pounding, and my hands are sweating.

I have to get out.

FEBRUARY 9TH, 7:21 P.M.

I realize as I sit in the Laundromat waiting for a machine to open up that I will have to do laundry much more frequently now that I'm not with Lucas. I hear the rhythmic whoosh and clink of the washing machines and begin to wander to the back of my mind, where I store all the secrets. I watch the scenes between Lucas and me in my mind as if they were in an old movie. Grainy, speckled and faded.

I remember the beginning, when it was all exciting, and I could fool myself into thinking the red flags didn't exist. I see him bringing me flowers, and I pretended they weren't flowers seeking forgiveness. I am looking at scenes that I should have seen differently when I was living them. Scenes of him coming out of the women's bathroom, followed by a guilty brunette. I see scenes of him hiding bottles and stashes of drugs in my apartment and his. I shake my head, as if to dispel the memories, but instead it brings up the worst ones. Instead of seeing his alcoholism, his drug addiction, his cheating, I see the beatings now.

I watch as he pulls me by my hair into the bathroom. I clutch his wrist with both hands to displace the weight and prevent him from tearing my hair out. I watch him squeeze shampoo onto my head so it dripped down and burned my eyes. I see myself reaching up for a towel to clean out my eyes, and Lucas taking advantage of my exposure and clubbing my ribs with closed fists. I hear the ringing in my ears that I would always hear when he open-palm slapped the sides of my head. He would push me closer and closer to the toilet. I held the bowl to pull myself up, and when I got close enough, he would push my head into the bowl and slam the seat down. The marks were always covered by my hair.

I'm looking at housekeepers and college students taking their laundry out of the washers and moving them over to dryers, but I'm paralyzed by the memories and I can't get up. I remember the metallic taste of blood in my mouth. I remember the feeling that if I just wait it out, he will eventually relent. I remember knowing that when he lit a cigarette, it would be over. I would always wait for the scratch of the lighter flint, and then I knew I could begin to heal again. He always pulled me into the bathroom, and only now, in this Laundromat, do I realize it was to give himself an easier cleanup. He didn't want to get blood on his furniture. In all that rage, and being so drunk, he was still a perfectionist.

These memories are filling me up and the adrenaline is making me shake. As the tears begin to fall out of my eyes, I throw my laundry bag over my shoulder and stalk back to my apartment, clothes uncleaned.

I open my apartment door and throw the laundry bag onto the floor. The tears are coming quickly now, and I fumble with a corkscrew and a bottle of wine. I told myself I was just keeping it here for guests and I didn't need to drink it myself. I fill up a giant stemless glass and take down two hearty gulps. With my back against the fridge, I slide down to the floor and pull out my phone.

I'm backsliding. I can feel the progress I've tried to make

toward putting myself back together again falling out of me with my tears. I can see the shadow of my future self gathering in a puddle on the kitchen floor. I'm looking around for old reliefs, for old solutions to old problems. I turn to old faithful, the best of old solutions, the wine, and I keep drinking.

My shakes have settled, but I can't clear my head. I'm filled with feelings of hate and resentment. Feelings of fear and worthlessness. I think of Richard's blackmail, the things he knows I've done. Adelle, Eddie, Jenni and her heroin-addicted sister. Shawn's medicine. The wine is helping but it's not enough. I need something to fill me up. Something to make me feel loved. I need AJ.

I unlock my phone and scroll through the old messages. I can't remember the last time I spoke to AJ. I haven't even been to Nick's. Come to think of it, this is the first time I have drunk myself stupid in what feels like ages. I look at the wineglass with a red ring of my old friend at the bottom. I fill it up again, but this time with white wine that I pull from the fridge. I told myself that my guests should have options. When's the last time I've had a guest over? I have to concentrate on focusing my eyes on the texts from AJ. The last time he wrote to me, he asked me to come to Nick's and I turned him down. And now I think I'm about to go crawling back.

The wine is going down like a two-dollar hooker and I can't seem to drink it fast enough. My tolerance isn't what it used to be, and the vague, downy haze of alcohol is descending upon me. I open up the pictures on my phone and remind myself what I'm missing. I've deleted most of his pictures by now, but I saved just a few. The best pictures. I try to bring back the old butterflies to my stomach. I try to let the alcohol make decisions for me.

I see the response I wrote to AJ, and I read it again and again. "Have fun without me." Have fun without me. And that's exactly what he's been doing. He had fun before me, he had fun with me, and he's now having fun without me. AJ hasn't changed. Lucas hasn't changed. But I have. I've changed. And the old solutions only solve the old problems, and this—this isn't what I need right now. I'm looking into the wineglass. The pinkish orange of the mix of red and white wine. I look at this bulbous glass and wonder why it had so much power.

I'm standing at the sink now, pouring the rest of the glass down the drain. The alcohol will not make these decisions for me. I pick the bottle of red and the bottle of white up off the floor and pour them into the sink. The smell is tickling my nose. I open the freezer and dump out the Tito's. Another offering for guests. I look to the living room and see the two bottles of scotch on the bookcase. Those bottles I had saved for so long to make it look like I could have alcohol in my apartment without drinking it. There's less than a shot in each one. I methodically remove them and pour the contents into the sink. The scotch burns my eyes. The combination of scents in making me gag; it's like the vomit I've hurled into my office garbage can so many mornings.

The bottles clank loudly in the recycling bag as I walk it down to the trash room. Back in my apartment, I wash the wineglass with apple-scented dish soap and peel off my clothes. I drop them on the laundry bag and step into my shower. I turn up the heat as high as it goes and watch as my skin turns pink.

FEBRUARY 10TH, 9:13 A.M.

I walk into the morning meeting and see everyone is already inside, sitting down at the conference table. There are packets distributed at every seat, and some of the staff is flipping through them. A couple of security guards, orderlies and custodians are standing along the back wall. They're all holding copies of these packets, as well. I have no idea how I'm late for this; I'm never late for this.

David pulls out an empty seat beside him and calls me over with a twitch of his head. He hasn't examined his packet yet. I plunk myself down in the seat next to him, and he taps his watch and gives me a condescending eye. *So, I'm late. So what? At least I didn't sleep with Julie.*

"Now that we're all here—" Rachel looks directly at me "—we can begin. Obviously, you've noticed we have some newcomers in our meeting today. These guys are here representing their teams and participating in this important meeting. For those of you who don't know, this is Sal from the maintenance staff—" Sal smiles and waves hello "—Gerard and Abdul, two of our orderlies—" Gerard lifts his coffee toward the crowd, and Abdul keeps his head down, squinting at the packet "—and this is Raul from security." Raul remains stoic and motionless. His gigantic steroid biceps are bulging against his uniform, and the little telltale acne spots are noticeable even through the fabric.

"I've asked that they join us today because we need to address some things that have been going on here that I'm beginning to get concerned about.

"The packets I've distributed are the revised ethical guidelines at Typhlos. All of you were given copies of these upon your hire, and you should be familiar with everything in here. Now and again, we get some new language from the administration, and sometimes there are new items added. I am going to need everyone's signature on a sheet that I'm passing around, indicating that you have read and understand these guidelines."

The social-work and counseling staff already have their noses buried in the packets. Except for Shirley. Shirley couldn't give a shit about ethical guidelines. She's been working here for probably five incarnations of these procedures and couldn't be asked to modify her behavior to please any administrators.

Gary is noisily flipping pages back and forth, trying to determine if he is breaking any of the rules. David's leaning back in his chair, drinking a coffee. He's ignoring the packet, but will surely study every word as soon as he's safely hidden in his office.

"You'll see in your packets," Rachel continues, "that you are not only expected to adhere to these policies while you are on the unit, but also any time you're in a public place. That includes the subways, out at dinner with your family and anywhere that you could be viewed as a representative of this institution."

"I'm not allowed to *curse* while I'm out at a bar in Bushwick?" Gary.

"Gary, you don't need to take every sentence literally. We're asking that you follow basic guidelines of ethical behavior, general decorum, because whether you're here or not, you work here, and we need to keep up a professional appearance both on and off the unit."

"Where is this coming from?" I toss my packet back onto the conference table and lean back like I'm above it all, but inwardly realizing and terrified that this is about me.

"Well, it's coming from a string of events that have been happening around here that seem to indicate some ethical violations, not to mention legal violations. So, to cover all our bases and keep the playing field level, we are *all* going to re-acquaint ourselves with the expected behavior of staff here.

"And this goes for all of you." She points around the table with a sideways index finger and thumb extended like a pistol. "Psychologists, counselors, security guards, everyone. No one is out of bounds here—even the psychiatrists have copies of this, and they'll be expected to sign the sheet, as well."

"What kinds of events?" Julie, knowing full well she would never be in violation of anything.

"Well, Sal and members of his staff have been finding alcohol on the unit." My ears *scream* a piercing squeal into my brain and my body catches fire. I am suddenly aware of my hands and arms, and I have no idea what to do with them. How can I ensure that I don't draw attention to myself? *Stay calm. No one is looking at you.*

"Alcohol?" David leans forward and sits at attention.

"Yes, small bottles like the ones you'd find in a hotel minibar. They've been found in the garbage cans of the men's rooms, in various group rooms, and pieces of broken bottles have been found strewn about." *Dammit, Richard!*

"They're glass? I always thought those things were made of plastic." Gary.

"Turns out they're glass, and there have been a lot of them.

Now, the patients don't have access to the outdoors, as you know. The smoking balcony is as much outdoor space as they've got while they're here, unless we're on supervised outings. Obviously, with the weather, there haven't been too many of those. Visitors are always searched, but these bottles are very small and I suppose could be snuck in."

"Is it possible that a patient brought a stash on intake?" Abdul, the orderly. *Oh, God, don't say* stash*!*

"It's very unlikely." Gerard, the other orderly. "We do thorough checks of all personal belongings whenever a new patient arrives. No alcohol, weapons, drugs or anything like that would be permitted. If anything is found, it's confiscated."

"Where does it go when it gets confiscated? Is there an evidence locker, or a storage room or something? If someone came in with a bunch of mini-bottles, and they're somewhere on the unit, then someone could have found them." Gary is beginning to sound guilty with all these questions. I hope the rest of the staff is getting the same impression, and I pray no one is looking at me. I'm holding my fist up to my chin, looking upon everyone like I'm completely disinterested.

"We keep an inventory of all the confiscated items before they're locked in a locker in the security office. No one has ever brought in a stash of liquor." Gerard will not be held responsible for this.

"And there's at least one of us in the office at all times, so no one would have the opportunity to walk in and steal things. Only the security officers know the code to the locker." Raul will not be held responsible for this.

"Are the bottles you're finding full or empty?" I will not be held responsible for this.

"Empty, obviously," Shirley sneers at me.

"I don't know that it's obvious they're empty. Patients could be leaving them for other patients. We've seen things like this before. Remember when Frankie and Harry did the Valium scavenger hunt? Leaving cryptic notes about the hidden locations of pills one of them was prescribed and the other one wanted? We have about a hundred alcoholics in here. It could be the answer." Create a diversion, make the staff look at everyone but me. *They can't fingerprint the bottles, can they? They can't trace them back to Richard, can they? Or me?*

"The bottles Sal's team have found have all been empty. Although it's true that patients have been known to find ways to get drugs and alcohol onto the unit before, I'm not sure that's what's happening here. What's very strange is that these are premium, top-shelf liquors. It's not tiny bottles of Georgi. We're talking Grey Goose, Patrón, expensive brands. And not one or two bottles here and there. It's added up to quite a few in the past couple of weeks." Rachel is ensuring she never looks at any particular staff member for too long while relaying the details of the situation. She doesn't want to appear accusatory or alienate anyone, but I can't help feeling eyes on me.

FEBRUARY 14TH, 11:01 A.M.

Richard seems uptight this morning. He sits rigidly, and keeps fidgeting with his papers and his fingers and his zippers. I'm eyeing him suspiciously, when he speaks.

"I know that you had a really hard time telling me about your diagnosis. So I figured it's only fair that I tell you the story that's hardest for me."

"We need to talk before you start in on any stories today." I lean forward with my elbows on my knees like Johnny Bench and look him square in the face. "Have you been leaving the empties around the unit?"

"What do you mean? The nips?" He snaps out of his trance.

"Yeah. What have you been doing with all the empty bottles? The custodians and other patients have been finding the empties. You can't blackmail me with this booze and this secret if you're gonna get yourself caught as well, you know."

"I've been throwing them away. Separately, in different garbage cans all across the institution. Never near your office, never near my room. Public places. Where it could be anyone. They're not going to know it's me. And they're certainly not going to know it's *you*."

"We had a meeting about the bottles. The staff is getting

suspicious. I've let this go on for long enough but now that's it—this is over. I can't have the bottles in here anymore. Keep them away from me and this office. I'm serious."

"Because you think they know it's you?"

"It doesn't matter why! It's over now. I am not drinking anymore, I'm definitely not drinking with *you* anymore, and we are done with this conversation. Now, please, go ahead with your story." I cross my arms indignantly and, with wide eyes and furrowed brows, challenge him to defy me.

"That doesn't mean that you're off the hook, you know. Even if we don't drink them together, I still have your stash. The deal remains the same." He points his huge finger at me.

"Fine." I nod along with him. "But they are not to come into this office again, do you understand me? I don't even know why we were drinking them to begin with! You should have just kept your contraband to yourself and not opened this can of worms. And you better keep them seriously well hidden because the staff is on high alert now."

"I figured some social lubrication would help you share your stories, get on board with our agreement."

"It would take a lot more than two airplane bottles to get me drunk enough to say yes. I said yes because you're black-mailing me, not because I'm hammered."

"Noted. I will keep the rest of your stash. As collateral."

"Right, collateral. I understand. No more booze in this office." I lean back in my chair defiantly.

He sits uneasily, waiting for the mood in the room to return to normal. He cracks his neck once to the left and twice to the right, and opens his mouth to begin.

"I have never told another living soul on this planet what happened that day." He's been rehearsing this.

"Why are you telling me?" My voice is soft and low.

"You're the only person I've ever met who could use this story to get better."

"You think you're going to make me better?" I smile and nearly scoff at him.

"Just listen to me, Sam. Please." My sarcasm and incredulity are not welcome for this story. "I was eighteen. I had been seeing a girl for a while, and she was probably borderline, too. That's something I learned in prison—that you end up attracted to people who have the same traits as your parents. Even if it's the bad traits. Because it's what you're used to and what you know. So, I guess I was attracted to women who were manipulative and kind of crazy—" He stops himself midsentence. "I'm sorry, I don't mean to call *you* crazy, it's just that borderline is really confusing. One day you're the best thing ever, and the next day you're the worst. I couldn't ever tell who I was going to get."

I nod and sip my coffee. I wave my hand, indicating he should continue.

"Anyway, I was dating this girl, and I think Frances was jealous, because when I would get dressed to take her out, Frances would end up throwing some kind of fit, and I would usually have to stay home and take care of her instead. I would sneak out to meet my girlfriend sometimes after Frances passed out at night. Her name was Samantha, actually. Huh." He scoffs at this realization.

"After a while, Frances started going out on dates, maybe to even the score with me since I was dating. Men were always falling in love with her. She would stay with them for a while, and then get bored, or angry, or tired of them, and move on to the next one. She was always very nice to me when she had just broken up with a man. This one time, there was a guy who came to the house, though normally I never met any of her dates.

"She had been in such a good mood for a long time, and I thought she was getting better. But, this one night, a man showed up to pick her up for a date. I was taller than him, and I think that was a problem, because he was immediately mean to me. He was condescending and rude, and he grabbed Frances, hard, by the waist. I remember I wanted to hit him, but then she started lacing into me along with him. They were both drunk already. They went out. I waited up for her at home. I was worried because he didn't seem like such a nice guy. I told Samantha that I couldn't see her that night and I had to stay home.

"Frances came back very late. It was spring and the sun was starting to come up earlier. It was already getting light out when she walked in the door. I had seen her angry so many times before. And she had taken out a bad night on me so many times before. But I had never seen her like this. Her dress was torn and her makeup was all messed up. She and the guy must have gotten into a fight." Richard starts breathing deeply, seeming to concentrate on pulling up the memories. He closes his eyes and continues.

"I remember she had dirt streaked on her shins. I was scared when she came home. She asked me why I bothered to wait for her. She said if I was just going to let her go out with a monster, then I shouldn't bother to wait up and see if she's okay. She said I knew she wouldn't be okay and I shouldn't have let her go. She had a cigarette in her mouth and started tearing through the drawers and cupboards in the kitchen. She picked up a frying pan and came after me. I was much bigger than her, but I still ducked and tried to cover my head. She kept hitting me over and over again with the frying pan, telling me that I don't love her, and I never should have let her go out with that man. She put the cigarette out on the back of my neck." Richard absentmindedly touches the burn scar on his neck as he tells me this.

"When the frying pan broke off its handle, I remember thinking it would be over. But no. Something bad had happened to her, and she needed someone to blame. She needed to even the score. She kicked me; she threw everything she could find at me. After a while, I just snapped. I couldn't take it anymore. She was whipping me with an umbrella and I wrestled it out of her hands. I threw it on the floor in the kitchen. Everything was on the floor. I have never heard anyone scream like she did when I stood up to defend myself. She sounded like the devil's rage. She started pummeling me with her fists and I tried to hold her by her shoulders and get her to stop hitting me, but she wouldn't stop. She was screaming and punching and flailing all over the place, and I was trying to keep her at an arm's length so she couldn't reach me. I was walking her into the corner of the kitchen so her arms couldn't swing, but as I was…but…as I was pushing her through the kitchen, I stepped on something and I fell forward." Richard is trembling and out of breath.

"I was still holding her shoulders, and I crashed into her. She lost her balance and fell backward and I fell on top of her. She hit her head on the steps into the pantry, and it made her forehead bounce forward and smack me in the face. I knew something was wrong immediately because of the silence. Her face was frozen in a horrible contorted scream. I didn't know if I had cracked her skull or broken her neck or what happened, but somehow I knew that she was dead. Just like that. One second I was trying to stop her from hitting me, and the next second she was dead. I remember I sat next to her and held a handkerchief to her face to see if she was breathing. I didn't know how to check for a pulse. I was on the floor trying to catch my breath, and the sun was up now, and then I heard Mrs. Choi slapping at the screen door."

My heart is trapped in my throat and I can't swallow. Richard's enormous presence is softening and shrinking, and he's turning into an eighteen-year-old boy in my patient chair.

"Mrs. Choi lived in another apartment in the house we lived in. She knew that Frances would hit me, and when she heard the screams, she sometimes came over to try to save me. Frances wouldn't hit me in front of anyone else.

"I heard Mrs. Choi slapping at the door, and I panicked because I knew something was wrong. But the door was never locked, so she came inside anyway. She must've been terrified. The scene was such a mess. There was the broken frying pan, the umbrella, me covered in booze and burns and welts, and Frances on the floor. All the glass and the debris all around us, and me out of breath, heaving into a handkerchief. She immediately ran out the door and called the police. It must have taken them twenty minutes to get there, but I didn't move. I couldn't move. An ambulance came, too.

"The ambulance workers rushed in and asked me what happened. I couldn't say anything. I started throwing up in the middle of the kitchen. The EMTs were doing all sorts of things to Frances and screaming at me to answer them. The cops didn't even come inside yet, but I could see them standing at the front door. One EMT asked me if I was okay, and I didn't say anything. I could see Mrs. Choi standing outside with the police, and she was just shaking her head and holding up her palms. I remember shivering and getting sick over and over again until I couldn't get sick anymore. An EMT covered me with a big wool blanket. Everything else is a blur.

"The police came inside and asked me questions, but it felt like they were talking in a different language. I couldn't understand them, so I couldn't answer them. I didn't know what had happened, and I didn't know what to say. I found myself in the back of a cop car, and I still had the EMT blanket, and two cops in the front were talking, but I couldn't really hear them. They took me to the hospital, and I went to one of those little curtained areas. The cops and nurses were in conversation, but I couldn't hear anything. It felt like the blackout again—there was all this chaos, but no sounds. I don't know how long I was there. Must have been hours. They brought me papers to fill out, and they kept asking me questions. I couldn't answer anything. I couldn't remember anything else until I got to the jail cell."

My mind seems to be operating in slow motion and I'm taking longer than I should to manage a response to this. "Richard, that wasn't your fault. How could you have been convicted of murder if you didn't murder her? That was obviously self-defense. That wasn't your fault!" I'm holding my hands over my mouth, speaking between the cracks in my fingers.

"Like I said before, you're the only living soul who knows that story."

"Why didn't you tell them? Why didn't you show them the bruises and the burns?" I'm nearly hysterical. I'm crying and pleading and trying to change the past.

"I couldn't. I couldn't bring shame to her by telling anyone what she had done to me. All I felt was guilt. For as long as I can remember, I knew that everything bad that happened to me was my fault. Frances had spent my whole life telling me that it was my fault that she hit me, my fault that she drank, my fault that she couldn't work. Even that night she told me it was my fault that man had hurt her." The way that he's retelling this story makes me feel like he still believes this. And to me, his story is all too familiar.

"Are you telling me there was no investigation? How is

that possible? How it is even remotely possible that you were thrown in prison for half your life on a fucking whim?"

"It wasn't a whim. It's hard to explain." He shakes his head and turns his eyes to the ground.

"I can't believe you wouldn't stand up for yourself and you went to prison for *half your life* as a result."

"I didn't go to prison because I didn't stand up for myself, Sam." His lips are trembling. "I went to prison because I *did*."

I'm crying hard now, and I'm desperately looking for the difference between Richard and me. Between me and Frances. I am Richard; I am the guilty, beaten child. I am Frances; I am the unstable, volatile wreck. I am stuck in all the roles in all these stories and I have to get away.

FEBRUARY 14TH, 12:11 P.M.

Richard's story is playing out in my life; I am hysterical with the notion that this is my fate. This is what will become of me, and I can't handle it. I stumble to the ground in David's office and plead with his knees to please forgive me.

"I can't be like this, David, I can't be! He killed her! He killed her because she was just like me, and he killed her!" I slobber these words out between sobs and leave smears on his pants. "People like me get killed, David!"

"Whoa, whoa, whoa. Shh, shh." David is smoothing back my hair and pulling up my chin. "Who did? Killed who?"

"Richard! That's why he was in jail—he killed his mother." My eyes are so swollen from the tears that squeezing out the next ones feels like pushing out water balloons. "She was borderline. *I'm* borderline! And he killed her because she's borderline!" I bury my face in his lap as I say it, hoping it will absolve me, but also hoping he won't really hear me.

"Shh. Sam, it's okay. Shh." David slides out of his desk chair onto the floor next to me. He wraps an arm around me and strokes my shoulder with the other hand. My violent heaves and sniffles are making me shake. David is whispering "shh" into my ear and kissing my hair. He is calming me.

The tears are falling from my swollen eyes, and the comfort David provides is slowing my breath. My chest begins to rise and fall normally. David and I are on the floor in a pile, his arm is snugly around my shoulder and my sweaty hair is matted to my forehead. He wipes it out of my eyes and looks at me staring forward.

"David," I begin calmly, "I have borderline personality disorder. The psych evals confirmed it. I knew I was fucked up, but I didn't know it was this bad. Rachel asked me to summarize the findings from OMH. I read my evaluation, and it's true. I have borderline." I take a deep, shuddering breath and steady myself to continue. "I've been meeting with Richard and making progress. He told me about killing his mom, and I told him I have borderline. Then he told me she was borderline, and it all became too much for me. I freaked out. I was just bawling my eyes out in my office in front of him, and I practically kicked him out before coming in here." I'm rocking back and forth, holding my ankles in my sweaty hands. "And I cheated on Lucas. With AJ. I slept with him a couple times. Every time Lucas fucked up, I ran to AJ. But I broke up with him, almost two weeks ago. I don't know why I didn't tell you sooner."

David isn't saying anything back to me. He's letting me get out what I need to get out, and he's still stroking my arms and petting my hair. Now and again he nods and says "shh." I'm still facing forward. The last tears have fallen and my eyes are beginning to sting. "I feel like everything fell down. I used to know who I was, and I knew what I was doing, and then they tell me I have this fucking disease, and everything is different. I wish I never knew."

"Stop, Sam. Stop. You can't sit here and shit on yourself like this. This isn't your fault. This is a diagnosis. And now you have it, and we will deal with it. This doesn't define you.

How could you say that?" He's pulling me back to face him as he tells me this. "You would never say that to your patients with BPD; you would *never* say that. Why the hell are you saying it to yourself?"

"It's different when it happens to you." I can't look at him.

"Why didn't you come to me to talk about this?" he says.

"I just didn't know how to tell you. I was afraid if I told you about AJ, you would be mad at me for cheating." Now I'm looking at him with pleading eyes.

"Sorry to tell you, but I knew about AJ. But I'm glad that's over and you broke up with Lucas."

I shake my head, knowing David has always been fearful of what will happen with Lucas. "But everyone else thinks he's so perfect."

"I see you every day, Sam. I see the bruises, I see the blood in your hair. I told you, you're not very discreet."

"Do you think everyone knows what's going on?"

"No. I don't think anyone knows. People want to believe that you guys were perfect. They don't want to know the truth. People like to pretend, because pretending is prettier." David has a way of making everything understandable.

"How am I supposed to build this back now? I don't know how to live like this."

"You're not supposed to build it back." Now we're both sitting cross-legged on the floor of his office, facing each other. I'm hunched down with my head in my hands. We hear patients and coworkers walking past the office doors, and we lower our voices.

"So, what do I do now? Everything I've always known is gone. My relationship is over. I don't have my perfect reputation here, I don't even have my sanity—I've got nothing left," I whisper.

"First, you breathe. You need some time to relax and get your bearings. Then we will figure out what's next."

"Are they going to fire me?"

"Of course they're not going to fire you. You're the golden girl; Rachel adores you. This place can't run without you." David doesn't know that I never turned in the summary for my report or filed my own evaluation.

"But shouldn't they fire me? I mean, doesn't this mean I am unfit for this environment?" I still need encouragement, even if I'm not telling him the whole story.

"No. Sam, you know this. Having BPD doesn't mean you can't do your job. You may even be better at your job because of this. Maybe that's why you're a better clinician than the rest of us." I can't help but laugh at this ridiculous comment. But maybe he's right; maybe I am so good at my job because I'm the blind leading the blind.

"Are you mad at me? I know I haven't been a very good friend to you lately. I just couldn't handle the thing with Julie."

"I'm never mad at you. Just worried."

"I'm sorry. I feel like things have to change now. I need to get my life together."

"Well, it's good you broke up with Lucas and that you cut off this thing with AJ. Neither one of those assholes was doing you any favors. Now you just need to stop drinking with patients at work."

I sit up ramrod straight. "How the fuck did you know about that?" I demand. My ears start to get hot and sweat begins to bead on my back. The office is growing smaller, and I feel the familiar sense of panic.

"After you had a session with Richard once, I heard you guys talking in there, and I know he has a reputation for silence. I thought it was strange, so I followed him when he left your office, and I saw him dump some empty airplane bottles into the garbage in the men's room."

"Do you think everyone in the meeting the other day knew that it was me?"

"No, you did a great job lying your face off." He smiles at me and hands me a tissue.

"Are you and Julie going to go out now?" I'm laying all my cards on the table. I'm getting out every question and every concern.

"No, Sam," he says firmly. "I know you think that, but I am *not* dating Julie, or anyone else for that matter. I've already told you this. She only approached me because she wants to get close to you."

"You know that's bullshit, don't you? She wanted to go out with *you*. I was just the excuse she used."

"I know you hate her, but, like I've told you, she's harmless. I'm sorry it upset you when you heard her in my office, but I promise you, there's nothing going on." He is sternly telling me this, forcing me to believe him.

"Someone should really fix these walls," I say. "It's really fucked up that you and I can hear through them."

He looks at me with concern. "Are you going to be okay?"

I chuckle nervously into my chest, uncomfortable that I have created another scene and come to David searching for salvation and absolution. "I think so. I have a lot to figure out. And, David, you cannot tell anyone what I told you. No one knows about this." I hold out my pinkie. "Okay?"

"No one except Richard," David reminds me, hooking his pinkie in mine.

PART THREE

PART THREE

FEBRUARY 21ST, 10:57 A.M.

I didn't eat breakfast, so I have a pile of offerings from the vending machine in front of me. I figure Cheez-Its and peanut M&M's are sort of real food. I'm constantly craving sugar because I'm not drinking, my body is in withdrawal. Richard is in my office, ready to keep moving forward, so I jump right in where we left off.

"What happened at the trial?"

"The trial still seems like a blur to me. I never told anyone what really happened. I never told my lawyer, I never told the judge, I never told the cops or anyone. The story they had was the story they pieced together from the evidence at the scene, and whatever Mrs. Choi told them." He reaches over and takes one of my Cheez-Its and pops it into his mouth. "Remember I told you the story of the blackout when I got arrested for looting?"

"Yeah, you and Jesse. They let you go, I remember."

"Well, remember they didn't book me under my real name because I didn't tell them my name?"

"Right." I offer him another one, but he turns it down.

"Originally, I was booked under John Doe. Then I was Williams Boy—Frances's last name was Williams. Then some cop found my fingerprints in the system and I was Henry James. Eventually, I told them my name was Richard McHugh. No one cares what your name is. My name was Defendant. My name was Murderer. That was my identity.

"There were no medical records of my broken arms because we never went to the hospital. There was nothing to say that my bruises and burns, the scars—there was nothing to prove that those were from Frances. Those could have been from a teenage boy roughhousing and acting a fool. From school-yard fights. They could have been from sports or self-inflicted. Without any story or testimony from me, they had nothing to go on. They painted me a monster. An abuser. A bad seed. They said the bruises came from Frances trying to defend herself. They said all the evidence of abuse they found on her, the marks from the boyfriend hitting her—they said those were from me. I never knew his name, so I couldn't even blame him."

It's just like the women in the survivor's group were saying—the authorities would never believe the victims.

"They said that I murdered my mother. You hear something enough times, you begin to believe it yourself. I had heard so many times that I was worthless, that I was bad and wrong..." His misty eyes are going far away and I wonder if he still believes it, even to this day.

"What was it like in prison?" I've got my elbows on the desk and my fists tucked underneath my chin like a child waiting to hear a ghost story.

"What was it like? Jeez. It was so many different things. There was a sense of solitude that I liked. No one bothered me. If you keep to yourself, they'll usually leave you alone. I started at Green Haven but I wasn't there long. I was transferred to a medium-security prison two and half years into my sentence. My lawyer explained about overcrowding and first-time offenses and whatnot. I was happy to go somewhere that had a bit more freedom." He wipes his salty fingers on a tissue and tucks it into his pocket.

"Where did they take you?"

"Ogdensburg."

"Really? I thought that was for sex offenders mostly. We've had a lot of patients come here after being released from Og-densburg."

"Yup, filled with sex offenders. They're not all bad. My time at Ogden was tough. After getting out of Green Haven, I started to get a better sense of what was happening to me. Most prisoners don't get transferred—they don't get a change of scenery or a change of security. I started to understand the reality of the situation, and I started to think about time. I was twenty-one years old, and I would be in there for longer than I had been alive. I thought about what I remembered from being a baby, and how long ago it felt. And I thought, for all the memories I have from my life, all of them will be replaced with memories from there. Memories from prison. The outside world would fade, and by the time I got released, I would have spent more of my life incarcerated than free. And that started to scare me."

"Fuuuck." I drag the word out like it's four syllables long. "You still had twenty years." I shake my head in disbelief. I was just getting out of high school twenty years ago. And in twenty years from now, I'll be nearly sixty.

"I started to get depressed. I stopped eating. I wasn't trying to starve myself or anything, I just stopped because I didn't get anything out of it anymore—no pleasure, no satisfaction. It never bothered me to be hungry, and I didn't like the food there anyway. So, I started to lose weight, and it was hard to sleep, so I would stay up at night. I wanted to be alone as much as I could, so I kept to my cell, and sat by myself in the mess, and I guess some admins started to notice.

"When I stopped eating, one of the admins had me see a psychiatrist. He said that I would benefit from talking to someone. I hadn't talked to anyone in years, and I didn't think I could. He told me to try it anyway and set up some appointments with this prison shrink, and gave me these pamphlets about group therapy. I went to some of the groups and my meetings with the docs; I was young and just did what I was told to do."

"Did you tell any of the doctors what really happened with your mom?"

He looks at me, wounded. "You know I didn't."

"What stopped you? It seems like that would have been the opportunity to work through your feelings about what happened with Frances."

"I had never admitted to anyone that it happened at all. I never told my friends growing up that Frances was the way she was. I never even told my girlfriend—all I said to her was that Frances had bad migraines and needed me to stay home. She always understood. And I loved her, my girlfriend. She was almost as crazy as Frances, but she would always understand when I had to stay home. If I couldn't tell *her* the truth, then I couldn't tell anyone."

"I want to hear more about the girlfriend." I gather the empty vending-machine bags and toss them into the garbage can.

"My girlfriend? I thought you wanted to know about prison?"

"I do, but next time I want you to tell me about her."

"Huh," he scoffs. "Okay."

"Keep going with the psych stuff. What were the sessions with the counselors like?"

"Not like these." He gives me an animated smile. "I had this one doc, a man. He was only a little bit older than me at the time, maybe thirty years old. He was always asking me what really happened. He didn't believe what the lawyers said and what the record said. He didn't think I was violent. He would ask me all these questions, and I never answered any of them. I stayed in his chair and I listened to him ask me, and I wasn't rude, but I just didn't answer him. I wouldn't ignore him or read the paper or anything, I just never answered."

"You were dead silent? You sat there without saying a single word? Not even *hello*?"

"I didn't say a single word for almost six years."

"*What? Six years?* I didn't think you meant that *literally*. I thought you meant you hadn't discussed your mother, or the trial, or the accident, or, or... I didn't know you went completely silent."

"I guess I just didn't have anything to say." Richard doesn't seem troubled by this at all.

"When did it start? When did you stop talking?"

"Around the time I started to get sick. I didn't say much of anything since the accident, but I answered when I had to and followed the directions of the judge and the legal folks, but beyond that, nah. I didn't have anything to say."

"That's unreal. I can't imagine not talking." His reputation for silence clearly followed him from prison.

"This doc that I'm telling you about, he was the only one who didn't try to get me to talk. A lot of people would get frustrated with me, start yelling. Some would get scared and just stay away from me. One inmate thought my tongue had been cut out, so he spent a couple weeks following me and telling everyone I had my tongue cut out for being a snitch. He told people I was the best person to be around because I could never tell anyone anything again. He would whisper secrets in my ear just to see if I would say something. His name was Victor. He molested two of his nephews and said he would do it again if they ever let him out." I cringe, pull my hands into my lap.

"But back to this doctor. He did what you did a little bit, had me come in for meetings in his office. He would ask me all kinds of questions, never really expecting an answer. Asked about what it was like for me in prison, day to day. Asked about what it was like at the trial, in jail, what it was like before the accident. He called it 'the precipitating event.' I guess he must have been a really good shrink, or I must have been answering him with my eyes or something, but he started to put together some kind of understanding. He figured that there was something wrong in my relationship with Frances.

"One day, he asked if I would be okay with getting a physical evaluation. I had never had a real one as an adult, not since I left St. Teresa's, so I guess I nodded, or shrugged, but he set me up to have one. He took me to the medical unit, and another doc came with us, and he set me up with the whole shebang. I had the blood tests and the X-rays, and the lung what-have-yous and everything."

"He was checking his theories, huh? He thought he knew something and wanted to see if he could find any evidence?"

"Bingo. He saw the breaks in my arms from the X-rays. He saw the cigarette burns and the scars on my back and my legs. I guess he got the picture, so he started asking me about it. I still never answered him. But he just knew."

"He just *knew*? He just figured it out?"

"Yeah, pretty much. He started bringing me books, too. Books about what he thought may be wrong with me. He brought me books on depression, books about what Frances was like, and shell shock, PT-whatever-you-call-it."

"PTSD, post-traumatic stress disorder. Similar symptoms used to be referred to as 'shell shock.'"

"Thank you, Doctor."

"You're welcome, patient."

"He gave me something on this thing called Stockholm syndrome. You know about this? Those hostages at the bank in Sweden?"

"Yeah, I know all about it. This doctor thought you were expressing similarities to Stockholm syndrome, just from looking at your X-rays and talking *at* you? Huh, traumatic bonding. That's incredible."

"He said he thought that might be why I didn't stand up in my own defense. He said if the bone breaks and the scars were from Frances, then it makes sense."

"It does make sense; it makes perfect sense." I sigh.

"So, he started to wonder what was going on with Frances. That's when I learned about borderline."

"This guy is amazing. What's his name? Whatever happened to him?" It's all becoming clear why Richard would need to get this off his chest. Why he sits in my office every Tuesday and tells me his story.

"Oh, I don't know. He left or retired or something while I was still in the can. I don't know where he went. He would come visit me in the general population after I stopped seeing him for therapy. Sometimes we would eat together. But I never spoke a word to him. Now I wish I could say thank-you."

"You don't remember his name?"

Richard hesitates. "It's been a long time. I just knew him as Dr. Mark."

"Great," I say sarcastically. "That's very helpful." I flippantly toss my pen onto my desk. "You really don't remember his last name?"

"I don't know. Maybe it was Scharf, or Stein or something Jewish like that."

"Okay, that's a start. Did you ever try to contact him?"

"After I left prison? No, I don't want to bother anybody."

"Richard, this man helped you. You said you wanted to thank him. Even with all the opening up you're doing with me these days, I would still like to talk to someone else who knows you!"

"I'm fifty-five years old; he must be sixtysomething by now. He doesn't want some ex-con knocking on his door."

"Do I have your permission to try to find him?"

"For *what*?"

"For help in your continued care! So I can talk to *anyone* who knows *anything* about you. I'm shooting blanks here, Richard. I would love to have some professional discussion about your case."

"My *case*? Is that all I am to you? You want to get to the bottom of 'my case'? See? That's *exactly* what I was talking about when I took your booze. You agreed that you wouldn't treat me like a *patient*." He huffs out a loud sigh, throws himself backward and glares out the window.

"You told me that if we went through with this deal, and we both shared our secrets, that I could give you the therapy you need to get better," I say sympathetically. I reach out and put my hand on the busted crook of his left arm. "Isn't that still part of the bargain? Isn't that still my job?"

He breathes in a deep lungful and slowly exhales out his mouth with his eyes closed. He puts his right hand on top of mine, and the hugeness of his hands and their softness and warmth startle me. He pats my hand gently.

"Fine. Go ahead. But you might not like everything you find."

FEBRUARY 21ST, 2:37 P.M.

I've just left a meeting in Rachel's office, and I'm walking down the back stairs with my handbag, my water bottle, a cup of coffee and two patient files. Every step I take, I seem to plant on the outside corner of my foot and wobble like a newborn fawn. The top of my water bottle has flown off, and the gravity in the stairwell is wonky. I tuck the patient files I'm carrying into my handbag and clutch on the railing for support.

The stairs are getting smaller and smaller, and by the time I reach the first floor and look for the big emergency-exit bar to push, I am twice the size of the door. I shake open the door and squeeze through, to find myself in a brightly lit hallway with Christmas decorations around the doorways. I could've sworn it was nearly spring. As I walk to my office, the bounce in my gait turns comical, and the gushes of water that slosh out of my bottle stay suspended in the air in front of me. As I walk through them, they soak my face and hair. It feels cold and refreshing and I shake the water bottle to release more.

My office door appears down the hall, and the doorframe is as big as a mountain. It's colorful and shining, as if it were inlayed with gemstones and mirrors. There is a small gray horse in front of my office. A spider monkey sits on his back, holding a martini and smoking a Marlboro Light. He laughs as I approach the door. I look down at him, and I see that the monkey is Lucas, and the horse is Sid, the bartender from Nick's. They push open my door, and I follow them in. Once we're inside, my office looks completely normal. The handbag that I just carried down the stairs is neatly hung from a coat hook behind the door, and a full water bottle and cup of coffee sit waiting for me on my desk. The patient files that I had in Rachel's office are back in the wire rack next to my phone.

Sid the gray horse jumps onto my patient chair and curls into a sleeping position. All four of his hooves are clumped tightly at his middle, and he yawns and settles his horse face over them to sleep. Lucas the spider monkey drains his martini, takes a last drag of his Marlboro Light and plops the butt into the remnant liquid at the bottom of the glass. He pats Sid's sleeping head and hops onto my desk.

"What are you doing here?" I ask him.

"I'm here to kill you. Something in this office has been poisoned, and when you find it, you won't survive." Monkey Lucas picks up my phone and starts dialing my mother's house.

"How can I find out what it is?"

"You'll have to test everything and see." He pulls the tangled cord of the phone straight and climbs up the wall. He pops one of the dirty tiles out of the ceiling and hangs by his feet with the giant phone propped in the crook of his neck. I scramble through my drawers, looking for something that has been tampered with. Looking for an old pharmacy bottle with the skull and crossbones from Saturday morning cartoons. I can hear monkey Lucas cackling on the phone, conspiring with my mother.

I feel the sense of panic come over me like a heart attack and I frantically dig through endless black holes in my office.

I sip and spit from my water bottle and coffee cup. I take a partially eaten bagel from the garbage can and test to see if it's poison. Nothing. Nothing is killing me; nothing is making the panic abate. The more I search, the more items appear in the room. It's getting filled faster than I can test everything. All I can hear is the static on the other end of the phone and the sickly cackling coming from the monkey.

I seem to be getting to the end of the piles. I can see the carpet beginning to show again beneath the heaps of patient files that I've been licking, the office supplies covered in sticky saliva, the drinks, the cigarettes, the garbage—all the things I've tested for poison in my office. I finally get to the bottom of the pile and I haven't found it. I haven't found the poison. I look up to the Lucas monkey to ask him what I missed, where it is, and as I turn my eyes upward I see a giant guillotine blade dripping with a toxic green liquid coming down too fast to dodge.

I immediately wake up with wet hair pasted to my cheeks and a pounding headache. I could feel myself crying in the dream, my chest heaving up and down in agonizing fear, and I touch my face to see that the tears were real. My subconscious must have known something because I have a text from Lucas waiting on my phone. Sam, I need to talk to you. I'm sorry. I pull open my drawers and look up to the ceiling to see if anything else remains. Everything from the dream is gone. But my morning coffee cup and my bottle of water sit at the edge of my desk. I delete the text.

FEBRUARY 24TH, 5:41 P.M.

I've called David into my office to help me locate the elusive Dr. Mark.

"David, you have to help me look through all of this." I'm on the floor with papers strewn about, flipping through intake materials and Richard's file, trying to see if I missed anything.

David sits down next to me. "What are we trying to find?"

I'm still having trouble looking directly at David, now that he knows everything, so I keep my eyes down on the papers. "I need to find out if we can locate this psychiatrist who treated Richard while he was in prison. Richard was telling me about him this morning, and this shrink seems to have some kind of insights into him that we have never been able to access before. We can find out if these stories are bullshit or not. Find out what the fuck got him here to begin with! I have *got* to talk to this guy."

"Which prison?"

"He was in Ogdensburg, and he saw a staff psychiatrist there. Mark something-with-an-*S*. He doesn't know his last name; he just called him Dr. Mark."

"Did you look at Ogden's website? See if there's any clinical-staff record?" David asks.

"No, I didn't bother because Richard said the doctor left sometime before his sentence was up. So, he got to Ogden in—what, '84? When did he go to Green Haven? Do you have that paper?"

"Umm…" David shuffles through the documents in his hands. "Yeah, hold on. Looks like he was arrested in May of '79, and then the trial started in September, also in '79. He went to Green Haven in February of 1980, and then went to Ogdensburg in September of 1982."

"Okay, so he said he was at Ogden for a while, and then he got depressed, and then they sent him to see a psychiatrist. I'm not sure of the dates. Doesn't it say?" I ask.

"No, there's nothing in the discharge info about any psychiatric treatment. It just states the terms of release and parole, some legal jargon that I don't understand, but there's nothing psychiatric here. Not in these documents."

"How the hell do you get transferred from one prison to another?" I flop the documents into my lap and look up to David.

"Didn't he tell you anything about that?"

"Yeah, he said something about overcrowding. Then he said it was a first-time offense, so they chose him? Something like that."

"I've never heard of someone convicted of murder getting transferred to a medium-security prison."

"Neither have I, but maybe it's because it was manslaughter. They didn't have motive during the trial, so he got convicted of manslaughter. Does that make sense?" I don't know anything about the legal system, sentencing, anything.

"Find this doctor, Sam. Something about this story is off."

"I know. Something's not right. The man is an enigma, a walking question mark. He's been telling me stories about prison, about his upbringing, but it doesn't clear up what the fuck he is doing *here*. Do you realize that I've been working with him for *months*, and I *still* have no idea what's wrong with him or why he's in a mental institution? We need to find this guy!"

Anxiously, David and I continue to shuffle and dig for anything that might lead us to this doctor.

"I'm gonna do some preliminary searches on the internet. It seems stupid to not try that." David pushes himself up off the floor and into my desk chair.

"Okay, it's Mark something-with-an-*S*, probably one syllable, like Stein. I'll keep trying to find answers in all this crap."

After typing only a few words, David has hundreds of hits. "Well, I've found every *inmate* at Ogdensburg." He gives the page a closer look, scanning for answers. "And I can write to them! There's a prison pen-pal site!"

"David, focus."

"Here's an OMH site related to forensic populations." He reads and rereads. He clicks through various pages that I can't see from my seat on the floor. "This is really unhelpful. They only list one clinician and it's the head of the department— hold on." David picks up my phone and dials a number he found on the screen. I'm holding my breath, losing hope that I will ever discover what Richard is actually doing at Typhlos.

"Hello, my name is David Bloomfield. I'm a staff psychologist calling from Typhlos Psychiatric in Manhattan. With whom am I speaking?" I strain to hear the other end of the conversation. "Hi, Kathy, how are you? I wonder if you can help me with something. I've got a patient here who was incarcerated with you at Ogdensburg, and I am looking to contact a physician he worked with there. Can you help me find him?" He looks at me, covers the receiver and whispers, "I'm on hold. Ugh, there's Muzak."

I take off my glasses and massage the bridge of my nose.

"Okay, I'm going to keep looking for something in all this nonsense."

David grabs a pen and snaps at me for paper. I reach into the garbage can and hand him the paper bag that held my morning bagel, with grease stains on the corners. He begins to scribble down whatever Kathy from Ogdensburg is telling him.

"Mark, the only name I have for him is Mark. I believe he was a psychiatrist, sometime in the early to mid-1980s." He continues scribbling. "Um, how far back *do* they go?" He covers the receiver and mouths to me, *They don't have pre-internet records of clinicians.*

I whisper back, "Well, how the hell did they do payroll? Weren't there computers in the fucking '80s? Tell Kathy to keep digging." David nods dramatically with wide eyes and dismisses me with a wave of his hand.

He listens attentively and nods along with me, understanding that this is our only lead, our only chance of finding out what's going on. David is on hold again while Kathy presumably digs up the answers we need. I'm continuing to riffle through the papers on my office floor, trying to find the needle in the haystack. Richard's file is nebulous, confusing, disorganized.

"Yes, a staff psychiatrist, I believe," David nearly shouts into the phone. "He treated our patient sometime in the early 1980s, probably starting around '82 or '83?" David covers the receiver, looks to me and whispers, "How long did Richard keep seeing this guy?"

I shrug and shake my head.

"I'm not sure, Kathy. Are you finding anything?" Pause, he listens. "That would be great; a name would be great. Thank you." He looks at me and crosses his eyes. He's leaning back in my chair with his feet up on the desk, his head lolled back with the receiver pinched between his shoulder and ear. *I'm trying*, he mouths at me.

David suddenly pops up and drops his feet to the floor, grabs the paper bag and begins furiously scribbling.

"No forwarding address, okay. No problem. How do you spell that? *O-a-n.* Okay, great." He stands and holds up his pen in triumph like the Statue of Liberty. "Got it!" he whisper screams at me.

Before we can celebrate, he turns his attention back to the phone, "I'm sorry, what?" Confusion and defeat register on his face. "Oh, I see. Okay. Well, why don't you give me the rest of the information, as well?" He holds a finger gun to his temple and pulls the finger trigger. He sits back down in my chair, exhales harshly and continues to write. After a series of mmm-hmms, it's over. "Thanks so much, Kathy. You have a great day." He hangs up the phone and spins in the chair to face me. "There's three of them. Three doctors named Mark something-with-an-*S* who worked there in the '80s. Do you have *any* more information from Richard?"

"No. Something short. Something Jewish. That's the best I can do."

"Well, great, because Woody Allen must have hired these guys. I've got a Mark Sloan, Mark Schiff and Marc Steele. Kathy gave me the last known phone numbers for all of them."

"Three guys named Mark something-with-an-*S* who *all* worked at Ogden in the '80s? *All* psychiatrists?" I shuffle the papers on the floor into a sloppy pile and pull the patient chair up to the desk next to David. "Either Mark was the most popular name in the world or Kathy fucked something up. We better start Googling."

FEBRUARY 28TH, 10:32 A.M.

Richard and I are sitting in my office, sharing a bagel with scallion cream cheese. He came earlier than expected, and I was midbreakfast when he walked in, looking hungry. We started this deal where we're both supposed to break down our walls because he had stolen my stash as leverage. I haven't had a drink in weeks, so the stash has become inconsequential. He knows my secrets and I know his.

"You have cream cheese on your lip," he says as he hands me a napkin.

"Thank you. So, back to business. Believe it or not, I still want to work on your file. Same shit I've been trying to get you to finish since you started here: psychiatric history, health information, previous arrests or hospitalizations."

"And what, my file didn't have any of that?" He has a mischievous grin on his face.

"No—why are you smiling?"

"I'm not smiling. Look, you know how I ask that you never write anything down? Well, I ask that a lot. I don't want to have records." He doesn't look at me as he says this; instead he fidgets with his cap on top of his stack of papers.

"What about at Ogden with Dr. Mark? Didn't you have to sign consents and release papers—anything?"

Richard shakes his head. "He never made me sign anything. He never even asked me to. I spent my life under the radar. I don't want paper trails."

"Were you formally diagnosed with depression in prison?"

"I suppose. Dr. Mark told me I had symptoms of depression, and shell shock, although I thought that was bullshit because I'm no combat veteran."

"Interesting you say that." I'm writing notes despite his protests and finally filling in the diagnostic sections.

"Interesting, how?"

"After living with Frances, I'd characterize that as some form of lifelong combat."

"Huh. Well, I still never had to fear for my life and carry weapons and follow orders and kill people."

"You sure 'bout that?"

Richard doesn't respond. His silence is pensive.

"What do you need to finish my file? I know I have my end of the bargain to keep up." He pulls himself to sit up straight.

"Well, we can start the family-history section of the psychosocial evaluation. The one you adamantly refused to complete."

"Family history, huh? Well, don't you know everything already? My father is a mystery. A dead mystery. I guess so is Frances, but we know her name and everything, so what else do you need?"

"Was Frances ever formally diagnosed with borderline?"

"Not that I know of."

"It wasn't called 'borderline' back then anyway. Do you know if she ever saw a doctor for treatment? Or took any medications?"

"I have no idea."

Do you know anything? "Okay. Any kids?"

"Just me, I think."

"No, I mean do *you* have any kids?"

"You don't think I would have mentioned that?" He glares at me, shocked I would even ask.

"Okay. Any pregnancies that didn't go to term?"

"I don't know!" He throws up his hands and leans back. "Women didn't tell you that sort of thing if it happened. They just took care of it. Sometimes they asked for money."

"Did any of your partners ever ask you for that kind of money?"

"No one asked me for money. But my last girlfriend before I went away, well, she made some implications. Nothing ever came of it. I think it was some kind of last-ditch effort to try to make me fight to stay out of jail. That used to be a normal thing. If you wanted things to change, or you wanted a man to commit, women would claim to be pregnant. Used to happen all the time."

"Are you in touch with her? Did you stay in contact while you were incarcerated?"

"Nope."

"Didn't you say she was, like, the love of your life?"

"What did I know? I was just a kid when I went away. They sent me out there for twenty years. I couldn't ask her to wait for me! She had a whole life to live. A whole life. I wasn't going to ruin her life because I ruined mine."

"Sorry, I didn't mean to hit a nerve."

"Look. She was a screwed-up girl. If she were in this office now, you'd probably tell me she was borderline, too. She was a real jack-in-the-box. She loved me, she hated me. But she couldn't stand it when I had to go away. She couldn't handle being left alone. She lashed out. I think she thought I could control it, like I was in charge of my sentence. She thought there was more I could have done. And she blamed me for leaving her. I'm sure she hates me, if she even remembers me."

"Of course she remembers you!" I reassure him. "Did you ever look into whether or not she was really pregnant?"

"Never occurred to me that she would be. Quite a liar, she was."

"What was she like?"

"Oh, she was beautiful. The prettiest girl on the block. Blue eyes, blond hair, the whole thing. Petite, elegant, delicate. But she had a mouth on her you wouldn't believe. Girls didn't talk the way you do back then. It was unheard-of. Even when you're burning your bras and voting, you still weren't cussing. But, my God, she could make a sailor blush. And funny. Quick-witted, fearless. She could knock you down with a quick jab and then bat her eyelashes as you licked your wounds."

"Sounds like quite a woman."

"She was. She most certainly was." Richard nods. "But that was her bright side. She was complicated and confusing. I always felt like I was nervous to be around her because I didn't know what version of her I was going to get. That was the same feeling I had with Frances, but with Samantha for some reason, I felt like I was more in control. I could actually do something to help her act like herself and not the lunatic she could be."

"Maybe because you were equals. On a level playing field. She didn't have inherent authority over you the way Frances did."

"Maybe. Maybe that's it."

"How did it end?"

"I went to prison. I didn't stay in contact with her because I didn't think it was fair. She had her whole life in front of her. I didn't want her to stop living because of me."

"Do you think about her still?"

"How is that relevant to my chart?"

"I'm just wondering."

"I think about her more since I've been here. In prison, at the beginning, I thought about her a lot, and I was afraid what she would do without me. But that fades. I'm sure she found another man, got married, had some kids. I'm sure she made the most of herself. When I got out of prison, even before I made it to the first halfway house, I thought about trying to find her. But it had been too long. I wouldn't want to come in and mess up her life."

"You seem to have a thing about not wanting to bother people from your past. You said the same thing the other day about Dr. Mark."

"Well, would *you* want your past sneaking back into your life?"

"No, I guess I don't." I turn away and grab the greasy bagel bag David used to write the names of the doctors from Ogdensburg. "Speaking of Dr. Mark…" I turn back to Richard. "Do any of these names sound familiar?" I read him the list. "Do you recognize those names?"

"Yeah, something Jewish. Those sounds about right."

"Which one?"

"One of 'em anyway." Richard turns back to looking out the window.

David and I discovered that Dr. Steele passed away in 1996, so hopefully, he wasn't the mystery doctor from Ogden. I've left messages for Drs. Sloan and Schiff, but I haven't heard back yet.

MARCH 1ST, 4:46 P.M.

I've got my heels up on my desk, and my shirt hanging off the back of my chair. Without booze, my body is a mess and the withdrawal is making me sweat like an animal. My shirt is wet as a mop. I lock my door while I make another attempt at reaching the two remaining possibilities for Mark something-with-an-*S*.

After six rings, a voice finally appears at the other end. "Hello?"

"Hello?" I flip my heels off the desk and sit upright. "Hi! My name is Dr. Sam James. I'm a staff psychologist over at Typhlos Psychiatric in Manhattan. I'm looking for Dr. Mark Sloan?"

"Yes? This is he." Finally!

"Hi. I'm sorry to bother you; I'm calling in reference to an old patient of yours at Ogdensburg, Richard McHugh? I've left you several messages."

"Oh, yes, I've gotten your messages. Yes, how can I help you?" *This is it! He's the one!* My heart jumps into my throat, and I leap out of my chair wearing just my bra.

"Well, Richard is mandated to treatment here at Typhlos, and I am trying to get some background." I struggle to hold the receiver and pull my damp shirt on. "He is very tightly shut, and I have hardly anything from his intake materials. He mentioned recently that he had a relationship with you during his time in prison, and I wonder if you could help me gain some insight?"

"What kind of insights are you looking for?" Dr. Sloan asks, and his voice sounds much younger than I imagined it would. "It's been a very long time since I've treated Richard McHugh."

"Anything that can help me understand him better. What was his diagnosis? Our intake materials show depression, PTSD, suicidal ideation, some comments about Axis Two characteristics, but no actual diagnosis. I have no formal family history other than what he and I have discussed together in my office. I've been seeing him for several months now but it's still not clear why he's institutionalized." I'm holding the phone in the crook of my neck, buttoning up the front of my shirt.

"I remember that he was one of the most fascinating patients I've ever encountered."

"Really? What captured your interest in him?" I'm thinking of Richard's warning—*you might not like everything you find*—and I want to hear what Dr. Sloan knows.

"Well, it's not often you find a man of his stature in prison—commanding size, young, strong—who chooses to keep to himself. When I was informed that he didn't speak or eat, I was intrigued. I imagined there must be quite a mind and quite a story behind all that."

"How did you decipher his story if he never spoke to you?"

"His eyes, mostly, and his posture. He was slumped down and round-shouldered when he first came in. He looked at me from below his brow, if you know what I mean." I know exactly what he means. "His eyes would light up when I touched on something significant. After a while of guessing, I gave him a physical and things started to make more sense."

"He told me about the physical. How did you know where the wounds came from?"

"I didn't know. But when I suggested it might have been his mother, his presence changed. As if he had been carrying the weight of that knowledge for so long, and my suggestion took the baggage from him. His head lifted, and his back straightened. It was remarkable, I had never seen such a rapid change in demeanor."

"Are you the one who told him about BPD?" I'm like an excited child ripping open Christmas presents—too consumed with asking questions to properly focus on the answers.

"Yes. After I realized that there was some level of abuse coming from his mother, he tuned to me more. He seemed to want an explanation, or some understanding of why she was the way she was. I would ask questions of her behavior, ask how he felt growing up. He seemed to respond to me in his own way, without ever saying a word. He would sit up, ever so slightly, or rub his thumbs together when something resonated with him. I started putting two and two together, and the profile he seemed to be implying was hands-down a borderline diagnosis."

"Unbelievable. You were able to draw the diagnosis of a dead woman from the silence of her son. Absolutely amazing." I can't believe this could be real. How could this guy know all of this, and *remember* all of this?

"Obviously, no formal diagnosis could ever be made for his mother—she was long dead, and I never treated her personally, saw any record or had anything else to go on. Just clinician's intuition, I suppose. Or maybe there was something to Richard's responses that convinced me. He was an avid reader in prison, kept to himself outside my office, so I gave him some literature—pamphlets and scholarly articles describing the diagnostic criteria for borderline personality disorder. Richard read every article I gave him. I imagine he became something of an expert in BPD by the time he left. He even borrowed my *DSM* and dog-eared the life out of it." Is Richard the one who left those copies open in the computer room?

"Is there anything else you remember that you think may be significant? Can you tell me anything more about what might have gotten him institutionalized here? I have no background information or diagnosis. Was he formally diagnosed in prison? I know he said he didn't fill out any forms, but did you? Do you have any records that could be helpful?" I'm scribbling notes, hopefully getting closer to putting the puzzle pieces together.

"Well, since retiring and leaving the prison system, I haven't got access to any of that anymore."

"You seem to remember so much detail from your interactions. Are you sure there isn't *anything* else that could help me out a bit?"

"Honestly, I can't remember if he ever received a formal diagnosis. I remember the silent interactions because they were so unique, but a diagnosis is commonplace among patients, I don't necessarily keep all that in mind."

"Did he have any visitors? Any friends in prison?"

"I wouldn't know about that." He's suddenly gone cagey.

"Did you ever find anything out about a girlfriend? He and I have been speaking recently about a girlfriend he had before he went to prison. Did you ever get anything about her?"

"Not that I can recall." He's starting to sound frustrated now, like he's tired of my inquiry.

"I'm sorry to keep prying, but I've been trying to figure out what's going on with Richard for months now, and you're the only solid lead I've got. Is there *anything*, really anything at all, that you can access that may be helpful to me? I just need to know what he's doing here at Typhlos. What his diagnosis was. How he ended up institutionalized. It's just not adding up."

Dr. Sloan expels an enormous, thick sigh. "I still have relationships with colleagues at the prison. I could look into some files and see if I can find anything relevant."

"That would be great. Absolutely any information would be incredibly helpful to me. Thank you."

"I will contact you if I find anything."

"Please do, Dr. Sloan. Thank you for your time."

As I hang up the phone, I can't help but feel that I am still exactly where I was when I started. Mark Sloan didn't have answers to any of my questions. What was Richard trying to warn me about?

MARCH 2ND, 3:20 P.M.

I'm at my desk, when I hear a knock on the door. I close my web browser and reach over to pull open my office door.

I have to slip off my glasses and stand up to adjust to what's in front of me. It's Lucas. Here, in my office. I search his hands and the hallway behind him, looking for the bouquet of roses that usually accompanies this scene. I sniff the air to see if I can smell his cologne, and if I can't, I'll know that it's a dream. The spicy amber scent fills my nose, and faint notes of alcohol and fruit from his hair spray present themselves. My arms feel heavy and my vision blurs. He doesn't carry flowers, but instead has a gray cardboard tray filled with four take-out cups of what must be pretentious coffee. The cologne and hair-spray aromas are replaced with the caramel and vanilla scents coming from the coffee cups.

I have had this dream so many times, I know I should feel scared, and I know I should slam the door and scream for David, but I can't move. It occurs to me that the coffee must be a gesture of apology or a peace offering. How long have I been standing here?

"Hello, Sam." His slick and rocky voice, like salt water over wet stones, fills up my office like a fog.

"I can't—" I don't have a greeting or excuse, and I'm trying to clear my head of this shock so I can compose a full sentence and get him off the unit.

"I know I shouldn't be here, but I needed to see you, and you haven't answered my texts, and I knew I would find you here."

Lucas's opener helps me to shake the cobwebs from my brain.

"You absolutely can't be in here. This is a confidentiality violation, and I am going to call security if you don't leave right now."

"Okay, okay." He holds up his free hand in defense. "I won't stay long, I promise."

"You won't stay *at all*, Lucas. I have nothing to say to you. Please leave."

"At least have a cup of coffee—that's all I'm asking. Just have a cup of coffee with me, and hear me out a second."

"No. I need you to leave."

"I brought all the good flavors; I have a caramel, and vanilla, and the one with the chocolate and mint. You can have whichever one you want. Or all of them? You can have them all, but please, can I come in? For a minute?" He gestures toward my patient chair with his tray of coffees and begins nudging his way past me. I see a visitor pass tucked between two of the coffee cups, and I hope that Raul gave him a full pat down.

He places the tray at the corner of my desk and hovers above the chair, waiting for permission to sit. His hands are over his thighs, eyebrows raised, wrinkling his forehead. I close the door slightly, and he takes this as an invitation. He pulls up his pant legs and sits with a deep sigh. He's looking around the office to get his bearings. He turns around to gaze out the window, and I momentarily wish there would be a construction accident across the street that sends a huge wooden plank flying through my office window, decapitating Lucas as he sits smugly in my patient chair.

I pull my desk chair in front of me, and stand between it and my door. The door remains ajar—far enough open that anyone outside could hear me if I raised my voice. I use my right foot to nudge the off switch on the white-noise machine that sits by the door to muddle any confidential conversations. My heart is beating hard, and I have to continually remind myself that I am *not* in the dream I've had so many times before.

I glance at my desk clock: 3:21 p.m. "You have four minutes, and then I'm calling security."

"Relax, relax—have a cup of coffee." He pushes the tray toward me. I don't budge. "Okay, fine." He pulls out the cup marked "caramel" and removes the lid. He blows on the contents, which have obviously already cooled, and lets the sweaty lid drop condensation onto my desk. "I'm here to make peace with you."

"I've already made peace."

"Fine, but I haven't yet. I am still very upset about everything that happened."

"That's your problem, Lucas, not mine."

"Yes. It is my problem. But the only way I can solve that problem would be if you could just find the kindness in your heart to hear me out. I'm working on my issues, and I'm trying to be a better man. I need your help. Your job is to help people, isn't it? Would it be professional of you to turn me away when I'm simply asking for assistance?" He grins and sips his coffee. Asshole.

"I get paid for doing my job. *You* are not my job."

"Here—" He reaches in his back pocket and pulls out a calfskin wallet. "How much do you charge for four minutes?

Twenty dollars?" He lays a crisp twenty-dollar bill folded in quarters on my desk and returns his wallet to his pocket.

I reach over and snatch up the bill and deposit it directly into his coffee cup.

"*You* are not my job. Three minutes."

"That's very big of you." He leaves the bill in the coffee and puts the cup down on my desk. He reaches for a tissue and dabs at the coffee splashes on his Thomas Pink shirt. "Well, I started seeing someone—" *Does he mean romantically or therapeutically? I can't decide which one would piss me off more.* "—and she thinks that the best way for me to move on from us would be to talk to you and work through everything. Come to some understanding."

"I have an understanding. You're an asshole. And now you're someone else's asshole." *Romantically or therapeutically.*

"I'm not going to get anywhere with you, am I?"

"No. Two minutes."

"How am I supposed to move on, and stop texting you and showing up at your office, unless you throw me a bone here?"

"A restraining order?"

"I mean it, Sam. I don't want to keep bothering you, but I need you back in my life if I'm ever going to move on."

"That doesn't make any sense at all. If you need closure, you can get it on the other side of my door. I'm finished talking to you. Now and any other time in the future. If you decide to continue to harass me, I will absolutely get an order of protection against you and make your life as impossible as I can. You have done enough damage, and it's time for you to tuck your tail and disappear. One minute."

"So you refuse to help me get better? You refuse to rescue a man who is clearly drowning?"

"Nice try."

"I'm not trying anything, I just want to be clear that I am asking you for help and you are saying no."

"Yes. That's correct. Time's up." I reach for the phone and immediately dial security. I don't wait for Lucas to stand, to stop me or to protest. Raul picks up the phone, identifies himself and asks who's calling.

"Hi, Raul, it's Dr. James. Can you do me a favor and send someone up here to escort a guest out? He's a little hesitant to leave." I stare at Lucas as I speak to the security guard, and he sees I'm not fooling around. "Thanks, Raul. I appreciate it."

Lucas promptly rises to his feet and smooths the front of his pants. He drapes his charcoal gray cashmere coat over his shoulders and squares himself. He looks down at me disapprovingly. "I thought you had more respect than *that*, Sam."

I pull my desk chair out of his way and gently swing open the door. He gives the office one last look over before he moves his feet to leave. As he inches past my chair, he leans his long, manicured hand over my desk and flicks over the open coffee cup so the soaked twenty-dollar bill and the sticky liquid fall all over my desk and patient chair. "Oops," he says as he walks out my door, and I hear Raul approaching down the hall.

MARCH 3RD, 1:14 P.M.

I thought of going to see David but I needed to get out of the office, so I'm walking in Riverside Park. It's that part of the year when the days are getting longer and the sun is bright, but it's still cool. I'm breathing in long, deep breaths to try to cleanse myself. The fresh air tickles my nose.

I sit down in one of the green folding chairs and watch the people. There's a big sign next to me that says No Smoking, and I use its base to put out my cigarette. No more booze, no more cheap thrills with cheap men, but I still hold on to my cigarettes. Everyone is rushing, with heads down, wearing jackets too light for the weather in an attempt to speed up the spring. They've got their arms wrapped around themselves, blowing into coffee cups.

As I'm gazing at the passersby, I light another cigarette, and I catch eyes with a homeless man sitting across the path from me. He's smoking, too. He holds out his cigarette and points to the No Smoking sign. He's wearing a pair of black fingerless gloves on top of another pair of gray gloves. I wonder how he wields his cigarette so well. I tuck mine between my lips and obligingly turn the sign around so it doesn't face either one of us. The man smiles, gives me a thumbs-up and turns to face the sun.

It's been a long time since I've felt the sun on my face. When I was drinking, I avoided the daylight. Daylight was for hangovers and wrapping myself around a toilet or a trash can. I couldn't hide the bruises in daylight; I couldn't hide the truth about Lucas. I couldn't sneak kisses from anonymous men. I feel like I've spent my whole life hiding from something— something I couldn't show in the light, someone I couldn't be when other people could see me—and now I'm exposed. I had a premonition that things were going to change when Richard appeared back in October, but I didn't know that *I* was going to change. His arrival seems timed with the departure of the me I used to know, of all the me's I used to be—the martyr, the superhero, the disaster, the caricature. I used to have a crutch to lean on; I could blame the alcohol for all my bad behavior. *I was drunk at the time, I would never do that if I were sober.* I could wallow in self-pity and play the victim, removing any responsibility from my own shoulders. Now all that's left is the raw material beneath all those masks I used to wear. It's time I find a way to get my feet on solid ground again.

I stand up to walk back to Typhlos and flick my half-smoked cigarette to the pavement. I feel taller than I ever have before. Like I used to carry a backpack that was too heavy and pulled my shoulders down, and now I've taken it off.

I pass Raul on my way back inside and give him a high five. My office is warm from the sun, and I feel sleepy as soon as I sit back down. I'll be out of here soon.

The phone jolts me back into awareness. At the third ring, I snatch up the receiver and growl into the phone, "Yes?"

"Dr. James?"

"Oh," I stammer and perk up. "Yes, this is she."

"Hi, it's Mark Sloan. How are you?"

"Oh, hi, Mark. I wasn't expecting a call from you."

"I wonder if you have a moment to spare?"

"Absolutely, yes." I lean back and sip cold tea from my dirty coffee mug.

"Well, after we last spoke, I did some digging back into the prison files to see what I could find for you."

"And? Were you able to find anything?"

"Yes. I'm still in contact with various people at Ogdensburg; very few who were there when I worked there have stayed, but a couple of people have. The records system before the internet is a mess, of course. But they still have all the records in paper files. I supposed when we do detective work, that kind of thing is useful!"

"It sure is. I'm sorry, can I stop you for a moment? I was reviewing our last conversation, and I'm still unsure about a lot of things. What was Richard's diagnosis? Do you have those records?"

"Yes, that was one of the items I was searching for when I looked into the prison records. Depression and PTSD. His prison medical records should have that information. Don't you have those?"

"No, I hardly have anything at all. Here's what's bothering me—though he was diagnosed with depression and PTSD while he was incarcerated, that was many years ago. He hasn't been diagnosed with anything since he was released from prison."

"Yes?" Mark Sloan seems to be unable to follow my train of thought.

"I can't diagnose him with anything because he doesn't fit the criteria for any disorders." I'm hoping Dr. Sloan will catch on.

"Yes, okay?"

My hopes falter. "So what is he doing in a mental institution?"

"Oh—" Dr. Sloan is stumped. "Oh, well, I'm sure you'll have to discuss that with him." Another dead end.

"Okay," I sigh, again defeated in my quest to figure Richard out. "What was it you wanted to tell me?"

"Well, this record I wanted to discuss with you isn't from Ogdensburg. It's in a note that came from his previous prison stay at Green Haven. You had asked me about friends or visitors."

"Yes. Does it say he had contact with anyone?"

"It shows that a blonde woman came to visit him several times. And each time she came, he refused to see her. She sat in the waiting room, went through the screening process, but never had any contact with him."

"A blonde? Is there any further physical description? Did they say she was petite?"

"That's the interesting part. The records say she was pregnant."

MARCH 7TH, 1:57 P.M.

Richard pops back into my office this afternoon after our session this morning. He's sitting in my patient chair, waiting for me to sign off on some changes he's proposing for his schedule. Even though he's been in that chair in my office so many times before, today the whole scene is different.

I put down his paper and look out the window at the construction team across the street. They've been working on that building for years now, and today, I see them pulling down the scaffold. Now and again, I hear a big crash of a plank being thrown into the truck. Richard watches me watching the men. He turns to see what the workers are doing.

"It's coming down, huh?" Richard says, facing me again.

"Yeah," I respond. "They finally restored that old building. It looks great now. So much cleaner."

"Like it got a new life."

"I was thinking. You know—" I put down my pen and take off my glasses "—you and I are the same. We believed everyone else's perceptions of us. Everyone else colored us in to be things that we weren't. You were a monster; I was a superhero. But, in the end, we're both just people. Equals. Just like you said."

"And monsters aren't real, Sam, and superheroes aren't, either." He smiles a knowing smile at me, picks up his hat and places it back on his head.

I smile and hand Richard his signed paper. He slips it into his pocket and pulls open the door.

We look up to see Shawn standing in the doorway. He appears anxious, like he may be in the wrong place.

"Hi, Shawn. Richard is just leaving." Richard nods, relinquishing his place.

"Oh, hey, Doc. Good, great, okay. I was worried that maybe I was here at the wrong time again." He breathes a sigh of relief as I gesture to Richard and stand up to welcome Shawn inside.

"Have a seat, and go ahead and put your stuff wherever you like." I sit back down in my desk chair, and Shawn arranges himself in his seat. He searches back and forth to find a place to put his plastic grocery bag filled with all his most prized possessions. As I look for a good spot with him, I see that Richard has left his newspapers on my desk. In the months we've been working together, he has always brought them with him at the end of his sessions. But for some reason, today he's left them here.

Shawn decides that there isn't a good enough spot to place his bag, so he tucks it onto his lap and looks to me to begin our conversation. Just as I'm about to start, my phone rings.

"Give me just a second, Shawn." I pick up the phone; it's Rachel. She's stuck at an administrative conference, and she needs to me to cover for her at a meeting in an hour. I hold up a finger in Shawn's direction and let him know that I need a minute. He starts sifting through Richard's newspapers, looking to occupy himself while I'm on the phone. I check my date book and schedule, and pencil in a few changes so that I can help Rachel out. Getting back in my golden-girl saddle, I tell her I will do whatever she needs. She thanks me profusely, and I hang up, satisfied. Things are finally returning to some semblance of normalcy.

"Sorry about that, Shawn. I'm ready to give you my undivided attention. So, tell me, how have you been doing?"

"Um, Doc? How come these papers you got are so old? This is old news." He holds out the top couple of papers for me to inspect.

"Oh, yeah?" I look at the cover of the *New York Times* and see the date is from the spring of 2012. I riffle through the other newspapers and realize they're all from the same time period. April and May 2012.

MARCH 11TH, 1:41 P.M.

I took Richard's stack of papers home with me, and I've been fortifying myself with coffee and Gatorade, bracing to look into them. They're sitting in my work bag on the floor next to the coffee table, and I'm pacing the apartment, nervously staring at them. I asked David to come over, and I'm waiting for him to get here.

I'm wandering around my apartment, trying to find something to do in the meantime. I've already tidied everything, so I keep refluffing pillows, willing the time to pass, checking my phone. I walk to my bathroom and pull some nail polish out from under the sink. I sit down at the coffee table in the living room, unscrew the and start filing my nails. I didn't realize how badly my hands were shaking.

The front-door buzzer startles me so badly that I drop the bottle on the carpet as I'm trying to open it. A gloppy line of gray polish shoots out of the top of the bottle and paints the leg of the coffee table. My heart pounds through my chest as I stumble to the intercom.

I see David's face in the grainy video and push the button to let him in. Through the camera, I watch him standing in the vestibule waiting for the elevator, holding a paper bag in his left hand and tossing his floppy hair with his right.

I wait in my doorway for the sound of the elevator opening, looking for David's face as he appears from around the bend. He glances up just as he turns the corner and seems startled to see me in the hallway.

He walks past me over to the couch and pulls a wax-paper package out of the bag. He sets the sandwiches on the coffee table and sits down without saying anything.

"Don't you want to know why I needed you to come over?" I grab some plates from the kitchen and sit down next to him. I realize the message I sent him probably seemed cryptic and unclear, but he doesn't seem focused on trying to figure out what I meant. "Aren't you intrigued? Why are you being weird?"

"Sam, I know you wanted me to come over and explore 'something crazy' with you, and I'm not sure what your text message meant, but I'm preoccupied and I need to talk to you before we start in on your adventure, okay?"

"Okay?" I twist my face into a concerned grimace, wondering what could possibly be more important than delving into the mystery of Richard's five-year-old newspapers.

David takes a deep breath and fidgets with the paper on his sandwich. I'm sitting with my feet tucked under me, my back on the arm of the couch, looking at him, and he is slumped forward over the coffee table. "I've been thinking a lot since you freaked out in my office that day."

"Yeah…"

"I know that you're scared that this diagnosis is a death sentence because it's got such a bad reputation, but I don't see it that way." He breaths deeply and starts unwrapping his sandwich. I take a bite of mine, my mouth dry, and wait for him to get to his point. "I always knew it, Sam. You telling me that OMH saw it, too, didn't change a thing." He gets up off the couch and walks to the kitchen to get drinks. "So, even though you were finding out for the first time, I always knew. It didn't change the way I think about you, even if it changed the way you think about yourself." He hands me a Sprite, still not looking at me. "I'm really glad that this happened, actually. Because it's obviously the motivation you needed to figure your shit out. And, I've been—" he takes a bite of his sandwich and continues with his mouth full "—I've been waiting for you to figure yourself out." He chews and swallows. He resumes speaking, looking into his sandwich. "And I figured, maybe once you got your footing back, and you were comfortable again—" he hesitates "—maybe we could…" He doesn't finish his sentence and instead turns his earnest eyes to me.

I know what's about to come out of his mouth and I need to stop him before he says it. I make a stumbling, uncoordinated attempt to reach my hand to his face and hush him, but instead my feet get caught and I drop my sandwich on the couch while trying to brace myself against crashing into him.

"David…" I sweep shredded lettuce from the couch onto my plate and try to reassemble my sandwich. I'm thankful for the distraction, so I don't have to look at him. "David, I think I know what you're going to say, and I—I *want* you to say it, but I don't think I can hear it yet." I'm graceless in my maneuvering of this conversation. "I need you to be my friend right now, and I can't be more than that for you, yet." I have mayonnaise on the fingers of my right hand, and I'm holding a plate with a dismantled turkey sandwich in my left, and David is watching me struggling to pull my feet out from under me. He's not quite smiling, not quite sneering, but looking at me with some auspicious expression that I can't identify.

"What do you think I'm going to say?" Now he's smirking.

"What?" I'm suddenly panicked that I read the situation all wrong. I thought he was going to ask me to be his girlfriend, or propose, or tell me he loves me or fucking *something* like that. "I thought you—I thought you were going to say you wanted us…" I trail off, completely mortified that I implied he wanted to be with me if that wasn't where his head was going.

He takes a deep and warming breath, and puts his plate down on the coffee table. He takes my plate from me and squeezes my hands in his. He kisses my right hand and gets mayo on his lips. "Sam, I was going to tell you that I have feelings for you. As more than just your friend. But, of course, you already knew that. You're always two moves ahead of everyone. I know you're not ready. I will wait for you. I've waited six years, and I will wait six more if I have to. Or sixty more." He kisses the knuckles on both my hands, licks the mayo off his lips and returns his attention to his lunch.

"You heard me when I said that I *wanted* you to say it, right?" He seems too satisfied with this outcome. I didn't expect him to be okay with waiting even longer.

"I heard you." His confidence is unnerving. "I know you, Sam. I just wanted you to know that I'm here. Like, *really* here." He smiles at me, and all at once, what awkwardness came into the room when he arrived has flown out the window.

MARCH 11TH, 7:11 P.M.

David is standing in the kitchen, cleaning up from our dinner, humming along with a TV theme song. He has a blue-striped dish towel thrown over his shoulder, and when he finishes each dish, he dries it off and puts it back exactly where it goes, as if he's been living here for years.

I'm sitting on the living room floor ready to investigate Richard's stack of newspapers, my work bag propped up against the leg of the coffee table. It still has the gray nail-polish stain. The bent corners of the papers are sticking out of my olive-green canvas bag, and as I tug them onto the floor, the smell of Richard fills my nose.

If Shawn hadn't shown me the dates on the newspapers, maybe I never would have known. It occurs to me that Richard has been bringing in the same stack since our first meeting five months ago. The flashbacks appear in my head, and I see traces and margins of the same pictures, and the ever-increasing wear and frays down the spines and along the edges. I never thought to look more closely at them. They were newspapers, the most commonplace, benign, everyday items. Why would I be suspicious? I was never interested in

Richard's papers. I never should have been. Not until Shawn showed me the dates.

Now I understand why he always took off his hat and placed it squarely on the front page of the top paper every time. Of course I would have noticed if, over all these months, the cover story was always the same.

April 17, 2012, is the date on the front of the *New York Times*. The *Post* is dated May 3. The rest of the papers are also early spring 2012. The pages have yellowed, the edges are frayed, and all the front pages are torn along the fold. There are greasy fingerprints and stains along the margins.

There are handwritten notes, Post-its and scribbles that usually start to appear toward the middle of the papers. From a preliminary glance, it looks like the bulk of the information is hidden in the *Daily News* and the *New York Post*.

Richard's cursive handwriting is small and, at times, illegible. Quick scribbles are interspersed with deliberate block letters. The crossword puzzle and sudoku boxes are filled with information. There are a few xeroxed pages taped along the insides of newspaper pages. The language is stark and clinical on the copied notes. And the Post-its seem to have come from various locations, as some have prescription drug names emblazoned at the top. Some of the notes are shorthand and I can't tell what they mean. I steel myself and prepare to read the details. As I'm shuddering out a deep breath, I see David's dirty Converse All Stars appear in front of me.

"Hey. I finished the dishes. What've you got going on down here?" He lowers himself to the floor next to me, kisses me on my forehead and picks up the *amNewYork*.

"*This* is why I asked you to come over. These papers are Richard's. These are the papers he carries around with him everywhere he goes. He left them on my desk on Tuesday and I took them home with me."

"So this is the big mystery, huh?"

"He's not reading these for the news."

"No? What's he reading them for?" David starts flipping through the *amNewYork*, sees the cover story about Mayor Bloomberg, checks the date on the front page, and confusion registers on his face. "Why is this from 2012?"

"Yeah, that's exactly what I'm trying to figure out. Look—" I show him the inside of my paper: the notes, the stickies, the memos. I show him that Richard has been studying his own writing inside the newspapers, not the editorials, not the stories.

"What *is* that?"

"This is data. It's information. Notes that Richard and someone else have written that he has hidden inside of these newspapers that he reads every day."

"Notes about what?" David is riffling through all the papers, too fast to see the details or make out the actual words, but slow enough to see that all the newspapers have hidden writing inside.

"Notes about *me*."

MARCH 12TH, 2:39 P.M.

All of Richard's newspapers are spread out in front of us, and David has moved a desk lamp onto the floor to illuminate our research. He has a notebook to keep a tab of themes and bullet points that we find hidden in the pages of the newspapers. His headings so far are "Sam," "BPD," "Typhlos" and "Recovery."

"There's a photocopy of a ripped-up psychosocial evaluation on page A6 of the *Times*," David is saying. "It hasn't been filled out, but it's got the Typhlos seal at the top. There's other intake stuff in here, too. Blank copies."

I can't figure out what he decided to save and what he may have tossed. Why were some documents in here but not others?

"Here's one, in the *Financial Times*." He drops the corner of the page and scoffs at me. "I can't believe you thought he was reading the *Financial Times*." He refocuses on the note and slides his glasses back up his nose. "He's got all the diagnostic criteria for BPD written out, in order. Some of them are circled with red pen."

"Which ones are circled?"

"Most of them, and there are initials next to the circles. S.J. and F.W. S.J. is obviously you, but who's F.W.?"

"Frances Williams, his mother."

"Oh, shit. He's got notes about both of you in here—which criteria you exhibit and which ones she did."

"Read them. Tell me."

"Okay, for number one, and I'm quoting the *DSM* here, 'Frantic efforts to avoid real or imagined abandonment'— he has your initials and his mom's. For number two, 'A pattern of unstable and intense interpersonal relationships,' blah, blah, blah, 'alternating between extremes of idealization and devaluation,' he has his mom's initials, and then yours, but with a question mark. For the third, 'identity disturbance,' he just has his mom's. For the fourth, 'impulsivity in at least two areas that are potentially self-damaging,' he has yours and his mom's, and then there's an arrow to some detailed notes." David squints at the bottom of the page. "I can't read that, can you?" He hands me the paper and pulls the light closer.

"It says 'F.W. drinking, men, smoking, not eating.' Next to S.J. it says 'drinking, men, drugs?' with a question mark." I shove the paper back in David's direction. I'm pissed to read what Richard thinks of me.

"How did he know you were drinking so much? And how did he know about the guys you were with?"

"This must be how—look at this one." I hand David the *Metro* I've been reading. There's a list of bars I go to, which days I usually go in, the names of the bartenders and the drinks I usually order. Next to it, there's a list of delis in my neighborhood, and liquor stores. He has *Chablis* misspelled next to *Miller Lite*. "Remember when you found that Post-it with my name on it? It had my address and the route I take to work in the morning. Do you think it fell out of here? It was Richard's note?"

David lets the paper droop into his lap and looks to me. "It must have been. But why would he have that?"

I look at David, apprehensive. Richard's words pop into my head like a shining marquee: *you might not like everything you find.*

I shake his words out of my head and continue the investigation. "What about the rest of the BPD criteria? Where was that one?"

"Here—" David hands me the *Financial Times* and moves on to analyze the other records.

Richard marked my initials next to three more criteria: number six, "affective instability due to marked reactivity of mood"; number seven, "chronic feelings of emptiness"; and number eight, "inappropriate, intense anger, or difficulty controlling anger." His mother's initials were next to those three as well, but he also put her down next to nine, "paranoid ideation or severe dissociative symptoms." He didn't consider either of us to be suicidal, so he didn't circle criteria number five. Did he figure out my symptoms just by watching me? Did he learn so much about this in prison that he was able to qualify my behaviors?

He has lists of books and references, shorthand notes with numbers and decimal points. Is it library reference sections? The Dewey Decimal System? Did he go to a library and look this up? As I uncover more hidden scrawls among the pages, I see he hasn't just been jotting down borderline symptoms and treatments, but also the symptoms of depression and PTSD. There are check marks, but no initials next to the diagnostic criteria for both disorders. Depression and PTSD, the disorders Richard was diagnosed with in prison.

"Okay, wait a minute, what the hell is all of this? Was he stalking you before he came to Typhlos? How does he know about Nick's? And Sid? Did he go there and talk to him?"

"It certainly seems like it, don't you think? I mean he wrote about drinking, so he must have seen me drinking. And then he found the ziplock bag of booze in my office, so that confirmed it."

"But what about the men? He wrote *men* next to your initials, right? How did he know about men? You were with Lucas for like a year, right? Did you cheat on him? I mean, other than AJ?"

"There was AJ, and I may have made out with a couple of other people. How could he possibly know that, though? How long has he been watching me?"

"I'm not as interested in how long as I am in why, Sam. Why does he need all of this information about you?"

"I don't know, David." I expel a huge breath. "Keep going." I put my reading glasses back on and sip from a cold bottle of Sprite. *You may not like everything you find.*

We flip pages and decipher cryptic logs and reports scrawled throughout the papers. We're filling up sheets of David's notebook with organized thoughts and something beginning to resemble a timeline. Along blank portions of the papers, we find several doodles in black pen that look like scaffolding.

"Holy shit." David's face goes white and he sits up ramrod straight. "Sam. He has your performance review in here."

"What? From when?" I snatch the paper from his hands and look over the familiar document, signed in Rachel's familiar handwriting. Portions have been circled in red pen. Individual words are triple underlined. It's a copy of my annual performance review from 2012.

"What did he underline?" David asks, craning his neck to see.

"All the parts that make me sound competent. The stuff about me being 'exemplary' at managing the difficult patients. 'Natural leader,' 'charismatic, understanding and empathic.'

In the section regarding potential for promotion, Rachel gave me the highest ratings on all the criteria, and Richard put red exclamation points next to them. How the hell did he get ahold of this?"

"Don't you keep a copy? I have copies of mine in my office."

"You do? We get to keep them?" I can't remember ever walking out of Rachel's office after these meetings with copies. Then again, there's a lot about the past that's fuzzy.

I remember leaving her office after the reviews feeling like a fraud, like I was Wile E. Coyote and a huge Acme anvil was going to fall on my head and I would have only a tiny umbrella to protect me. But now, as I picture that scene, I remember that as the anvil crushed my cartoon self into oblivion, the performance review floated down like an errant leaf in the dust cloud. Maybe I *did* have copies. What could I have done with them? "Jesus, I mean if he could go through the shit in my office and find the stash of booze, I'm sure he could find all of this, too."

"Except this is from 2012. Why would he have chosen this particular year? And how could he have had time to go through all the pieces of paper? The airplane bottles were in a big ziplock bag, right? That's easy to spot. This would have taken forever to find—with all the other documents and files you have in your office. And why would he have known to take *this* in particular? It doesn't make sense. He must have had this since 2012."

"I don't… I don't understand this." I collapse the papers down between my knees and look up to David for comfort. This is surreal. We can entrench ourselves in the excitement of this discovery and temporarily displace the feelings that this is completely insane. Why the hell has my patient been following me? When did this start? There's so much information in here, but there are no answers.

"There's a whole section here on forgiveness. Look—" David has moved on, too enthralled with his discoveries to waste too much time on each finding. He scoots closer to me. "He drew over these words so many times they've bled to the next two pages. It says 'forgiveness,' 'self-absolve' and down here it says 'exonerate.' And it looks like a how-to book, some kind of self-help mumbo jumbo. It's so blurred from all the overwriting; I can't make it all out. And look in the crossword puzzle—'self-forgiveness is freedom.' He even made it fit in the boxes."

Self-forgiveness. It's a manifesto. It's the gospel according to Richard. It's a series of insights into his psyche. It's the real answers to all his evaluation questions.

"Whose is the other handwriting? It's so clinical." David is holding most of the papers now.

"Yeah, that's what I'm trying to figure out, too. I've got the *Post*, and it's filled with recovery-oriented stuff. But not self-directed stuff, I'm talking treatment protocols, emotion regulation techniques, all sorts of shit. It's got details about dialectical behavioral therapy, for Christ's sake! What the fuck is going *on* with this?" I am trying to keep my emotions separated from our investigation, but I'm getting frustrated and scared.

"Well, DBT is the most effective therapy for treating personality disorders."

"Thank you, Dr. Bloomfield!" I holler sarcastically with my hands up in the air. "Why does *my patient* have a list of treatment protocols for personality disorders shrouded in a newspaper from fucking years ago? Huh? I get that he is interested in all of this. I get that his mother had BPD, and he has enormous guilt associated with killing her and not helping her! I get that. I understand he needs to find forgiveness and peace. But why am *I* all over these pages? What does this have to do with *me*?"

"Oh, my God. I know whose handwriting it is."

"Whose? How do you know?" I scramble to my knees to see what David has found.

"It's the prison shrink. Mark something-with-an-*S*. The guy from Ogdensburg who we dug up? The one who figured out what Richard went through even though they never spoke?"

"Dr. Sloan? How do you know that?"

"Look—" David holds up the *Daily News*. "There's a note card with 'M.S.' on the letterhead over the photocopy of this letter, right? And it's clearly a letter responding to a question, see? Because the opening line says he's got the information Richard was looking for. And the letter has a pretty comprehensive list of BPD treatments. It's fuzzy in some spots, but that's what it looks like, right? And the date in the corner says March 27, 2012. Just before the dates on these papers."

I'm reading over the letter, faded from photocopy and wear, with Richard's handwritten blurbs in the margins. At the bottom of the page, the original letter was folded over, so only a piece of the last sentence was copied. It was written in flourished handwriting: "good luck finding…" But the last words are gone.

MARCH 13TH, 9:22 A.M.

I'm sitting in the morning meeting, staring out the dirty window. The sun is peeking out from behind a building; it's illuminating all the grime and dust pasted to the outside of the windows, and it's obscuring the view completely. It looks like a wall of dried cat vomit.

My knees are bouncing erratically. I skipped breakfast because I have a nervous stomach, and I'm afraid if I eat anything, it'll fall directly out of my ass. I'm pounding coffee, and it's making me grind my teeth and clench my jaw.

I have Richard's papers in my bag, and I keep looking down and checking on them under the conference table, as if they would jump out and slip away if they saw an opening. I'm willing Rachel to fly through the morning meeting so I can get the hell out of here and go find Richard.

I'm not paying attention to anything, and I see the staff and Rachel drone on about mundane happenings on the unit. I feel like Charlie Brown watching the teacher's ankles and hearing nothing but a vibrating murmur. I'm stuck in slow motion and the room is going at its usual pace.

I see my colleagues start to pull their piles of stuff together; they stack notebooks on top of other notebooks, wiggle keys out of tight pockets and begin making moves to walk out the door. David gives me a nod, and I slam back the last drops of my second coffee and throw the strap of my bag over my shoulder. Before anyone can bother to make niceties at me, I fly out the conference-room door, down the hall to my office.

I remove Richard's file from the wire letter organizer next to my computer and gently lay it in front of me. I look down at my shirt and see my heartbeat pulsing the space between the buttons. My fingers are trembling from the caffeine.

The first loose page in his file is a photocopy of his daily schedule, and I place it on top, blink away the floaters in my eyes and look for Monday at 10:00 a.m. Try as I might, I have never memorized a patient's schedule, and as I focus on the 10:00 a.m. box on Mondays, I see he should be only a few short steps from my office in the computer room. My desktop clock tells me I have six minutes until ten.

I use the time to set the scene. I slowly pull the newspapers from my bag, careful not to cause any more damage to the pages. David and I ensured that we didn't disturb the placement of the notes and records within the papers, and I tried to remember the order of the stack. Richard is meticulous, and the edges of the newspapers were always perfectly lined up and even. I shift and tuck and reorganize until it looks like *he* laid the hoard on the corner of my desk closest to his chair, my patient's chair.

Not since I first met him, while we were all speculating about his crimes, his demeanor, whether or not he would kill one of us, have I felt so nervous to see him. I've been setting up my office for this confrontation for what feels like hours, and I look at the clock to see it's just four minutes to ten.

I open my bottle of water and take slow, deliberate sips while breathing deeply through my nose to bring a sense of calm and serenity that never comes. Although time feels at a standstill, the seconds are passing, and when I see the tiny, white digital numbers click from 9:59 a.m. to 10:00 a.m., I push my chair back and stand up.

I find Richard sitting in a chair with his eyes squinted at the computer screen. There are only two other patients in the computer room—Barry and Tashawndra. Tashawndra is sitting in front of a computer, pushing the mouse around, but the monitor isn't on. Shirley is supposed to be in here, but she's nowhere to be found.

Richard's head turns to me, but his expression stays as it was while he strained to see the screen. He points a heavy finger to his chest and mouths, *Me?* I nod and tilt my head toward my office. He takes a last glance at whatever he was researching on the computer, clicks the page closed and switches off the monitor. As he scoots his faded blue plastic chair back, the scraping sound on the linoleum alerts Barry.

Barry twists at the waist and clutches the back of his seat to see who's moving around. He locates Richard and watches him rise to come meet me. Understanding registers on Barry's face, and he offers me an enormous wave. I smile tightly and usher Richard out of the room.

MARCH 13TH, 10:04 A.M.

I have been rehearsing this conversation in my head since David and I stayed up until sunrise trying to piece together the mystery of Richard and his newspapers—but all the words get stuck and bottleneck in my throat.

Richard sits in the chair in my office and looks at me with hesitation. "Were we supposed to be meeting now?"

I stare at him as I try to dislodge the sentences and inadvertently shift my gaze from him to the newspapers.

"Oh." He sees me looking at the papers, inspects them himself, returns to me. "Oh, those."

"Yes. Those." All the brilliant comments and questions I crafted so meticulously in my head fall out of my ears into a pile on the floor.

Richard breathes several deep, husky breaths and interlaces his fingers over his stomach. He looks out the window, back at the construction site across the street, which is nothing more than a shiny new facade surrounded by dusty remnants of scaffold and hardware. "Did you read everything?" He's casually leaning back, seemingly oblivious to the magnitude of this conversation.

"I did. What I could decipher."

"And?"

"And? *And?* You're asking me? 'And,' yourself! What am I supposed to make of all of this? You've been stalking me? Are you even a patient here?" The calm is gone, and now I'm starting to freak out.

"Whoa." He sits up quickly and faces me. "Of course I'm a patient here! My name is Richard McHugh, and I have never lied. Well, I've *mostly* never lied. I never lied to *you*, directly."

"What does that even mean?" I'm sweating; my knees are bouncing; I am regretting the last cup of coffee.

"I may have employed some dishonesty to get into this institution." He rubs his thumbs together nervously.

"You *may have*? You're not really a patient, are you?" I'm pushing my chair back toward the door, afraid of him again. Feelings from when he first walked through my door are rushing back to me.

"Technically, I am. I was sent here by a doctor. But no, it was not a condition of my parole. You don't get sent to the loony bin years after leaving prison as a condition of parole. You should probably know that. And, no, I'm not here because I need treatment." He's holding his hands up in a gesture of submission.

"Then what are you doing here? And how the *hell* did you get in here?"

"Getting in here wasn't very hard. All you really need is a doctor to call another doctor and a couple of forms to get filled out. And then I'm on your doorstep."

I'm beginning to breathe heavily, and I can feel the snot in my left nostril blocking my panicked breaths, and it's making a whistling sound. I pull tissue after tissue out of the cube on my desk and begin blowing my nose. I'm honking loudly, and this is unnerving Richard, who now looks disgusted.

"Calm down, Sam."

"You realize that everyone is here because they need to be," I snap, tissues still to my face. "They're here for treatment and to get better, and then get out of here. And *you* coming in for your own selfish, bullshit agenda, for your own psychotic—I don't even *know* what—you're compromising the treatment of everyone else here! Did you even consider that? Did you consider how faking it, and manipulating the system— Did you consider how that could fuck other people over?"

"Honestly, no." His composure is in glaring contrast to my flustered resentment, and it looks like we're in two different movies.

"What were you thinking? Explain *this* to me!" I slam my hands on top of the stack of papers and, infuriatingly, they don't budge.

"I *am* explaining it, but you need to calm down. This isn't easy for me, either, you know. And I won't talk to you when you're like this." He crosses his arms and cuts off the conversation.

I inhale an enormous breath. "Please, proceed. I will *calm down*." I'm incensed. I want to shake his shoulders until the truth rattles out of him and I can understand who the fuck has been sitting in my office all this time.

"May I? Thank you." He uncrosses his arms and continues, "As I was saying, getting committed to a mental institution is easy. All you need is someone in the right position willing to make a referral. I never lied, Sam. I never told you anything that wasn't true, either. It's important that you know that."

"Dr. Mark. He's the 'someone in a position,' isn't he? Did he make the referral?"

"He did, yes. He and I stayed in touch. I told him that I needed further treatment, and I had been doing research on institutions. I told him I wanted to come to this one."

"You told me you never talked to him again after he left Ogdensburg."

"Yes, you're right. I did say that. And I'm sorry that I lied, but I couldn't have you finding out what was going on until I was ready."

"Ready? Ready for *what*? What the hell is going on?" I want to cry, I want to throw a temper tantrum and stomp my feet until he answers me!

"Yes. Ready to tell you everything."

"And you're ready now?"

"Well, I guess I have to be ready now. You've found the papers and you've read my notes. I don't want you to feel confused or scared. I need to tell you." He's holding out both his palms, imploring me to calm down.

"I have security on standby! How could I not be scared? I did read your notes, your detailed, invasive, bizarre notes! About *me*! What did you think I was going to find out from reading them? All the answers? I have more questions than *ever* now." I stand up and kick on my white-noise machine when I realize I'm screaming in my office.

"Maybe it's easier if you just *ask* me about the things you don't understand."

I fall back into my chair, exasperated. "Everything. I don't understand any of it. Why did you have all the diagnostic stuff in there? The *DSM* criteria?"

"I don't remember things as well as I used to. I had to remember how to behave. When you're depressed, you naturally behave as if you're depressed. But when you're better, it's hard to remember what depression looks like. I needed to look the part. You're the best doctor here, that's what I found out, so I knew you'd see through me if I didn't do it right."

"So you had the criteria listed so you would know how to act depressed? And the PTSD? It was all a lie?"

"No—Sam. You're not listening." He vehemently shakes his head, frustrated. "None of it was a lie."

"Did you really kill your mother? Was that bullshit?" I feel like the room is spinning and I don't know anything anymore.

"Everything that I said happened, happened. Exactly as I said it did. I wasn't lying while I was talking with you. Never. Not once."

"But you needed to behave a certain way on the unit so no one would be the wiser that you don't belong here?"

"That's what the plan was, but it turns out I didn't really need to do anything that didn't come naturally to me. I never felt like I was acting. I was being myself. It's easy to feel depressed in here."

"So why are you here, if you don't belong here?" I put my head down between my knees and wheel my chair as far away from Richard as I can. The images of the notes are flying through my head at breakneck speed and I can't concentrate on specifics. I had so many lucid points to make. This is confusing, and I'm not getting the answers in order. I still don't understand.

He doesn't respond to me, instead interlaces his fingers and crosses his ankles as he leans toward me.

"You wrote about forgiveness." I raise my head slightly to look at him. I'm trying to remember the individual questions I wanted to ask. His lucidity and cooperation are helping my fears subside, and I'm beginning to calm down. His voice is slow and methodical; he's trying to help me understand.

"Yes. That was from Dr. Mark. When I was at Revelations, the halfway house, I wasn't getting better. Leaving prison was harder than I thought. I figured the freedom would wash over me and I would build a life. But I couldn't. The feeling of freedom never came. No matter how many books I read, or mantras I repeated, no matter how many times I assured myself that I was allowed to move on, I couldn't. I felt like my punishment wasn't up. I had no family left. And the reason I had no family left was because I killed the only family I ever had. When it got to be too much, and I was afraid I would never get better, I called the closest thing to family I had. I called Dr. Mark. We set up calls for therapy over the phone. He didn't want me to leave Revelations; he said it was important for me to be in a safe space while I was recovering. So we had weekly calls."

"That's why he remembered so much about you. But he didn't tell me that when I talked to him. Why wouldn't he tell me that he had been your therapist?"

"Yeah—" he looks at his feet and fidgets with his thumbs "—that's why I was nervous when you said you wanted to talk to him. So I told you I didn't remember his name, to make it harder for you to find him. I called him and told him I wasn't ready to talk to you yet, and I didn't want him to share my stories if you ever found him. He said he couldn't lie to you, and he didn't want to be involved in any deceit, either. I asked him to be vague. I guess I lied more than I thought I did. I'm sorry about that. My intentions were never to deceive you."

"I'm hoping you're going to tell me exactly what your intentions are."

"Dr. Mark was the one who put the forgiveness idea in my head. The same thing you said to me right here in this office not too long ago. He said to be able to move on, and to find the sense of freedom, I would have to forgive myself for what I'd done. He said, 'Self-forgiveness *is* freedom.' So, I tried to find out how to do that.

"I talked to the staff at Revelations; I asked them about forgiveness. I asked them how. That's the thing about you people, you always tell us *what* we need to do, but you never tell us *how*. So, I read books. I stopped asking questions, and I buried myself in books. Philosophy books, psychology books. Memoirs, biographies. Looking for the answers. And it occurred to me—amends. I needed to make amends. 'An eye for an eye.' I killed someone. So, I had to save someone."

"So, you went looking for someone to rescue? Why didn't you join the fire department or something?" I scoff sarcastically and shake my head.

"Remember Jesse? My friend from Woodside?" He reaches his meaty paw across my desk.

"Yes, from the blackout. You got arrested together."

"Right. When I left Revelations, I looked him up. I didn't have anywhere else to start, back out in the world. So, I looked for Jesse, and he was right there in the phone book, still living in the old neighborhood. I reached out to him, and he met me for a coffee at a diner in Manhattan, down near where the towers used to be. He looked exactly the same. Same puff of hair, same lanky limbs. He seemed happy to see me, I guess. He was working as some higher-up in a construction company. After we talked awhile, I asked if he could help me with a job. I wanted something off-the-books, and Jesse said he could arrange something for me at one of his sites." Richard's gaze slowly returns to the window.

"So he got you a job at the site across the street? You were working construction across the street? That's how you found me?" I look out the window again to see the ghost of a construction site. Richard was there?

"I *asked* to go to that site. I had already found you, but I needed to know more about you before I could approach you."

"Richard, this is insane. How long were you there before you came *here*?" I'm tugging at the hem of my shirt and pulling my sleeves down over my wrists. I'm instinctively trying to protect myself, and everything is starting to get itchy. *You may not like everything you find.*

"A few weeks, couple months—no more. I followed you a few times. I wasn't sure what I was doing when I first found you. I needed to get to know you. From a distance, obviously."

"That's why you took the Typhlos documents? To get to know me? How did you get ahold of my performance review?" My mouth is dry, and my throat is starting to cramp up.

"That was an incredible stroke of luck, actually. When I was first looking for information, I went through the recycling bags in the alley. Most of the documents in there were shredded or torn to pieces, but now and again I would find a whole one. Usually, it was stuff that hadn't been filled out, but it was useful. Intake documents, psychological tests—things that helped me figure out how to behave, if I was ever going to get inside. But then I found your performance review. Something that was really about *you*. It was crumpled up and had coffee stains on it, but it was signed, so I thought it must be significant. So, I tucked it into my pocket.

"It said you were practically perfect. Best doctor here. Saving everyone's day. But when I followed you, and I saw you away from work, I saw you weren't okay. I knew all about borderline from researching it for so many years after Frances, and it was easy to recognize. I knew you were suffering."

A strange stillness falls over me like a warm blanket. My breathing has softened, and long, slow tears are streaming from my eyes. I'm beginning to understand.

"That's why you had the lists of treatments—you were coming to treat me. You learned how to make it better, how to make *me* better, and you got yourself institutionalized so you could 'save me.' So you could find the forgiveness you needed for freedom." The newspaper notes are appearing in my head—highlights are popping out in bolded print. I'm putting all the pieces together, and I know exactly what he was doing.

"Yes. I came for you."

"But why? Why *me*?"

MARCH 21ST, 7:44 A.M.

There is a funny thing that happens on the train. You're neither here nor there, and it's transformative in that way. I leave the person I was at the Fourteenth Street station and become the person I'm going to be at the last stop.

As I get off the train car, I drop my OMH evaluation into a sticky garbage can on the 1 train platform and watch as the maintenance guys empty it along with the other trash into a yellow canvas Dumpster. I've stopped fighting against the truth of who I am; I've unclenched my fists, and now it's time to save myself.

There's a wind tunnel between the train station and the unit, and it will kick up everything the city has to offer in tiny tornadoes of flotsam. I'm not ready for my day until I pick something gross out of the corner of my eye and get the debris out of my hair.

I take David's hand when we meet at the corner. He kisses my cheek and my heart gets warm. He hands me a coffee, and we walk toward Typhlos. It's Tuesday.

As we enter through the front doors, David looks at me. "What time is your session with your dad today?"

"Eleven a.m.," I say, "as usual."

★ ★ ★ ★ ★

ACKNOWLEDGMENTS

Endless thank-yous to my brilliant agent, Marian Young, without whom I would be sitting alone at a coffee shop wondering if I could publish a book. Thank you for your support and dedication, your guidance, encouragement and advice. Thank you for your belief in me, and in *The Blind*, and for your tireless efforts.

To my incomparable editor, Liz Stein, thank you for taking a chance on me and *The Blind*. Thank you for helping Sam and Richard become their best selves, and for making me into a real writer.

Thank you both for your patience and understanding and your willingness to tolerate my eccentricities and bizarre predilections.

What a team of superheroes we can be.

Thank you to the talented and dedicated team at Park Row Books/Harlequin/HarperCollins for all your work and all the help along the way.

Thank you to my family for your love and support, pride and counsel.

To my husband, Bobby, for being absolutely everything.

For reading and rereading ad infinitum, listening and relistening ad nauseam. I couldn't do much of anything without you.

To Dr. EB, Dr. EF and JLBZ for the professional opinions, the unwavering support and the ability to keep me being me.

To M, for saving the day.

ONE PLACE. MANY STORIES

Bold, innovative and
empowering publishing.

FOLLOW US ON:

@HQStories